LOVE IS STRANGE

STORIES OF POSTMODERN ROMANCE

♥ ♥

Edited by Joel Rose and Catherine Texier

W. W. NORTON & COMPANY

NEW YORK ♥ LONDON

Printed in the United States of America.

First Edition

Portions of this book have been previously published in *Story*, *Conjunctions*, *Christopher Street*, *Peau Sensible*, and *Between C & D*.

Grateful acknowledgment is made to the following for permission to reprint previously published material:

"Breaking Up with Roger," copyright © 1989 by David B. Feinberg, from *Spontaneous Combustion* by David B. Feinberg. Reprinted by permission of Viking Penguin, a division of Penguin Books USA, Inc.
"Yellow Rose," copyright © 1989 by William T. Vollmann, from *The Rainbow Stories* by William T. Vollmann. Reprinted by permission of Andre Deutsch Ltd.
"A Real Doll," copyright © 1990 by A. M. Homes, from *The Safety of Objects* by A. M. Homes. Reprinted by permission of W. W. Norton & Company, Inc.
"Shifter," copyright © 1991 by Lynne Tillman, from *Motion Sickness* by Lynne Tillman. Reprinted by permission of Poseidon Press, a division of Simon & Schuster, Inc.

The text of this book is composed in 10/13 New Baskerville,
with the display set in Bernhard Fashion and Kabel.
Composition by PennSet, Inc.
Manufacturing by The Courier Companies, Inc.
Book design by Jo Anne Metsch.

Library of Congress Cataloging-in-Publication Data

Love is strange : stories of postmodern romance / edited
by Joel Rose and Catherine Texier.
p. cm.
1. Love stories, American. 2. Short stories, American. I. Rose,
Joel. II. Texier, Catherine.
PS648.L6L67 1993
813'.08508—dc20 92-15411

ISBN 0-393-30965-7

W. W. Norton & Company, Inc., 500 Fifth Avenue, New York, N.Y. 10110
W. W. Norton & Company Ltd., 10 Coptic Street, London WC1A 1PU

1 2 3 4 5 6 7 8 9 0

To the memory of
David Wojnarowicz

CONTENTS

♥ ♥

INTRODUCTION

♥ ♥

What is this thing called love? And what is its place in American literature? Is the American love story Jake Barnes, *sans* his privates, chasing after Lady Brett Ashley, or Gatsby taking a bullet for the love of Daisy? Or is it just about a bunch of guys going fishing?

The classic American love story, literary critic Leslie Fiedler tells us in his book *Love and Death in the American Novel*, is not at all about the passion of man for woman, but about the enamoration of the white American male for his dark-skinned brother: Ishmael for Queequeg, Huck for Jim, Natty Bumppo for Chingachgook, the Lone Ranger for Tonto.

Is this still true in contemporary American literature? Has the modern story of *amour* been relegated to the insatiable realm of Harlequin romance novels and traditional blowsy fiction? Do "serious" young writers write love stories, and if they do, are the tales they tell dripping with cynicism or dripping with tenderness? In today's world can love still possibly be romantic? Has AIDS killed any chance of writing about love and sex? How do young American authors depict love? Is love about intimacy, is it about desire, is it about obsession, or hard-edged, and only about attitude? Is love dismissive of itself, does it take itself seriously, too seriously? Can it? Or is love none of the above, or all?

Love Is Strange tries to answer these questions by collecting the work of sixteen writers who prowl the edges of human experience and literary form to evoke the landscape of American love from deepest downtown New York and decadent California to politically correct campuses and surreal suburbia.

The stories have wit and style. They range from the tender to the abrasive, the sunny to the darkly sexual, the poignant to the savagely ironic.

Some of the characters, like those of Lynne Tillman, Daytona Beach, and Kathy Acker, are young and urban, but no yuppies. They live on society's edge with no money and few prospects, trying their best to make sense of their lives in utter confusion. David B. Feinberg's characters are gay and hide their tenderness and terrifying fear of love behind a deadpan and unrelenting cynicism. There is William T. Vollmann's bittersweet love affair of a San Francisco bad boy with an utterly unsentimental Korean girl, and Lisa Blaushild's sardonic love letter from a young woman to her rapist. David Foster Wallace's characters are not hip. You might call them "New Age," or less charitably, "young hippies at sea in the nineties." Yet the obsession of Barry Dingle, "cross-eyed purveyor of bean sprouts," with Myrnaloy Trask, "operator of Xerox and regent of downtown Northampton's most influential bulletin board at Collective Copy," is as contemporary and cutting as any "hip" love story.

There is Lynne McFall's country love story, played to the tunes of Patsy Cline and Hank Williams, David Wojnarowicz's harrowing monologue of a young hustler lost and desperate and on the prowl, A. M. Homes's weird tale of a teenage boy who falls in love with his sister's Barbie doll. There's an outlaw, white-trash, southern lesbian romance by Barry Gifford, a black-and-white romance in diary form by Trey Ellis, and tossed in for spice an English adultery story of gothic proportions by Patrick McGrath. Darius James, writing under the cognomen of Doctor Snakeskin, affords us the inside dope on "The Blackman's Guide to Seducing White Women with the Amazing Power of Voodoo."

That most stories end in distress rather than with wedding bells or even peaceful cohabitation may not be an indication of the impossibility of love in the treacherous nineties so much as the illustration of the old adage "If you're happy you don't have a real story to tell."

What these stories do have in common is an edge, a grittiness, an eye for what's really out there, and a voice to tell it. Gutsy, erotic, tender, unsentimental. Most important, by writers with original talent.

Love Is Strange proves that an era of safe sex can still produce dangerous and exhilarating art about the universal experience of romance.

Catherine Texier
Joel Rose

New York City
February 1992

LOVE IS STRANGE

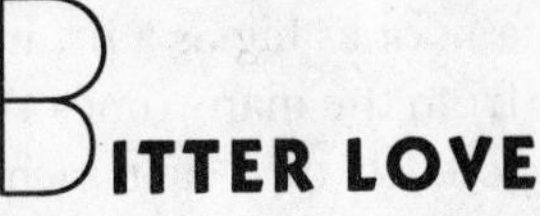

BITTER LOVE

♥ ♥

Lynne McFall

I lost my right eye in a pool-playing accident in the Sea Horse Saloon on January 27, the day of my thirty-ninth birthday. I'd tell you the story but everyone I've told it to so far—man or woman—starts making retching noises and backing away. But you can use your imagination: a pool cue, a jealous woman, one blue eye.

I would like to tell you about the man, however. His name was Jake and he was a steam-pipe fitter. He drove a rusted-out, puke-green Maverick that he bought with some money he won playing liars' dice. There was a hole the size of a bowling ball in the floorboard. No rugs except for some little frayed pieces of green still stuck to the metal. The tape player ate every tape you put into it. I remember how I cried the day it ate my Bonnie Raitt. When you turned the heater on it smelled like dirty socks burning, and it didn't put out any heat. His driving was worse than his car. Every time we went anywhere together, I'd end up with a knot as big as a fist in my stomach and violent inner trembling from the many times I'd nearly died. An eighteen-wheeler would screech to a halt inches from my door, and he'd smile like a manic child. He looked behind him *after* he changed lanes, used his rearview mirror mostly for picking his teeth, which he'd do with a silver dental instrument while driving eighty miles an hour. When the light, any light, turned green, he'd floor it, apparently untouched by the months of gas rationing most of us remember. He took every corner like he was at Indy, cut people off without even a gesture toward his blinkers, turned on his lights at night only as an afterthought. He was dangerous.

Two weeks after he left me he wrote me a letter. He said he felt like he'd been driving for a long time through the dark toward some glorious city. That he'd taken the back roads because he couldn't find the main highway. It was a longer route, he knew, but he thought he'd get there eventually. Sometimes he thought he could see lights, but like a mirage of water they would vanish as he got closer. But he kept on driving, too stubborn and stupid to stop and ask someone. What they would have told him, he said, is that that road didn't go there.

I guess I was supposed to be the glorious city. Or maybe it was "true love" he was driving at. I'm not sure. I wanted to write back and say that maybe, it's just a thought, per*haps* he should consider this: the reason he didn't make it to the glorious city is that his car is shit and he's a lousy driver. I wanted to say that there are some good places you can't find on a map. I didn't, of course. I wouldn't want him to think I was bitter.

But he cured me of country music, I'll give him that. I used to drink rum and Coke and play Patsy Cline or Hank Williams and cry myself sick. He taught me the true meaning of self-pity. I no longer need the cheap fix.

I remember Patsy was singing the night we met. I had gone to the Sea Horse Saloon in a mood of drink-yourself-blind. I was upset, not about anything in particular but just about the general strain of living—that a person has to *work* for a living, for example. I am a photographer by chosen profession, but I was working for Ted's Typing Service at the time, on Geary Boulevard. Drunks off the street would bring you in some legal form to type up—they were suing their landlord, they were writing up their last will and testament—and they would breathe whiskey in your face and threaten you with nonpayment for fixing their spelling errors. Working at some low-level job for peon wages at great aggravation instead of pursuing one's *art*, what kind of life is that?

He came in and sat down with two barstools between us. Friendly but not pushy. I looked up out of polite curiosity but just quickly, no smile. Dark hair, a beard, heavyset. Pretty brown eyes, so kind, they reminded me of my grandmother's. Some guys, you look into their eyes and know it's only a matter of time until they pick you up and throw you against a wall. This guy wouldn't do it. Or if he did, he'd regret it instantly and forever.

When he smiled I wanted him. It was the kind of smile that would not only take you home and tuck you in afterwards, but would fix you breakfast.

"I want! I want!" This is something I would yell at odd moments during our days together. Then Jake would come to me, take off my clothes, first the blouse, unbuttoned slowly from the bottom, each article of clothing—taking his time with me, making me wait, teasing me with his hands, his tongue. "What do you want?" he would say and smile at me like I was really something. Something precious. Something you would always want in your line of sight.

I guess not.

I should have seen it coming. But in his life no one had ever been loyal, had ever stood up for him, stuck with him when things got tough. I wanted to be the one. Noble me.

Maybe he didn't like having someone around who was always pointing out the half-eaten worm in the rotten apple. I have a gift for the negative, I admit. But even those who are difficult need to be loved, and in that I am no exception.

He had a complicated system of merits and demerits as to love. How harsh you were last night to my friend Alex. That's seven demerits. Janice and Rick *liked* you, that's three for you. Why must you keep badmouthing Big John? Don't you know that'll cost you an arm and a leg? Big John was his boss, but I think Jake thought of Big John as his father. His real father walked out on him and his mother when he was little. Maybe that's where he got the talent.

He was always walking out. This is the picture that sticks in my mind: him slamming his things together and stuffing them into the trunk of his Maverick. It would take several trips, and he would keep his face in a rage the whole time. He walked this ridiculous indignant cartoon strut when he was mad. I'd be crying, wondering what went wrong this time, saying I was sorry, or saying I wished I'd never put myself in his hands, whichever was appropriate.

He hated what he called "scenes." That's me screaming and him stuffing his things into the trunk of his Maverick. But he wouldn't talk to you in an ordinary human voice about anything of significance. I would try to get him drunk, hoping he would tell me where I stood, once and for all. But he could never tell me the truth, as if it took some superhuman courage he just couldn't summon. So I was always trying to read the signs, begging for bad news. "It looks like you don't love me enough," I would say softly. "But maybe you don't have the guts to tell me." We'd be at the Surf, listening to "You're Not the Man" on the jukebox, that saxophone like someone moaning. "No," he'd say, too carefully. "I love you." But the look of his eyes in the light of the Coors sign was not convincing. Finally it was me who'd get drunk and start screaming. Patience is not its own reward.

He was very punishing but in a passive way. He wouldn't call, he would be silent long hours of a Sunday, he would pinch his lips together and harden his eyes to a fine glint. He withheld the word "love" from his cards and letters for the entire last six months, then he signs his goodbye letter "Love, Jake." It was, to put it simply, more than I could take. It's the small things that destroy us.

If I knew his side of the story, I would tell it. But here I am as usual having to make it up, trying to stuff all these painful memories and ragged feelings into some kind of trunk. I hate people—I'm trying for a light tone here—who have no sense of an ending, no need of a proper burial.

I've been going through some letters he wrote me. Reading them over for clues. He said in one that what he felt for me was not love because love was not fierce enough. But reading that didn't make me feel better. If someone has decided to rewrite the past, old letters prove nothing.

When I got a temporary job down in L.A. (photographing zoo animals) and he moved into the latest new place that was chosen without me in mind, he got rid of my favorite chair. Looking back, that was a sign.

He took up with this woman, Sally. Dumb as shit and bright pink lipstick. That was the second sign. I guess she was a glorious city he could find on his frayed atlas. She liked to torment me with it. For example, she'd say, when I saw her at the bar, that she and Jake had spent last weekend fucking their brains out. I said I bet it didn't take all weekend. Her idea of independence was to always have more than one lover. I used to ridicule this.

Some people, when they are gone, leave you less than you were. He wasn't one of these. There were good things. But remembering them pierces me.

I bought him this white silk teddy for his birthday. Me in it was the present. But I was too shy to put it on. He kept asking and I finally did. He had me turn this way and that in the soft light in the dark room. He looked at me then like he loved me enough. I can remember every instant of that night, the urgency, my pounding heart, the way I moved above him. Those are the things that make the loss of an eye seem a kindness.

It was hard that last year to keep taking off my clothes, to keep making myself vulnerable to him, when he was doing the final tally. Sometimes I would look at him and see him moving his lips and know that he was adding things up, trying to be fair. It would be interesting to know which point was the clincher.

I have a talent for sleeping. Nine or ten hours a night is usual. When he left I woke up crying every night at three a.m. and couldn't get back to sleep. Images of us together, in different postures, filled my head. Every night, like a video, I would see us.

Pale thighs against a dark-haired chest. I am sitting on his lap, in the large red leather chair, my knees up under his armpits. I am rocking back and forth, back and forth. He is making a sound I have never heard before, his eyes half closed, his mouth open. I kiss him hard, bite his bottom lip until I taste blood.

After a month I went to see Dr. Glass. I said, "I can't sleep." There were blue shadows under my eyes. I said, "If you're not careful you can see through my skin." I held up my translucent wrists, helpless. "I see him. I see him everywhere." She said it was only grief.

Then she recommended something called counterimagining. "For example." She held up her two forefingers like goal posts. "Imagine putting all his letters in a box in the backyard. Burn it. Or," she said, "put *him* in a closet. Firmly close the door."

I liked this idea. But it didn't work. I cried at the pyre of letters, let him out after five minutes.

But she'd given me a thought. That's when I started trying to imagine a better ending, thinking this might allow me to put this man behind me, give me some peace.

This is the way it really happened. He called me to say it was over. Just like that. (I didn't think you could walk out over the telephone; that's one on me.) I had been supposed to come and stay with him that weekend, to celebrate my birthday. I thought we had been working things out. I had been trying to change in some of the ways he needed (for example, quit screaming), trying to fathom what it was like to be him, trying to understand what made him the tender man he was. Now I know: too much sympathy can kill you.

Anyway, he calls up and after five minutes of clearing his throat like he was choking on a goddamn chicken bone—and slow me saying, "What? What is it? Can't you *breathe*?"—he just says this: "I don't want us to be together anymore. I don't want you to come out here this weekend." I asked him why. He said he didn't think he could make it clear. He said that living with me was like riding on a roller coaster and he wanted to get off. He said he loved me but not enough. He said there was someone else. "That's pretty clear," I said. "Jesus Christ," I said, "any one of those reasons would have been sufficient." But he said he was trying to be honest for once. Nice change for him, I thought, but I was trying to keep from being beaten to death by my own heart. And I'd bought a nonrefundable ticket. There I was, all fucked up and no place to go.

Telling me over the phone like that—I didn't think it showed respect for what we had been to each other. We'd had a life together (four years, on and off) and I deserved better than a phone call. I was only thirty-nine but I'd already learned that it's not so much what is done to you as the manner in which it is done.

So I used the ticket. Air West. Free drinks. During takeoff I closed my eyes and the images started to come. Now it wasn't just at night, when I couldn't sleep. Thoughts of him were taking over my life. I closed my eyes tighter but the images still came.

This time we're standing on the balcony overlooking the ocean. It is night. I have my long black nightgown on. I stand in front, the top railing just above my waist, an edge against my ribs. He is behind, the only warmth in the cold night, his thighs against the backs of my thighs. He slips the spaghetti straps off my shoulder, cups his warm hands under my breasts, uses his thumb and forefinger to make me arch my back. I feel him lift the slippery material up to my waist, feel him push himself inside me, easy at first, then harder. I stand on tiptoe, feel my feet rise off the wooden planks as I watch the white of the slow-breaking waves.

Liar! I started tying him up, first his arms, behind his back, handcuffed to emphasize a point, then his legs. When I was through he couldn't move. I made the rope so tight it burned his ankles. Betrayer! I put masking tape over his mouth. He made a "Mm-mmm" sound, but this time I didn't give in. A person has limits.

I got into town around eight that evening and took a cab to the Sea Horse, knowing he would be there with his latest glorious city. I thought I deserved a more fitting ending and I intended to have it.

The cab driver was tight-lipped and sullen but I gave him a ten-dollar tip, for flair and courage, then walked through the heavy black curtains. Made an entrance, you might say.

This woman, call her Poughkeepsie, was bigger than I expected. Hair the color of mouse. Thin. Pale. Not too glamorous. No Paris.

I remember the song on the jukebox. Lenny Welch. "Since I Fell for You." Jesus.

I walked up to the bar where they were sitting with their backs to me. I said, "Hi. My name's Sarah," and stuck out my hand. I can be civilized when I have to be.

But she didn't seem to understand my desire to have things out with the man whose thigh she had her hand on. So I tried to give her a little history, let her know where I stood in the order of things.

"Fuck off," she explained.

I grabbed the dice cup and shook the bartender, Judy, for the music. I lost. But she gave me four quarters anyway. I put on Hank Williams singing "Your Cheatin' Heart" with "I'm So Lonesome I Could Cry" as a chaser. Six times.

I had a few more Bacardi and Cokes and then tried to convince her again. "Four years," I said. "You are only a few nights. Maybe *good* nights, but still . . ."

She was not impressed with this line of reasoning and pushed me backwards off the barstool where I had been trying to make my case.

All this time Jake is looking at me like I'm in the wrong movie. I thought, *Jake*. It's *me*. Sarah. Don't you recognize me? At my final undoing, I had believed, at my attempted massacre, he would be on my side. At a minimum. No. Maybe she was a few more nights than I imagined.

I was down and I didn't have the will to get up. I just lay there, near defeat, close to a whimper. The boots around my head seemed way too big for human feet.

When I picked myself up off the floor Poughkeepsie was right in my face. That's when I picked up the pool cue. Never pick up a pool cue if you don't intend to use it. Never brandish a pool cue at someone larger and meaner than yourself. I play these useless admonitions over and over in my head, the way a person might repeat a prayer for improved health over the deceased.

I had believed the human eye to be a tenacious thing. I think that woman must have been an oyster shucker before she took up with Jake. She popped that thing out of there as easy as opening a longneck, like removing a cork with a crowbar, like playing tiddlywinks. I thought my face was on fire. I tried to put it out with my fingernails.

I was in the hospital for six weeks. You can have too much time to think. I stared at the white walls so long I went snow-blind. Once in a while I would put my right hand over the bandages on the right side of my face, the way you do when you're trying to see something more clearly. I thought about Jake, the old movies, the old reruns. No counterimagining could touch the way his skin felt next to my skin, like you're in warm water and sinking.

This time we are in bed, on Christmas Eve. He has given me a toy and we are trying it out, children laughing in the dark. "Like this?" he says, moving the head of the machine. "Like this?" I wiggle until it's where I want it, then I begin to writhe, making sounds of mock ecstasy. He takes me almost roughly, his thrusting hard and steady, his hands on my shoulders, holding them down, as if he were trying to teach me a lesson, his thrusting now hard and irregular, probing, as if he were trying to locate the wound. I don't know him. My eyes are wide open and the only sound in the room is the muffled whirring of the small motor trapped in the blue comforter.

My last week in the hospital the candy striper lady brought in some books on a cart, but she didn't smile. She looked at me as if hers were a serious mission, full of mortality and risk. I picked out *Crooked Hearts. Endless Love*. I looked up at her. She shook her head, back and forth, eyes that saw everything. I put the books back on the cart.

Instead I started rereading Nietzsche—something I hadn't looked at since my days at Modesto J.C., something I thought I'd never use, perfectly useless, like trigonometry. The part I concentrated on is the part about *amor fati,* loving one's fate even when it's harsh, especially when it's harsh. What he's talking about is pain, great pain, that long, slow pain in which we are burned with green wood, pain that takes its time with us, like a good lover.

The morning they took the bandages off and I saw the place where my eye had been, I cried. Tears seeping through the red twisted skin. An obscene wink. It was the most sickening sight I had ever seen, and it was a permanent part of my face. But I refused the black patch. I have made a lot of mistakes in my life but I am not a coward.

Nietzsche says that only this kind of pain forces us to go down into our depths, to put away all trust, all good-naturedness, all that would veil, all mildness, all that is medium—things in which we have formerly found our humanness.

For weeks I howled like a coyote. I could not look in a mirror. I wanted, more than to be whole again, someone to hold me. I said, "Nothing is as good when you have it as it is bad when it's gone." It didn't ring true. I said, "Rejection is the great aphrodisiac." So what? I said, "I have been wounded in an accident of my own choosing, and there is no way I can undo it."

Out of such long and dangerous exercises in self-mastery, Nietzsche says, one emerges as a different person, with a few *more* question marks—above all, with the will to question more persistently, more deeply, severely, harshly, evilly, and quietly than has ever been questioned on this earth before. The trust in life is gone; life itself has become a problem.

I'm not a religious person, but when I read that part I said it out loud: "Amen."

Yet one should not jump to the conclusion, Nietzsche says, that with all this a man (or a one-eyed woman, I would add) has necessarily become a barn owl. Even the love of life is still possible—only one loves differently. It is the love for a woman who raises doubts in us.

Maybe I've got him wrong but I think what he's talking about is bitter love. The kind of love that sees the withered eye in the mirror and doesn't cringe. It's a love that comes out of strength rather than weakness, but it has no illusions. It does not expect something for nothing. (It does not expect something for something.) It knows that for every inarticulate joy there is some bright grief.

People are always saying, "You're so bitter." As if this were something one should endeavor to avoid. I say, "Look at this eye." I say, "If you're not bitter you haven't been paying attention." But would there be so much bitterness if there wasn't still love? That's the hard question I have to ask myself.

I haven't got the answer yet but last night, for the first time, I could sleep. I slept through almost to morning, without dreaming. When I woke up I didn't raise the blinds. In that shallow half-light, with my one good eye, I could see his real face. The soft brown eyes so like my dead grandmother's, the heavy nostrils flaring, full lips, those straight white teeth, the ugly mole just beneath his jawline.

I don't know why but I decided to let him go. It was at first merely an internal gesture, like intending one person rather than another when you use a common name. But then it gathered momentum. I untied his arms and legs, unlocked the handcuffs with the small key I keep on the chain around my neck, loosened the straitjacket in back, so it no longer looked like he was hugging himself, ripped the masking tape from his mouth—fast, so it wouldn't hurt.

In spite of the rope burns and the welts, I think he smiled, nodded a thank-you. Is this what love is? Out of gratitude he took a step toward me, looked at me for the first time as if I were human. But before he could open his arms, I gave him his heart back.

He didn't know how to take what was his. I understand that

now. That's why he always laughed so hard at the part in *Midnight Cowboy* where Ratso Rizzo is stuffing the salami into his pockets. That's why he needed me: gifted and greedy.

In my imagination I could see him opening outward. I set him free to become whatever he is. Thief. Ordinary man. Truth-teller. I watched him bloom, even in the dark, like a nightflower.

ORDER AND FLUX IN NORTHAMPTON

♥ ♥

David Foster Wallace

Barry Dingle, cross-eyed purveyor of bean sprouts, harbors for Myrnaloy Trask, operator of Xerox and regent of downtown Northampton's most influential bulletin board at Collective Copy, an immoderate love.

Myrnaloy Trask, trained Reproduction Technician, unmarried woman, vegetarian, flower child tinged faintly with wither, overseer and editor of Announcement and Response at the ten-foot-by-ten-foot communicative hub of a dizzying wheel of leftist low-sodium aesthetes, a woman politically correct, active in relevant causes, slatternly but not unerotic, all-weather wearer of frayed denim skirts and wool knee socks, sexually troubled, ambiguous sexual past, owner of one spectacularly incontinent Setter/Retriever bitch, Nixon, so named by friend Don Megala because of the dog's infrangible habit of shitting where it eats: Myrnaloy has eyes only for Don Megala: Don Megala, middle-aged liberal, would-be drifter, maker of antique dulcimers by avocation, by calling a professional student, a haunter of graduate hallways, adrift, holding fractions of Ph.D.s in everything from Celtic phonetics to the sociobiology of fluids from the University of Massachusetts at Amherst, presently at work on his seventh and potentially finest unfinished dissertation, an exhaustive study of Stephen Dedalus's sublimated Oedipal necrophilia vis-à-vis D. in *Ulysses*, an essay tentatively titled "The Ineluctable Modality of the Ineluctably Modal."

Add to the above Trask-data that, though Barry Dingle's spotlessly managed franchise, The Whole Thing Health Food Emporium, is located directly next to Collective Copy on Northampton's arterial Great Awakening Avenue, Myrnaloy has her nutritional needs addressed at The Whole Thing's out-of-the-way, sawdust-floored competition, Good Things to Eat, Ltd., the proprietor of which, one Adam Baum, is a crony of Megala, and add also that The Whole Thing is in possession of its own Xerox copier, and the following situation comes into narrative focus: Myrnaloy Trask has only the sketchiest intuition that Barry Dingle even exists, next door.

For Barry Dingle, though, the love of Myrnaloy Trask has become the dominant emotional noisemaker in his quiet life, the flux-ridden state of his heart, a thing as intimately close to Dingle as Myrnaloy is forever optically distant or unreal.

Suspend and believe that the consuming, passionate love of Myrnaloy Trask has in fact become defined and centered as a small homunculoid presence inside Barry Dingle, a doll-sized self all its own, with the power of silent speech and undisguised ambitions to independent action. Barry Dingle's love sees itself as the catalyst that can transform Barry Dingle from a neutral to a positive charge in life's delicate equation. It sees itself as having the power to remake, reform, reconstitute Barry Dingle. In fact—since facts are the commodity at issue—Barry Dingle's love of Myrnaloy Trask wants in some ultimate sense to *be* Barry Dingle, and has lately launched an aggressive campaign to assume control of Dingle's life, to divert and even divorce Dingle from his seven-year definition as manager of The Whole Thing, from his hard-learned disposition to passivity and mute fear: in short, for those who know him, from the very Dingleness of Dingle.

The birth of Barry Dingle's love for Myrnaloy Trask can be fixed generally at a present some two years back, when The Whole Thing, like the rest of the health-food industry, is scrambling wildly to capitalize on the American consumer's growing enthusiasm for bran. The precise two-year-old moment when the crossed eyes, healthy heart, modest mind, and tame history of Barry Dingle consummated their need for intersection at the point of object-choice can be identified as the moment 4:30 p.m. on 15 June 1981, when Dingle, arranging a cunningly enticing display of bran-walnut muffins on the recycled-aluminum shelves of The Whole Thing's display window, finds himself staring, as only the cross-eyed can stare, into the smoke-dark window of a Northampton Public Transit Authority bus, halted on the street outside by one of Northampton's eternal red lights. In the sunlight off the sienna glass is the muted reflected image of Myrnaloy Trask, next door, outside Collective Copy, in her denim skirt and Xerox apron, editorially scanning CC's public-announcement bulletin board's collection of fliers and hand-lettered ads, searching out the irrelevant, the nonprogressive, the uncleared.

To see and feel anything like what Barry Dingle feels as he stares slack-jawed through his glasses, his store's glass, into the darkly reflecting glass of the frustrated bus, the student of the phenomenon of Barry Dingle must try to imagine the unimaginable richness, range, *promise* of the community bulletins before which Myrnaloy establishes herself as culler and control, the board aflutter with bright announcement, Establishment-opprobrium, introduction—bids for attention from kyphotic-lesbian support groups, Maoist coffeehouses, organic-garden plot rentals, dentists who eschew all mercury and alum, obscurely oriented political parties with titles longer than their petitioned rosters of names, sitar instructors, anorexia crisis lines, Eastern and Mideastern expanders of spiritual consciousness, bulimia crisis lines, M.D.s in healing with crystals and wheat, troupes of interpretive tap dancers, holistic masseurs, acupuncturists, chiropractic acupuncturists, Marxist mimes who do *Kapital* in dumbshow, typists, channelers, nutrition consultants, Brecht-only theater companies, Valley literary journals with double-digit circulations, on and on—a huge, flat, thumbtack- and staple-studded, central affair, sheltered from the apathetic vicissitudes of New England weathers by a special Collective Copy awning. The board is the area's avant-garde ganglion, a magnet drawing centripetally from the center of town on the diffracted ions of Northampton's vast organizational night, each morning bristling brightly with added claims to existence and efficacy, each late afternoon edited, ordered, wheat-from-chaffed by Myrnaloy Trask, who stands now, reflected in the dun shield of the bus's glass, snake-haired in the June wind, one nail-bitten finger on a shiny leaflet of debatable value or legitimacy, deciding on the words' right to be; and at this moment, 4:30 p.m., 15 June 1981, she brings up behind herself her left leg—in the bus window a distant right leg—bends it at the pale knee to effect the ascension of an ankle, pulls a sag-laddered wool knee sock tight up the back of a white calf; and the movement, the unconscious gentle elevation of the thick ankle, is so very demure—reminiscent finally of the demure elevation of Sandra Dee's own sturdy calf as Gidget kissed interchangeable emmetropic young men in the climaxes of all the interchangeable Gidget films that informed so much of Barry Dingle's childhood—the movement so very young, tired, unself-conscious, sad, right, natural, reflected, distant, unsexily sexy, slatternly erotic . . .

. . . so very *whatever*, in short, that off the bus's window and through the TWT display pane and Dingle's thick hot angled glasses the parallaxed leg-image tears, rending Dingle's sense of self and place, plunging with a crackle of sexual ozone into the still surface of the stagnant ankle-deep pond that defines at this moment the Dingleness of Dingle; and through the miraculous manipulations of primal human ontemes, too primal and too human even to be contemplated, probably, it gives birth to life:

from the clotted silt of the uninterestingness at the center of Barry Dingle there emerges the salamanderial zygote of a robust, animate thing, a life, Barry Dingle's immoderate homunculoid love, conceived out of the impossibly distant refracted epiphany of Myrnaloy Trask, demure in her now-not-fallen socks, a Myrnaloy who is as unaware as carbon itself that she has effected the manufacture of life through her role in the interplay of forces probably beyond the comprehension of everything and everyone involved.

Northampton is located on the northern fringe of Massachusetts's Pioneer Valley on the eastern edge of the Berkshire Mountains. To the south lie Amherst and Springfield and Hartford, Connecticut. Incorporated in 1698, Northampton is the eighth-oldest township in the state. It is the home of Smith College for Women. The college's Congregational Church, still semi-erect, saw the 1711–17 delivery of the Great-Awakening jeremiads of dentist/theologian Solomon Stoddard, in which the reverend foretold the world's cold and imminent end, characterizing that end as a kind of grim entropic stasis already harbinged by, among other portents: poor nutrition and its attendant moral and dental decay; the increasing infertility of modern woman; the rise of the novel; the Great Awakening itself.

The city grew to economic prominence in the late eighteenth century, after more space was cleared for development and commercial intercourse. Space for development and commercial intercourse was cleared all over the Pioneer Valley by the British commander Lord Jeffrey Amherst, who in 1783–84 won a telling victory over the sly, putatively "peace-loving" native population by providing its tribes with free blankets, each carefully preinfected with smallpox.

Northampton today enjoys the nation's second-highest percentage of homosexuals, calculated on a per capita basis, a distinction that has earned the city the designation "the San Francisco of the East." It also enjoys the nation's sixth-highest percentage of homeless persons, again per capita, countless capita to be seen each winter night clustered around the tattered flickers of countless trashcan fires. Most enjoyable of all is the nation's lowest percentage of registered Republicans, with the brow-raising total of exactly zero within the corporation limits.[1]

Fact: certain unlucky persons exist as living justifications of those phobias peculiar to mothers. Barry Dingle is such a person. His childhood, his whole life, stands darkly informed by Mrs. Dingle's failure ever to be incorrect. Examples range through the history of the man. The tiniest pre-dinner treat does spoil little Barry's appetite. The briefest exposure of his unrubbered Hush Puppies to rain or snow ensures, with mathematical reliability, disease. The dullest of sharp things wounds, the safest of playground games injures, the scantiest inattention to oral hygiene sees the dark time-lapse sprout of an instant caries.

The Barry Dingle who dislikes drinking milk, avoids it at all costs, does fail to grow up big and strong like his sister, a field-hockey prodigy.

Also a fact: certain persons, especially mothers, come in time to resemble more and more closely their automobiles. Mrs. Dingle is outdated, rust-chassis'd, loud, disposed to the emission of fumes; she is wide and rides low and has a poor turning radius; but she is ideally suited for the transport of much baggage, and her mileage is phenomenal.

Picture her, then, entreating the child Barry Dingle never, never *ever*, to cross his little eyes. She believes, with the complete conviction of the phobic mother, that the child who crosses his eyes Stays That Way. She cajoles, enjoins; the indoctrination's movement is as broad and slow and irresistible as the Dingles' station wagon. The orientation of his eyes becomes for the little Dingle an object of black fascination. He dreams, in the night's dark part, of his eyes crossing by accident, their paths never again to diverge. He avoids sighting on any but the stablest objects. He resists the natural urge of the child to look down at his own

[1] For much more here see W. Deldrick Sperber, "The Sensitive Community: Nutritive, Sexual and Political Ambiguity in Northampton, MA," *Journal of American Studies in Sensitivity*, v. IX, nos. 2&3, 1983.

nose. With Mrs. Dingle riding herd on their mutual neurosis, Dingle treasures the clean binocularity of his sight like a never-miss aggie. He makes it through fifteen years of exquisite temptation without so much as a retinal wobble.

Fact to be feared: the rebelliousness of fearful youth, no matter how momentary, can itself be a fearful thing. On 15 June 1961, Troy, New York, enraged by the imposition of a domestic sanction soon lost to memory, Barry Dingle stands before his mother in the warm checker-tiled Dingle kitchen and gives in to the terrifying, wonderful temptation of the ultimate transgression against natural and maternal law. The cross is delicious; his eyes roll toward each other with the sweet release of catharsis long delayed. Two Mrs. Dingles scream and raise four arms skyward, pleading for intercession against the inevitable. . . .

Cross-eyed Barry is shunted from specialist to specialist. As Mrs. Dingle tearfully predicts, they are powerless to help. For six binary, true-and-false-filled months Dingle veers, bumbles, bumps his way through the doubled system of peccatum and punishment he has wrought. Finally, December, Buffalo, an optician at technology's cutting edge fits Dingle with an elaborate pair of glasses—thick angled lenses that catch and reorganize the disordered doubleness of things into a unity that fuses at a focused point several yards in front of Barry's own ruined apparatus. Relief is purchased, at a cost: the glasses work, unify, but objects for a bespectacled Barry now appear always twice as far away as they in fact are. Smaller, more distant. So that for twenty years Dingle has chosen minute by minute between doubleness and distance, between there being, for him, exactly twice or exactly half as much as there really is.

The point here being that a key ingredient of Myrnaloy's allure for Barry Dingle, and an irreducible constant in the sensuous half-equation whose sum is the immoderate love that even now makes its move for control of Barry Dingle's present and future, is the fact that Myrnaloy must always remain either fundamentally distant *from* Dingle, or else doubled, and so unreal, *for* him. Meaning that the "real" Myrnaloy Trask is for Dingle not even a possibility: he is in the (not unenviable?) position of a man able to want without the disturbing option of ever truly being able to have. Hence a classic, almost classically static romanticism as fundament, as primal element, precondition for the very experience of being B. Dingle.

Additional fact: Mrs. Dingle predicts, long ago, over vermouth, that love will someday make Barry Dingle hideously, hideously unhappy. This, too, is come to pass. Dingle is, as it were, beside himself, in a state of utter emotional flux whereby up and down, good and bad are as indistinguishable as right and left. Here, though, it is necessary to distinguish between the unhappiness of Barry Dingle and the happiness of his interior homunculoid love. Barry Dingle's immoderate love is itself happy as a clam. It thrives, grows, gets off on the existence of a telos at once right next door and horizon-distant, at once really one and apparently two—in short, of a love-object invested with all the flected ambiguity that makes Romance itself possible.

But one last fact: Barry Dingle's love is still a human love. With the illogic that defines all autonomous but entombed emotional homunculoids, Dingle's immoderate love is possessed of a desire for the attainment of the very love-object whose fundamental *un*attainability is that love's animating breath and bread. It is by nature dissatisfied, and that dissatisfaction is, via the hermeneutic circle of love's illogic, its life and mission. It needs Barry Dingle to appropriate, possess, use and encompass Myrnaloy Trask. It harbors in its doll's heart a desire for a strong new Dingle shell, the outward instantiation of an immoderate inner force. It envisions Dingle capturing Myrnaloy's heart and fashioning inside her a demure-calved homunculoid of her own, a love for Barry Dingle that will, in the union of Dingle and Trask, merge with the homunculoids themselves and render them complete (i.e., no longer animate, inside). A genuinely human emotional armillary, Dingle's immoderate love's life strains ever forward toward the death that love's life loves.

Think of it this way, Dingle, says Dingle's love as Dingle inventories herbal teas on a May afternoon, 1983. Think of your love as being by nature an incomplete, questing thing. I was born in you half a love. My end is the unity I am by definition denied.

Dingle is silent over ginseng and camomile.

The homunculoid taps its foot patiently. The point, it says, is that I've got a nature to be true to, just like you. I'm compelled by its nature to spend my time, therefore our time, questing and striving for my other half. This is so, no matter how much you buck and snort. Think of me as a chivalric knight, you as my dragon. And obversely. Each other's torments, but also our salvations.

Salvations? Dingle says. Dragons?

You give birth to a love in Myrnaloy Trask; she forms her own half-a-love homunculoid, curved, gentle, round-faced, doll's eyes that open with the pull of a heartstring, concave where I am convex. You do such a thing; Myrnaloy gives birth; her half-a-love and I get together; I leave you in peace. Everybody's a winner. *Verstehen-Sie?*

And the toe problem? whispers Dingle, biting a cracked lip.

Your toes are once again your own psyche's own, says Dingle's love, making its presence felt with a playful twinge in one red Dingle digit.

The fact of the May '83 matter here is that Dingle's love, as of some six weeks past, has decided to play hardball. It has moved to consolidate its authority over Barry Dingle by focusing its attention and influence on Dingle's most vulnerable parts. Here these parts are due south of even the most sensitive dangling chinks in all men's armor. They are the tortured ingrown toenails of Barry Dingle. (Possibly worth noting here that Mrs. Dingle was and is a fanatic on the subject of foot care.) Barry Dingle's love is using the curved culcates of Dingle's nails, together with the tender genital/emotional complex that birthed the immoderate homunculoid in the first place, to force an intrinsically passive Dingle toward some decisive romantic action.

Love has turned the order of Barry Dingle's life into flux; Dingle is now at war with himself; divided; schismed; finally wounded, behind the lines.

Yes, cross-eyed Barry, thirty-five, perennial wearer of leather sandals, bell-bottoms, and Central American ponchos, high of forehead, long of incisor, thick of spectacle, is in possession of

(2) feet presently in torment from the negative-reinforcement regiment of his immoderate love. Since adolescence (specific moment of origin coincident with that of the optical transgression), the toes have detracted from Dingle's quality of life: corticate yellow nails curving in of themselves, sinking into the tender meat of his red toes, the toes taking turns at self-harm, swelling, shining with erumpent infection, to say nothing of pain. Dingle, of routine, takes all possible preventive steps. He trims the nails daily, paring them straight across, leaving perfect planks of protruding cartilage, into the corners of which each morning he tucks tiny cotton pellets soaked in camphor and oil of clove. Sandals, affording the toes movement, oxygen, freedom from pressure, are worn at all times. In cold seasons Dingle even forfeits the privilege ever of being taken seriously as a person: he wears sandals with socks.

Now for naught: B. Dingle is literally staggering under the incurving influence of his immoderate love for Myrnaloy Trask. The love, from its central facility in Dingle's clean red heart, now commutes daily south to an annex in Dingle's clawlike nails, from which annex it makes its presence, wishes and directives acutely known. The campaign is insidiously subtle, the pain carefully gauged to impel cooperation without ever quite causing incapacitation. Barry Dingle's love begins moving against his feet in April 1983. By June Dingle knows something must be done. Myrnaloy Trask must somehow be appropriated, Dingle's cherry-colored homunculoid completed, sated, silenced. The love has worn Dingle down—to years of flux and now two months of rampant ingrowth: his tortured feet, his keening heart, the disorder and disruption of the neutral Dingle equation are driving Dingle quietly toward breakdown and tilted stasis.

Cf. he has become unable to concentrate at work. He becomes lax, his employees demoralized, intransigent, carbohydrated. The owner of the whole The Whole Thing chain pays a personal visit, 2 June, to the Northampton franchise. He takes a significant look at Dingle's blackly circled cross-eyes, his well-chewed lip, his obscenely swollen feet. The owner straightens his suede vest and fingers his Scientology medallion. He advises Dingle in no uncertain terms that he, the owner, knows that things here at the Northampton facility are on the decline. That sales have been slipping, that freshness is on occasion being compromised, that TWT's employees, not to mention Northampton's health-rabid customers, are losing a focus for their nutritional vision. Even the bran, he says pointedly, though not without a smile at his own wit, lately isn't moving like it should. He asks Dingle what *he'd* do, in the owner's place, here. Dingle's love, from deep inside him, puts in its own two cents' worth—an electric thrill of podiatric pain. A pale Dingle removes his glasses, sets his jaw. He reassures the twin images of the owner. Things will turn around. The store will soon be back on its feet. Seven years of careful management; passionate devotion to the marketing of health; the dingy Good Things no competition: he waxes briefly eloquent, an aggressive sincerity that surprises the owner and distracts even the bloated TWT employees from their game of rummy. The owner eventually nods, acquiesces, checks his sundial, and makes for the glass doors, leaving in his cinnamon-scented wake a system of insinuations that both reaffirm and cast doubt on his faith in Barry Dingle. The store is silent; a halted bus's motor can be heard at the traffic light.

For two unprecedented sick days Dingle stays home, brooding, his feet in hot salt water and eucalyptus. Nigel, the assistant manager, temporarily assumes The Whole Thing's helm. Dingle communes with his love. With himself.

The result of which is the prenominate realization that something must change, coupled with a robust new determination really, truly, finally to act. After two days (date now 6 June 1983), Dingle leaves his bath, returns to TWT's many windows, and resolves with a coldly febrile set to his tall forehead to set his unsteady sights on the distant Trask and to bring her, by fair means or otherwise, swimming into his romantic ken. His homunculoid love smells the metal smell of strength in Dingle's blood, and approves it. It loosens the grip of Dingle's own nails just a bit. It encourages Dingle, exhorts, plays interior good-cop-bad-cop, says it discerns in him a nascent newness, a courage.

Courage! says Dingle's homunculoid love, defining the term in

Gothic script on Dingle's heart as a willingness to bring the comfortably distant into a unified proximity, to risk stasis as completion. The words pump against the fishwhite skin of Dingle's shallow chest and appear on his body in faint pink calligraphy. Dingle reads himself double in the night's salty bath. Touches the blurred words.

The fly in the emotional ointment here being the initially mentioned Don Megala, eternal student, dulcimer-*craeftig*, whose connection with Myrnaloy Trask, visible through Collective Copy's window via the reflecting umber glass of the ever-halted Northampton bus, is undeniable, though ambiguous—Megala being in his heyday an epic drinker and chaser of skirt, both the denim skirts of Northampton's straight female leftists and the tartan skirts of the aesthetically inclined Smith College set whose poetry readings, madrigal recitals, and sherry-and-scone mixers Megala haunts, earning himself the designation *Der Doppelbanger* by Smith's artistes-in-the-know—and Myrnaloy being shy, withdrawn, clearly inexperienced, and, even more clearly, deeply ambivalent about men.

It is now appropriate to note that Barry Dingle and Don Megala enjoy some slight acquaintance through the University of Massachusetts at Amherst, that Megala had been going through the motions on an abortive sociobiology dissertation while Dingle completed his undergraduate studies in Digestive Science, that they had had in common a mentor and adviser—one W.W. Skeat, a socio-digestive biologist best known for his thesis that the underlying and true cause of cancer is in fact plain old human saliva—and had both done substantial research under and lab-assisting for this mentor, adviser, Skeat. Noted further is the fact that Megala regards Dingle with the jolly condescension reserved for the cross-eyed, buck-toothed, and sock-and-sandal-shod, while Dingle, lately under the emotional aegis of his homunculoid love, harbors for Megala a mute dislike, an active wish to do him harm, from a distance.

Megala being the fly in the ointment of romance vis-à-vis Myrnaloy, it is understandable that Barry Dingle, whenever the opportunity presents itself, arranges to observe Myrnaloy and Megala together—not actually *following* M & M, mind you, given documented eye and mobility troubles, but rather just arranging to be located, unconspicuously, wherever they are likely to appear together.

Opportunities for such observation are not few, Myrnaloy and Megala to be seen by Dingle variously: sipping four-dollar espressos at Northampton's Leftward Ho Café; strolling hand in hand through any one of the city's fifty-six used-book stores; waving a shared banner at weekly rallies of the Northampton Anti-Nuclear And Non-Aligned Nations' And Neighbors' Alliance, Myrnaloy having been recording secretary of NANA-NANANA since its mid-seventies inception; exercising together on the town's common's public aerobics palestrae; etc.; and, of course, variously talking, confiding, nuzzling, arguing, being ambiguous, all in the bus-reflected Collective Copy window.

Not to mention patronizing Adam Baum's own Good Things to Eat, Ltd., The Whole Thing's chief sit-down competition, a tiny-windowed establishment which Dingle, incurring substantial professional risk, begins inconspicuously patronizing as well. Picture Dingle, in early '83, hunched, poncho-swaddled, his cotton pellets grimed with the floor's sawdust, in a Good Things booth as M & M establish themselves over a whole-grain dinner at their usual table directly behind him. They are deep in conversation. Barry Dingle and his immoderate love listen. Myrnaloy seems just to have finished pouring her ambivalent heart out to Megala on the subject of men and sex. Dingle's ears are aprick, his carrot cake hardening and peppermint tea chilling, untouched.

Myrnaloy, on the last leg of a redditive narrative journey, is revealing, fragilely, with many stuttered pauses, that she is terrified of sex. Thoroughly terrified. She alludes to some shadowy, long-ago trauma, some betrayal, the details of which Megala, judging from the sympathetic and reinforcing soft sounds he keeps making as he chews, already knows. Barry Dingle's love gnashes its teeth at Barry's not knowing what Megala knows. Myrnaloy's voice is trembling; she is revealing that she is, at thirty-five, flower-child past and all, still technically maiden. She states that sex holds a great, albeit undefinable, terror for her.

Don Megala gives Myrnaloy Trask to understand that he understands, that he regards—nay, *genuflects to* her attitude as one more than just understandable, don't you know, but as deeply somehow sexually-politically *correct*. He reveals that he lost his own innocence at fifteen and has been terrified ever since. That he lives in sexual terror. That sex is, by nature, terrifying.

To Dingle's horror he finds himself in significant agreement with Megala.

But what Megala is about here, Barry is roughly told, is clear. Yes Dingle's love smells impending seduction. Dingle searches through his angled glasses for some reflecting surface in the restaurant, anything in which to study Myrnaloy's facial reaction to Megala's inevitable upcoming arguments. He imagines her looking down, rouged with self-revelation, dabbing at nothing with a recycled napkin, smiling hesitantly, gratefully, at Megala's understanding, his willingness to share a vulnerability. Yet it's the willingness-to-share gambit: the homunculoid establishes itself in an orbit of impotent rage around Dingle's carved heart.

Because But wonderful, too, Megala is going on to muse out loud. His voice is pocked with the tiny hesitations of purposeful sincerity. Sex, Megala means. Even the terror of sex is, in fact, wonderful, in a terrible sort of way.

Dingle envisions Megala's delicate white hands covering Myrnaloy's delicate white hands. Dingle is pale, helpless, staring into the distant fossil of his dinner.

Because sex also being, let's both be honest with ourselves and admit it, a pretty big thing in this predominantly short and unhappy life, Megala adds. How sad it would be to depart the coil without taking, as it were, a look around at life, to see what's what. Surely sex is one of the big whats in life, to be at least looked at, no? Or so he tells himself, he tells her, whenever his perfectly appropriate terror threatens to get the best.

Dingle envisions clean binocular eye contact between M & M.

And it's hard to think of a more *natural* thing in this life, Megala muses out loud, than intimacy between a man and a woman who share mutual concerns and respect and correctness. Who *care*.

No? A natural, natural thing. Like the coruscating flora of autumn. A cotton Nehru jacket dried on the line. A bird wheeling before a stiff gust. And, irony of ineluctable ironies, are not the very most *natural* things in life often the most terrifying? Does . . . *could* Myrnaloy share this feeling, this insight? This sad, wonderful, terrifying irony?

Dingle hears Myrnaloy make a gentle noise variously indicative of: agreement, gratitude, admiration, the recognition of something unseen that's been recognized *for* her. Dingle's love twirls, staring balefully at its blurred reflection in Dingle's clean pounding courage-scripted heart.

There is the violent sound of Megala vacuuming the bottom of his glass with a straw. Each of Dingle's eyes contemplates its reflection in the other.

An absolute scuttling mink, hisses Barry Dingle's love.

Pardon? whispers Barry Dingle.

This guy is a sterling example of a mink, says the homunculoid.

A mink?

A technical term for a certain kind of low-rent player in the love game the love says, "Mink," noun, meaning basically someone who's smooth on the outside, but inside still just a weasel.

A smooth weasel?

The guy is minkness in motion, says the love; and here we sit, inert. It goes for a shiny metatarsal's tip, in the sawdust.

Megala and Myrnaloy exit Good Things. Dingle can finally see them, far away, through the cashier's little round window to which he's half-run, limping. They are detaching the leash of Myrnaloy's Nixon from a Good Things leash-hook. Disappearing in a direction opposite that of Collective Copy. Leaving behind a slim trail of Nixon's digestive distress.

The following couples grapple into the wee hours of this early-June night: Myrnaloy Trask and Don Megala; Barry Dingle and Barry Dingle's love.

Fly-ridden ointment or not, recall that Barry Dingle has, as of 6 June, reoriented himself, that the needle of his emotional compass now points, shakily or not, toward the pole of action. Action number one is taking place right this minute, on the morning of 6 June, as Dingle sits at his fiberboard TWT desk, absent his thick glasses, composing an advertisement for a new line of wheat germ with coconut and date-dust mixed right in. He hand-letters a flier outlining nutritional virtues and introductory discounts. He finishes flier, caps his Magic Marker, submits flier to Nigel for the correction of doubled letters and incongruities of scale, and lets Nigel edit while he, Dingle, drifts pensively through the store's bulk aisle, past broad side windows, past clean sunwashed plastic trashcans brimming with granolas, past nuts, dried fruit, protein powders, bran barrels, trowels, degradable baggies, scales, to The Whole Thing's frontal display pane. In the window of the idling bus can be seen Myrnaloy, fetchingly distant at the control of her Xerox behind the CC customer counter. The arched-bridge-esque figure of Nixon is to be seen ranging over a spread-out pile of invalidated bulletin-board submissions. Against the CC counter leans Don Megala, flushed and shiny, speaking out of one side of his mouth to Baum, the Good Things proprietor, whose fliers enjoy, through the influence of Megala, a consistent place on a Collective Copy board whose facilities Dingle has never had the gumption to request.

Nigel pronounces the flier clean copy. Dingle finds the thing in his hands, alludes to a vague problem with the copier in The Whole Thing's stock room, and says perhaps he'll just whisk over next door to Collective Copy. Nigel mans the TWT con while Dingle embarks on what is possibly history's slowest whisk, three wide elliptical passes at the copy center's entrance, last-second veerings, sudden reversals of flight at the compulsion of the homunculoid, who has only to feint at Dingle's sandals to get its point across. The closure of ellipse number three sees Dingle pass under the bulletin board, fumble between the old wooden door's two apparent knobs, *glom* finally on to the genuine article, hear the *ching* of the customer bell, and enter the lair of M & M. The place is hot, full of the dry chemical wind of roaring copier and rattling automatic collator. Flier in hand, Dingle steps over the tortured figure of Nixon and makes for the customer counter.

Baum having decamped at TWT's approach, here is Megala, alone, under his arm a used copy of Stuart Gilbert's *Ulysses* guide. Megala greets Dingle with broad enthusiasm, extends a doubled hand. Dingle hopes very much he won't be clapped on the back. Smells of cork and yeast exit Megala's mouth; his eyes are red as certain toes, a filigreed road guide to the state of post-lunch fermentation he now enjoys. Dingle's tense smiling cheeks spasm as two Myrnaloys leave the copier and approach; Megala has called for a look at this flier of Dingle's, here. Myrnaloy Trask is close. Two denim skirts, two work shirts the pale blue of tired laundry, Xerox aprons, four knee socks. Eyes and forehead framed in tiny dry wrinkles and squeezed in a kind of tight pain against the hot June window-light, but Dingle can see only two milky facial outlines that resist resolution or rapprochement. A customer enters, as does a unit of spring wind, carrying to the counter the rich smell of Nixon. Megala wrinkles his nose, reaches across the pitted counter for what appears to Dingle as the twin-towered facade of a Bass ale.

Megala, with a flourish, introduces Dingle to Myrnaloy. Her hand is white and delicate, if a bit unsoft. Dingle's tongue is dry meat in his mouth. Myrnaloy acknowledges Dingle as somehow connected with The Whole Thing, next door. Megala outlines Dingle's curriculum vitae for Myrnaloy. Dingle brandishes the advertisement, requests copies. Costs are negotiated, specifications specified; Myrnaloy retreats to her machines. Nixon sniffs with ominous interest at Dingle's sandals.

Megala comments on the weather, the bus, the lager, the Laffer Curve's impact on the whole-grain and dulcimer trades. Largely without punctuation. At least two of his three sheets are flapping. Dingle can tell, standing here at the counter, fingering the collar of his poncho, that Myrnaloy is still within earshot, despite the roar of Xeroxes, from the unmistakable way Megala directs his voice to the wide empty parqueted space between Dingle and Trask. There are twine-gnarled subtexts here to which Barry is not privy: Megala's loud voice is making Myrnaloy strangely tight-lipped; Dingle watches her face expand at the sides. His love tightens the screws on a digit, shrieking silently at Dingle to act, to speak, reveal something of himself before this woman and her mink of a beau.

So I see you have at least one Stuart Gilbert, there, under your arm, Dingle says to Megala. I guess I'll assume, he says, that the Stuart Gilbert you have there under your arm is material for a dissertation.

Assume away, says Megala, who's been counting heavily on the source in question and is now disappointed, to say nothing of pissed, to find that Gilbert's work on what Megala keeps calling "The Big U" is just a reference guide, not an analysis—original, as opposed to recapitulatory, scholarship is not a Megala-strength.

Assume away, he says; worthless though, the man vastly overrated, important implications overlooked, mere surfaces scratched, Dedalus's Oedipal psyche stands unrevealed, the metamorphosis from young artist to Telemachoid heir a blank, his dead love-object a scholastic deletion.

So a challenge, then, says Dingle.

Or a study in futility, smiles Megala, less wryly than he means to, eyeing a red triangle on the Bass bottle in some sort of thousand-yard expectation.

At this point Dingle finds himself staring at the images of Myrnaloy Trask bent reproductively over the photographic strobe of the copier. He makes certain observations—mute, internal, lyrical—about her breasts, which happen to be budging almost geologically against her worn work shirt; about the hip-induced swells in her denim skirt; about the bristly shine of her white legs, above the wool. Standard metaphors are invoked. Now, in a gesture of thoroughly unconscious cooperation, Myrnaloy brings her right ankle up behind her and tends to the top of a tired sock. Dingle perspires freely. His eyes stare into each other over the bridge of his nose. There is a sinister protrusion near the hem of a certain poncho. Dingle shifts closer to the protective counter. Megala drinks at his bottle. Nixon diddles on a box of Hammermill bond.

Megala, soaring on the wings of futility's study, waxes nostalgic, collegial. He asks after Skeat. Dingle has not seen Skeat for years, believes him to be out West, living on grants. Myrnaloy glances through the flash of photocopy at the postprandial foot traffic on the sidewalk outside. Megala calls to her, jolly, regarding a Dingle-anecdote, set in the UMass research laboratory of W. W. Skeat, an incident dated 1968. He says the incident concerns Dingle. Dingle's immoderate love whispers encouragement. Myrnaloy's eyes register what could be called interest. Dingle clears his throat. Two Myrnaloys move through blinking mists, toward the counter, the copier on automatic pilot. Dingle tells.

Picture this. It is 1968. Barry Dingle, burning the midnight fluorescence in the basement laboratory of Skeat, is bent over the special microscope he, Dingle, requires to fuse a slide studied into unified, eyelash-free focus. He wears a white lab coat and thongs. He is using the microscope to observe the activities of some routine germs, paramecia in a droplet of saliva from the mouth of a melanoma patient. The germs swim aimlessly around, engage in activities. Dingle observes them. Then, on a whim.

On a whim, mind you, he says, he removes the slide from its clips, turns it around, reinserts it, and again bends to observe. He notes something curious in the movements of the germs at issue.

Megala belches, incurring the empathy of Nixon. Myrnaloy betrays distaste, looks back again at Dingle, who's still crowding the counter.

Dingle, in the past, in the lab, becomes excited. He turns the scope's slide again. Looks. Sure enough. The germs are swimming north. Not aimless. Not just around. North. Only aimless if seen from one angle. Turn the slide, the wily germs take sharp lefts and rights, head due north again.

Megala chuckles. Myrnaloy's four eyes are on Dingle, perplexed.

North? she says.

Not just around, Megala says. The aimlessness only apparent.

North, Dingle says. They swim north. Sense the ephemeral pull of some deep geologic magnet. Heed its call.

North for the summer, says Megala.

Dingle manipulates the hood of his poncho. And the whole on-a-whim insight a matter of *perspective*, was what excites, he says. See? Look from just one angle: things seem aimless, disordered. Flux reigns. Change the angle: illumination. Pattern. Order.

His love whips a checkered flag downward.

Look at a thing from some variety of perspectives, Dingle says; input from let's say even just two completely different angles: see matters in a whole new light, potentially.

Northern expedition, ruminates Megala.

It was so excited, Dingle says quietly.

Except it was Skeat was the one who wrote it up, Megala says. Got himself a Guggenheim out of it.[2] Dingle here got no credit. Skeat gave him the academic shaft. The big femur.

Dingle smiles shyly. Credit not important. The insight itself important. Epiphany under cold lights. Beside myself with joy, that night.

The homunculoid thumbs-ups its approval, reclines on a shiny ventricle, polishing its fingernails against the front of its tunic.

Myrnaloy: And now you manage The Whole Thing?

Yes. Problems in terms of medical-school applications. Finances. Vision.

The Skeat thesis, laughs Megala. Watch what you swallow, Myrnalove.

The relevant Xerox grinds into automatic shut-off. Myrnaloy retrieves Dingle's original, hands him a stack of warm noisome copy.

Fine, fine copies, Dingle says, flipping through, willing himself not to squint. Myrnaloy punches up his bill.

Megala gestures over at the register. Why not let Dingle put one up on the old board, Myrnaloy, he suggests, grinning. A quo for his quid.

[2] See W. W. Skeat, "The Intrinsic Northern Orientation of the Paramecium in Neoplastic Human Saliva," *Principium Salivato*, v. 2, nos. 2&3, 1970.

Really a first-rate new product, Dingle stammers, gratitude and resentment toward Megala swirling together oily in his heart, which pounds. Excited about the chance to be part of, he says; happy to arrange a complimentary.

Why not, Myrnaloy says tightly, figuring tax.

Dingle's immoderate love senses tension between tight Myrnaloy and scabrous Don.

I sense tension here, it says. It takes care of Dingle's potentially disastrous poncho-protrusion so that he's free at last to leave the pelvic shelter of the store's counter.

Thanks, mutters a relieved Dingle.

No problem, says Megala. The inevitable dreaded back-clap descends; Dingle's small coughing fit is also quashed. Megala and Nixon head for the rest room. Myrnaloy removes tools from a double-locked drawer marked BOARD, heads for the door, Dingle and Dingle's love in emotional tow.

Dingle stands in sunlight before the complicatedly colored bulletin board with Myrnaloy Trask. He is dizzy from the ripe, distinctively feminine fragrance that surrounds this slatternly woman who is not unerotic.

Really a well-edited board, he says; admired it in passing on countless.

Myrnaloy says nothing. With practiced tweezes of a staple claw she amputates a slick proclamation for a trampoline-a-thon benefitting the Quebecois Separatist Party, the final gymnast having succumbed June 8. Dingle's wheat-germ-and-dust notice inherits its position, is staple-gunned into place.

Dingle's own personal notice has been attracted by two professionally typeset, black-and-white notices that sit dead center on the board's prized eye-level row. The images almost focus. He squints, covers an eye, reads slowly, transfixed by the following flier's text:

WANTED: MALE DOG, SETTER/RETRIEVER MIX, FOR **MATING** W/1-YR.-OLD SETTER/RETRIEVER **BITCH**. OBJECT: **LITTER**.

PICK OF **LITTER** TO SUPPLIER, MALE **DOG**. ESTIMATED TIME NEXT **HEAT**, **BITCH**: C. JUNE 15, 1983. INQUIRE WITHIN, MS. M. TRASK, COLLECTIVE COPY.

That okay? Myrnaloy asks, stepping critically back from the TWT flier.

Appreciate it, croaks Dingle, half strangled by an inspired homunculoid's sudden appearance in his throat.

I'll try to get over sometime, try some of the germ.

Please do. On the house.

Myrnaloy goes for the doors. Dingle contemplates the boards.

Myrnaloy has paused at both knobs. She is looking at Dingle. Dingle sees her. She is a hydra, her dirty-blond hair a mess of muted light. Her faces assume an expression. Germs really know where north is? she says; swim there?

Dingle's smile is unforced, though complexly motivated. It turns out they do, he says.

I find that pretty interesting.

Me too.

And it was just an accident.

Pure whim.

She looks past him at the street.

I'll hope to be seeing you around the store should you want some, the new wheat.

She both nods and smiles absently, disappearing back inside, Dingle trying to thank her through the glass.

The board rustles in a sweet wind, a system of circled squares around a bullseyed invitation to mate. The bus revs at the traffic light. Myrnaloy's outline reappears on the other side of the CC machines. Dingle flops back to The Whole Thing, his bellbottoms swirling. He is clutching the warm copies to a lettered chest heaving with the implications of what has passed before him.

An abridged history of the dog Dingle is now buying, late afternoon, 9 June 1983:

This dog, a three-year-old Setter/Retriever male, currently in residence at Pets And More Pets, Northampton, is a fine-looking animal . . .

Fine-looking animal here or what? says the toupee'd Pets And More Pets salesman.

Looks good from here, says a bespectacled Barry Dingle.

. . . and a potentially first-rate pet; with, though (2) features that cry out for classification as Flaw. The first is an advanced case of ocular venerean sub-stamus,[3] a progressive atrophy in the ocular cavity's web of muscle that causes one of the dog's eyeballs to roll chaotically in its socket, making the dog look, more often than not, cross-eyed.

I sense an affinity between you and this dog, sir, says the salesman, dapper in a checked sportcoat and white leather loafers. He fingers a flea collar speculatively. Am I off-base? You feel some sort of affinity here by any chance?

Dingle considers the distant dog through his angled lenses. His homunculoid love lies low, chewing a knuckle.

Think maybe I do, Dingle is saying. The dog, a veteran of uncountable near-purchases, scratches endearingly with one tentative paw at the bars of its cramped cage.

The second flaw represents the reason why the dog was originally let loose at rush hour along the Valley's busy Route 9 by his original owner, a scholar of Korean funeral pottery at nearby Amherst College. Information regarding this flaw is being withheld from Dingle at the professional discretion of the pet salesman, who is even now working at the lock of the dog's receptacle, flashing an uneasy smile at Dingle as the dog, freed, immediately lunges slavering at a Smith student who stands nearby, tapping on the glass tank of a comatose terrapin. The understandably withheld information: this three-year-old male Setter/Retriever suffers from a disastrous enthusiasm for the special scents unique to the privates of the human female; has proved untrainable, unbreakable in this regard; leaps without hesitation, snuffling wetly, up the skirt of any woman unfortunate enough to enter the unfortunate orientalist's home. (Imagine your own embar-

[3] See, for instance, photographs E. Dickinson, B. Streisand, J. C. Oates.

rassment as, say, cocktail host of a colleague and his wife, seated on divans, over gin, surrounded by somber dynastic thanography, trying to make polite conversation as the dog steadily disappears ever farther into the colleague's wife's nether regions, she and you and the colleague all too mortified to pull the dog away, since any such move would signify acknowledgment of what is going on, while what is going on signifies that the colleague's wife possesses genitals, with a scent, a reality the suppression of which is absolutely key to maintaining the thin veneer of civilization that separates the behavior of, say, you and the colleague from that of, say, the dog.) A more complete history would countenance the dog's repeated olfactory advances at the orientalist's feminist-ideogram-theorist fiancée, who eventually realizes, not without horror, that she is coming to prefer them to the pottery scholar's own caresses, and today belongs to no fewer than three support groups. 1982: the dog is finally the object of abandonment, is found and saved at rush hour by a cruising abandonee-scout for Pets And More Pets, rather a more high-pressure pet shop than Barry Dingle would have preferred, but the only present possessor of a male S/R in the whole Pioneer Valley phonebook.

Also frisky, the salesman says, getting a headlock on the frantic animal, whose toenails scrabble on tile as the Smith student drifts off toward the venomous-reptile aisle. No shortage of *joy de vive* in this animal, the salesman says.

Definite Setter/Retriever mix? asks Barry Dingle. He eyes the distant, dull-gold dog writhing under a tiny salesman.

Word of honor.

Sexually mature? Intact? Inclined?

As the day is long, sir.

Name?

No name. A nameless dog. Be creative.

The dog barks.

Price? Dingle asks.

Highly negotiable. Plus necessary canine paraphernalia thrown in, as well.

Done, then.

Thank you, God.

Excuse me?

The salesman is making for a cage-lined back room, dragging the dog by the scruff. Right back, he promises. Vaccination checks, paperwork . . . Price negotiations moments away. He shuts a heavy door.

Moments later Dingle departs Pets And More Pets with: one flea collar; one reinforced military leash; one bag food; one plastic crater of a dish; one set vaccination papers; one surprisingly cheap, covertly (in the back room) tranquilized dog, which trots grinning, stoned, next to Dingle, one eye on Great Awakening's sidewalk and one on his owner. Dingle heads for home, sandals and pants flapping.

Good man, exhorts Dingle's immoderate homunculoid love for Myrnaloy Trask.

Thank God, the salesman repeats for the benefit of Pets And More Pets' cashier, who uses violet talons to remove a hair from his checked lapel.

Fine-looking animal, the love says.

The purchase of Dingle of a dog, 9 June, represents part of a whole broad homunculoid-inspired plan. The plan unfolds ideally thus: One day next week, Myrnaloy Trask, accompanied by Nixon, leaves Collective Copy at lunchtime, as is her wont. She heads south on Great Awakening, toward the town common, where her lunch is picked and eaten while Nixon is encouraged to make complete use of the limitless facilities. As M. heads south down the broad Northampton sidewalk, Barry Dingle, down the street, theoretically emerges from a convenient vantage point and moves north on same sidewalk, holding the leash of one well-rested, libidinous, pep-talked, male Setter/Retriever. As he and Myrnaloy begin to converge, Dingle contrives something clever—tripping, bumping into the odd passing spike-haired pedestrian—to render his hand plausibly absent from leash handle. Dingle's dog, driven to erotic frenzy by its time in confinement and the proximity of a premenses female S/R, is on Nixon like a shot. Etc., but ideally not too much etc., because Barry Dingle suddenly flops onto the scene and extracts upright dog from hunched bitch before uninvited indiscretions are committed.

The plan having the ideally threefold result that: (a) Dingle is able to meet and reestablish social ties w/Myrnaloy Trask w/o the oppressive fly-in-ointment atmosphere that attends the presence of Don Megala, who devotes his preprandial hours to his antique dulcimer craft; (b) Dingle appears sensitive, conscientious, possibly chivalric, in rescuing Myrnaloy's dog from drooling amorous assault right there on the main thoroughfare's sidewalk; (c) Myrnaloy sees that the sensitive, chivalric, etc. Dingle is in possession of one (1) male dog of just the right lineage and enthusiasm for the bulletin board's published assignment.

The above results, then, according to the projections of Dingle's homunculoid love, lead with arithmetic inevitability to the mating of the two pets, the symbolism of which vis-à-vis Dingle and the increasingly Megala-dissatisfied Myrnaloy Trask escapes neither party; thus to a Megala-free connection between Dingle and Myrnaloy, one based on mutual anxieties, shared dietary concerns, and the common offspring of their lives' closest companions (Dingle figures he'd better come up with a name pretty quick: he's acquired a catalogue for parents-to-be, and pores nightly); thus to nature taking its natural, terrifying course. Yes Dingle appropriates the heart, soul, moderate love of Myrnaloy Trask of Collective Copy. Megala is kicked in the emotional ass. A new Barry Dingle emerges from the cracked chrysalis of chastity and clotted hankie—complete, of the world, fulfilled, requited, ordered of heart and head, sound of mind and toe. A unified Myrnaloy/Dingle homunculus moves stately and plumply away, heading possibly north, disappearing into a cadet-blue horizon that darkens to a gloam of unity, eternity, immoderate love's good night.

So 9 June, Dingle maneuvers his dog, rattling with Dalmane, listing ever so slightly to port or starboard at females' passage, home without major incident. The dog eats three plastic bowls of Purina, sleeps for seventy-two hours, and establishes itself in front of the television. Dingle's love bides its time.

Nighttime, 14 June 1983, Troy, New York, Mrs. Dingle lies next to Mr. Dingle and dreams the following dream:

Nighttime, 14 June 1983 B.C., Kingdom of Ithaca, the King of Ithaca, played in the dream by Nelson Eddy, has a dream. He dreams that a ship carrying plague from the Ionian Sea's south enters the port of Ithaca the following day. He dreams that, soon thereafter, plague erupts in the kingdom, and ravages it. He dreams that the plague eventually carries off his devoted Queen of a wife, played by Mrs. Dingle, and his handsome Prince of a son, played by the straight-eyed young Barry D. on whom Attic sandals had looked so darn dapper.

The King of Ithaca awakens 15 June 1983 B.C. and is so distressed by his dream that he brushes aside his Queen's advice and neglects to eat a good Mediterranean breakfast. His summons his Royal Adviser, played here by Don Megala, which is passing strange, since Mrs. Dingle has never met Don Megala. The Adviser listens to the distressed King's dream. He strokes his well-groomed beard. Like the King, like all prehistoric pagan-types, the Adviser takes dreams very seriously. He reflects. After substantial reflection, the flaming torch of inspiration appears over his head: he advises the King simply to stop, on this day, any ship approaching from the south before such ship can enter the port of Ithaca, to keep such ship far out to sea, south, downwind, and to quarantine it, in order to ensure that whatever is on this theoretical ship, plague-wise, stays out there, far, far away.

Sure enough. By lunchtime, a ship, tacking chaotically, sporting an ominous obsidian sail, manned by a moaning, bubo-studded crew, appears on the southern Ionian horizon. The King sends his most formidable man-o'-war out to halt the ship, has the ship quarantined, and then just to be on the safe side has the formidable man-o'-war *itself* quarantined, all far, far out to sea, downwind.

Sure enough. The black-sailed ship turns out to be a veritable petri dish of plague germs. The Adviser's advice to keep it out of the port looks to be sound. The King, the Queen, and the big and strong and emmetropic Prince all rejoice over a lavish supper rich in high-density lipids.

Except a few days later (represented in Mrs. Dingle's dream by the fluttering palimpsests of a Hellenistic daily planner) yes a few days later, plague erupts in the kingdom of Ithaca. It ravages even the more respectable neighborhoods of the capital city. It eventually carries off the devoted Mrs. Dingle and the binocular fine-sandaled Barry D. Nelson Eddy plunges into well-coiffed despair, not to mention rage. He summons Don Megala. The two men are to be seen facing each other, perfumed hankies fastened over their mouths and noses, in a linen-draped castle chamber festooned with garlands of olive leaves, roses, garlic, various herbal propititions to big-bicepsed gods.

The King sketches for his Adviser his despair, rage. Thanks to the Adviser's advice, he says, the dream-foretold plague ship was stopped, isolated, kept at a big-time distance. And yet here, in Ithaca, as the dream foretold, is some pretty goddamn clear evidence of plague. The King demands an explanation, hinting that the continued connection between the Adviser's well-bearded head and toga'd body could well depend on the force of that explanation.

There is a long silence while both Nelson Eddy and Don Megala utilize the filmy June sunlight through the windows' woven linen to present profiles, respectively agonized and pensive, to Mrs. Dingle's dreamvision. Really long silence. Then the Adviser changes expression below the tattered torch-flame of a tardy but near-epiphanic realization. He smiles a slow smile, one of sadness as at the inevitable, taking the King by the elbow and guiding him confidentially to the chamber's corner, even though no one else is around. The King, looking about, impatiently clears his throat while the Adviser feels delicately at his own.

He advises the King: it was, unfortunately, nothing other than the King's dream itself that has brought plague to Ithaca, the kingdom.

The interval 11:50 to 11:57 a.m. EDT, 15 June 1983, finds a tiny percentage of the planet's persons involved in a tiny percentage of the planet's various and ineluctably modal situations.

8:50 a.m. DDT, Dr. W. W. Skeat, Fullerton, California, driving north on the Brea Highway toward an Osco to obtain an esoteric brand of peroxide mouthwash, finds himself, in his car, afflicted with an enormous jumping muscle in his right buttock. The muscle jumps, bouncing him around in his seat. Skeat whimpers; his car begins to weave.

11:50 a.m. EDT, Myrnaloy Trask, Collective Copy, concludes a pain-racked and I-should-have-known-flavored conversation with Don Megala, professional student, re the issue of her having entered his loft last night to find a nude Smith postgraduate (actually one Pamela Drax, 25, Ithaca, New York) astride Megala's doubly bearded face. Megala, at his dulcimer work table, perspiring over a little brown forest of blunt Stout bottles, claims that it had not been as it appeared. Myrnaloy responds with a shrill expanded variant of Oh sure. Megala, looking about him, launches into something about a contact lens lost under circumstances so bizarre he guesses he couldn't expect anyone to believe him about it outside an environment of very special sharing and trust. Myrnaloy laughs, cries, invects. Running his hand through the memory of his hair, Megala alludes with transparent patience to Myrnaloy's still narratively shadowy personal troubles regarding sexuality and men. From here things deteriorate faster than clinkers in fists. Myrnaloy hangs up and crumples onto the form feeder of her Xerox. The form feeder coldly continues to form-feed.

6:51 a.m. MT, Patricia Dingle of Rock Springs, Wyoming, Hyper-Arctic Correspondent for *Geo* Magazine, wakes alone in a mummy-shaped bag by a dead fire on the northern shore of Coronation Gulf, North-Northwest Territories, Canada, to discover that the fingers of her right hand have escaped the bag's faulty zipper and are frostbitten solid. An odd windy June snow is falling, flakes skittering like mad insects over the solid crust of the shore. She looks at the dark remains of her campfire and the bright polka dots of frozen blood in her hand's cyan.

11:51 a.m. EDT, Mrs. Dingle, Troy, New York, sits over a corn toastie and peach tea and tries to articulate an unspeakable fear to Mr. Dingle, who is arranging leaders and flies on a tackle box's second tier.

11:51 a.m. EDT, Barry Dingle, Northampton, Massachusetts, sans glasses, avec best poncho and conic cotton slacks, lurks in the recessed doorway of the Leftward Ho Café, just south on Great Awakening from The Whole Thing and Collective Copy. His ominously frisky dog held tight between his knees, Dingle is awaiting the public appearance of Nixon and Trask. Courage defined glows bright along his ribs, illuminating the glazed doll's-eyes of an immoderate love, sitting lotus on Dingle's heart, staring straight ahead beneath the steady sixty-watt glow of a plan's fruition. The last of a shelf of spring rainclouds is moving away east, carrying with it the drepanoid nub of a descending rainbow.

11:53 a.m. EDT, K. K. McFadden, Stenographer to the Assistant Press Secretary to the President of the United States, Washington, D.C., makes a stenographic error, asserting, in a presummit statement to be read to the Cyrillic media by Press Secretary Speakes, that the President is, as he's iterated time and again, willing to go the extra diplomatic mile to ensure that the terrible possibility of unclear war never becomes a reality.

11:54 a.m. EDT, Mrs. Dingle is at the telephone, dialing the Northampton number of The Whole Thing, her heart ridden with a nameless angst.

11:54 a.m. EDT, Myrnaloy Trask, an automaton of distress, takes her zucchini bread and mineral water and dog and exits Collective Copy, moving south into the lunchtime sidewalk crowd's spectrum of hair and Kabuki paint. She feels humidity, sees a thoroughfare's rising steam, hears the brief rustle of her sheltered board, smells ozone and the sweet diesel of the idling public bus.

6:54 p.m. ADT, Aristotle Onassis, on his yacht, four degrees west and six north of Lord Howe Island in the Tasmanian Sea, ruminates over a celery juice at his yacht's wet bar. He sits on a teakwood barstool. The seat of the stool and the wet bar's top are covered in an exquisite cyan leather processed from the scrotums of sperm whales under Mrs. O's personal supervision. Onassis twirls his ice cubes with a thick finger.

8:54 a.m. PDT, W. W. Skeat narrowly avoids contact with a

Trailways bus in the highway's left lane. He shifts on his bottom, raising the offending ham off the driver's seat. The Trailways bus falls in behind him, the driver honking at Skeat's inclined-to-port image through two layers of thick glass.

11:54 a.m. EDT, Don Megala redials Collective Copy, is informed that a very upset Ms. Trask has left for lunch. Megala peels at the triangular label of a moist bottle, staring at a half-strung instrument.

6:55 a.m. MT, Patricia Dingle, eyes rimmed with ice, palate hanging with the oystery starlight of extreme outdoor fear, makes a clumsy incision in the first finger of her frozen hand with a camp knife. The incision is a deep one just beneath the nail. She begins squeezing her finger with her left hand, moving the frozen blood up the finger and out the incision. The blood leaves the finger in a bright solid mass, protrudes in an arc into the snow-skittered and very cold air. Patricia Dingle remembers her covert passion for sweet cherry Freezer-Pops as a milk-drinking child and is suddenly unwell onto the royal gulf's sloped shore.

11:55 a.m. EDT, Barry Dingle emerges from the doorway of the Leftward Ho and moves north on the broad sidewalk toward the tiny, divergent, dual images of Myrnaloy Trask and her life's companion. The sidewalk before him, aswarm with mohawked women, weak men in leather, children in dyed smocks, branches in his sight into two vivid columns. Dingle makes for the distant root where the columns converge, where two Myrnaloys and two incontinent dogs will come together. His sandals slap on the wet pavement. Dingle tastes the material of his heart on his tongue. His white knuckles are redly dotted with clench on his dog's heavy leash; he's numb; he does not feel the dog's abortive lunges at the crewcut Sapphoids passing just outside Dingle's crossed-inward ken as they whirl on spurred boots, most of them, glaring at the male animal and either saluting as in Rome or assuming martial-arts postures. Dingle is blind to what passes; he stares straight ahead; his immoderate love's eyes roll over white beneath its lit bulb.

11:55 a.m. EDT, Mrs. Dingle exchanges terse greetings with Nigel, temporary helmsman of The Whole Thing, lunchtime. She asks for Dingle.

8:50–8:57 a.m. MT, the Eskew brothers, Ronnie and Boone, both remanded to the custody of the Arizona Department of Corrections for terms not to exceed twelve years, attach a centerfold to the back of the new inmate Dean-Paul Doyle, age 18, and sodomize him repeatedly on the floor of a crowded dormitory in Cell Block D, Arizona State Correctional Facility, Florence, Arizona.

11:56 a.m. EDT, Myrnaloy Trask moves south on the sidewalk, seeing little past her curtain of hot tears but a miasma of colored hair, khaki pants, the twinkle of emergent sun on single earrings. Her past and present whirl together and yield a tornado of pain. Nixon trots cheerfully beside her.

11:56 a.m. EDT, Mrs. Dingle, on the phone, finds herself weeping for no good reason. Nigel tries to soothe her with a recipe for gazpacho.

6:56 p.m. EDT, Aristotle Onassis, on his barstool, on his yacht, sees on the radar dish's monitor behind him the videotaped face of Cliff Robertson, speaking on behalf of AT&T, which Aristotle owns. Robertson looks tan and fit. Onassis can see both their faces' reflections in his polished mirror over his wet bar, on his yacht.

11:56 a.m. EDT, Don Megala, waiting for the special Weather-That-Wood brand shellac to dry on a soon-to-be-antique dulcimer, smokes a Dunhill, looking out his workshop window at the whitewashed New England brick wall the window faces.

8:56 a.m. MT, ten-week-old Shauna Doyle, Olney, Arizona, lies on the carpet of her absent mother's trailer. She sees the sun shine faint pink through the upright ear of the white Husky puppy standing guard over her as Barry Dingle moves forward into convergence. His white-eyed love chants prayers for the living. The teams close. Nixon, in new heat, strains at the approach of Dingle's restrained male. The clouds, a dark eastern blight on an immoderate blue sky, rumble as their commalike nubbin of rainbow hangs there, indecisive. Myrnaloy is blind.

Dingle smiles wildly as he reaches the columns' union, smiling, poorly feigning a shock of recognition. He goes into a rehearsed stumble of ideal surprise—this time, though, unideally stubbing a swollen toe on the pole of the bus stop's tall sign—loosening his grip on his length of chain. Dingle's dog is uninterested in Nixon: its rolling eyes lock on a point just below the denim waistline of Myrnaloy Trask, upwind. Dingle goes all convincingly for his hurt toe, howling, his right foot brought up and held with both white hands: the Retriever is set free, its military chain a suitor's jewelry. It clears a bright puddle in one horny bound. From below, the puddle reflects upward the not-pretty, bright-red arousal of the male dog. Myrnaloy stops. Dingle stops. Dingle's dog hangs in midair, entombed in color, fixed and fused in an unutterable focus.

A REAL DOLL

A. M. Homes

I'm dating Barbie. Three afternoons a week, while my sister is at dance class, I take Barbie away from Ken. I'm practicing for the future.

At first I sat in my sister's room watching Barbie, who lived with Ken, on a doily, on top of the dresser.

I was looking at her but not really looking. I was looking, and all of a sudden realized she was staring at me.

She was sitting next to Ken, his khaki-covered thigh absently rubbing her bare leg. He was rubbing her, but she was staring at me.

"Hi," she said.

"Hello," I said.

"I'm Barbie," she said, and Ken stopped rubbing her leg.

"I know."

"You're Jenny's brother."

I nodded. My head was bobbing up and down like a puppet on a weight.

"I really like your sister. She's sweet," Barbie said. "Such a good little girl. Especially lately, she makes herself so pretty, and she's started doing her nails."

I wondered if Barbie noticed that Miss Wonderful bit her nails and that when she smiled her front teeth were covered with little flecks of purple nail polish. I wondered if she knew Jennifer colored in the chipped chewed spots with purple Magic Marker, and then sometimes sucked on her fingers so that not only did she have purple flecks of polish on her teeth, but her tongue was the strangest shade of violet.

"So listen," I said. "Would you like to go out for a while? Grab some fresh air, maybe take a spin around the backyard?"

"Sure," she said.

I picked her up by her feet. It sounds unusual but I was too petrified to take her by the waist. I grabbed her by the ankles and carried her off like a Popsicle stick.

As soon as we were out back, sitting on the porch of what I used to call my fort, but which my sister and parents referred to as the playhouse, I started freaking. I was suddenly and incredibly aware that I was out with Barbie. I didn't know what to say.

"So, what kind of a Barbie are you?" I asked.

"Excuse me?"

"Well, from listening to Jennifer I know there's Day to Night Barbie, Magic Moves Barbie, Gift-Giving Barbie, Tropical Barbie, My First Barbie, and more."

"I'm Tropical," she said. I'm Tropical, she said, the same way a person might say I'm Catholic or I'm Jewish. "I came with a one-piece bathing suit, a brush, and a ruffle you can wear so many ways," Barbie squeaked.

She actually squeaked. It turned out that squeaking was Barbie's birth defect. I pretended I didn't hear it.

We were quiet for a minute. A leaf larger than Barbie fell from the maple tree above us and I caught it just before it would have hit her. I half expected her to squeak, "You saved my life. I'm yours, forever." Instead she said, in a perfectly normal voice, "Wow, big leaf."

I looked at her. Barbie's eyes were sparkling blue like the ocean on a good day. I looked and in a moment noticed she had the whole world, the cosmos, drawn in makeup above and below her eyes. An entire galaxy, clouds, stars, a sun, the sea, painted onto her face. Yellow, blue, pink, and a million silver sparkles.

We sat looking at each other, looking and talking and then not talking and looking again. It was a stop-and-start thing with both of us constantly saying the wrong thing, saying anything, and then immediately regretting having said it.

It was obvious Barbie didn't trust me. I asked her if she wanted something to drink.

"Diet Coke," she said. And I wondered why I'd asked.

I went into the house, upstairs into my parents' bathroom, opened the medicine cabinet, and got a couple of Valiums. I immediately swallowed one. I figured if I could be calm and collected, she'd realize I wasn't going to hurt her. I broke another Valium into a million small pieces, dropped some slivers into Barbie's Diet Coke, and swished it around so it'd blend. I figured if we could be calm and collected together, she'd be able to trust me even sooner. I was falling in love in a way that had nothing to do with love.

"So, what's the deal with you and Ken?" I asked later after we'd loosened up, after she'd drunk two Diet Cokes, and I'd made another trip to the medicine cabinet.

She giggled. "Oh, we're just really good friends."

"What's the deal with him really, you can tell me, I mean, is he or isn't he?"

"Ish she or ishn' she," Barbie said, in a slow slurred way, like she was so intoxicated that if they made a Breathalyzer for Valium, she'd melt it.

I regretted having fixed her a third Coke. I mean if she o.d.'d and died Jennifer would tell my mom and dad for sure.

"Is he a faggot or what?"

Barbie laughed and I almost slapped her. She looked me straight in the eye.

"He lusts after me," she said. "I come home at night and he's standing there, waiting. He doesn't wear underwear, you know. I mean, isn't that strange, Ken doesn't own any underwear. I heard Jennifer tell her friend that they don't even make any for him. Anyway, he's always there waiting, and I'm like, Ken we're friends, okay, that's it. I mean, have you ever noticed, he has molded plastic hair. His head and his hair are all one piece. I can't go out with a guy like that. Besides, I don't think he'd be up for it if you know what I mean. Ken is not what you'd call well endowed. . . . All he's got is a little plastic bump, more of a hump, really, and what the hell are you supposed to do with that?"

She was telling me things I didn't think I should hear and all the same, I was leaning into her, like if I moved closer she'd tell me more. I was taking every word and holding it for a minute, holding groups of words in my head like I didn't understand English. She went on and on, but I wasn't listening.

The sun sank behind the playhouse, Barbie shivered, excused herself, and ran around back to throw up. I asked her if she felt okay. She said she was fine, just a little tired, that maybe she was coming down with the flu or something. I gave her a piece of a piece of gum to chew and took her inside.

On the way back to Jennifer's room I did something Barbie almost didn't forgive me for. I did something which not only shattered the moment, but nearly wrecked the possibility of our having a future together.

In the hallway between the stairs and Jennifer's room, I popped Barbie's head into my mouth, like lion and tamer, God and Godzilla.

I popped her whole head into my mouth, and Barbie's hair separated into single strands like Christmas tinsel and caught in my throat, nearly choking me. I could taste layer on layer of makeup, Revlon, Max Factor, and Maybelline. I closed my mouth around Barbie and could feel her breath in mine. I could hear her screams in my throat. Her teeth, white, Pearl Drops, Pepsodent, and the whole Osmond family, bit my tongue and the inside of my cheek like I might accidentally bite myself. I closed my mouth around her neck and held her suspended, her feet uselessly kicking the air in front of my face.

Before pulling her out, I pressed my teeth lightly into her neck, leaving marks Barbie described as scars of her assault, but which I imagined as a New Age necklace of love.

"I have never, ever in my life been treated with such utter disregard," she said as soon as I let her out.

She was lying. I knew Jennifer sometimes did things with Barbie. I didn't mention that once I'd seen Barbie hanging from Jennifer's ceiling fan, spinning around in great wide circles, like some imitation Superman.

"I'm sorry if I scared you."

"Scared me!" she squeaked.

She went on squeaking, a cross between the squeal when you let the air out of a balloon and a smoke alarm with weak batteries. While she was squeaking, the phrase *a head in the mouth is worth two in the bush* started running through my head. I knew it had come from somewhere, started as something else, but I couldn't get it right. *A head in the mouth is worth two in the bush*, again and again, like the punch line to some dirty joke.

"Scared me. Scared me. Scared me!" Barbie squeaked louder and louder until finally she had my attention again. "Have you ever been held captive in the dark cavern of someone's body?"

I shook my head. It sounded wonderful.

"Typical," she said. "So incredibly, typically male."

For a moment I was proud.

"Why do you have to do things you know you shouldn't, and worse, you do them with a light in your eye, like you're getting some weird pleasure that only another boy would understand. You're all the same," she said. "You're all Jack Nicholson."

I refused to put her back in Jennifer's room until she forgave me, until she understood that I'd done what I did with only the truest of feeling, no harm intended.

I heard Jennifer's feet clomping up the stairs. I was running out of time.

"You know I'm really interested in you," I said to Barbie.

"Me too," she said, and for a minute I wasn't sure if she meant she was interested in herself or me.

"We should do this again," I said. She nodded.

I leaned down to kiss Barbie. I could have brought her up to my lips, but somehow it felt wrong. I leaned down to kiss her and the first thing I got was her nose in my mouth. I felt like a St. Bernard saying hello.

No matter how graceful I tried to be, I was forever licking her face. It wasn't a question of putting my tongue in her ear or down her throat, it was simply literally trying not to suffocate her. I kissed Barbie with my back to Ken and then turned around and put her on the doily right next to him. I was tempted to drop her down on Ken, to mash her into him, but I managed to restrain myself.

"That was fun," Barbie said. I heard Jennifer in the hall.

"Later," I said.

Jennifer came into the room and looked at me.

"What?" I said.

"It's my room," she said.

"There was a bee in it. I was killing it for you."

"A bee. I'm allergic to bees. Mom, Mom," she screamed. "There's a bee."

"Mom's not home. I killed it."

"But there might be another one."

"So call me and I'll kill it."

"But if it stings me I might die." I shrugged and walked out. I could feel Barbie watching me leave.

I took a Valium about twenty minutes before I picked her up the next Friday. By the time I went into Jennifer's room, everything was getting easier.

"Hey," I said when I got up to the dresser.

She was there on the doily with Ken, they were back to back, resting against each other, legs stretched out in front of them.

Ken didn't look at me. I didn't care.

"You ready to go?" I asked. Barbie nodded. "I thought you

might be thirsty." I handed her the Diet Coke I'd made for her.

I'd figured Barbie could take a little less than an eighth of a Valium without getting totally senile. Basically, I had to give her Valium crumbs, since there was no way to cut one that small.

She took the Coke and drank it right in front of Ken. I kept waiting for him to give me one of those I-know-what-you're-up-to-and-I-don't-like-it looks, the kind my father gives me when he walks into my room without knocking and I automatically jump twenty feet in the air.

Ken acted like he didn't even know I was there. I hated him.

"I can't do a lot of walking this afternoon," Barbie said.

I nodded. I figured no big deal since mostly I seemed to be carrying her around anyway.

"My feet are killing me," she said.

I was thinking about Ken.

"Don't you have other shoes?"

My family was very into shoes. No matter what seemed to be wrong my father always suggested it could be cured by wearing a different pair of shoes. He believed that shoes, like tires, should be rotated.

"It's not the shoes," she said. "It's my toes."

"Did you drop something on them?" My Valium wasn't working. I was having trouble making small talk. I needed another one.

"Jennifer's been chewing on them."

"What?"

"She chews on my toes."

"You let her chew your footies?"

I couldn't make sense out of what she was saying. I was thinking about not being able to talk, needing another or maybe two more Valiums, yellow adult-strength Pez.

"Do you enjoy it?" I asked.

"She literally bites down on them, like I'm flank steak or something," Barbie said. "I wish she'd just bite them off and have it over with. This is taking forever. She's chewing and chewing, more like gnawing at me."

"I'll make her stop. I'll buy her some gum, some tobacco or something, a pencil to chew on."

"Please don't say anything. I wouldn't have told you except . . ." Barbie said.

"But she's hurting you."

"It's between Jennifer and me."

"Where's it going to stop?" I asked.

"At the arch, I hope. There's a bone there, and once she realizes she's bitten the soft part off, she'll stop."

"How will you walk?"

"I have very long feet."

I sat on the edge of my sister's bed, my head in my hands. My sister was biting Barbie's feet off and Barbie didn't seem to care. She didn't hold it against her, and in a way I liked her for that. I liked the fact she understood how we all have little secret habits that seem normal enough to us, but which we know better than to mention out loud. I started imagining things I might be able to get away with.

"Get me out of here," Barbie said. I slipped Barbie's shoes off. Sure enough, someone had been gnawing at her. On her left foot the toes were dangling, and on the right, half had been completely taken off. There were tooth marks up to her ankles. "Let's not dwell on this," Barbie said.

I picked Barbie up. Ken fell over backwards and Barbie made me straighten him up before we left. "Just because you know he only has a bump doesn't give you permission to treat him badly," Barbie whispered.

I fixed Ken and carried Barbie down the hall to my room. I held Barbie above me, tilted my head back, and lowered her feet into my mouth. I felt like a young sword swallower practicing for my debut. I lowered Barbie's feet and legs into my mouth and then began sucking on them. They smelled like Jennifer and dirt and plastic. I sucked on her stubs and she told me it felt nice.

"You're better than a hot soak," Barbie said. I left her resting on my pillow and went downstairs to get us each a drink.

We were lying on my bed, curled into and out of each other. Barbie was on a pillow next to me and I was on my side facing her. She was talking about men, and as she talked I tried to be everything she said. She was saying she didn't like men who were afraid of themselves. I tried to be brave, to look courageous and secure. I held my head a certain way and it seemed to work. She said she didn't like men who were afraid of femininity, and I got confused.

"Guys always have to prove how boy they really are," Barbie said.

I thought of Jennifer trying to be a girl, wearing dresses, doing her nails, putting makeup on, wearing a bra even though she wouldn't need one for about fifty years.

"You make fun of Ken because he lets himself be everything he is. He doesn't hide anything."

"He doesn't have anything to hide," I said. "He has tan molded plastic hair, and a bump for a dick."

"I never should have told you about the bump."

I lay back on the bed. Barbie rolled over, off the pillow, and rested on my chest. Her body stretched from my nipple to my belly button. Her hands pressed against me, tickling me.

"Barbie," I said.

"Umm humm."

"How do you feel about me?"

She didn't say anything for a minute. "Don't worry about it," she said, and slipped her hand into my shirt through the space between the buttons.

Her fingers were like the ends of toothpicks performing some subtle ancient torture, a dance of boy death across my chest. Barbie crawled all over me like an insect who'd run into one too many cans of Raid.

Underneath my clothes, under my skin, I was going crazy. First off, I'd been kidnapped by my underwear with no way to manually adjust without attracting unnecessary attention.

With Barbie caught in my shirt I slowly rolled over, like in some space shuttle docking maneuver. I rolled onto my stomach, trapping her under me. As slowly and unobtrusively as possible,

I ground myself against the bed, at first hoping it would fix things and then again and again, caught by a pleasure/pain principle.

"Is this a water bed?" Barbie asked.

My hand was on her breasts, only it wasn't really my hand, but more like my index finger. I touched Barbie and she made a little gasp, a squeak in reverse. She squeaked backwards, then stopped, and I was stuck there with my hand on her, thinking about how I was forever crossing a line between the haves and the have-nots, between good guys and bad, between men and animals, and there was absolutely nothing I could do to stop myself.

Barbie was sitting on my crotch, her legs flipped back behind her in a position that wasn't human.

At a certain point I had to free myself. If my dick was blue, it was only because it had suffocated. I did the honors and Richard popped out like an escapee from maximum security.

"I've never seen anything so big," Barbie said. It was the sentence I dreamed of, but given the people Barbie normally hung out with, namely the bump boy himself, it didn't come as a big surprise.

She stood at the base of my dick, her bare feet buried in my pubic hair. I was almost as tall as she was. Okay, not almost as tall, but clearly we could be related. She and Richard even had the same vaguely surprised look on their faces.

She was on me and I couldn't help wanting to get inside her. I turned Barbie over and was on top of her, not caring if I killed her. Her hands pressed so hard into my stomach that it felt like she was performing an appendectomy.

I was on top, trying to get between her legs, almost breaking her in half. But there was nothing there, nothing to fuck except a small thin line that was supposed to be her ass crack.

I rubbed the thin line, the back of her legs and the space between her legs. I turned Barbie's back to me so I could do it without having to look at her face.

Very quickly, I came. I came all over Barbie, all over her and a little bit in her hair. I came on Barbie and it was the most horrifying experience I ever had. It didn't stay on her. It doesn't stick to plastic. I was finished. I was holding a come-covered Barbie in my hand like I didn't know where she came from.

Barbie said, "Don't stop," or maybe I just think she said that because I read it somewhere. I don't know anymore. I couldn't listen to her. I couldn't even look at her. I wiped myself off with a sock, pulled my clothes on, and then took Barbie into the bathroom.

At dinner I noticed Jennifer chewing her cuticles between bites of tuna-noodle casserole. I asked her if she was teething. She coughed and then started choking to death on either a little piece of fingernail, a crushed potato chip from the casserole, or maybe even a little bit of Barbie footie that'd stuck in her teeth. My mother asked her if she was okay.

"I swallowed something sharp," she said between coughs that were clearly influenced by the acting class she'd taken over the summer.

"Do you have a problem?" I asked her.

"Leave your sister alone," my mother said.

"If there are any questions to ask we'll do the asking," my father said.

"Is everything all right?" my mother asked Jennifer. She nodded. "I think you could use some new jeans," my mother said. "You don't seem to have many play clothes anymore."

"Not to change the subject," I said, trying to think of a way to stop Jennifer from eating Barbie alive.

"I don't wear pants," Jennifer said. "Boys wear pants."

"Your grandma wears pants," my father said.

"She's not a girl."

My father chuckled. He actually fucking chuckled. He's the only person I ever met who could actually fucking chuckle.

"Don't tell her that," he said, chuckling.

"It's not funny," I said.

"Grandma's are pull-ons anyway," Jennifer said. "They don't have a fly. You have to have a penis to have a fly."

"Jennifer," my mother said. "That's enough of that."

I decided to buy Barbie a present. I was at that strange point where I would have done anything for her. I took two buses and walked more than a mile to get to Toys "R" Us.

Barbie row was aisle 14C. I was a wreck. I imagined a million Barbies and having to have them all. I pictured fucking one, discarding it, immediately grabbing a fresh one, doing it, and then throwing it onto a growing pile in the corner of my room. An unending chore. I saw myself becoming a slave to Barbie. I wondered how many Tropical Barbies were made each year. I felt faint.

There were rows and rows of Kens, Barbies, and Skippers. Funtime Barbie, Jewel Secrets Ken, Barbie Rocker with "Hot Rockin' Fun and Real Dancin' Action." I noticed Magic Moves Barbie, and found myself looking at her carefully, flirtatiously, wondering if her legs were spreadable. "Push the switch and she moves," her box said. She winked at me while I was reading.

The only Tropical I saw was a black Tropical Ken. From just looking at him you wouldn't have known he was black. I mean, he wasn't black like anyone would be black. Black Tropical Ken was the color of a raisin, a raisin all spread out and unwrinkled. He had a short afro that looked like a wig had been dropped down and fixed on his head, a protective helmet. I wondered if black Ken was really white Ken sprayed over with a thick coating of ironed raisin plastic.

I spread eight black Kens out in a line across the front of a row. Through the plastic window of his box he told me he was hoping to go to dental school. All eight black Kens talked at once. Luckily, they all said the same thing at the same time. They said he really liked teeth. Black Ken smiled. He had the same white Pearl Drops, Pepsodent, Osmond family teeth that Barbie and white Ken had. I thought the entire Mattel family must take really good care of themselves. I figured they might be the only people left in America who actually brushed after every meal and then again before going to sleep.

I didn't know what to get Barbie. Black Ken said I should go for clothing, maybe a fur coat. I wanted something really special. I imagined a wonderful present that would draw us somehow closer.

There was a tropical pool and patio set, but I decided it might make her homesick. There was a complete winter holiday, with an A-frame house, fireplace, snowmobile, and sled. I imagined her inviting Ken away for a weekend without me. The six o'clock news set was nice, but because of her squeak, Barbie's future as an anchorwoman seemed limited. A workout center, a sofa bed and coffee table, a bubbling spa, a bedroom play set. I settled on the grand piano. It was thirteen dollars I'd always made it a point to never spend more than ten dollars on anyone. This time I figured, what the hell, you don't buy a grand piano every day.

"Wrap it up, would ya," I said at the checkout desk.

From my bedroom window I could see Jennifer in the backyard, wearing her tutu and leaping all over the place. It was dangerous as hell to sneak in and get Barbie, but I couldn't keep a grand piano in my closet without telling someone.

"You must really like me," Barbie said when she finally had the piano unwrapped.

I nodded. She was wearing ski suit and skis. It was the end of August and eighty degrees out. Immediately, she sat down and played "Chopsticks."

I looked out at Jennifer. She was running down the length of the deck, jumping onto the railing, and then leaping off, posing like one of those red flying horses you see on old Mobil gas signs. I watched her do it once and then the second time, her foot caught on the railing, and she went over the edge the hard way. A minute later she came around the edge of the house, limping, her tutu dented and dirty, pink tights ripped at both knees. I grabbed Barbie from the piano bench and raced her into Jennifer's room.

"I was just getting warmed up," she said. "I can play better than that, really."

I could hear Jennifer crying as she walked up the stairs.

"Jennifer's coming," I said. I put her down on the dresser and realized Ken was missing.

"Where's Ken?" I asked quickly.

"Out with Jennifer," Barbie said.

I met Jennifer at her door. "Are you okay?" I asked. She cried harder. "I saw you fall."

"Why didn't you stop me?" she said.

"From falling?"

She nodded and showed me her knees.

"Once you start to fall no one can stop you." I noticed Ken was tucked into the waistband of her tutu.

"They catch you," Jennifer said.

I started to tell her it was dangerous to go leaping around with a Ken stuck in your waistband, but you don't tell someone who's already crying that they did something bad.

I walked her into the bathroom, and took out the hydrogen peroxide. I was a first aid expert. I was the kind of guy who walked around waiting for someone to have a heart attack just so I could practice my CPR technique.

"Sit down," I said.

Jennifer sat down on the toilet without putting the lid down. Ken was stabbing her all over the place and instead of pulling him out, she squirmed around trying to get comfortable like she didn't know what else to do. I took him out for her. She watched as though I was performing surgery or something.

"He's mine," she said.

"Take off your tights," I said.

"No," she said.

"They're ruined," I said. "Take them off."

Jennifer took off her ballet slippers and peeled off her tights. She was wearing my old Underoos with superheroes on them, Spiderman and Superman and Batman all poking out from under a dirty dented tutu. I decided not to say anything, but it looked funny as hell to see a flat crotch in boy's underwear. I had the feeling they didn't bother making underwear for Ken because they knew it looked too weird on him.

I poured peroxide onto her bloody knees. Jennifer screamed into my ear. She bent down and examined herself, poking her purple fingers into the torn skin; her tutu bunched up and rubbed against her face, scraping it. I worked on her knees, removing little pebbles and pieces of grass from the area.

She started crying again.

"You're okay," I said. "You're not dying." She didn't care. "Do you want anything?" I asked, trying to be nice.

"Barbie," she said.

It was the first time I'd handled Barbie in public. I picked her up like she was a complete stranger and handed her to Jennifer, who grabbed her by the hair. I started to tell her to ease up, but couldn't. Barbie looked at me and I shrugged. I went downstairs and made Jennifer one of my special Diet Cokes.

"Drink this," I said, handing it to her. She took four giant gulps and immediately I felt guilty about having used a whole Valium.

"Why don't you give a little to your Barbie," I said. "I'm sure she's thirsty too."

Barbie winked at me and I could have killed her, first off for doing it in front of Jennifer, and second because she didn't know what the hell she was winking about.

I went into my room and put the piano away. I figured as long as I kept it in the original box I'd be safe. If anyone found it, I'd say it was a present for Jennifer.

Wednesday Ken and Barbie had their heads switched. I went to get Barbie, and there on top of the dresser were Barbie and Ken, sort of. Barbie's head was on Ken's body and Ken's head was on Barbie. At first I thought it was just me.

"Hi," Barbie's head said.

I couldn't respond. She was on Ken's body and I was looking at Ken in a whole new way.

I picked up the Barbie head/Ken and immediately Barbie's head rolled off. It rolled across the dresser, across the white doily, past Jennifer's collection of miniature ceramic cats, and *boom* it fell to the floor. I saw Barbie's head rolling and about to fall, and then falling, but there was nothing I could do to stop it. I was frozen, paralyzed with Ken's headless body in my left hand.

Barbie's head was on the floor, her hair spread out underneath it like angel wings in the snow, and I expected to see blood, a wide rich pool of blood, or at least a little bit coming out of her ear, her nose, or her mouth. I looked at her head on the floor and saw nothing but Barbie with eyes like the cosmos looking up at me. I thought she was dead.

"Christ, that hurt," she said. "And I already had a headache from these earrings."

There were little red dot/ball earrings jutting out of Barbie's ears.

"They go right through my head, you know. I guess it takes getting used to," Barbie said.

I noticed my mother's pincushion on the dresser next to the other Barbie/Ken, the Barbie body, Ken head. The pincushion was filled with hundreds of pins, pins with flat silver ends and pins with red, yellow, and blue dot/ball ends.

"You have pins in your head," I said to the Barbie head on the floor.

"Is that supposed to be a compliment?"

I was starting to hate her. I was being perfectly clear and she didn't understand me.

I looked at Ken. He was in my left hand, my fist wrapped around his waist. I looked at him and realized my thumb was on his bump. My thumb was pressed against Ken's crotch, and as soon as I noticed I got an automatic hard-on, the kind you don't know you're getting, it's just there. I started rubbing Ken's bump and watching my thumb like it was a large-screen projection of a porno movie.

"What are you doing?" Barbie's head said. "Get me up. Help me." I was rubbing Ken's bump/hump with my finger inside his bathing suit. I was standing in the middle of my sister's room, with my pants pulled down.

"Aren't you going to help me?" Barbie kept asking. "Aren't you going to help me?"

In the second before I came, I held Ken's head hole in front of me. I held Ken upside down above my dick and came inside of Ken like I never could in Barbie.

I came into Ken's body and as soon as I was done I wanted to do it again. I wanted to fill Ken and put his head back on, like a perfume bottle. I wanted Ken to be the vessel for my secret supply. I came in Ken and then I remembered he wasn't mine. He didn't belong to me. I took him into the bathroom and soaked him in warm water and Ivory liquid. I brushed his insides with Jennifer's toothbrush and left him alone in a cold-water rinse.

"Aren't you going to help me, aren't you?" Barbie kept asking.

I started thinking she'd been brain-damaged by the accident. I picked her head up from the floor.

"What took you so long?" she asked.

"I had to take care of Ken."

"Is he okay?"

"He'll be fine. He's soaking in the bathroom." I held Barbie's head in my hand.

"What are you going to do?"

"What do you mean?" I said.

Did my little incident, my moment with Ken, mean that right then and there some decision about my future life as queerbait had to be made?

"This afternoon. Where are we going? What are we doing? I miss you when I don't see you," Barbie said.

"You see me every day," I said.

"I don't really see you. I sit on top of the dresser and if you pass by, I see you. Take me to your room."

"I have to bring Ken's body back."

I went into the bathroom, rinsed out Ken, blew him dry with my mother's blow dryer, then played with him again. It was a boy thing, we were boys together. I thought sometime I might play ball with him, I might take him out instead of Barbie.

"Everything takes you so long," Barbie said when I got back into the room.

I put Ken back up on the dresser, picked up Barbie's body, knocked Ken's head off, and smashed Barbie's head back down on her own damn neck.

"I don't want to fight with you," Barbie said as I carried her into my room. "We don't have enough time together to fight. Fuck me," she said.

I didn't feel like it. I was thinking about fucking Ken and Ken being a boy. I was thinking about Barbie and Barbie being a girl.

I was thinking about Jennifer, switching Barbie's and Ken's heads, chewing Barbie's feet off, hanging Barbie from the ceiling fan, and who knows what else.

"Fuck me," Barbie said again.

I ripped Barbie's clothing off. Between Barbie's legs Jennifer had drawn pubic hair in reverse. She'd drawn it upside down so it looked like a fountain spewing up and out in great wide arcs. I spit directly onto Barbie and with my thumb and first finger rubbed the ink lines, erasing them. Barbie moaned.

"Why do you let her do this to you?"

"Jennifer owns me," Barbie moaned.

Jennifer owns me, she said, so easily and with pleasure. I was totally jealous. Jennifer owned Barbie and it made me crazy. Obviously it was one of those relationships that could only exist between women. Jennifer could own her because it didn't matter that Jennifer owned her. Jennifer didn't want Barbie, she had her.

"You're perfect," I said.

"I'm getting fat," Barbie said.

Barbie was crawling all over me, and I wondered if Jennifer knew she was a nymphomaniac. I wondered if Jennifer knew what a nymphomaniac was.

"You don't belong with little girls," I said.

Barbie ignored me.

There were scratches on Barbie's chest and stomach. She didn't say anything about them and so at first I pretended not to notice. As I was touching her, I could feel they were deep, like slices. The edges were rough; my finger caught on them and I couldn't help but wonder.

"Jennifer?" I said, massaging the cuts with my tongue, as though my tongue, like sandpaper, would erase them. Barbie nodded.

In fact, I thought of using sandpaper, but didn't know how I would explain it to Barbie: *you have to lie still and let me rub it really hard with this stuff that's like terrycloth dipped in cement*. I thought she might even like it if I made it into an S&M kind of thing and handcuffed her first.

I ran my tongue back and forth over the slivers, back and forth over the words "copyright 1966 Mattel Inc., Malaysia" tattooed on her back. Tonguing the tattoo drove Barbie crazy. She said it had something to do with scar tissue being extremely sensitive.

Barbie pushed herself hard against me; I could feel her slices rubbing my skin. I was thinking that Jennifer might kill Barbie. Without meaning to she might just go over the line and I wondered if Barbie would know what was happening or if she'd try to stop her.

We fucked, that's what I called it, fucking. In the beginning Barbie said she hated the word, which made me like it even more. She hated it because it was so strong and hard, and she said we weren't fucking, we were making love. I told her she had to be kidding.

"Fuck me," she said that afternoon, and I knew the end was coming soon. "Fuck me," she said. I didn't like the sound of the word.

Friday when I went into Jennifer's room, there was something in the air. The place smelled like a science lab, a fire, a failed experiment.

Barbie was wearing a strapless yellow evening dress. Her hair was wrapped into a high bun, more like a wedding cake than something Betty Crocker would whip up. There seemed to be layers and layers of angel's hair spinning in a circle above her head. She had yellow pins through her ears and gold fuck-me shoes that matched the belt around her waist. For a second I thought of the belt and imagined tying her up, but more than restraining her arms or legs, I thought of wrapping the belt around her face, tying it across her mouth.

I looked at Barbie and saw something dark and thick like a scar rising up and over the edge of her dress. I grabbed her and pulled the front of the dress down.

"Hey big boy," Barbie said. "Don't I even get a hello?"

Barbie's breasts had been sawed at with a knife. There were a hundred marks from a blade that might have had five rows of teeth like shark jaws. And as if that wasn't enough, she'd been dissolved by fire, blue and yellow flames had been pressed against her and held there until she melted and eventually became the fire that burned herself. All of it had been somehow stirred with the lead of a pencil, the point of a pen, and left to cool. Molten Barbie flesh had been left to harden, black and pink plastic swirled together, in the crater Jennifer had dug out of her breasts.

I examined her in detail like a scientist, a pathologist, a fucking medical examiner. I studied the burns, the gouged-out area, as if by looking closely I'd find something, an explanation, a way out.

A disgusting taste came up into my mouth, like I'd been sucking on batteries. It came up, then sank back down into my stomach, leaving my mouth puckered with the bitter metallic flavor of sour saliva. I coughed and spit onto my shirt sleeve, then rolled the sleeve over to cover the wet spot.

With my index finger I touched the edge of the burn as lightly as I could. The round rim of her scar broke off under my finger. I almost dropped her.

"It's just a reduction," Barbie said. "Jennifer and I are even now."

Barbie was smiling. She had the same expression on her face as when I first saw her and fell in love. She had the same expression she always had and I couldn't stand it. She was smiling, and she was burned. She was smiling, and she was ruined. I pulled her dress back up, above the scar line. I put her down carefully on the doily on top of the dresser and started to walk away.

"Hey," Barbie said, "aren't we going to play?"

EVERYBODY GOT THEIR OWN IDEA OF HOME

♥ ♥

Barry Gifford

Big Betty Stalcup kissed Miss Cutie Early on the right earlobe as Cutie drove, tickling her, causing Cutie to swerve the black Dodge Monaco toward the right as she scratched at that side of her head.

"Dammit, Bet, you shouldn't ought do that while I'm wheelin'."

Big Betty laughed and said, "We're kissin' cousins, ain't we? Sometimes just I can't help myself and don't want to. Safety first ain't never been my motto."

Cutie straightened out the car and grinned. "Knowed that for a long time," she said.

"Knowed which? That we was kissin' cousins?"

"Uh-uh, that come later. About the safe part. You weren't never very predictable, Bet, even as a child."

Big Betty and Miss Cutie had spent the week in New Orleans,

then the weekend in Gulf Shores, Alabama, and were headed back into Florida at Perdido Key. The Gulf of Mexico was smooth as glass this breezeless, sunny morning in February.

"Jesus H. Christ, Cutie, tomorrow's Valentine's Day!"

"So?"

"We'll have to make somethin' special happen."

"Last Valentine's we was locked up at Fort Sumatra. Spent the whole day bleachin' blood and piss stains outta sheets."

"Still can't believe we survived three and change in that pit."

"Don't know if I'd made it without you, Bet. Them big ol' mamas been usin' me for toilet paper, you weren't there to protect me."

Big Betty shifted her five-foot-eight, two-hundred-pound body around in the front passenger seat so that she faced Cutie Early. At twenty-four, Cutie was twelve years younger than Betty, and Miss Cutie's slim-figured five-foot-one-inch frame engendered in Big Betty a genuinely maternal feeling. They had been lovers ever since Miss Cutie had tiptoed into Big Betty's cell at the Fort Sumatra Detention Center for Wayward Women, which was located midway between Mexico Beach and Wewahitchka, Florida, just inside the central time zone. Cutie's curly red hair, freckles, giant black eyes, and delicate features were just what Betty Stalcup had been looking for. It was as if the state of Florida penal system had taken her order and served it up on a platter. Big Betty brushed back her own shoulder-length brown hair with her left hand and placed her other hand on Cutie's right breast, massaging it gently.

"You're my baby black-eyed pea, that's for sure," said Betty. "We ain't never gonna be apart if I can help it."

"Suits me."

"Cutie, we just a couple Apaches ridin' wild on the lost highway, the one Hank Williams sung about."

"Don't know that I've ever heard of it."

"Travelin' along the way we are, without no home or reason to be or stay anywhere, that's what it means bein' on the lost highway. Most folks don't know what they want, Cutie, only mostly they don't even know that much. Sometimes they think they know but it's usually just their stomach or cunt or cock complainin'. They get fed or fucked and it's back to square one. Money makes 'em meaner'n shit, don't we already know. Money's the greatest excuse in the world for doin' dirt. But you and me can out-ugly the sumbitches, I reckon."

"How's that?"

"Just by puttin' two and two together, sweet pea, then subtractin' off the top, one at a time."

"I ain't sure I understand you, Bet, but I'm willin' to learn."

Big Betty threw back her head, shut her wolfslit green eyes, and gave out a sharp laugh.

"Young and willin's the best time of life," she said. "You got to play it that way till you can't play it no more."

"Then what?" asked Cutie.

Big Betty grinned, threw her heavy left arm around Cutie's narrow shoulders, and squeezed closer to her companion.

"Start cuttin' your losses," she said. "All that's left to do."

"Along with cuttin' throats, you mean."

"Why, Miss Cutie, honey, you way ahead of me."

The two Peruvian seamen, brothers from Callao, Ernesto and Dagoberto Reyes, went straight from the *Madrugada*, a 30,000-ton container ship registered in Liberia and berthed for eighteen hours at the Esplanade dock, to the Saturn Bar on the corner of St. Claude and Clouet in the Ninth Ward. Since Encanta's Tijuana, their former primary New Orleans hangout, had closed down two years before, the Reyes boys had frequented the Saturn—pronounced with the emphasis on the second syllable by the locals—whenever they hit town. It was a lively though sometimes deadly little place, where the brothers could drink, dance with an assortment of neighborhood doxies and slumming college girls, shoot some pool, and otherwise entertain themselves before heading back out to sea. This trip, the *Madrugada*'s next port of call was Port-of-Spain, Trinidad, a place neither Ernesto nor Dagoberto cared much for, which is perhaps why they drank too many Abitas with Jim Beam chasers at the Saturn.

The two women they left with, the bartender, Bosco Brouillard, later told police, were strangers to him. One was large, Bosco said, about five-eight and heavy, even muscular, buxom, maybe in her late thirties. The other was small, just over five feet, boyish, pigeon-chested, a lot younger.

"Them ladies moved over those guys like Hypnos and Thanatos," said Bosco.

"Who're they?" asked the cop, who had discovered the butchered bodies of the Reyes brothers behind Swindle Ironworks on Burgundy over in the Eighth Ward.

"Sleep and Death," Bosco told him. "Twin children of Nyx. You know, Night."

"No, I don't know," said the cop, who had not slept since he'd seen the pair of brown Peruvian heads hollowed out like cantaloupes scooped clean at a Cajun picnic.

"Gals had 'em covered, okay."

"Anyone else leave with them?"

The bartender shook his bald head no.

"Could be Morpheus was waitin' outside, though," Bosco said. "He's usually not far away."

"Who's this Morpheus?"

"The god of dreams, Nyx's sidekick. Say, you law enforcement types ain't 'xactly up on your mythology, are ya?"

"Not really."

"Then I don't guess you know somethin' else is important."

The cop looked at the bartender, who was grinning now. The four television sets above the bar, each tuned to a different station with the sound off, flickered above his clean head.

"What's that?" the cop asked.

"Sleep, Dream, and Death, they all only one generation removed from Chaos."

The policeman, whose name was Vernon Duke Douglas, and who was a direct descendant of H. Kyd Douglas, author of the book *I Rode with Stonewall*, folded his notepad and put it away.

"Obliged, Mr. Brouillard. We'll be around again, I'm certain."

Bosco winked his weak-lidded left eye at the Confederate

scribe's great-great-great-nephew and said, "Sir, I ain't no kind of travelin' man."

Other than the four years he'd spent as an undergraduate at the University of Chicago, and the four in New York while he worked the counter at Hartley's Luncheonette on 116th Street and Amsterdam Avenue when he wasn't attending law school at Columbia, from which institution he had received his degree, Rollo Lamar had spent his entire life in Egypt City, Florida.

His mother, Purity Mayfield, had worked as a maid for Arthur and Delia Lamar for ten years, from the time she was fifteen until she was twenty-five, at which age she died giving birth to her only child. Since the father, a juke joint piano player named Almost Johnson, was married to another woman and had been murdered in a mysterious incident soon after Purity's pregnancy became evident, and Purity Mayfield had no relatives in the vicinity, the Lamars, who were childless, adopted the boy and raised him as if he were their own son, even though they were white and he was black. They named him Rollo Mayfield Lamar, after Arthur's father and Rollo's mother.

The Lamar family had long been proponents of equal rights for all people, regardless of race or religion. Rollo Leander Lamar, Arthur's father, had been the first federal judge of the district in which Egypt City was situated, a post Arthur attained a generation later. Both Arthur and his father had attended Columbia Law, and so, of course, young Rollo followed suit.

Young Rollo, as he was known in Egypt City even into adulthood, was educated prior to his college years at home by Judge Lamar and his wife. Blacks were at that time not admitted to other than exclusively black southern universities, so Young Rollo was sent to Chicago, a city he came to loathe. He spent his years there mostly sequestered in his dormitory room, studying, seldom venturing beyond the immediate area of the campus. New York he liked only a little better. Both places he found too cold, corrupt, and unfriendly; the black people too aggressive. Rollo was relieved once his studies had been completed and he was able to return permanently to Egypt City.

Back home, he went to work for the firm of Lamar, Forthright & Lamar. Abe Forthright, Arthur Lamar's best friend and professional partner for twenty-seven years, had died of pleurisy shortly after Young Rollo's return, four years to the day after the Judge's fatal heart attack that occurred during the Miss Egypt City Beauty Contest, of which the senior Lamar was, of course, a judge. Just as Breezy Pemberton strode onstage at the Gasparilla Livestock Center, wearing only a zebra-skin two-piece and ruby-red spike heels, Judge Lamar keeled over sideways and fell off his chair. He was dead before he hit the ground, the doctor said, of a massive coronary.

Breezy Pemberton, who the following day was unanimously named by the four remaining judges as that year's Miss Egypt City, made this victory speech:

"I'm entirely honored to have won but equally entirely horrified that my beauty might have caused the death of such a prominent citizen of our great town as Judge Lamar. I want the Lamar family to know that it never was any intention of my own to upset the Judge by wearin' a zebra two-piece, certainly not to inspire such a terrible tragedy as has occurred. But I guess sometimes this kinda thing happens, whether required by God or not of course I am in no position to understand, and it ain't no person's fault. I am sixteen and one-half years old and Judge Lamar was much, much older, I know, and seein' a young lady, namely me, like that caused a shock to his tired-out system he was no longer capable of standin', and it's too bad. I'm sorry for the Lamars that is left, but I'm also thrilled to've won the title of Miss Egypt City on my first try, and I just want to say I'm dedicatin' my reign to the mem'ry of the dead Judge. Thank you all, you're very sweet."

Rollo was accepted by the community as a Lamar and treated, as far as he could tell, like any other man, despite the fact of his being black. There were very few black citizens of Egypt City, the population of which remained constant at approximately fifteen thousand. Rollo had never married, living on alone in the Lamar house after Delia's death. Delia had kept a signed photograph of Breezy Pemberton that Breezy had presented to her in a gold-edged frame on the piano in the front room for several years, but as soon as the news reached Egypt City that Breezy had died of acute alcohol poisoning in a room at the Las Sombras Motel in Hermosa Beach, California, Delia took the photo, frame and all, and threw it into the trashbin.

"Why'd you do that, Mama?" Rollo had asked her.

"For every good reason, son," Delia said.

Cutie Early was born in Daytime, Arkansas, pop. 1150, to Naureen (née Harder) and Arlen "Left" Early. Soon after her birth, Cutie moved with her parents to Plant City, Florida, where Arlen found work as a bridge tender on the Seabord Rail Line. Over the next four years, two more children followed: a boy, Ewell, called You, and another girl, Licorice. Cutie being the eldest, it fell to her to tend for her siblings as soon as she was able, especially after Naureen developed an unfortunate affection for Southern Comfort.

At about the same time that his wife found a friend in a bottle, Arlen found one across town, a divorcée named Vanna Munck, with whom he soon kept more than casual company. When Cutie was ten, her daddy left the family and went to live with the Munck woman. One year later, at suppertime, Naureen drove her yellow Voláre over to Vanna Munck's house and left it idling in front while she went inside and shot Left Early and his paramour to death with a .38 caliber handgun her delinquent husband had given her to protect herself with when she was alone in the house. After murdering Arlen and Vanna, Naureen, who was apparently stone-cold sober at the time, got back into her vehicle and drove it as fast as it would go smack into a brick wall behind the Reach Deep Baptist Church. The police concluded that she had died practically on impact.

The children were taken in by Arlen's brother, Tooker, and his wife, Fairlee, who lived in Tampa. You and Licorice accomplished a relatively seamless transition, but Cutie had difficulty adjusting. Her first serious misstep occurred when she was twelve and a half years old. Cutie had been on a date with a Cuban boy named Malo Suerte, who was seventeen, and they had driven in

Malo's Mercury through the exit at the Seminole Outdoor Auto Theater. The drive-in security cop, Turp Puhl, a former prison guard at Starke, had a particular hatred for kids who tried to sneak in without paying. After spotting the red Merc as it crept stealthily with its lights off toward a vacant stall, Turp Puhl pulled out his revolver and made a beeline for the intruder.

As soon as the illegal entrant was berthed, the security guard ordered Malo and Cutie out at gunpoint. Malo swung the driver's-side door hard into Turp, who dropped his revolver. While the boy and the man struggled, Cutie came around the rear of the Mercury, picked up the fallen weapon, and shot Turp Puhl once behind his left knee, causing him to curse loudly and release his grip on Malo. Malo grabbed the gun from Cutie, jumped back into his car, and drove away, leaving Cutie standing next to the wounded guard, who took hold of the girl and held on to her until the police arrived.

Cutie was sent to the Nabokov Juvenile Depository for Females at Thanatos for eighteen months. Shortly thereafter, Malo Suerte went off the Gandy Bridge in his Mercury after it blew a front tire while being chased by the highway patrol and drowned.

By the time she was sixteen, Cutie had established herself as a regular problem, both for her family and for the Tampa police. You and Licorice loved her, but they had their own little lives to sort out, so they kept their distance. After Tooker discovered a cache of knives, including a Hibben Double Shadow dagger, a fifteen-inch Mamba, a quarter-inch-thick Gurkha MK3, and several Italian switchblades, hidden under Cutie's bed, he confiscated the weapons and turned them in, along with Cutie, to the authorities. The knives had been stolen by a boyfriend of hers named Harley Reel, a part-time shrimp salesman who lived with his wife and four children in a trailer home in Oldsmar. He had asked Cutie to keep the knives for him until he found a customer. Harley Reel got four years in Raiford and Cutie, whom Tooker and Fairlee told the judge they never wanted to see again, was sent back to Thanatos until she turned eighteen.

Since then, Cutie had supported herself mostly by waitressing with some soft-hooking thrown in. Her definition of a soft-hooker was a girl who worked without a pimp and made dates privately, without advertising or standing on a corner. Cutie usually went out with older men who didn't mind paying for her time. Most of them couldn't get it up anyway, Cutie found out, which made her job easier, although occasionally a john's frustration over his inability to perform caused him to physically abuse her. Cutie quickly learned to take the money at the beginning of the evening, which ordinarily included dinner, rather than have to go through what could be a difficult scene afterwards. Working without a pimp to protect her had its drawbacks, but Cutie liked not having to be responsible to anyone other than herself.

Cutie had ended up at Fort Sumatra after a bad date, during which she'd been forced to stick a customer in the ribs with a Tanto boot knife. The john had paid Cutie a hundred dollars for letting him piss on her hair. Ordinarily, she didn't do perv, but this was an old guy, in his seventies, he seemed nice, and he promised not to get any urine on her face. He lost control and sprayed her all over, and she jumped up before he'd finished, which angered him. The old man began beating on her, so Cutie cut him. There just happened to be a cop standing outside the motel room when the stuck customer started screaming and Cutie, still dripping wet from the golden shower, ran out.

Big Betty looked out for her now. Cutie knew she could trust her, they could trust each other, and that, Cutie felt, was about the most one woman could ever hope to expect from another. Men hadn't even progressed that far, she figured, and now it was too late. She and Bet were at the end of their rope with them.

Dubuque "Big Boy" Stalcup, Betty's father, was fully grown at six foot six, two hundred thirty-five pounds by the time he was sixteen. He was raised on a south Georgia farm next to the Suwanoochee Creek close to the point at which the Suwannee River crawls out of the Okefenokee Swamp. The Stalcup place wasn't so much a farm, really, as a junkyard hideout for criminals. Big Boy's father and mother, Mayo and Hilda Sapp, maintained an infamous safe house for thieves, moonshiners, and killers on the run. Whenever the law got up enough nerve to invade the Stalcup sanctuary, which was not often, the various fugitives in residence used a secret trail to the swamp, where they would remain until one of the Stalcup kids came to tell them it was safe to come back. The Stalcups made no real attempt to work their land, which had been homesteaded in 1850. The War Between the States passed the Stalcup clan by; they were too remote and the males considered extraordinarily crazy and too dangerous by those few who were acquainted with them to be pressed into service of the Confederacy.

Big Boy and his wife, Ella Dukes, had four children, of which Betty was the youngest and also the only girl. Her three brothers, Sphinx, Chimera, and Gryphon—each of whose names was chosen by Big Boy from *Bulfinch's Mythology*, the only book other than the Bible that he owned—never left the farm. Betty, named by Ella after her grandmama, Elizabeth Hispaniola, a niece of the Seminole warlord Osceola, had run off at the age of fourteen with Duval and Sordida Head, a brother and sister from Cross City, Florida, who had robbed a bank in Valdosta and paid the Stalcups to hide them. Their descriptions of city life intrigued Betty, and she agreed to leave with them when they felt the time was right. Betty never said goodbye to her parents or brothers and never returned to the farm.

After Duval had used her several times, he tired of Betty and passed her to his sister, whose sexual proclivities involved mainly the participation of women and dogs. Sordida introduced the adolescent Betty, who at fourteen was already rather a large person, to the delights of female love, which Betty found preferable to the rough ways of the men who had handled her; namely her brothers, who had deflowered their sister when she was nine and subsequently took their pleasure with her whenever one or more of them felt the urge, and Duval Head. Betty told Sordida that Sphinx, Chimera, and Gryphon really preferred cornholing one another anyway, and figured she'd hardly be missed.

Big Betty stayed with the Heads for a few months, during

which time they knocked off dozens of convenience stores and gas stations and burglarized homes all over the state of Florida. Duval and Sordida went off one day to rob a bank in Fort Walton Beach, leaving Betty to wait for them in the Greyhound bus station, and they never returned. A man and his wife who were traveling to Miami gave Betty enough money for a ticket to New Orleans, a city that for no reason she could think of Betty told the couple was her destination. Betty never did learn that both Duval and Sordida had been killed in a head-on crash with an eighteen-wheel Peterbilt transporting commodes when Duval drove their 1972 Dodge Coronet onto an off ramp of Interstate 10 while attempting to elude a police car in hot pursuit.

Betty found work in New Orleans as an exotic dancer at the Club Spasm on Opelousas Avenue in Algiers. She was big enough to pass for twenty-one and nobody questioned her. Between her dancing gig and turning occasional tricks on the side, Betty did all right. She stayed away from drugs and alcohol, neither of which particularly agreed with her, and entered into a series of lesbian relationships with other dancers and prostitutes. Many of the women with whom Betty consorted were married or had boyfriends, a situation to Betty's liking; she was not interested in committing herself to any one person and discovered that she enjoyed living alone. Privacy, a condition she had never truly experienced either at home or on the road with the Heads, was her greatest pleasure.

Eventually, Betty moved on to Houston, then Dallas, where she took a small-caliber bullet in her left ankle from a drunken patron named Feo Lengua, an illegal from Nueva Rosita, while she was dancing onstage at Rough Harvey's Have Faith Sho-Bar. After she was shot, Betty's days as an exotic dancer were finished, and she worked as a bartender, card dealer, waitress, seamstress, car wash cashier, and hooker; just about anything and everything, as she drifted from Texas back through Louisiana to Alabama and Florida.

It was in Orlando, where she was working in a janitorial capacity, cleaning up a medical building after hours, that Betty was brutally raped and beaten by two male coworkers one night on the job. Betty reported the attack to the police, who several days later informed her that there was insufficient evidence to pursue the case. She bought a Beretta .25 caliber automatic at Emmett's Swap City off the Orange Blossom Trail near the Tupperware International headquarters, went to the apartment of one of her assailants, a glue-sniffing freak named Drifton Fark, found him in an olfactory stupor, and shot him just below the heart. She then hunted down Drifton Fark's companion, Willie "Call Me Israel" Slocumb, a black man who claimed to be a Micosukee Indian and who had converted from Disciples of Christ to Judaism after reading Sammy Davis Jr.'s account of his own conversion in his autobiography, *Yes I Can!*, and shot him once in the right knee and again in the groin while he sat at the bar in the Blind Shall Lead Lounge across from the Flying Tigers Warbird Air Museum.

After Betty shot Willie "Call Me Israel" Slocumb and watched him drop to the floor, writhing in pain and clutching at his affected parts, she laid the Beretta on the bar and told the bartender to call the cops. She sat down on the stool next to the one that had been occupied by her most recent victim, picked up the glass he had been about to drink from prior to the interruption, and drained the contents, a double shot of Johnny Walker Black on the rocks. Just before the police arrived, Betty told the bartender, "You know, that's the first time liquor really tasted decent to me."

Betty was sent to the Fort Sumatra Detention Center for Wayward Women, where, until she met up with Cutie Early, she kept mostly to herself. Miss Cutie was the one for her, all right, Betty decided, the only person she could rely on for ever and ever, her ideal friend. Betty had an agenda, of course, but Cutie, Big Betty vowed, would always rate just as high on the big chart of life as she did herself.

As Rollo Lamar drove from Egypt City toward Trocadero Island, he thought about B. Traven, the writer who had insisted on keeping the details of his life, including his birth, real name, and heritage, secret so long as he was alive. Rollo, who had always been a dedicated reader of fiction, was a great admirer of Traven's work, such as *The Treasure of the Sierra Madre*; *The Death Ship*; *The Cotton-Pickers*; his jungle series, which included the novels *March to the Montería, The General from the Jungle, Government*, and *The Carreta*; and many others.

Traven had deliberately attempted to cover his tracks, with good reason, since he had been a radical journalist and activist in his native Germany and become a wanted man there. He escaped to Mexico, changed his name more than once, worked as a merchant seaman and in the mahogany forests, finally marrying and settling down to the life of a novelist and short story writer in Mexico City. Traven and his wife raised two daughters there, and when director John Huston made a film of *Treasure*, starring Humphrey Bogart, Traven received a certain amount of notoriety, even though he attempted to masquerade, during his stint as technical adviser to the production, as a friend of Traven's named Hal Croves.

Rollo liked not only Traven's novels but his repeated statements that the man who produced the work was of no real importance, that only the work should be examined, not the life of the author. Of course, Traven was paranoid, concerned that his early life and supposed crimes might be revealed. Whether or not he would still have been held accountable for any incendiary acts was doubtful; nevertheless, "the man nobody knows," as he fictionalized himself, developed a strict philosophy based on the insignificance of the creator.

It made sense to Rollo, and as he wheeled along he decided that it would not be the worst condition in the world to become utterly anonymous, known only to oneself. That way, the truth would disappear and there would remain only the brutal evidence of a life, the greater truth, without the unnecessary pain of reexamination. Life itself is difficult enough, Rollo thought. Retrospective investigation, Traven knew, could reveal nothing of real value, so he did his best to conceal his origin. It was a difficult maneuver, given the amount and quality of the work he produced, and the fact that it was intended for public consumption.

Rollo, who at sixty-four bore an uncanny resemblance, though of darker hue, to the actor Broderick Crawford as he appeared in the 1955 movie *Big House, U.S.A.*, had no desire nor any reason to disappear. There was nothing in his past he needed to cover up. In fact, he realized, his life had been rather dull, marked by no really emotionally searing events, despite the death of his mother when he was a young boy and unusual circumstance of his subsequent upbringing by the Lamars. He had no responsibilities other than himself, and no outstanding complaints. As he headed his car across the Trocadero Bridge, he wondered if it were too late for things to change.

Once across the bridge, Rollo pulled into the yard in front of Jasper Pasco's Fishin' Pier and Grocery, a regular stop of his on this run. Rollo needed to stretch his legs, and he usually enjoyed his visits with Jasper Pasco, whom Rollo had known since the Judge started taking him along on trips to the orphanage fifty-three years before. Jasper had to be at least eighty-eight now, Rollo figured, but still more than able and willing to carry both ends of a conversation without much encouragement.

Rollo stretched his arms and legs, bent over at the waist as best he could, and then walked into the store. Before the screen door could bang shut behind Rollo, Jasper was at him.

"You look like a man in need of a ringer for squeezin' meat from a muskrat," the old man shouted from his perch on a high stool behind a wooden counter laden with a motley assortment of items, such as purple tennis shoes, a bucket of used golf balls, net dip for treating trawls, loaves of Wonder bread, all sizes and varieties of nails, red potatoes, an LP album of Conway Twitty's Greatest Hits, green Red Man tobacco baseball caps, and more. Behind Jasper on the wall was a nine-by-twelve-inch framed photograph of John F. Kennedy, autographed by the slain president and inscribed, "To J. Pasco, for whom may the catfish continue to bite and bite hard."

"Lost my taste for muskrat when I was a boy," Rollo said.

"Then I guess to hell you're after chicken necks," said Jasper, "you're goin' fishin'."

"No, thanks, Jasper. I'm on my way to check on the orphans,

as usual. See they ain't bein' made to sleep on their same pee-stained sheets nights."

Jasper grunted. "Ain't wet the bed myself since my pecker seized up six, seven years back. Used to be I was only full of vinegar, now I'm full of piss and vinegar. Haw!"

Rollo smiled and shook Pasco's liver-spotted right hand. Jasper reached down with his left and massaged his bare left foot.

"Got the athlete's foot, Rollo. Doctor told me wear socks, but I hate 'em. Hate wearin' socks almost as much as I hate most my neighbors abandoned me for the Piggly Wiggly soon as it went in up the highway. I used to be a sweet fella, Rollo, you knew me about when. Then that lyin' sumbitch Scaramouche, when he was state senator, promised me the game warden's job if I swung the local vote his way, never come through. That was the start of my bad luck, okay. He gone up to Washington with the U.S. Congress, asked him to pre-vent the Piggly Wiggly comin' in, ruinin' my business, but the sumbitch never even wrote me back. Wouldn't take my phone calls, neither. Well, I ain't easy-goin' no more, you can bet. I'm gonna laugh lastest and longest, though. You'll see."

"Oh, Jasper, shut," said a thin, eagle-beaked woman sitting on another stool behind the counter. She was smoking an unfiltered cigarette and looked to be about ten or fifteen years Jasper's junior.

"Hello, Hermina," Rollo said to old man Pasco's wife of forty-six years. "How you been keepin'?"

Hermina emitted her version of laughter, an extended screech, which sounded as if she had unexpectedly been doused with a bucket of ice water.

"Protectin' this jackass from himself is about all I ever do," said Hermina. "No man on earth better suited to guaranteein' grief to a body than Mr. Pasco, you know it."

"What you expect, the world decayin' the way it is?" Jasper shouted. "Can't expect people to keep a promise! Look at that truck passin' there," he said, pointing at the road. "Shrimper with a butterfly net. Butterfly nets are the ruination of human creation! Can't get the refrigerator man to come out. Tobacco man shows late. Remar the cracker man ain't been in two weeks. And Bowlegs Linda the cupcake girl we ain't seen since she went to Pensacola to bury her mama."

"Bury her mama, my bony ass," said Hermina. "That girl gettin' buried under by the Navy, is what."

"I been around," Jasper said. "Dogpatch U.S.A., Six Flags over Texas, Rock City, Disney World. Ain't much I haven't seen. Had me a Co-Cola once with Connie Francis in Dothan, Alabama. Or was it a beer with Crystal Gayle in Calhoun, Georgia? Which was it, Hermina?"

Hermina screeched and coughed, expelling a small cloud of cigarette smoke as she did.

"Go on and laugh, woman! Rollo, you ask people up and down the Gulf Coast about this place and if they don't know me they ain't never been a cow in Texas."

"Just stopped by to say hello, Jasper," Rollo said, "and to pick up a roll of Spear-O-Mint Life Savers, you got any."

Jasper reached into a pile, fished around, and came up with something.

"Only got Pep-O-Mint," he said.

"Good enough," said Rollo, taking the candy from Jasper and handing him four bits.

" 'Preciate it, Rollo. You come by again soonest."

"Next time I'm here, Jasper. Take care, now. You too, Hermina."

Jasper's wife sat and smoked. Wrinkled, sagging skin hooded her eyes.

"Everybody got their own idea of home," she said.

Rollo walked to his car, unwrapping the Life Savers as he proceeded, popped one into his mouth, and was about to get in when a voice behind him inquired, "Mister, you believe the devil needs a witness?"

Rollo turned around and saw a large, dough-faced woman with small pink eyes standing there, holding a gun in her right hand. She pointed it at Rollo's belly.

"It's okay, honey," Big Betty said, "you can drive."

Betty opened the driver's door, got in, and slid over to the front passenger seat.

"Come on, get in," she ordered, and Rollo obeyed, dropping the roll of Life Savers on the ground as he did.

"Well, what do you think?" she asked, as Rollo started the car and put it in gear.

"About what?"

"The devil needin' a witness."

"I wouldn't know."

"You will," said Big Betty.

YELLOW ROSE

♥ ♥

William T. Vollmann

1

When I put Jenny's picture up against my glasses her face fogs into a pale yellow moon mistily aswim in the darkness of her hair and high school uniform, because as aging progresses (so I once read), the minimum distance required for the eye to focus on an object increases, which depresses me and incites me to strategies of avoidance, such as chewing psilocybin mushrooms. Two bitter grams of these infallibly "increase the absolute blue space/ Which alienates the sky from my embrace," as Baudelaire said about something else. I still pretend that when this expansion takes place, easing my surroundings farther outward on the circumference of a wheel radiating spokes of isolation, then whatever I look at crawls beyond that fatal focal length of vision, like a dreamer fleeing through the molasses of a nightmare, reaching the end of the world at last and jumping into indigo where monsters can never reach. So Jenny herself moves farther and farther away into a freedom the more clear for being lonely; now, through the intergalactic telescopes of my widening pupils, I can decipher the *I love you* that she wrote on the back of her photograph, which before was a disquieting mammogram of blue-ink veins. To a bacterium upon the dot of an *i*, no doubt, the meaning must be less distinct for being more closely embraced.

The night that I decided to declare myself to Jenny, I was at my connection's house, laughing until I ached (convulsions being a side effect of the drug) and drinking Coronas at the kitchen table with friends for whom I had much esteem. The bubbles in my friends' yellow beers as they tilted the bottles to their mouths one after the other seemed to me indescribably COOL, like jazz solos performed with glass instruments of perfect subtlety. I suspected that my friends were drinking that way on purpose, to show off to me, but I did not mind because I had never seen beer drunk so professionally. In fact, I admired myself for having such amazing friends. All of us slammed our bottles down on the table laughing. I was sure that we would come into some money soon and never have to work again, just sprawl around on the sidewalk drinking wine coolers and bloating ourselves with leisure. This thought circulated through my body like a bubble. While it was passing through my cranial arteries I remembered what it was and understood it down to its electrons; but as it left my head it became unknowable again, though I did not mind much because it tickled pleasantly down my neck, my thigh, the top of my big toe. Soon thereafter the open-eyed dreams began. It is needless to say that I retained control of myself, for I saw oddities only in the shadows, which were insignificant in the context of the golden kitchen and golden beers ripening with light. My friends were now playing more than their Coronas; they had added their lips and teeth to the orchestra, scattering sparkles whenever the light struck their gleaming incisors, and pumping their lips in bellows movements against the necks of their beers. I tried not to look at their mouths too much because what they were doing was dangerously complicated. But when I turned my head away I saw prickly greenish entities in the darkness beneath the table. Studying the sink for relief, I was stunned to find that the drainboard was not a drainboard at all, but a *Helmet Rack*, for steel mixing bowls gleamed upon it with dull military efficiency, as they had when I was three and my father had pretended that I was a German soldier and put a bowl over my head and shouted *"Achtung!"*—My friends whooped at this discovery and slapped my back, yelling, "Helmet rack! Helmet rack!" until I could see their tonsils palpitating like a colony of cherry-colored mussels, even after they had closed their mouths. Presently we all lurched to the living room, watching spots of various hues, but primarily lavender, crawl upon the rug like spiders. At first I considered the spots to be hostile eyes that might destroy me, but as I became acclimated to the living room I saw that I had simply lacked confidence, as was my fault with strangers, and that the eyes were delightfully friendly. For this reason I started feeling good as I walked upon the carpet, which struck me as being a meadow in bloom;—never before had I realized that the distinction between inside and outside was but an invention of the academicians. The ceiling, for instance, could easily be a white sky without heat, expressing neutrality for me and all that I stood for. This was how it would feel to be the narrator of Wells's *Time Machine*, strolling moodily on the beach at the end of the world and watching the giant crabs. My friends had vanished. As I traveled across the plain of spots, perfectly aware that it was still the living room, I began to feel a desire to go, although where I wanted to go I did not know; yet as I thought about it I felt a secret glee that indicated that I did know where I wanted to go after all; I just didn't know that I knew; and once I had deduced this, flattening the dough of concepts into substance with strenuous use of my biggest rolling-pins, it became clear that I was going to see Jenny. Then I put on my coat, laughing until I cried.

The night was marvelously clear, as if varnished in epistemological peppermint. I walked up Haight Street faster and faster, until I almost thought I was running, but the street unrolled block after block of ultramarine shops, dreamy cafés, and humid window-fronts, in order to besiege me with options, confused as I already was, first by the multiplicity of bars, next by the comic book stores, then by the record stores where millions of disks chafed inside their cardboard sleeves. Streets radiated from me. But I knew that all of them except Haight Street were streets that I should not take. As for Haight Street itself, wide and bright though it was, like some interstellar boulevard, it would have an end; and though it was expanding faster than I could run, my urgent purpose would empower me to traverse it somehow, just as an insect can travel many times its own length. The sidewalks swam with shadowy crowds going counter to my direction, as if pulled by an undersea current. Their hair floated; I thought I saw bubbles coming out of their ears. Were I to stop or even hesitate, I would be ingested into that remorseless stream and fall backwards past the blackness of Buena Vista Park and down the steep hill behind it, so that I might never see Jenny again. But I kept smiling. (Sometimes I had to stop to laugh into my hand.) A pale woman with cropped brown hair drifted mockingly toward me and waved her fingers in my face. I walked on, but for hours I felt the presence of her fingers still twining themselves over my eyes like seaweed. Then I knew that if I was not careful I might lose myself forever in this unknown world. It was essential that I devote my mind to Jenny, the goal, enfolding my brain lobes around her in tightest concentration until her edges cut into the cerebrum and cerebellum, the same way that when I was a child going to buy candy I used to squeeze my dime in my hand to be sure at every step that I hadn't lost it. The silver dime of my determination ached behind my forehead. Deliciously (I now had to laugh for a long time, hardening myself against the fishy stares of the fish-people), the knowledge began to bubble up inside my chest, where I had kept it secret from myself out of fun, that I was in love with Jenny. Whenever I forgot about her I began to drift into the painted side-alleys where the skinheads lounged in their ultraviolet jean jackets; or else that current of flitting faces pushed me back step by step, draining silently out of theaters and late-night delis; but before any harm came to me I always felt the star of Jenny glowing in her second-story flat to bring me to her. Naturally she did not know that I was coming; she was studying. But I could feel her radiations. Of course she was awake; otherwise the tickling in my chest would have diminished to a drowsy tingling. So I strode on, block after block, not letting myself feel panic that I had not yet reached the end of that vast wide street, the thoroughfare of a chess empire, where up ahead Golden Gate Park occupied a greenish-black space in the night. More hours went by, though Jenny's energy transmissions refreshed my tissues like mint-tingling lymph; and finally I passed the ice cream store and reached Stanyan, which was a sloping gray ribbon of a street that stretched on north of me for several thousand miles, all the way to Geary with its diesel dragon-buses. Now that I had come to Haight Street's last block, the night people roiled behind me like minnows in an eddy; but they were not a menace anymore, since my buoyancy alone would win the fight, carrying me beyond the headwaters, past source-springs and strata and water trickling down sewer gratings; and at precisely this moment, as I saw that Haight Street had been a subterranean river, I emerged from it into the thin air of the wilderness. I was now in the Sunset district. The windows of the apartments were all laughing at me. Every few steps I had to turn aside and laugh into my hand. But there were windows on every side to see me. I felt Jenny not far away, studying calmly like a light bulb. I turned alternately right and left, in hopes of finding windowless walls where I could laugh, just as a drunk will look for a peaceful place to urinate. But there were none. So I continued on my way, turning left, then right, my footsteps very loud on the streetlit sidewalk, until I reached the block where Jenny lived. The darkness was playing dominoes with the housetops. Into my mind came a variety of aphorisms, since I was now in the fiendishly loquacious stage of the drug, and I was eager to see Jenny and express them to her: pins are just like hyphens if you cut the heads off; love is two crickets hopping in the same direction. Clearly there had been no effect on my PK, that is psychokinetic functions.

I stood across the street and looked up at the second floor. Her light was on behind the curtains. She was preparing for her medical boards. I wondered if I should leave her alone. I could go up to the third floor, where my own flat was, but then if I went to my bedroom and turned on the light there would be nothing in there but Jenny's vacuum cleaner (which I had borrowed), alert, but, like all appliances, opaque in any discussion; and it was not for the sake of the vacuum cleaner that I had successfully gamed these complex turns of streets; and I also knew that if I did go upstairs and turn on the light just to see Jenny's vacuum cleaner watching me I would begin to laugh, and all the neighbors across the street would hear and see through their windows, which my windows were transparent to. I could avoid this publicity by taking off my shoes and leaping around my flat in the dark, chuckling very quietly, but inevitably the darkness itself, though it easily subsumed Jenny's vacuum cleaner and indeed the whole apartment, would despite its impressive range not be as good as Jenny (who did not know that I was in love with her) because I would begin to feel restless and so would go eventually to the window to see the lights outside. Then I would start laughing. That would be defeat. And, bubbling up inside me, as I stood on the doorstep, was the knowledge that whether or not these considerations were valid I was going to show myself to Jenny anyway. Gleefully, I rang her doorbell. It was one in the morning.

2

Jenny was Korean. She came from a very traditional family. If her mother ever suspected her of being involved with a Caucasian, Jenny would be cast off. Her mother had just booked her a ticket to Seoul for her vacation so that she could get engaged to a nice Korean boy.

3

"So, will you be upset if I get engaged to somebody else?" said Jenny, looking at me with her flat black eyes.

"Yes," I said.

"Why?" said Jenny.

I didn't say anything.

Jenny had a beautiful round face like a sun or a golden coin. She had chubby arms because she loved cookies and ice cream. She eternally wanted to lose twenty pounds. Whenever she called home her mother told her that her legs ought to be thinner by one-third. She had studied biochemistry at Harvard and graduated with honors because she worked with diligence—"No-Ryok" in Korean, which has ideogrammatic roots in "strength" and in "slave," which latter in turn breaks down into "woman" plus "hand."

Jenny was Soon-Jin (innocent), "Soon" being a fresh shoot sprouting from the ground on the right of the ideogram and a string of twisted silken fibers beneath a cocoon on the left to indicate purity, while "Jin" was a man's head nodding, meaning "genuine." One often sees "Jin" in Korea on the labels of liquor bottles. My pretty Jenny was always smiling and loved to go to Macy's. She kept her room perfectly clean. For me she symbolized above all rest and happiness, an escape from my own gangrened calculus. I wanted to have children in her womb.

"Do you mind that I don't love you?" she said.

"No," I said. "Do you mind that I love you?"

"Don't say that," she said.

We sat on her couch together, and I rubbed yellow marker all over my face to show my resolve to be acceptable to her family. They would not like it at all if she married a white boy. Maybe her brothers would beat me up. That was why Jenny had done her best not to love me. She saw no future in the affair. But I myself still hoped for Kyeol-Hon, matrimony (that is, lucky tie-up woman clan-name day). This must have been why I was awakened in the mornings by the anxious beating of my heart. I do not believe that I have ever cared for anyone as strongly as I did for this Korean girl, because I knew that she was not right for me. In California, where I was born, where I have lived most of my life, wants are satisfied so easily, so cheaply, for the Boo-Jas (rich people) and the bourgeois, that stagnating lusts vent themselves in gambles with fortune. If one is so unfortunate as to win, one moves on to other drugs, to art films and absurdly expensive kiwifruits, each one personally picked by a Maori chieftain in New Zealand. Or so I sometimes told myself—that my affair with Jenny was only a shrink-packed novelty like a new compact disk. And yet later, when she said she loved me I felt a funny weakness localized three inches above my liver. I soon found that I would do anything for her.

4

"I just picked up a really cute guy," said Jenny, down in L.A. "Boy, it was so hard to ride the Windsurfer out there; he had to help me. Actually, he's not that cute, but he has a cute personality. It's really difficult trying to tack. Also, wind died out. Well, here he comes. All right, all of you get lost. Just kidding."*

The man came across the sand, scrunching his golden toes. Jenny gave him beer from the cooler and he thanked her easily and was gone.

"Where's the Windsurfer now?" said Martin in his deck chair.

"Over there," said Jenny, pointing at the buoys.

We were at Marina del Rey, the five of us: Jenny, Martin, Lilith, Anna, and myself. Lilith was out on the Windsurfer; far away she could be seen riding, riding in her blue-and-green

* Jenny spoke the sweetest English that I ever knew. Whenever it came time to tidy her room, she'd announce, "Gotta tighten up now!" —Every minute that she was not studying saw her rushing on errands, saying to herself, "I'm gonna—I gotta—" until it was time for dessert. "I'm so bad!" Jenny cried. "I've been eating chocolate truffles till they came out my tears!" —At the fish store there were turtles and there were frog legs. Fat banded shrimp glistened like resistors. Jenny's eyes went wide with excitement. She saw some squirting clams. "*Ooooh!*" she said. "They're *alive!* They're trying to hide. Ooooh! I wanna *eat* them."

bathing suit, freed from the land and its problems, more or less as she was on the beach, curled on her towel, Japanese eyes almost closed, a soda in the sand beside her as she lay tanning herself like some golden honey plant, nourished by her personal stereo, which was Thoreau's different drummer that only she could hear, rocking her beautiful head (which was more beautiful still than Jenny's) in time with that intimate music which we others had never been privileged to hear or hear of, her face swimming through her long black hair in a coolly masturbatory rhythm, not unfocused ecstasy as I had first imagined, since Lilith was still capable of tabulating the land's ill-conceived interactions behind her eyelids, so that whenever anyone ate a chocolate Tootsie pop she'd slowly open her eyes and say, "Mmm, it looks like you're eating shit on a stick!" and smile brilliantly and almost close her eyes again. Her face was sensuous, cruel, well cared for (she made a lot of money). She would be frightening when she aged. Jenny went to Macy's and bought Clinique makeup but forgot to use it, while Lilith had her compact with her at every moment and took every measure possible to preserve her skin, rubbing ice cubes on it in the living room and no doubt bathing herself in fresh blood like that fifteenth-century Hungarian vampire-countess. Martin had been interested in Lilith the previous year, but other girls had manifested themselves to him in a sweet whirlwind of skirts; other coconuts had fallen off the tree, cracking open just right for Martin so that all he had to do was suck the juice and wait for the next one to drop, just as we now waited for the Windsurfer to blow Lilith back to us, no one caring that much about taking a turn; but not opposed, either, to sailing out in a chilly mist of salt sea-droplets, seeing that the day had to be eased through somehow; there was no sense in rushing it because if we did we might get tired or sunburned and then we wouldn't want to go out drinking that night, and if we didn't go out drinking there would be nothing to do except a movie or the television in the hot living room; for we did not converse, considering each other companions of convenience with sweet-smelling Play-Doh souls unsuitable for interactive entertainment; bluntly, it did not matter if we never saw each other again (for my wooing of Jenny was a secret thing which embarrassed Jenny, so that she had forbidden me to give others any indication; mute lovers tell no tales). At night Lilith hung around me by the TV, wanting to take me for rides in her Porsche past the used car lots and pizza parlors of Santa Monica, where I was born, but I never went with her because Jenny was the only one for me. And in the mornings I'd whisper every new secret thing to Martin, while Jenny and Lilith and Anna changed in the bedroom, rubbing suntan lotion beneath the straps of each other's bathing suits for luck; and it was another hot perfect morning, the beach anyone's only conceivable destination, and Jenny (whose real name was Ji Yun) asked somebody to help her carry the Windsurfer out to the car, and I got up fast to be the first one to lift an end of the Windsurfer, walking backwards with it out the apartment door to look into Jenny's eyes, Jenny my giggly love, my yellow rose, my Korean girl, my butterfish, my kimchee delight; and this was California, my glorious California, where I would never want for anything. Martin felt much the same. A native of Orinda, he knew how it was to be tanned and wear pastel-colored shirts. In San Francisco, Martin and Sheila, Martin and Sherri, Martin and Shoshanna went off to the symphony in formal dress. Once Martin and Jenny went. Martin was pretty sure that he could seduce Jenny whenever he wanted to, but so far he had not gotten around to it. Shoshanna was always bringing him flowers and baking him cakes; and Lilith called him on the bedroom phone, but he had to work late that night at the lab. —"You know, I feel a little guilty," he said in his softhearted way, for he never wanted to hurt girls. And outside in the fog, Sherri honked her horn. —We were, in short, Guk-Mins; that is, citizens; literally, if one researches the source ideogram, walking eyes with obstructed vision. The ancients were cynical about mass thought.

"Do you think Lilith will fall off the Windsurfer?" I said.

"God only knows," said Jenny, bored. "I swear."

Lilith's figure receded slowly among the other brightly colored sails.

The hours went by slowly but effortlessly, as if we were in a convalescent home. Jenny was in a giggly mood. She shook the seawater out of her curly black hair, spraying me. "Windsurfing is a good way to do this, to pick up these guys. Don't worry; he's a nice Caucasian guy. Not all that cute. Very nice guy, nonetheless."

When one lies facedown on a beach mat, the whole world is nothing but yellow and white stripes framed by blue sky. Martin's hairy knees were in the periphery of my view. Jenny's feet were chubby and pinkish-gold. She lay back in her beach chair, chewing gum and dangling her hands from the armrests. Her white teeth were the color of the expensive boats in the lagoon, as could be seen when she laughed. Her heavy round face glistened in the sun. I looked at her and felt Ae-Jong, sincere love, or, to be more precise, a blue heart crowded with slow movement. More than anything I wanted to settle into habits of well-fed intimacy with her. Over and over I told her that I loved her. Our conversations on this subject continued for months, in the shade of various apartments. Sometimes the whole business seemed futile, like attempting to sleep with a bad head cold, but I could not stop. Unbeknown to Jenny, I had decided that if I failed to make her love me I would shoot myself in the left eye.

"I love you," I said. "Sweetheart."

"Don't call me sweetheart," she said.

But we screwed in the backseat of her car.

"Let's do it again," she said.

"As many times as you like," I said.

"Don't assume anything," she said.

We fell asleep together on her waterbed.

"You're my first man," Jenny said. "I hope the others will do it this well."

"Why do you want the others?" I said.

"Kiss me goodbye," she said, and gave me her innocent tongue.

"I love you," I said.

"Oh, never mind," she said. "Another thing I said in my letter. Don't love me too much. It's bad for your health."

"This is the last time," she said.

I sat imagining the cool barrel of the gun against my left eye.

"I see no future in this," Jenny said.

"I love you," I said.

"I'll have to think about what that means," she said.

"I love you," I said.

"I care for you," she said very softly. "My heart is breaking for you. It's my heartbreak that I cannot love you more. I am not going to marry you. I just can't do this to my family. So you have to be lighthearted about this. Otherwise, I'm not gonna come back here. I'm not kidding. You're going to be lighthearted about this. Promise me you will."

"No," I said.

"I am not worth it. I am not worth it. I am not worth it. I am not worth it. Tell yourself I am not worth it. Seriously."

I cried.

"Do you promise not to love me too much?" Jenny said.

"Sure," I said.

She sighed. "You're so transparent."

"Baby," she said. "You're so good. I love it when your legs go all over the place."

"I'd do anything for you."

"Do you like it when I hold you like this?" I said.

"Kind of!" she whispered with a giggle.

"Mom would stab me with knives," said my Korean girl. "Mom would fry me alive if she knew. I'm becoming steel-faced, as my mother said these days."

"Well," I said, "I hope someday I can get on Mom's good side."

"No way," said Jenny. "She'll never accept you. Not your fault, kiddo, but you're never gonna be acceptable. I just can't do this to my family. That's why I'm gonna leave you."

"Oh," I said.

"Don't look at me like that with those glassy eyes!" she commanded.

"Sorry," I said. "I didn't know I was looking at you that way."

"I don't know what to do," she said.

"I love you," she sniffled. "How could you do this to me?"

"I love you, too," I said.

"Oh!" she cried in exasperation. "Suck my tit! At least that way you'll shut up. And I can't believe you tried to screw me when I was on the phone. You are so bad!"

A month later I was living in her room, as Jenny looked at big red pictures of eyeballs in her ophthalmology textbook, lying cozy on the water bed. "I'm recharging my little eye thing," she said to me. "Then I'm gonna want to practice on you because you have blue eyes, you know." Every evening she came home in her white medical smock, smiling at me. "Hand me my Board scores," she said on the bed. "Actually I'm kinda glad you're around so you can get me things." —But we never held hands where Koreans might see. If we drove to Chinatown she might have me put my hand up her dress, but we both had to look straight ahead so that the crowds outside the windows would suspect nothing. Jenny had Chinese friends, too.

5

Jenny loved taking trips, so in the summer we either went down to L.A., stopping at the Carl's Jr. in Kettleman City, the halfway mark, to cool off from the desert while Jenny ordered soft drinks and fries; or else we drove north and east for the weekend, tenting by a picnic table fifty feet from Jenny's car so that we could get whatever we needed (and Jenny always had everything imaginable in the trunk, having worked for fifteen hours the day before to make salad and salsa and Korean barbecue which went into her cooler with the beer), but we never went by ourselves for a trip in those days because I made Jenny nervous; she did not want to be my girlfriend or to marry me, so often my flatmate Martin came along, talking about genetics and opera with the latest girl from the lab whom he was trying to screw. Martin was always sincere. Each time he believed he'd found true love. But true love seemed to transfer itself with austere completeness from Martin to the girl he'd just mounted; and then there was the agony of getting rid of her, the phone ringing for Martin every evening, every weekend, with Martin not returning the calls because he was up at the lab working late, meeting and recruiting other girls; and the harder he had to work to screw a girl the more and the longer he loved her. So Martin motored along with us to the north, he and his new girl up front, while Jenny and I hung the back windows of her white car with towels and white sweatshirts to keep out the sun; and Martin drove steadily down the freeway, his foot pressuring the fuel injector with the same care he devoted to pipetting one of his genetic liquors; and around noon we checked in at some manmade lake resort. —"So hot!" exclaimed Jenny. "I swear." We carried Jenny's cooler down to the water, and Martin and the new girl waved and proceeded to an adjacent cove, the new girl wary but potentially tender, while Martin secreted the maximum doglike sincerity into his eyeballs. We did not see them again for hours. —"Don't lie there! Come on—swim, swim, swim!" said Jenny, and I waded in slowly as Jenny, already immersed, burst out of the water and splashed me, and we made our progress across the uninterested lake, I hugging a yellow air mattress and she breast-stroking beside me like a seal puppy. The channel was about a quarter mile wide. Jenny was going slowly for my sake, being a much better swimmer than I. She was a very strong girl. Sometimes I would kick fast and hard to catch up with her, and I'd pull her to me over the air mattress and turn her wet face to me so I could kiss her. She'd laugh and splash me.

I invented conversations with her in my mind:

"Someday I'll show you Korean thing, a total intimacy kind of thing."

"What kind of thing?"

"I'm not gonna tell you. First you have to marry me, buy me things."

"But what is it?"

"I don't know."

(There is something to be said for attaining the end goal of one's passions as slowly as possible, lingering over each stage: the first kiss, the declaration of love, the progressive sexual exercises; because there is in life a continuous urge to escalation, and it may well be that after you have her and she has you there is nothing else to do.)

Being in love unloved is not unlike rowing in a glass-bottomed boat, which allows you to see both the shimmering green light of the pond and the muck at the bottom; unimpeded in your love by her virtues and vices (since she is indifferent to you), you proceed across the surface of your beloved, leaving behind you the shortest-lived ripples imaginable; and flowers and pine boughs dance upon the breezy bank. You are alone. —How much more difficult it is, unloving, to have *her* in love with you. The boat weighs on you and exposes to her gaze your private depths, until there is nothing for you to do but work in concert with the next available storm to capsize her. When, on the other hand, you love her and she loves you, in your desperation to reach each other you will forget who is in the boat and who is in the water, and one or the other of you will break through into the green light and *SEE EVERYTHING* with rapturous drowning eyes before tumbling slowly into the muck.

When we got to the other shore Jenny wanted me to screw her on the air mattress. I was nervous because I could see passing speedboats through the trees, which meant that through the law of reciprocity they might be able to see us; and besides we were within a hundred steps of the rest rooms—but I did not want Jenny to think me timid. (That was another reason that I took psilocybin.) —"Come on, silly boy!" she giggled. "Suck my tit!" —I could not understand why she was suddenly so much rasher than I, I the Mushroom King. How afraid she had always been that Martin and the others might find out that she was my secret girl . . . and now, in front of anybody who might amble by for bowel or bladder relief, she was taking off her bathing suit. I was her boy; I pulled my swim trunks to my knees, holding her wet brown body in my arms to protect her from whatever it was that I continually watched for even as Jenny's hips and my hips did the necessary. But nothing happened within my visual range (which was bounded on the near side by ballooning focal length and in the distance by haze and nearsightedness), though I surveyed the water like an Aztec apprehensive of Cortez. —"Once you told me I was too shy for you," said Jenny, kissing me and kissing me. "Am I too shy now?" —I felt the same fear that even the expert drug abuser has when the dose is too great, and controlled consciousness disintegrates, the soul whimpering as it senses that it is now strapped to the electric chair of destiny. I didn't realize that she wasn't screwing me out of brazenness, that I had not corrupted her and made her into a jade, but rather that she loved me desperately.

6

Regarding Jenny's mother, I reminded myself that "there need not be proof of the emission of semen; proof of penetration only is necessary to constitute proof of sexual intercourse. Nor is it necessary that penetration be full and complete; but the slightest penetration of the male organ of the man into the female organ, or vulva, of the woman, as penetration sufficient to rupture the hymen, will constitute sexual intercourse, or carnal knowledge." I am, of course, quoting from the decision of State v. McCann, *18 Ohio Dec 64, 5 Ohio Law R. 388, 389, 52 Wkly. Law Bull. 563*, as interpreted in *Words and Phrases*, published by West (St. Paul, Minnesota, 1953). As yet, however, I have said nothing regarding sodomy res veneria in ano, per os, and per anum.

"Oh!" said Jenny. "I don't *believe* I tried oral sex. It wasn't so bad, though. It's like a slippery lollipop."

Jenny's father, whose picture I never saw, had died after they had immigrated. Spinal meningitis had killed him. Because he could not walk, the doctors told Jenny's mother that he was lazy. His final coma, which lasted a year, had destroyed the family savings; and Jenny's mother, who now stood silently in her kitchen frying meat and watching me, had the look of someone who had worked hard for life, a strained slenderness of hands and features, and black curls going gray. She ran a grocery business (in Korea she had been a concert pianist). It was clear to me at once that what I was doing to Jenny would hurt this woman, that I had less right to be in her house than she had to be in my California, where, in the words of Hassan the Assassin, "Nothing is true; all is permissible," when back in Korea it had been so well understood what her daughter was to become, even when Jenny was the class leader of her elementary school back in Seoul, deciding who among the other pupils had to sweep the classroom, who had to get coal for the stove in winter; and then when she was eleven Jenny was picked by a magazine to be a child model, and Jenny's mother had to buy her a whole new outfit, but she told none of the relatives because she didn't want Jenny to be spoiled, and Jenny wasn't spoiled; and when Jenny's mother came to school to greet the teachers she looked so young then, so pretty, that everyone said to Jenny, "Who's that? Is that your sister?" and then Jenny went to high school and graduated with honors and was accepted by Harvard and then medical school, her mother thinking that she was still Soon-Jin, but there were to be no full-blooded Korean children out of her; already her womb was being ruined by a Caucasian with no rights to her; and though Jenny cried sometimes she did not entirely comprehend the spermatic tragedies nightly enacted; but Jenny's mother surely would if she knew the case. Then she and Jenny would both hate me. —"Thanks for the shower," I said. "It felt good after the ride through the desert." —Jenny's mother laughed politely, as if I had made a joke. Jenny told me that her English was not good.

The house overlooked a golf course. It was very hot there. "Do you ever get golf balls in your backyard?" I said, considering this to be a charmingly casual, even witty question that would solve all difficulties. —"All the time," said Jenny's younger cousin politely. Later I found that Martin had asked the same thing when I was in the shower.

Jenny snapped her fingers and gave orders. "Carry my clothes up," she said. "Hurry up! Wash my clothes. Clean my room. Make two gin and tonics." She was the darling of the family. She could do whatever she liked.

7

"It was an outdoor Sunday service kind of thing," my Korean girl was saying in the car as she drove us all to the beach. "They had about five thousand foods."

We got to the beach and set up the Windsurfer. Jenny ate plums and fanned herself. "What a weather! My mom's about to eat me alive because of the little tan I got. She goes, 'You stay out of the sun!' She's pissed 'cause I'm so dark."

When Martin went out on the Windsurfer, Anna took a shower and Lilith went to the bathroom, we were alone for a minute. Jenny lay on Anna's towel. I slid my hand down the top of her bathing suit. She opened her eyes slowly. "Well well well well well," said my Korean girl.

All of us lay on the beach doing nothing for hours. "I love sun!" laughed Jenny. When it was dark we drove through Westwood in her little white Nissan, the windows all the way down, while Jenny chewed her sugarless gum. The sidewalks were crowded with teenagers trying to pick each other up, anxious to clasp each other like sea anemones in beachfront bedrooms. Jenny shook her head at them. "These kids are so bad!" she said. "All my friends were pretty much virgins when they married." —But she added slyly, "They got married early."

After this, Jenny took us to her favorite bar, "Yesterdays." Jenny and Anna had sweet pink drinks. All the rest of us had beer.

8

Having been previously disappointed in love, my flatmate Martin had become very confiding of all romantic developments, feeling, doubtless, that in the act of telling his love to the indifferent world he could reassure himself that he *was* loved. Anyone who encouraged him was his friend. I was almost the same way.

Martin and I were flatmates because we had gone to an experimental school together in eastern California, where females were excluded for the sake of strong libido development, making us Trustees of the Nation in a very real biological sense, as our founder had desired. Acting upon these principles, Martin and I used to go off together to smoke pot beneath the green desert moon. We'd roll out our sleeping bags side by side in the marble canyons, drink beers, and talk about girls, thereby inculcating in each other a constellation of expectations which winked and blinked nightly as we lay staring up and thinking; so it was inevitable that when we graduated we would go chase all the women we could, in a low-key sort of way involving Valium and Sonoma wine. I enjoyed telling Martin about my high school girlfriend, who had dropped me, but whom nonetheless I had laid beneath her father's desk, which made me, I believed, quite special. The first girl that Martin screwed was named Virginia Lemmons, in a dome house in some commune or other that Martin was hitching through on his academic break. Such episodes used to be as common as measles, back in the days before Acquired Immune Deficiency Syndrome, Martin not grasping that promiscuity is a failure to understand the basic sameness of vaginas, of women, of oneself, of one's own deliberate entrapments. Virginia Lemmons wrote Martin, but he never answered.

There were days, months in our twenties when Martin and I had such good times talking about women that I loved the grin of his big white teeth as we sat on the beach, Jenny and Martin's new girl out swimming; or Martin and I loitered around our dining-room table, eating a chuckling granola breakfast right over the heads of Jenny's roommates. Then I knew that Martin and I would be successful with our girls and marry them, and have terrific extramarital affairs.

"Are you going to marry Sherri?" I asked.

"It's not inconceivable," said Martin in a tone of academic thoroughness, so that I knew that he was about to scan every phenomenological side of this Moebius strip. "I know the real and imaginary blocks, and I've discussed them with Sherri, so I think, yes, there's a chance. But I wish she'd clean up her room, and she should brush her teeth before she kisses me. Also, she's always borrowing money, which I find annoying. I tend to count my pennies. But I went to this party for this professor who got tenure, and this girl from the other lab was there; she was drunk, and it was so tempting to just sort of walk her home and . . ."

"Was she pretty?" I said.

"Oh," said Martin, "I think she's pretty enough. She's actually about Rhonda's height. She can look pretty, yes, kind of a coy little-girl expression, you know how it is . . ."

And that pleased me, that Martin knew that I *KNEW HOW IT WAS.*

Martin and Jenny and I sometimes went sailing in the Bay. Jenny kept failing her licensing exam, so she had to continually go out, never quite learning how to bring in the jib or how to tack. Martin had to do all the work. —"I know how to tack," she insisted. "I know how to bring the boat in the Bay and out of the Bay. It's just like driving. It's just a matter of confidence. I also have very little sailing experience compared to Martin. He's sailed Sunfish, and I don't know what else. But someday I'll get it down. But before that I need to do reading for a couple hours, on points of sail and things like that." —It was peculiar watching Martin metamorphose from a hanger-on at Jenny's Korean meals (which she cooked for everybody) to the omnicompetent skipper, shouting at Jenny to take in sail or take out sail. —"There isn't much wind," Jenny said defensively. "We're just putzing around for a long time. And we keep getting close to Angel Island. I keep telling Martin to put the motor on." —"Jenny, get ready to come about," said Martin. —"Oh, give me a break!" cried Jenny. —I lounged on the stern side, squirting Jenny with my plastic replica of an Uzi pistol. We floated on the blue Bay until the fog came. When it got rainy, Jenny huddled in her slicker with her hair frizzing out from her hood, as if she were a poor wet Eskimo (Eskimos, being Mongolian in type, are closely related to Koreans, I once read), crying, "I want to go home, I want to go home," down in the hot cabin that reeked of diesel, and Martin and I sat companionably at the ropes, rain gear zipped up to our chins, winking at each other like old sailors.

It was Martin who first got Jenny to smoke pot. She never thought that she would do it. Martin persuaded her that it would be a good scientific experiment. Jenny smoked too much the first time and got dizzy and Martin had to hug her. That was O.K. with him. Martin enjoyed hugging girls. After Jenny became my girl he kept hugging her. Sometimes he'd rest his head on her shoulder for a very long time, or kiss her cheek while I watched.

Martin genuinely liked Jenny. He told me that her breasts looked really good. He often borrowed her car. He liked going on trips with Jenny because he could use her car and she would usually make something to eat. Jenny was very convenient for Martin.

Down in L.A., Martin gazed like a lord at Anna and brown-skinned Jenny carrying the hull of the Windsurfer into the water, like a pair of Melville's Pacific island women with an outrigger canoe. Then they unrolled the sail and snapped it to the mast. ("Where's the batten?" said Anna. —"Maybe we must have forgot that ropy kind of thing," replied Jenny, endearingly.) —"Martin, you go first," Jenny said. —"Actually," said Martin, half-asleep on his deck chair beside me, "I don't feel like it." —"I'll go," said Anna. "But I want you all to watch me. As long as I'm going to hurt myself I may as well entertain others doing it." —"Lilith, help us push her off," said Jenny. —Lilith disconnected herself from her headphones and raised her eyebrows and stood up, hugging herself so tenderly that she seemed her own lover. For a moment I myself almost loved her, so confident was she of her own splendor that her faith moved me, amorous agnostic though I was; but then she turned to Jenny with a little sneer, and I was released. —Martin and I watched the three girls walk slowly down the beach to the Windsurfer. They slid it into the sea. Anna stood upright on it, clutching the mast and looking diminished by her assignment. The three girls stood in the water as if they were having an oceanography seminar. Jenny was a dark brown figure in the water, which came up to her knees. She extended her arms, as if to help Anna magically before Anna fell. Anna toiled with the sail and drifted, Jenny wading after while Lilith stood in the water watching. I could see Jenny following, her arms ready. Jenny pointed and pushed off. Anna sailed a short distance and fell.

"You notice that she's moving and hasn't ever gotten the sail up," said Martin from his deck chair. "It's a lot of work. Still trying. Still trying." Martin, being a scientist, habitually observed and commented on the phenomena around him. When something happened, he could not help but take notice (Ee-mok, literally, "ear-eye"). —Jenny swam out to help. —"Well, she's standing up," said Martin, surveying things through his white-framed sunglasses. The hot breeze stirred the hair around his nipples. "I always forget whether you move the sail forward or back," he said.

"Well," said Lilith, who had just reached us, "it's all a matter of getting used to things. Could you pass the fifteen lotion? It's going to be a rough day in the sun." Lilith was an engineer at a nuclear plant, because, as she quipped, she had a glowing personality.

9

"Mom says, 'Jenny, why are you getting as brown as a nut? What are you doing Windsurfing today? Remember, Jenny, white is beautiful.' "

"Right," said Lilith in a world-weary tone.

Jenny knew all the department stores in town. On Sundays she liked to sit in the living room, eating blueberries and reading in the paper about sales. "These blenders are so cute," she'd tell me. "Macy's is having special. But here they are at this other place. Probably a better place to go than Macy's, no matter sale or not. Anyhow, I already have a blender."

One night I lay in her bed watching her get undressed. When she looked at me I waved. —"You're so silly," she giggled, removing her earrings. "Any case, I'm so tired, I can't believe I have to write this goddamn pediatrics case out. Very big head circumference. Pulse is fifty-six. In the playground she buries a lot of toys in the ground. What's wrong with this TV? This TV has funny problems at times."

"I want you," whispered the actress on Jenny's TV. —"Dana, I've found the traitor!" said the male firmly. I swam in Jenny's water bed . . .

10

Concerning psilocybin, we must not forget that even the love of Tristan and Iseult, as admirable an achievement as it seems, was only the result of a potion, and can thus hardly be credited to the two songbirds. This being the case, we should be fair and admit that negative emotions may similarly have chemical causes, preventing us, however much we would like to, from assigning blame.

Lifting her plump wrist, she squinted at her watch in fascination. "I don't believe it!" she cried. "It's all opposites!" —Jenny and Anna lolled back in their chairs, screaming with laughter. The straps of the beach chairs dug into their fat thighs. Jenny's face was purple. She was laughing so hard that she was gasping for breath. She clutched Anna's red-and-orange towel and kept twisting it and chewing on it. To me in my own drug state, the towel glowed fatefully, investing the entire beach with sullen hues of lava and vomit, no matter how I turned my head away from it. —Jenny kicked her legs in the air. —"I see your gums!" she said to Martin. "Oh, this is so weird!"

Now she was getting the mushroom sweat. Her round head fell back helplessly, and I thought of the way she had stroked my face and said, "I love your sunken Caucasian eyes." Fat drops of moisture ran down her cheeks and arms and legs. Then, as I lay on the sand watching her, the mushrooms took me also, and she began to change in my eyes, her body getting redder and older until I saw her as she might be twenty years from now: heavy, indolent and shameless, sitting out on the porch screeching and laughing and yelling day and night so that I got no sleep because she was MY WIFE, the kind of wife who would be the shameless laughingstock of the awful neighborhood that we had to live in thanks to my cruddy income, for I would never be either Boo-Ja or bourgeois; and Jenny sat rocking on the top step, whisking away the flies and bellowing for me to bring her things and tidy up the house; while my own kids, a platoon of half-Asian youngsters with serious faces, organized the household as directed by her, passing me by silently as a worthless lump of white meat ridden with the maggots of a bygone empire; as well they should in a culture where the word "Pu" (father) was derived from a picture of a hand holding a whip; I did not live up to that; and Jenny's mother ("Mo," a woman with nipples), now so old as to be just a gray stick with glaring eyes, hobbled down the stairs once a day to beat me for having degraded Jenny; but I didn't care about any of it because I still loved Jenny, because I remembered how she had been that night when I first rang her doorbell, high on mushrooms, and Soon-Jin Jenny came downstairs in her nightgown and she opened the door not really knowing me, and she had never seen anyone on drugs before. —"You're drunk," she said tolerantly. "God only knows. You want me to unlock your door for you?" —"No," I chuckled. "It's not that." I beckoned her very close to me and began to whisper to her a secret story which I knew she would find irresistibly funny. —"Jenny," I whispered. —"What?" she said, shivering in her nightgown. —"Jenny, when I was at my friends' house . . ." and I began to tell her how the rooms had been different, all about the helmet rack and the spots on the rug, "and the spots were watching me," I explained, leaning right up against Jenny's ear. She was staring at me. —"At first I thought they didn't like me, but"—I was already beginning to grin, because the punchline was so good—"then I realized that they were very friendly!" —I laughed so hard that I almost fell down. And dear Jenny looked me up and down and shook her head and laughed, too. I really loved her then.

"Kiss me with your tongue!" she commanded. "It makes me feel kind of nauseous, but I like it! Because, you know, I'm kind of a flittery girl."

I kissed her.

11

While Jenny was in Korea I went down to Haight Street to smoke hash and watch rock and roll videos. Late at night I met a blond addict who appeared surprisingly clean-cut until I got close and saw how pale he was and he pulled me into a dark storefront doorway and showed me his skimpy slimy filthy little joints. —"They're covered with hash oil," he assured me. They looked as if he'd spat on them. —"How much for one?" I said just to get out of there. —"Two dollars," he said, "just two dollars, and if you give me three I'd really appreciate it because I need my fix, man; I've just gotta get cranched." He was trembling. I gave him two and a quarter in disgust.

A guy was yelling outside the record store. "*HEY*!" he said. "I'm new in town. Where do I get to *MEET* somebody?" —Everybody laughed.

Although every day I craved Jenny, within me I think I already saw the days so soon to come when she admitted that she was ashamed of me, and when I put my arms around her in the bed she cried, "Get the hell out, I hate you! I hate you! I'm gonna go to church and pray." And yet, even granting that she might be perpetually ashamed of me, I still knew that our life together could be almost seamless. One day in Berkeley when I sat waiting for her to come home from Korea, I got ribs at Flint's Bar-B-Q. One might as well do something while waiting. (I eat.) We are always waiting for something new to happen. So time passes, and so do our opportunities. —I sat under a tree in Ho Chih Minh Park, eating. Two dogs came up to me. I told them to go away, but one stayed, and I kicked him. He looked at me very patiently. Finally I decided to give him the bone that I had just finished, because he was being very patient and dignified; and anyhow it seemed a waste to drop the bone in the trash can, from where it would only be conveyed to some contaminated landfill. I threw the bone to him. He picked it up very quietly, hunkered down, and began to grind it in his mouth. Every now and then he snarled, and I hypothesized that he was either (a) pretending to kill it, or (b) engaged in an irregular war with the barbecue sauce. I had ordered the hottest kind they had. It occurred to me that even if Jenny kicked me and yelled at me, I would be satisfied with whatever bone she threw me, even if it hurt to eat. So I made my peace with myself.

12

Dust to dust and lust to lust: Suppose I died, and when I got my postthanatonic bearings it turned out that the dead were passionless, after all, as has often been postulated, but I wasn't, because I had killed myself out of yearning for Jenny despite the fact that as she lay there in her death–water bed she made me promise to remarry and screw other girls, but her last words were "I love you," so I decided to shoot myself in the head in order to remarry HER in Ghostland; but once I had done it I found her aloof, so I still couldn't have her even though I was dead along with her, and I felt terrible, like one of those dumb petulant poltergeists trying to get attention, and Jenny offered to take me to a dead doctor like Martin who could fix my brain so I wouldn't mind anything, and then that way I'd get reincarnated faster, but I wouldn't do it; I just stood in a corner of Hell getting more and more transcendently miserable because secretly I had the idea that maybe if you got more miserable than anyone thought possible you might achieve a special transcendence superior to whatever dumb transcendence this dumb Zen renunciation stuff offered; and if I did that I'd triumph over everybody; and then Jenny, who like other Asians was status-conscious, would come back to me.

13

"I don't care about solidarity; I care about commonality. It's so much more *immediate*," as I heard a Haight Street anarchist say.

Jenny and I, I decided, were going to make love on her water bed, wearing separate but equal headphones plugged into the same tape deck, so that we could go up and down in synch to the Eurythmics doing "Sexcrime" at maximum volume, and then we'd dance around naked shooting my air pistol at pictures of Kim Il Sung and his appropriately named Yook Goons (army military), and then we'd get back in bed and do sixty-nine and I'd leap out of bed and flip the cassette so that the Eurythmics would sing, "Plusgood, doubleplusgood, plusgood, doubleplus-good!" and finally we'd walk through Golden Gate Park on psilocybin, talking and talking to each other like birds, endlessly expressing our love to each other in the greenness.

(Sublimely perfect communication, like the bird-cries, would actually be imbecilic, would be blissful cries that meant nothing and might even be mistaken for cries of pain, would accompany tropical colors, like those of the slate-blue birds with fan-shaped crests, swiveling their heads in martial increments, while rain ran off the leaves, and the birds (blue-crowned pigeons, *Goura cristata*, New Guinea) puffed themselves up and marched through the mud, glaring with their red eyes; and green-banded black talking-birds uttered baffling cries in the branches of trees; and the water wavered with green reflections stirred by ducklike birds (Layson teal) that swam in fleets, leaving V-shaped wakes; they drank the water eagerly; and other birds sang with resonant metallic sounds.* Plump white birds banded with black and red eased themselves into the water silently, paddling with fat orange feet, and then sauntered through the rain like tourists, glancing round idly in the mud beneath the trees; and blue-bellied brown hens pecked at worms under stones. Yellow-and-black birds swooped down from round-leaved branches like tigers glorying in their own colors; and gray-green birds roosted in the trees patiently. Great needle-leaved palms stabbed the sky, but the birds did not fly to them. The blue pigeons picked at their own chests and shook their feathers. When alarmed, their wings shot up darkly

* It was these sounds that Jenny seemed to me to imitate when she talked Korean to her mother. I once transcribed the alien syllables that I heard her say: "Omja, kumija goo-o, gooey-gooey! Handala! Kulego kulegrum. Gahio." —But when I read them back to Jenny she could not understand them at all.

from their backs. Other birds were golden-beaked, rearing tarnished heads and showing brown belly-feathers that looked like shingles; while the flamingoes bent and stabbed down in the streams like mosquitoes; and bridal-white birds veiled with trailing feathers stood in shallow pools. Overhead, birds cried like groaning fan belts. The saffron-colored ones turned their backs and hunched, like high-shouldered Buddhist monks. Egrets coiled their snaky necks and flexed their twiggy feet . . .)

"You've got me hooker-sinker line," said Yellow Rose.

"You mean hook, line, and sinker," I said.

"That's what I mean. Any case, you sure got me now. In Asian tradition, when a man penetrates a girl he's gotta be responsible for her for the rest of her life. I hope you're feeling responsible."

"I'll try," I said.

"You have upper hand now," she said. "I'd do anything to keep you. My heart is aching for you. Oh, dearie, my heart is dying for you."

Now began the happy time when Jenny spoon-fed me ice cream and bought me chocolate bars, and we lay in bed all day and I rested my head on her shoulder listening to her talk on the phone. "I feel so stupid compared to you," my Korean girl told me. "I want you to tell me all about those philosophers—Aristotle and Pluto and those Greek kind of guys." In the living room she lay on top of me on the sofa, her skirt unzipped. "I'm not just a steel-face, I'm an iron-face!" she giggled. "Mom would die." Whenever I went anywhere Jenny came to the top of the stairs in her nightgown, begging me not to go. I tongue-kissed her and stuck a finger up her golden ass.

The ring was a wavy gold band crowned by a diamond. Examined through the jeweler's loupe, the diamond itself seemed a transparent bud, composed of a hundred tight-clasped petals of crystal veined to the core with yellow refractions from the gold below. I could not determine whether the diamond was yellow, blue, purple, or perfectly colorless. —This was the engagement band. —The wedding band was a golden circlet of the same wavy shape, made to interlock with the engagement ring.

It was going to be a surprise for Jenny. I had obtained the

complicity of her housemate, Margaret. Margaret was a shy gentle girl with a freckled face. All the girls downstairs were Soon-Jin. Margaret, when asked by Jenny for a rope with which to lash her sleeping bag onto her pack, furnished a pretty red ribbon, at which I smiled, while Jenny and I went backpacking in the Olympic Rain Forest, Margaret's ribbon flying from Jenny's pack as the trail took us through Spanish moss and maidenhair. Water glistened on the toes of our boots, making them brown and shiny like champignons. Secret Creek was hidden under tall cinnamon ferns. We peered through them to see black water glinting with cold gold light. Jenny grinned, climbing up the mountains. But since she was a city girl I had to give her my hand to help her across brooks. I had been with her for so long that I had what Asian-Americans laughingly call "yellow fever," for when I closed my eyes I still saw the gold light from her; and the autumn leaves in their oranges, browns, yellows, and golds could almost have been butterflies born from her, each leaf fixed with a particularity of gold derived from her shimmery skin, the blood pulsing in her cheeks when she looked at me and told me that she loved me; and Margaret had watched the courtship smiling, so now when my pillow burned me at night and my dreams were of golden Jenny I turned to Margaret and confided in her, telling her that I had to marry Jenny at once; and Margaret, astonished that matters had gone so far, but trusting me, drove me down to Post Street, where the shop windows shone yellow with gold. Margaret and I were both nervous. Neither of us had ever done this before. —The jewelers all thought that Margaret was my fiancée. They put the rings on her finger one after another, while she held out her hand, blushing slightly. In the second store we found the ring that was perfect. The jeweler was an elderly man, plump and benign, who waited on us with attentive courtesy. There was something about the cut of his suit, the smell of his cologne, that reminded Margaret and me of distant exotic places where jewels come from; and I imagined him traveling to the Demilitarized Zone, writing out a check with his liver-spotted hands, unperturbed by the *PHWWwwwinnnNG!* of bullets, as his contact, a North Korean private, came leapfrogging over the barbed wire, on his head a conical hat stuffed tight with gold (for gold, too, was a drug; and no doubt its purchase and manufacture was attended by the usual risks). — As the afterimage of my treasure-buying imaginings faded I looked at the jeweler's tie and let my heart pound at the romance of my own absurdly expensive purchase, Margaret also goggle-eyed; and Jenny was going to be astounded. The jeweler waited out my silence patiently. When I told him that I was unemployed he did not lose his gentleness. He got out the padded pews of diamonds and placed the rings on Margaret's finger for us to see. One of Margaret's fingers was bandaged. For some reason, the sight of her hardworking hand (she was a night waitress, carrying trays of cruel gleaming cutlery and heavy wineglasses that could shatter into a million dangerous jewels), with its Band-Aid and all its temporary diamonds, filled me with tenderness.

The fourth ring was the right one. Both of us knew it. —"Oh," said Margaret quickly, "it's really cute. I mean, but maybe cute's not the word for something this important." And she looked timidly down at the ring, in case she had offended me. —"Yes," said the jeweler. "See how pretty it is." And he withdrew the ring from her finger and gave it to her to hold.

There was a sapphire ring at the Shreve Company that Margaret and I liked almost as well, but we knew that Jenny was a traditional girl, and sapphires were not traditional, although the saleslady tried to convince us that they were mainstream now that Lady Di had gone with one. —"Let's get the diamond ring," I said.

We went back to buy it. When Margaret saw it again she nodded. "You have good taste," she said.

"Of course I do," I said complacently, "because I have Jenny."

From my shabby pants pocket I counted out the sum, in a great heap of tens and twenties on the glass counter, with a solitary hundred thrown in for garnish. Margaret told me on the way home that the jeweler had smiled just a little at my youthful display of cash. I did not see his face because I was looking at all my money for the last time. —"When's the big day?" said he, anxious, no doubt, to distract me from considerations of poverty.

—"It hasn't been set yet," I said. "I'm about to ask her. When she sees this nice ring, I guess she won't be able to resist." —"Yes," said the jeweler in his stately manner, sweeping my money off the table. He gave me two clean copper cents in change. I gave one to Margaret for a luck-penny.

"Well," I said, "that's done. Let's hope I never have to do it again."

"You can't say that now or the ring will be cursed," Margaret said. "I know it's going to be your lucky ring." She smiled at me. She loved Jenny.

Jenny was home. "Where have you two been?" she said.

"Oh, just around," I said.

Margaret winked at me behind Jenny's back and left the house.

I gave Jenny the two little packages. I had even figured out what to say. "Jenny," I said, "once I told you that I wasn't worth your little finger. After you put these on that'll certainly be true."

"Oh, no," said Jenny, sitting down on the bed as if she had just discovered that she was ill.

She unwrapped the boxes and opened them. "There's so much tissue paper in here," she said. "Christ sake. I'm never gonna get to the bottom of these little things. I sure hope you didn't get what I think you got."

"That's the engagement ring," I said, "and this is the wedding band. Margaret said you're supposed to wear the wedding band nearest to your heart."

Jenny put the rings on her finger. "They're beautiful," she said, looking down at the bed. "You know I am not gonna wear them. You know I can't accept them."

"Oh," I said.

"Why are you putting this pressure on me? You know I'm not about to marry you. If I were head over heels with you, I'd say, hell with the whole world. I'd marry you right now. But I don't love you to that degree. You're so impractical. You've made me so unhappy." She put the rings back in their boxes and wrapped the boxes up again. "You've made me so unhappy," she said. "I can't believe you did this dumb kind of thing. How unhappy are you, on a scale of one to ten?"

"I don't know," I said.

"Ten would be all my family killed in an airplane crash. One is, you know, slight disappointment. That's the scale, Mister."

"I don't know," I said.

"You've put such a big burden on me. I'm a six. No, I'm a five."

"I see," I said.

"How about you? I've told you; now you tell me."

I considered. Ten would mean that I was ready to kill myself. I had already loaded my guns upstairs. "Seven," I said. "No, seven point five."

"I want you to return the ring right now."

"No," I said.

"Return the ring."

"No."

"I know! I'll tell you I don't like it. I hate this ring. I hate it. It's so ugly. Return the goddamn ugly ring. Now you'll have to return it, won't you?"

"No," I said.

"Boy," she said, popping her gum. "I tell you."

I turned away.

"Fine, fine, fine, get away from me," she said. "You just don't want to be near me anymore."

"That's not it," I said.

"I want you to return the ring. You are so impractical. Do you hear me? I say, return the ring. Anyhow, what finger's the engagement ring supposed to go on?"

"The ring finger," I said.

"Anyhow I never wear rings," Jenny said. "With all the scrubbing and scrubbing of my hands in the operating room, soon it would be worn down to nothing." She put her arms around me. She had never held me so sweetly. "You know I love you, you silly boy," she said.

That night Jenny tucked the covers of her bed around me gently and went out. I had dreams of severed heads. After a long time I woke up with Jenny's arms around me. —"You're having a terrible night, aren't you?" she said. —I said nothing, pushing my face hard against the cold wall. When Jenny finally fell asleep, I got out of the bed as quietly as I could and put my clothes on. She said something in her sleep. I opened the door and closed it behind me without looking back. I walked past Margaret's room and went downstairs. Outside, I unlocked the door to my apartment, went up to my room, and lay on the floor. My stomach squirmed in its acids inside me, and my chest was so tight that I could hardly breathe. After a long time it was still dark. But I could hear cupboards slamming in the flat downstairs; I heard a voice in Margaret's room; I heard streetcars rattling by and birds singing. No doubt aging had set in with a vengeance, overcoming my many doses of magic mushrooms, increasing my focal length of vision further and further in the course of this night so that I would never again be able to see anything closer than Jupiter.

Brother Do You Talk Black but Secretly Wish to Sleep White?
Put Your Dick Where Your Mouth Is and Read . . .

THE BLACKMAN'S GUIDE TO SEDUCING WHITE WOMEN WITH THE AMAZING POWER OF VOODOO

♥ ♥

Doctor Snakeskin

INTRODUCTION

Back in the bubble-toed seventies, after Jimi choked on his vomit, but before Nixon faced the bull(shit) in the arena, my posse of platformed homeboys and I hid behind the hedges in the high-school parking lot, smoked toothpick-thin sticks of reefer rolled from shot-glass nickel bags, swigged chilled Strawberry Hill, and discussed the future following our impending graduation.

Sporting broad-brimmed *Mack* hats on the sides of our big, bushy, and bulbous Afros, we had nicknames like Shaft, Sweetback, Truck Turner, Superfly TNT, and Willie Dynamite.

My tag was Hell up in Harlem. And, like my polyester party-pals, I wanted to be a pimp.

Why I thought I'd be more successful at pimping, instead of, say, *drug dealing*, is a question I'm baffled by to this day.

My entire range of sexual experience, at that point in my young life, consisted of one isolated incident with a fourteen-year-old pepper-faced blonde I dry-humped against a Coke machine in the New England boarding school I attended some years before.

My virginity notwithstanding, I was determined to be a pimp. Not a gorilla pimp like Iceberg Slim, but a *guerrilla* pimp who understood the world according to Fanon, and had the physical prowess of Bruce Lee, but dressed better than the average member of the Black Panther Party.

As I explained this to my pack of pot-puffing playmates, Sweetback looked up from his joint, coughing reefer smoke.

"Shit, nigga, is you trippin' out wid dem whyte boys on dat acid again or what?"

"Naw, brutha, I'm gonna be a pimp with a *revolutionary* agenda! My face is gonna be *stenciled* on walls throughout the third world, right alongside Che Guevara!"

"Sounds like somebody slipped som' Led Zeppelin in da sleeves o' yo' Funkadelic albums, nigga! *You trippin'!*"

"Naw, nigga, I *reads* my Uncle Ho! I gots the Cong down cold! My shit is *skulled!* Remember, the Panthers said: "*Political power begins at the lips of a pussy!*""

"Pimpin' be 'bout controllin' da bitches, not some Black Panther bullshit! When da bitch hol' out on yo' money, what you gon' do? *Quote Chairman Mao?*"

My comrades roared with laughter. Once the laughter subsided, I struggled against my feelings of embarrassment, and outlined my simple pimping plan.

I envisioned a bloodless coup. I was going to hypnotize the pale-haired daughters of the oppressor with the rhetoric of third-world liberation SLA General Field Marshal Cinque style, turn 'em out with some acid dipped on the tip of my black nigger dick, and then instruct my cadre of politically correct 'hoze to fuck the white man to death in the name of oppressed peoples everywhere.

I had no conception of how to initiate my plan until I enrolled in college a full five years later. It was the college the sixties wouldn't forget. Never mind the Sex Pistols. John Travolta didn't happen. The campus was located on fertile grounds near the Long Island Sound. God-eyes twirled in the doorways of candle-lit bedrooms perfumed with incense. Voices droned tunelessly over battered folk guitars in the hallway. Heavy-bosomed women in floral-patterned peasant skirts believed reading *The Hobbit* would somehow mend their drug-addled brains. It was John Lennon and Yoko Ono singing "All We Are Saying Is Give Peace a Chance" *twenty-four fucking hours a day!!*

Many went mad and hung themselves. Suicide by macramé.

The women outnumbered the men on campus but among the men there were two brothers—myself and a cat with a gigantic, wild-man Afro from rural Alabama who had a large library of Blowfly albums. I called him Alabama Blowfly.

Alabama insisted if you quoted Eldridge Cleaver's *Soul on Ice* white girls magically dropped drawers and gave up the pussy. Obviously, he hadn't read Susan Brownmiller.

He was also a Muslim. I hadn't realized this until a buxom, grain-fed wondergirl of the midwestern heartland had grossly misinterpreted his intentions.

With salty tears balanced on the rims of his lower eyelids, Alabama fell to his knees, and in the name of universal love for all humankind, *begged* her for some pussy.

She said *no*.

The nigga went nuts!

Overnight, his jeans, the two ducks fucking on his "Fly United" T-shirt, and his Chuck Taylor Converse All-Stars were replaced by a white robe, a skullcap, and a pair of cloth slippers.

Every morning at the crack of dawn, he knelt on his prayer mat, howling at Mecca, fervently begging Allah's forgiveness for being led astray by that "devil white girl" with the big *Playboy* titties.

I didn't have his problem.

I squandered my time on campus by guzzling cheap Californian jug wines, gobbling psychedelic fungi, and laying up with busty, big-nippled nymphs who stank of patchouli oil and stale reefer smoke—Women of pure pagan *instinct*.

One woman had an affinity with night and taught me to traverse its blind darkness with surefootedness. Another communed with water and could divine the future by its rippling surface.

This water witch and I would make love on the shores of the Sound at night, our brains basting in savory psychedelic sauces; her sandy hips rolling beneath me, crashing like waves on the beach.

Most coeds, though, had no more doodled on the slates of their Etch-A-Sketch brains than reggae lyrics and the outline of Bob Marley's cock. I'd approach a group of these young women squatting in a circle on the grass, strumming guitars and smoking pot, saying:

"If smoking dope doesn't damage your brain, why do so many Jamaicans believe a dead Ethiopian is god?"

Smoke would sputter from their mouths and their eyes would narrow into hateful slits.

Still, I got laid. *A lot.*

And by women with an amazing, tantriclike control of their pussy muscles. I don't mean bland, lackluster pussy with the consistency of wet Wonder bread. I'm talking about *trained* pussy. *Athletic* pussy. Pussy with a firm undulating grasp, clamped so tightly around the shaft of your cock, you don't cum unless it says so.

And when you do cum, the pussy snaps, barks, and farts in eruptive orgasm, sending bolts of heat spiraling through the barrel of your dick, and out your asshole, leaving a luminous blue ring revolving above your head.

Good, home-breakin' pussy.

Now I don't have any money, my breath stinks of beer and stale cigarette smoke, and my hair is a scraggly nest of unkempt pickaninny knots. So why did I get all that abundant white-girl pussy whereas Alabama Blowfly was left to beat his meat to the Koran?

I practice Voodoo—the *true* religion of the Amerikkkan Blackman!

Timing is the key factor in the practice of Voodoo and any other form of magick (Spellcasting, Witchcraft, Ceremonial, etc). As Crowley wrote in *Magick: In Theory and Practice*, "the proper Force in the proper manner through the proper medium to the proper object" *at the proper time*. In order to do this, a good witch must know how to read the signs.

I learned to pay close attention to menstrual cycles. On campus, I observed that women who lived together menstruated almost simultaneously. One woman's menstruation, a dominant, initiates the cycle for the others. This situation frequently occurs among roommates, biker babes, and women in all-girl rock bands, especially if the band is on tour. (One New York band in the early eighties would only perform publicly "at that time of the month." Before mounting the stage, they would all ritually smear themselves with each other's blood. And the sound emitted by their amplifiers was so abrasive, it would turn Axl Rose's testicles ice cold.)

Why is this information you need to know?

Many women are very horny either before, after, or during their menstruation. And sex eases the pain of menstrual strain.

So prepare to chow down, brutha, *and earn those red wings!*

The height of menstrual activity on campus occurred when the moon was at its fullest. This is consistent with the nature of the Triple Goddess who symbolizes the moon in its three phases. The Goddess in her full-moon phase, her warrior aspect, represents the sexually active woman.

By keeping track of the phases of the moon, I could calculate who was bleeding and when. I became so proficient at this practice I actually developed a nose for detecting its warm, earthy aroma in the air.

WARNING: MENSTRUATING WOMEN CAN BE UNUSUALLY AGGRESSIVE.

Living in a coed dorm with few men during a full moon is like being trapped in a den of cats in heat. I endured shrill whining, tits brushed "accidentally on purpose" against my arm, and, sometimes, I literally had asses pointed in my face.

YOU HAVE NO CHOICE. YOU MUST GIVE UP THE DICK. REPEAT. YOU MUST GIVE UP THE DICK. IF NOT, IT WILL BE RIPPED FROM ITS SOCKET, MOUNTED ON A STICK, AND USED IN SOME UNSPEAKABLE GIRL RITE UNDER THE FULL MOON.

Lastly, in the Hoodoo tradition, a mixture of African and Celtic folk magick, it is said that if a woman feeds a man her menstrual blood he will fall hopelessly and uncontrollably in love with her. So, if she invites you over for a home-cooked meal, I advise bringing along a dog, slipping the animal a portion from your plate. And if the dog humps your leg . . . .

CHAPTER TWO: HOW NOXIOUS NEGRO ODORS CAN WET THE CRACKS OF THOSE YOUNG WHITE PUSSIES

Odor from a strong, foamy lather of underarm perspiration is a pretty effective people repellent—*but*—that social liability can be turned into a social asset.

Smells attract as easily as they repel. Animals are aroused by smell. People are too.

With the right combination of scented oils, you can enhance your natural body odor to arouse the sex urge in others. Mixed in balanced combination, those oils are:

Cinnamon, patchouli, almond, sandalwood, and *jasmine*.

Blended with your body's natural oils, the mixture enhances your animal sex appeal. One fourth of this mixture is cinnamon oil, an oil believed to exude the essence of Scorpio, the astrological sign ruling the sex organs.

This oil should be applied sparingly or poured into a bath. The cinnamon burns a bit, a sensation lasting under thirty seconds, so I don't advise rubbing it directly on your balls.

Don't overuse the oil. If you do, you'll end up smelling like some tie-dyed neo-hippie, killing the oil's overall effect by masking your real odor rather than enhancing it. Your natural odor is what draws a potentially compatible sex partner to you. The scent is subtle and detected subliminally. As she approaches, you will notice her nostrils flare with desire.

Once you've been sniffed out, and you have a potential bedmate standing before you, gaze into her eyes and begin to work your spell of *Fascination*.

CHAPTER THREE: HOW YOUR SIGNIFYING MONKEY-ASS CAN WIN FRIENDS, INFLUENCE PEOPLE, AND SCAM PLENTY O' WHYTE-GAL BOODY TO BOOT

According to *The Dictionary of Contemporary American Usage*, to fascinate is to hold by enchantment, *to charm*. This means your most important magickal weapon is your *personality* but you must follow these three basic rules:

1. Intent eye contact
2. Physical contact
3. Breath contact

One classic tactic of girl-hustling involves a basic element of Fascination—whispering in a woman's ear. It's intimate, erotic, and effective.

Slouch against a wall, standing so your mouth is level with her ear. Speak softly or mumble. She will automatically draw closer to you in order to hear what you have to say. Keep her pinned with your gaze, hold her there, and don't let your eyes wander.

As you speak, breathe on her neck and gently drape your arm around her shoulder. Be casual, but most important, be *empathetic*.

Watch and listen to the woman snuggled in the crook of your arm. You want her to understand that you are interested in *her* and not what unusual tricks she might know with your cock in her mouth.

Read her feelings, respond intuitively, and speak in a soothing tone of voice. It inspires confidence. The sound of your voice projects how you feel. How you express what you feel and what feelings you inspire is of primary importance. Words *stir* the emotions. Chose strong, evocative, and emotionally charged words.

"Verbal magic is a skillful combination of meaning and sound, effecting an almost alchemical change in the thinking of the listener." —Eric Maple, "Incantations and Words of Power"

In a state of heightened emotion one is susceptible to hypnotic suggestion. So don't waste time blathering about semiotics, deconstruction, postmodernism, or some other useless gibberish you might read about in the art & lit sections of certain New York weeklies. Use your words wisely and stir up a heady intoxicant. Your goal is to make her wet and tingly between the thighs. The ear is an erogenous zone. You can accomplish almost as much by whispering in her ear as you can by tongue-flicking her clit.

Practice the Taoist principle of Wei Wu Wei "to do without doing." Or, in other words, *seduce without seducing*.

With this attitude, you'll find that most women will do the work for you.

CHAPTER FOUR: SPELL-CASTING

Spell-casting is only necessary when all other means have failed. Why work your will over a lock of hair when a bouquet of roses and a book of poetry might accomplish your goal?

Often, love obtained by magick is unauthentic, short-lived, and delusional. It lasts only as long as it takes the moon to complete one full cycle. It is all you want and all you don't want. In the end, it proves insubstantial and has nasty side effects. *Disease. Impotence. Bankruptcy*. Venus can be a hellish bitch.

On the other hand, *sex* obtained by magick can be a *blast*.

The attraction spell I'm about to detail is a form of "lower" or "lesser" magick. Its use will not bind another's will to your own. The key is not to waste valuable psychic energies by projecting onto one desired person but rather to produce a scattershot effect and keep your options open.

By opening the sexual channels of your psyche through spellwork, you can activate the sexual energies in your environment and attract the corresponding energies. In this way, you draw the right person(s) suited to your particular psychosexual needs. This method teaches you about your sexuality and sensitizes you to your preferred sex partner. (You may not want to fuck White-women at all, brutha. You could be just frontin' the shit off and might really want a young Whiteboy with a *ripe pink behind!*)

When practicing any form of magick, the first step is deciding what it is that you truly desire, and the next step is asking yourself what are the best circumstances under which you might acheive that goal.

Your goal must be realistic. No matter how expert your spell the centerfold babe taped to your wall will not mysteriously come to life and materialize in your bed. You must have a clear and realizable magickal objective based, not on fantasy, but on real emotional need.

Clarify your intent in a journal. Ask yourself why you want what you desire. Try and understand the psychological needs associated with your desire. Describe your desire. What are its attributes? Its strengths? Its weaknesses? Reduce the information recorded in your journal into a few concise sentences, then visually codify these sentences into symbols for use in the ritual you will perform later. These are important steps in the spell-working process.

Next, select objects you associate with your desire, objects which appeal to your senses: music, scents, foods, textures, drawings, etc. These serve to intensify your emotions during the actual ritual. In fact, it's a good idea to actually draw pictures of what you desire or create images out of wax, clay, wood, etc.

This activity can be compared to programming a computer. You're etching a function on your psyche. Through these preparations, you are building up an energized emotional force you will later release in a focused and directed fashion during ritual.

In order for this force to travel, you must create a "magickal link." If this is not done, the force will either dissipate or strike you in the ass like a lightning bolt.

Hair, toenail clippings, soiled clothing, jewelry, etc. are normally used for this purpose.

As we are discussing creating a general auric field of seductive power, I suggest selecting objects dear to Venus as a "magickal link." It is Venus who has dominion over the kind of gifts you seek. Study Venus, try and understand who she is and what meaning she has for you. Offer her gifts with personal meanings you both share.

Venus, like the other deities, is not an external spiritual force. She is an aspect in all of our psyches, an archetype buried in our collective unconscious. Through ritual, the conscious is intergrated with the forces of the unconscious. We invoke a God or Godette form by drawing it out of ourselves. It then becomes an operative force within our personalities.

CHAPTER FIVE: THE RITUAL: OR "THE MONEY-SHOT"

Seal your ritual area with a triangle of sea salt. The triangle should be vaginal in appearance. Some will suggest a circle. I prefer the triangle because of its associations with the womb and birth. The sea salt confines the psychic energies released during ritual to one area.

Set up your altar with the previously selected, emotion-evoking objects. Arrange your drawings and carved figures. As you want to appeal to Venus's lascivious side, drape women's lingerie, preferably stained with menstrual blood.

Now, back to your journal. Turn to the visually codified sentences. Symbols are the language the unconscious understands best. Consider the strange imagery and surreal situations of dreams. This is how your subconscious talks to you. One can use traditional symbols but I suggest creating your own. You are communicating with your own subconscious. It knows its own language. Let your subconscious tell you what that language is.

Once you've found your symbols, carve them on a red candle. Red is the traditional symbolic color of sex, lust, and passion. This is called "sigilization." It is the most simple form of ritual.

Anoint your carved candle with the previously described oils and armpit perspiration. Or use the sweat from the underside of your testicles (let's keep our eye on the old ball here: the point is to magickally energize the seductive power of your pheromone essence). Anoint the candle by stroking it upward three times from the middle and then stroke three times downward.

Set the candle on your altar and place the "magickal link" in front of it.

As stated before, timing is a key factor. You must decide when is the proper time to perform your ritual. The moon is a good and simple guide.

The new moon is the best time to initiate new projects. It is the time of planting and growth. The full moon is the time of harvest, when things have ripened to their fullest. The old moon is a time for dark deeds, hexing, for sweeping away the withered.

Never start a new love on an old moon. This ritual should be performed during a new moon or when Venus is in good aspect to the moon, Mars, and Mercury. Ultimately, you must deduce when conditions are most susceptible to your influence. The phases of the moon and the alignment of the planets are merely guides. In the end, you must objectively analyze the situation in order to know when to make your move.

Drink a glass or two of good Bordeaux. Undress. Enter the ritual area, burn incense, and light your candle. Enjoy the food you've laid out. Admire the drawings. Fondle the lingerie. Excite yourself into a heightened state of lust. Sit before your altar. Slick your hand with Vaseline. Are you ready? Good.

Now beat your meat. Hold your dick in a "Black Power" grip, visualizing fire-red sex energies swirling around you in an egg-shaped cocoon, shot through with needles of gold, and shake that muthafucka harder than a pair of dice. *Feel* the magnetic pull of hundreds of naked Whitewomen floating toward you, casting the cocoon of radiant red energies around the "magickal link."

Imagine yourself cradled between two strong thighs fanning open and closed with the grace of two palm fronds in a languid breeze, the pelvis rolling like a wave churning across the sea. A phantom cunt draws your cock deeper and deeper into its moistness with a gently flexing grip, its sweating walls rippling along the stem, kneading it like soft Plasticine.

A phantom sphincter tightens around your finger.

The cunt bubbles beneath you. It convulses with violence, and nibbles the bulb of your cock, snapping like a steel beartrap.

Cum spatters in your Vaselined hand.

On the altar, the candle's wick is a charred stump in a puddle of beaded red wax. Prick your finger, rolling the web of cum, the drops of blood, and blob of wax into a ball. Toss it into a live body of water under a new moon.

The ritual is over. The spell is done.

In the unlikely event my prescription fails you, walk the streets with your cock out. I guarantee—women will *stare*. And you'll get offers. Maybe only from scabby-legged bag women who neglected to take their Lithium. But, hey, *it's not called a "magic wand" for nothing*.

CALISTA

♥ ♥

Trey Ellis

September 9, 1979

CALISTA

I've been back at Andover a week helping run the Search & Rescue section of the freshman and transfer orientation. I had taken the course last year and now as a senior I'm a student leader. Let's hope it helps me into Stanford.

It's wonderful to be back at school with no classwork to do. Every day I take another group out to Den Rock and lead them up very simple faces. Every night there's a movie or ice cream or something to do. Going through it last year I was too nervous to enjoy myself. But that's not why I'm writing. I'm writing here in the room (alone! Kurt doesn't arrive until Thursday) after tonight's flick, *Cabaret*, because I'm in love with a white girl.

Today I was putting the ropes and helmets for my sections away in the supply cage when I see her bent low laying her section's ropes on their pegs. Her leader sprained her ankle so Calista, an Upper from New York State somewhere, volunteered to stow the gear. Did I tell you she was wearing blue velvet clogs? The vulnerable underside of her pretty foot yawned at me invitingly as she crouched. I almost kissed it. We just grunted hellos and pleasantries at each other. I asked a friend her story and he said, "She's a bitch, everybody's tried talking to her." I have a feeling she too will get the chance to get her hits in on my feeble heart before this, my glorious senior year, closes.

September 15, 1979

CALISTA

The finale of Search & Rescue orientation is the bell tower rappel. It was great to see all those kids terrified and in complete awe of me when I calmly scooted over the ledge and rappelled the 113 feet down to the ground. Maybe for once people weren't looking at me and thinking, "Virgin."

Our section used one side of the tower, Calista's the other. I was belaying some poor freshman, which you don't even do on a real rappel. So not only was he just sliding down the rope, which is easy, he had another rope attached to his harness that came up to me. Even if he let go and just jumped I'd catch him. That didn't matter to him. Logic didn't matter. The white bones were about to pop out of his knuckle skin he was so scared. I asked him to smile and he scrunched up his cheeks.

"Just take it one step at a time." I felt like the experienced pilot in the control tower talking down the hysterical stewardess in the first *Airport*.

This Upper who's real cute but just a friend, Ellen, she looked down the other side, saw Calista, who was already halfway down the brickface of the bell tower like she did it every day.

"Austin, lend me your sweats. I don't want to look like her."

I was paying out the belay rope as the wimpy freshman inched down my side. I could've killed to see what everyone else was looking at but if the kid freaked out and died who knows what college would take me. But I heard from the rest of my section it was great. Calista was just wearing these cutoff shorts and the harness comes up between your legs. When you're rappelling your waist holds your body weight and her harness had sucked up her shorts. Everybody whispered that it looked real freaky. Ellen was mean though.

"Ohhhhh," she impersonated Calista. "Let me ride again, *please*." I should have defended her but I didn't. It was right on the tip of my tongue to say, "That woman you're making fun of will be my wife."

February 26, 1980

CALISTA

I think I had a nervous breakdown last week.

I'm teaching cross-country skiing since I was the worst skier on the ski team last year but my form's pretty good. Calista's taking skiing too. We see a lot of each other and are great friends. I wouldn't think of jumping her (maybe if she were black, who knows). It's weird. I brag to my friends about what good friends we are, but when they tease me and say it's more than that I get pissed. Of course I whack off about her often but the fantasy is always that we're just friends stuck in a tent on a mountainside and one thing leads to another.

I wrote this on a piece of paper last week. I was in AP Calculus, but the lesson was a snap:

> Austin deluded himself. Natalie ("Nat"), Calista, Sue, Ellen, Jenny, Stephanie ("Stef") are all beautiful girls he considered his friends and only one was black and he had tried to make her more than a friend and had just recently given up. Did he chose his girlfriends just because they were beautiful? Did he punish himself by surrounding himself with the very most beautiful women on campus? Austin even fantasized about making love to his woman "friends." If he had ever allowed himself to think about his strange

relationships, made stranger still by his absence of a steady girlfriend, he would have been puzzled.

I don't know why I wrote that in the third person. I haven't written about Nat, Sue, or Stef because it's the same old story. They are gorgeous and popular girls who sometimes let me eat with them. Like Pumpkin, my dog at home, it must be nice having an animal always trotting behind you, living for the crumbs of affection you toss.

April 17, 1980

CALISTA

At school we had talked about John Anderson and how we hoped he would mess up the Republicans. Now it's Spring Break and I'm back in Hamden. She's from Rye, New York, and there's a big rally for Anderson in New York City tomorrow. I called to ask her if she'd like to go but she said she was going hiking with her parents. Then we started talking about the outdoors and I let slip my plans to hang glide and get certified to scuba dive this summer. I was thinking of going hiking this Spring Break myself, I said.

"Why don't we go together?"

I'm sure she could practically *hear* my smile through the telephone wires. "Sure!" I said, my voice fucking cracking for the first time in months. But it didn't matter, joy, bliss exploding in my insides. The day started so normally. I was almost looking forward to going back to school since I'd lost track of most of my Hamden friends. But her simple sentence triggered a chain of images to flicker before my eyes from a kiss to marriage to kids. I didn't want to even talk to her anymore. I wanted to just sit in my room and feel this wonderful feeling.

"There's a free Judy Collins concert in Central Park tomorrow night. We could meet there with maps and plan. But the Appalachian trail is always nice."

I don't remember what else she said. My brain was filling up with ecstasy, short-circuiting all worldly thoughts.

April 18, 1980

CALISTA

We met in front of this statue of *The Tempest* by the side of the big lawn in the middle of the park. I was proud of myself for finding it easily. A good sign, I thought.

Bows and flows of angel hair,
And ice cream castles in the air,
And feather canyons everywhere,
I've looked at clouds that way.

Judy Collins was warbling and clanking her guitar. I can't believe I used to like music like that back in eighth grade. Fucking Muzak. But Calista is a Judy Collins type of woman so I didn't mention my musical evolution to the jazz/fusion of the Return to Forever band.

Calista's black hair glistened like lacquered wood, her black eyes seemed a sticky, romantic trap, a La Brea tar pit of broken hearts. I tried to look at her as little as possible during the concert. Lying on a quilted piano blanket, she had brought Stella d'Oro cookies and apple cider. I forgot to bring anything. Every time I looked into her eyes I felt them draw me to her, hoisted up into those eyes by my stomach. We talked for hours and she laughed constantly.

Nearly every black man there was with a white woman. My folks actually said they expected me to someday marry a white girl since, after Michigan, they brought us up around the poor white ignoramuses of southern New England. Yet I was always determined to prove them wrong. I never ever went out with a white girl (all right, all right, I've never gone out with any girl, but I've only *tried* to go out with black girls).

I've looked at life from both sides now,
From here and there and still somehow,
It's clouds' illusions I recall,
I really don't know clouds, at all.

April 20, 1980

CALISTA

It's twelve-twelve! Go to sleep! You have to get up at five for the trip and do you want her to see you and say, "Are those bags under your eyes for carrying miniature first-aid kits?" Many trips get canceled at the last minute so don't get your hopes up until you're actually inside her sleeping bag. Yes, you've packed the rubbers in the real first-aid kit (if she finds them I'll tell her they're to "isolate a finger wound, keep moisture away from it" or something like that). Besides, with Search & Rescue you shared a tent with a girl and nothing happened then. Of course she was a hateful druggie witch, ugly in mind, body, and spirit. Go back to sleep, creep.

"Austin, I can't believe I'm calling this late but this is Calista . . . I . . . I don't know how to say this . . ." It was one o'clock, an hour ago, when she called. "My parents changed their minds. I can't go."

"Oh. Why."

"I don't know. They're just being unreasonable. You . . . you know, it wouldn't be so bad if they hadn't waited till the last minute. This really stinks, I know, but their mind is made up. We've been fighting all evening but I had to call you before you left for the city tomorrow morning."

"But . . ."

"I know, but what can I say . . . ? Listen, why don't we go to Montauk for the day. They'll let me do that . . ."

We talked until two in the morning about everything from how to make your life extraordinary, to the worthlessness of money, to sex. Eye bags be damned.

April 21, 1980

CALISTA

I took the seven-o'clock train into the city and we met by the Chemical Bank cash machine in Penn Station and caught the

9:02 Long Island Railroad bound for the beach. She kissed me on the cheek hello and the warmth from her lips heated my whole face. It's early in the season and I wouldn't even have thought about going out there until July but I wasn't about to say no. The day was so beautiful, it must have been at least 75, that there were quite a few other lovers on the train. Our conversation was light and witty and delightful as always.

She got us off the train at Amagansett, a ritzy fake New England village, and hiked us miles and miles to the town beach. The beach grass was sprinkled with tiny blue flowers, the wind was already kind and warm. How soft the sand, how clean the beach, how clear the sea. We passed three other interracial couples on the beach, older people, and they seemed to wink to us, "Keep on keeping on," they seemed to say. Maybe they all have a secret high sign like the Masons that we're supposed to know.

We walked far enough away that the other premature beachgoers were small enough to give us some privacy. Then I showed her my beach trick: I scooped out a deep chaise longe for her out of sand and laid her towel upon it.

"Thank you, sir."

Then I created a hole for myself. We both kept our clothes on. Then I took off my shirt even though it was still too cool. When clouds curtained the sun, goose bumps sprouted on my arms, my nipples pulled at my pecs. I've been lifting a lot this year—180 pounds is my max, twenty pounds over my weight (lifting your weight is already above average). I tried not to look like I was flexing like a jerk but obviously I wanted her to get hot and jump my bones.

"You lift weights? You don't seem the type."

"Vat do you mean I do not seem the type." I impersonated Arnold Schwarzenegger, Mr. Olympia from the movie *Pumping Iron*. "You tink ve are all ze stupid?"

She laughed until spittle leaked from her mouth. My heart soared like a bird.

"You've got a great body."

Yooo! I wanted to leap up and do a sand dance, chase and

scatter sea gulls along the beach, somersault my way across the Sound back to Connecticut.

"You ain't so bad yourself."

She blushed, I swear to God she did.

Then I did it. I pushed myself out of my sand chair, double-checked to make sure I'd put on swim trunks instead of underwear, dropped my jeans to my ankles, and ran to the water, SCREAMING. I hate cold water and even in the summer the water in the Northeast makes my balls recede up to my chest and they won't come down again until I beg and apologize. But if she would take off her clothes so I could just see her in a bikini, then who knows what magic would follow. So there I was, splashing through the shallows, splattering myself with needles of melted ice cap and all I was thinking was this: What a stupid idea. You will die in this ice water and even if you live, it'll take a week for an erection to come back. But I couldn't stop, I felt her eyes on my Speedos. I threw myself forward and in, and all the air from my lungs spat out and I sank.

Later, when I stood up, I didn't turn around because I didn't want her to learn from my mistake and not come in. Down the beach a dozen old people frolicked in the surf as if it were possible. Old people are incredible, if it were big enough, they could swim in a Slurpee. Then I heard it, a splashing behind me.

I turned and realized I was wrong. My brave dick ignored the cold and worked just fine in these arctic conditions. She came bouncing toward me in a string bikini I would never have expected from a liberal and a backpacker. I thought then of begging, of giving her my bicycle, sixty percent of what I earned in my lifetime just to make love to her once.

I thought she must have read my perverse mind by the look of horror she flashed, then the wave she had been worrying about slammed the back of my head, rubbed my face into the coarse sand I had just been standing on, flung my feet skyward, and skidded me onto the shore. My terrorized Speedos allowed the interested a view to the top half of the crack of my ass before I pulled them back up. The suit would have sped past my ankles and back out to sea if my boner hadn't held it in place like a coat rack's horn. I turned to where I had rolled past Calista but she was gone. Then she surfaced, her bikini top askew to the limit of an areola. But another wave pounded her head just as she stood again and tumbled her toward me. She stood up, her long hair masking all her face except her nose. Her bikini bottom now low-slung and her bikini top (yes, her bikini top, go on) was COMPLETELY OFF! I would have fainted if I could have closed my eyes. Her nipples were so hard and tiny, the areoles so small and concentric. *My first live naked tit!* She struggled her breasts back into her top, dragged the wet curtain of hair from before her eyes. By that time I had turned away and turned back only after she was decent as if I had not seen the single sexiest live image of my seventeen years.

"She's just a friend, she's just a friend, she's just a friend," my brain said to me. But I also heard, even more clearly, my dick talking. "Get me inside of her or I'll pee down your new three-piece suit at graduation," it said. "I'll burn, I'll itch. I'll pop a boner in the boys' shower, wilt on your wedding night."

The train back was an old, old wooden-benched car. Gray-and-black it was, steel and mildewed upholstery.

"I love this old train." Calista loves a lot of things but this time I knew just what she meant.

"It's pathetic but homey. And at least it's not like the new ones feebly trying to impersonate jets."

She agreed and from that our conversation progressed to the joys of train travel. (I actually am not crazy about them but I wanted to agree with her. I had taken the Greyhound across country last summer to visit Stanford. At least buses turn, and they drive right through the middle of cities. Trains are always segregated to the industrial wastelands, the backsides of towns.) We talked about how overpriced and bad prefabricated train food is, finally ending on the subject of how hungry we were. With that, Calista pulled a cucumber from her bag (I'm not making any of this up, I swear!) fresh from her Rye, New York, garden. (We had eaten the squash, the carrots, and the tomatoes on the beach.) I don't hate cucumbers, who could hate what doesn't taste. I expected her to snap it in two but she just bit off the end and pointed it at me. I took it, bit off some, and pointed it back to her. The cucumber quickly shrank as it passed between us and the rules of the game became quickly obvious—give your opponent a final piece, too small to divide. So Calista giggled and passed me a sliver as small as her large black pupils, deliciously shiny from her saliva. I tried my best to bite it in half but only managed to coat it in even more spittle.

"Oooow, gross!" she said and I gave in and lapped up the last of it.

"You win."

"And don't you ever forget it."

At Penn Station she had to hurry off. Her parents wanted her home by eight-thirty. She kissed me on the cheek again but this time added a squeeze to my shoulders. I don't know when I've been so happy. I won't try anything with her because I love her and couldn't stand it if she freaked out and didn't ever talk to me again.

Dad's a sociology prof and he says, "Adolescents cannot have friends of the opposite sex. These people you may mistake as friends are actually frustrated lovers." But I think that's horseshit. Sure, I don't doubt that tonight I'll whack off to Calista in an "unfriendly" way. But I know, I guess, that she'll never do anything major with me. We're pals now, though I am in love.

June 30, 1980

CALISTA

First, while I was scouring the neighborhood looking for white fuel for my camping stove, I passed a bum sitting his butt in a metal wire trash can on a street corner. His knees and calves and feet, half of his back, and his arms and head dangled free, but the center of him was lodged there. This city is so weird.

We'd planned a camping trip to the Pine Barrens, chaperoned by her big brothers, who still live in Rye. I met her on the street near FAO Schwarz and immediately confessed to be happy she was wearing a dress. She smiled, then introduced me to her two friends, Maya, who's Indian, and Rich, who's black. They are friends of hers from her public high school in Rye. It's disgusting but I was immediately jealous of him. My back went up, I instinctively wanted to protect my territory from this other black guy.

As they said goodbye I realized that he was as in love with her as I. He rocked back and forth on his feet and kept staring at her. Where a mustache might someday grow, snot glistened from his leaky nose. He pitched forward, his lips right on course for hers. Thankfully, Calista wagged her head left, then right, converting his pass into two continental pecks.

I am still wondering if that is how I look to the world. Perhaps my condition is worse than I had suspected.

I pulled her away, down the street to the garage where my uncle's car was being fixed.

Of course the car wasn't ready by five as the mechanic had promised. Calista and I waited on the old front seat of a big American car leaning against the wall. The wall across from us was papered with centerfolds and bikini'd and naked spokesladies for air filters and fuel-treatment systems. I made sure I didn't look too much. I was wearing an old T-shirt from St. Thomas and I swear I think I caught her staring at my pecs.

At six-thirty the Gremlin was fixed and I drove onto the West Side Highway. I tried not to let her realize how scared I was. I'd never driven in the city before and was positive I was going to kill or at least paralyze us both. On the highway itself the traffic was awful. And then the Gremlin just stopped. Immediately every asshole in New York City was honking at me. Calista didn't scream, though. She was great. Finally, a nice foreign guy (Polish?) pushed us and I jump-started the car. We went about another half mile when it just stopped again. This time a car full of Puerto Rican guys about my age inched their Elektra to the Gremlin's bumper and pushed us over a hill and with the help of the downhill it jump-started again. This time I got off the highway at the next exit, 178th Street.

Calista's cool the whole time, in fact, she reached up the sleeve of my shirt and stroked my biceps—the first time we'd ever really touched. A wave of goose bumps erupted across my chest and I flinched away from her. Immediately I wanted to squeeze and kiss her, even in just a friendly way, but I didn't want to make her think I was a studly hound dog, but I also didn't want to make her think I was cold. But I should have done something back, dammit.

I turned the wrong way down a one-way street.

"Austin, uh . . . I think . . ."

This garbage truck cruising the right way down the street almost took us out.

"Shit! I'm sorry. But if we stop again we'll conk out and I don't want to stop here."

The car stopped anyway. We walked to a gas station. The night was starting to rise. I felt awful being afraid of my own people, but I didn't even know Manhattan had a 178th Street. I untucked my T-shirt and tried to think tough. We walked past some actually OK buildings to a Citgo. There she called her brothers to tell them we'd be late. I walked a bottle of gas back to the car, expecting to find it already stripped and aflame. It wasn't but the gas didn't help. I flagged down a gypsy cab (I'm learning all the NYC lingo) and he jump-started the car for free.

I noticed that the guy who ran the gas station, he was white or white-Spanish, carried a sawed-off baseball bat wrapped in silver duct tape. He said whatever was wrong with the car he couldn't fix tonight. Calista called her brothers to come pick her up. I called my uncle. Her brothers came first. They snatched Calista home and I felt like Romeo and Juliet, our relationship torn asunder. Of course I didn't go in for the Rich-like, leaky-nose kiss.

July 3, 1980

CALISTA

We've gone to the movies a couple of times this summer but nothing's happened to write home about until today.

She's leaving for a bicycle tour of the Basque region of Spain in three days and today was our goodbye. She had asked me to come along but I have to make money for Stanford.

I went to this cutesy gay-run gift shop near my uncle's house, P.S. I Love You, because I had gotten my sister's Christmas present there. It took me forever to decide on a gift. It was hard to chose something romantic/friendly and definitely unsappy. Then the guy puts it in a pink box and closes it with a big red heart sticker that says the name of the store, P.S., I Love You, on it. I tried to peel it off but it was ripping up and fuzzing the box itself. I tried to think of jokes to acknowledge the sap factor of the box.

I was excited and springy all day. She wanted to go to the Museum of Broadcasting. She said she loved museums and "most of my other friends aren't the types to go to museums." I wasn't crazy about being called a "museum type," especially since I think of myself more as an "outdoorsy, rugged, macho, mercenary/ mountainman type." But at least she said I was her friend.

In front of the place no kiss hello but the first thing she said was that I looked "dapper." I could have levitated. I was wearing my brand-new white pleated pants, a long-sleeve button-down shirt but I'd rolled up the sleeves, and loafers. She looked fantastic too. New cowboy boots, stylish lavender pants, and a matching velour top.

After the exhibit on the history of TV news, we wandered around midtown and I was proud and for once not stoop-shouldered. We came upon a businessman's minipark with a waterfall with a tunnel you can walk right through and it was her idea to stop.

My heart sapped the rest of me and I had a hard time not making any noise while I breathed. The tiny gift box also seemed to swell. I wedged my hand into the pants pocket folded as closed as a purse by my sitting. I had to arch out of the chair to enter the pocket and a corner of the paper box was smushed.

"Austin, what did you do!"

I thought I had food on my cheek or farted.

"Oh! It's nothing special. Just a going-away present. The sticker is just, uh . . ."

"I'll be back in a month."

I delivered the little box to the space above her lap, stickerside down. Her hand contacted mine, a lot, while she removed the boxlet from my palm.

"I don't want to rip the sticker, it's so cute."

I don't remember what I said. Probably nothing at all or some unintelligible grunt.

The pink-and-purple ceramic unicorn with the safety pin in its back lay on its side in the cotton batting inside the tiny box as if in a coffin, dead.

"It's beautiful. Thank you. It's . . . uh . . . thanks."

"It's five-fifteen. You're going to miss your train."

At Grand Central I said goodbye as if I were saying see you later. She stepped into the car and I said it, the dumb thing only an idiot says to someone going to Spain. I said *Adios*.

August 18, 1980

CALISTA

She got back from Spain three days ago and I'd already called her mom three times. I'm leaving for Stanford in four days and Calista will have to go back to Andover in a week. Every ring of my uncle's phone triggered my practiced, unstressed conversation with her. Finally she called today. The words "I love you" and "I can't live without you" barely stayed down with the entire box of Pop-Tarts I had just eaten. She's house-sitting her old Tai Chi instructor's apartment on 88th Street and invited me over for "a drink."

It wasn't the first time I'd bought booze but I was still pretty nervous. The Indian guy didn't care and even asked me if I wanted the Freixenet gift-wrapped. I did. She said to come over at eight but I was late trying to find a newsstand with decent breath mints. I couldn't wait for them to dissolve so I crunched six.

Her door opened and her hug nearly broke me, the heat from her cheek I still feel in mine.

"I wasn't back an hour before my mom said, 'Calista, I have

to talk to you.' I thought she was going to talk about sex, but it's a little too late for that."

The world then fell away from me. I couldn't hear whatever it was she continued to say. I was all heartbeat. I forced my face into what I hoped was an unshocked expression but she caught on and backpedaled, embarrassed. I teased her about it, congratulated her, and tried to impersonate a laugh by huffing out quick exhales. I think I said things like "Way to go," and maybe even lied "Welcome to the club," but I honestly can't remember. As she talked, all I saw in front of me was Calista under a Spanish oak, under a Spanish man, naked.

Sabino. He was herding his sheep on horseback just outside of Pamplona when the American cyclists tried to pass. They did it in a youth hostel.

"Don't they have rules against just that? Don't they separate guys and girls?"

"Austin, it's a youth hostel, not a prison."

I waited as short a time as I could, then checked my watch. "Oh, my uncle's taking me out to dinner. Then I have to pack my stuff to take back to Hamden, then repack for school."

"I'll miss you, *laguna*, that's Eskuara for friend. Eskuara is what the Basque speak." She opened the front door, stepped close enough to bump my knee.

She kissed my cheek (actually, closer to my ear). Still my heart fluttered and I must have been smiling foolishly by the sad smile she gave back. Her lips were rose petals near my ear.

July 5, 1981

CALISTA

This summer I'm moving people for a company called For This I Went to College? It's run by Dianetics devotees so the other movers tell me to double-check my paychecks. I'm getting stronger lifting pianos and refrigerators up New Haven's countless five-flight walk-ups. Maybe I will inflate and maybe that will help me in my expedition to Mount Calista this summer.

Yesterday, my first attempt. I took the train into the city to see her. We went to the Gordon Lightfoot concert in Central

Park. She couldn't see over the crowds, so I hoisted her up on my shoulders. Her thighs were so deliciously warm around my neck and ears that I longed to turn around, listen to her squeal with delight. The goodbye kiss on the lips was longer than the hello.

August 28, 1983

CALISTA

This past weekend was the twentieth anniversary of the march on Washington and Calista said I could stay in her dorm room at Georgetown. I'd like to think I would have gone anyway.

High school and college students masquerading as 1960s-era hippies, nuns, the Red Communist Youth Brigade, and various black Baptist deacons and deaconesses filled every seat on the Amtrak and every spot in the aisles. I stood between the cars with the noise.

The heat and the wet and heavy air along the Potomac weighted my lungs. Calista led me quickly from the station to "Synergy," her dorm/deadhead commune (once an SAE frat house before they were kicked off campus for peeing on a pledge). The white, be-tie-dyed communards all stood up with finishing-school grace and reverentially shook my hand with both of theirs.

"How *are* you."

Their wide eyes looked so sad. They must have all just watched *Sounder*.

They all painted "Reagan! Stop the Lies!" and "Imagine" placards and staple-gunned them to halved broomsticks. Calista and I made one quoting Elvis Costello: "What's so funny 'bout Peace, Love and Understanding." I tried to feel like Paul Robeson in the Spanish Civil War, but the whiny John Lennon music kept spoiling my mood.

I bought a pair of blue bikini-style underpants at Woolworth in New Haven just before boarding the train. Her futon on the floor was small. When she leaned over to open her window wider to let enter the only fractionally less muggy outside air I noticed down the V of her nightgown her hanging breasts. The vision of Amagansett, Long Island, and the angry waves' scorn for her bikini top instantly replayed in my mind.

"We'd better get a good night's sleep. Tomorrow might get a little rough."

You know that wasn't me talking.

The shower room is coed and communal. Calista, however, had wisely woken before me and showered while I slept. When I went in, there were only woolly, bearded men and this stringy, junkie-looking pale girl with breasts sharp and thin like an animal's.

The march was inspiring and wonderful and all that. Hundreds and thousands of people—a lot of black folks but I wish there'd been more. Busloads of union people, old civil rights and Hollywood celebrities, Buddhists, Spanish Civil War veterans, and rastas lined the long reflecting pool before the Lincoln Memorial. A stunning, topless white hippie waded through the water on the shoulders of her tall and naked boyfriend with a concave chest.

Jesse Jackson spoke at the end and everybody, all the hundreds of thousands, held hands and sang "We Shall Overcome." Calista held my hand high as a TV camera panned the crowds. She was crying. I only let myself feel the tiniest wave of a chill.

At the commune it was Calista's shift to wash dishes. The (surprisingly delicious) tofu spaghetti sauce was burned and fused to the pot and the stove top. We didn't finish cleaning until it was time for bed.

"I don't know if my shoulder is sore from the march or the pots and pans." I windmilled my arm and winced every once in a while.

"Oh."

I waited, she brushed her hair in the mirror under her " 'IRIE!' " rasta poster.

"You must be sore too. Would you like a massage?"

"I'm going to fall asleep as soon as I hit the pillow, but thanks, sweetie."

Later, no matter how much I kept shifting and scooting around on the futon, she wouldn't wake up. Luckily, the night air was hot and dead and declared a stage-five pollen alert night by the TV news. You could almost see the millions of ragweed bits surfing the air. She woke up coughing. I handed her a Kleenex before she even asked. She squeezed two hits of nasal spray up each nostril. She squinted at the clock radio and huffed. Three-ten.

"Would you still like to give me a massage, or is it too late?"

She must have noticed the physical manifestation of my exuberance (my bursting boner on top of her butt), but she just kept on sighing and groaning in sexy comfort as I pressed away the knots in her muscles through the cotton of her nightgown. I slid my middle fingers over the sides of her breasts, the parts that swelled and spilled out from under her body. And she let me.

Then she massaged me and while she worked on my shoulders her breasts massaged my back.

"Oh, right there. Ohhh!" I tried to make sexy sex sounds so deep they'd reverberate my chest cavity and hence vibrate her straddling thighs.

"You have the body of a god."

I forced myself over and she rose up as I rolled. She rolled the muscles in my arms between her thumbs and the rest of her fingers. I kissed her hands.

"Let's get some sleep."

"I'm not sleepy."

"You're so sweet. But those antihistamines are really knocking me out."

She leaned off me and slumped to the pillow at my side.

Late for my train, in the morning I woke suddenly to a weighty wetness in my underwear, smelled the bleach and mowed summer lawn of more spilled and wasted life.

The shower together was cruel. At the station, in front of the long and stainless-steel-sided American Zephyr, she patted my butt goodbye.

The body of Shlemiel, the seldom-worshiped god of failure, premature ejaculation, and drizzle.

April 6, 1983

CALISTA

I'm on a 727 bound for Santa Fe. Seat 12D. She's doing independent study at a women's center for Hopi Indians in Gallup, New Mexico. We're going to travel Mexico together. I haven't seen her since last summer's march. I'm hoping we'll at least make out.

I needed to get out of Hamden. I was so bored with the winter so snowless, dry, cold, and cracked. The black streets were grayed by dead salt. Graduating early was stupid. I thought the spring would have healed me. I sit up until two or three in the next day quietly beating off under the ugly orange caftan my grandmother crocheted to whatever R-rated garbage is on HBO downstairs in the TV room. I almost want to get caught by the folks so I'll stop.

Gay guys just go to bars, wink or nod knowingly, or wave their bandanna semaphore, and they've found someone for the night. I couldn't pick up a girl at a fucking Bennigans, I'd feel too stupid. And what kind of girl would go home with a stranger?

A stewardess would be terrific. It's a shame that today almost all are either ugly, old, or male. When I was a kid I remember a stewardess was a stewardess, none was over twenty-five. When they tried to put them out to pasture they must have sued and won. So the same ones I ogled in the sixth grade are the same moms shoving a microwaved towel in my face.

I hope I don't fuck up this friendship too. You know, planes make you think.

April 7, 1984

CALISTA

Last night, lying there next to her, on my back, the sheet making an obvious big-top tent pole between my legs, I tried to will her to kiss me. I tried to psychokinetically draw her lips to mine. It didn't work. Maybe if we talked about it?

"Water beds make me horny."

"Austin, they're actually awful for making love on. You can't ever find a good rhythm. It's like this. . . ."

And she, also on her back, jerked her hips into and out of the waves, activating the bed with ricocheting surges from foot to headboard and craziness in between. It didn't calm for minutes.

"Calista, do you think our making love would be a good idea?"

"Wow!"

"My thoughts exactly."

"Oh, I don't think so. We're friends and I've tried that with other friends and life just gets too complicated."

"It doesn't have to be if two people are clear with each other in the beginning."

"Maybe you're right, but not tonight anyway. I'm telling you, water beds suck. It just came with the apartment."

April 8, 1984

CALISTA

Mexico is fantastic! So close and yet so far. It's more different than Italy. And before coming I'd been watching the Spanish stations on TV, and with my Italian, I can pretty well let them know that I'm hungry or sleepy. Of course, Calista is so fluent they think she's one of them.

We took a Greyhound to El Paso, Texas, then a cab across the border to a Mexican train that wheedled through the desert and La Barranca del Cobre, "Copper Canyon." It's deeper than the Grand Canyon, carved by the Rio Grande. We spent the night in Chihuahua, home of Zapata. I think she asked for two beds but I'm not sure. Anyway, we got two beds in a cute little *posada*.

"Would you like to make love tonight?"

"Oh, I'd feel strange, because, oh I told you. One of my clients at the women's center went back to her husband and he put her in the hospital again."

April 9, 1984

CALISTA

We slept on the train across the country to Mazatlán. I tried to hug her every once in a while but she wasn't too into it. This trip might have been a horrible mistake.

April 10, 1984

CALISTA

Mazatlán, what a wonderful place. We're in the old, colonial part of town, away from La Zona Dorada where all the drunken Stanford students pound margaritas and seviche. Our place has a kitchen, four beds in two bedrooms, a terrace overlooking L'Avenida del Sol and the Pacific, prettier here than up north. We're on the beach all day long and I could swear she's wearing the same bathing suit she fell out of that magical day years ago in Amagansett. She fell out of it here also, today. I took it as a good sign from God.

"I'm so happy to be out of Hamden. I was drowning there of loneliness."

"Why don't you go back to Florence?"

I'm thinking about it. I've got the rest of my life to sit behind a desk, or make sure actors arrive on time for instructional videos. I don't feel like I've had enough fun yet in my life. . . . "Speaking of fun, how about tonight?"

"Do you always have to talk about it? Fine. But just wait till I'm ready."

It's twelve thirty-three. She's in her own bed, very asleep. I leave the door open and flush the toilet. The frontier of my reading lamp's light just catches her eyelids. I'm about to open the French doors in the front hoping some late-night drunken *taxista* will honk.

April 11, 1984

CALISTA

Never have I felt a sun so hot. It presses you to the sand. You feel the sweat pool, then run down your sides past your armpits. After a day of heat, wonderful people, and lime-cooked raw fish, making love with a good friend would be the perfect, perfect ending. On the beach I lie next to her thinking of how she will look orgasming under and above me, just in case she can read my mind. I mean, if you like someone, don't you want to make him happy? If she only knew that I WILL DIE if we don't DO IT, I'm sure she'd give in.

Wait, I have to stop. She's coming back from the straw-hut bar with our Tecates.

"You know, after sex with my old boyfriend, we used to masturbate each other."

She just said this, out of the blue. We were talking about seviche and how magical it is that lime juice can cook fish. She also said:

"You're a god. Look at your body compared to these men around here."

Back in the hotel, she dug the sand out of her bikini bottom.

"Oh, if I don't stop I'll come."

I didn't close the door before I stepped into the shower and before stepping out I played with myself a bit just to get it less stubby, but not yet hard. She passed the open door just as I was drying my balls. I peeped in the mirror that she didn't.

April 12, 1984

CALISTA

It's our last night. She's flying back to New Mexico; I'm taking the overnight train to Mexicali, on the Mexico-California border (right across the invisible line from California's Calexico).

We ate at a wonderful restaurant called El Patio. It's right on the beach, candle-lit and straw-roofed.

"I've had more lovers these four months in New Mexico than ever in my life. Some of the Indian men are amazing."

"My great-grandfather was Cherokee."

"Really?" She smiled. "On peyote especially, they last forever, and you come before they do, which of course is the best way. . . . I can't believe I'm telling you all this."

"You know, in Washington I wanted so desperately to make love with you but I didn't want to scare you. And also, I haven't done it much and I was afraid I wouldn't be, you know, superhard, or I'd come too quickly, or, I don't know. . . ."

Walking back to our hotel barefoot on the cold night sand, I held her waist and leaned my lips down to hers. She turned and I struck cheek. I left my lips there, sadly stranded on the side of her face like a boat whose keel is stuck in the mud at low tide. I tried again but this time got the other cheek. She started walking again.

"Oops."

"Austin, I don't want to, all right? It's weird. When I was house-sitting in New York and had just come back from Spain, I wanted you *a lot.* I dreamed about your muscles for months. But now it's just not right."

This gorgeous friend was warm for my form *FIVE YEARS AGO!!!* I could have been laid when I was SEVENTEEN YEARS OLD!!!! I wanted to scratch and claw, chew my way back to the past. If we had made love back then I'd be a suave stud even Lyle Wagoner would envy. I'd be a flesh-and-blood, smoking-jacketed, gourmet-cooking *bachelor* that Hef would call for advice.

"Are you all right, Austin?"

"I'm just going to take a walk on the beach."

Mexican beaches in the moonlight, alone, fill your mind with dark wisdom.

I thought about how fucked up I have behaved. I've ruined our vacation. I was *exactly* like her sniveling black friend, years ago in New York City, begging for a kiss on a street corner while snot drooped from his nose to his upper lip. The only way you can sleep next to a body you like for nearly a week and never want to play with it is if you are absolutely repulsed by the personality of the attached brain.

I wanted to sleep on the beach, curled into the cold sand by the side of the road. Instead, I snuck back inside our lovely room.

Calista called out, "You can turn on the light. . . . I got roasted today. I can't believe you didn't burn."

"If I were still in Africa I'd be under this sun every day. For you this is unusual, a tan, but for me, New England winters are the unusual, the 'anti-tan,' or 'pale.' "

"Anyway, could you put suntan lotion on my back."

She rolled over on her belly, hoisted my T-shirt that she was wearing high up her neck. Her breasts puddled beneath her. I was already in just my white BVDs when I climbed on her back. I rubbed it in daintily, struggled to avoid the sides of her breasts.

"All done." I climbed off her, pushed off the overhead light, and found my own twin bed in the dark.

"I'm mad at you."

At first I couldn't locate her voice in the black.

"I'm mad at you for making me feel guilty. If we do make love, it won't be out of pity. I've got to think, by myself."

Of course I don't want it out of pity. Unless that's the only way.

She left our room overlooking the water, for our wasted bedroom in back (all for just five dollars a day). I was waiting for her answer when I fell asleep. When I awoke it was one-thirty. I snuck into her room and peeped. She was asleep. I guess that was her choice.

In the morning I woke up and sat on her springy bed.

"Calista, if you want to hit the beach before your flight, you'd better get up."

"I'd rather stay in bed." She yawned and smiled sweetly, stretched her arms, her body, long as if diving into a pond. Under the sheets, she was naked. "I'm really fried." She held the sheet to her breasts, presented me the bottle of Sea & Ski, and turned on her breasts. I drew down the sheet just to the low valley of her back. Then I massaged her, OK, a little sexily this time.

"I'm sorry for mucking up this vacation. I could make it up to you by going down on you." That way, she wouldn't have come out of "pity."

"No thank you. But I was just going to ask you to make love."

"Really?"

She nodded, rose from the bed, nude, snatched up her purse on her way to the bathroom. She had brought her diaphragm. That made me happy (unless she thought she might have met some tourist or Mexican).

My dick wasn't doing so well. It wasn't soft but it wasn't superhard. I helped it a bit harder manually.

She came out, she pushed me to the bed and smeared herself

over me as we kissed. She cried when I sucked on her breasts. I rolled her over, entered her, she moaned for a minute before I came.

Same as it ever was.

I thought the guy was supposed to ask, "Did you come?" It was all pretty horrible, but I deserved nothing less. I was mad at her for not letting me go down on her first, to guarantee her at least one orgasm.

She was already up and off me, had already grabbed her towel for her shower.

"I wish we had more time. The second time I'm not so, you know, whatever."

"I'll miss my plane."

"Isn't there another one in the evening?"

"Can I borrow your shampoo? Mine's already packed."

Big black muscle man of her dreams prematurely ejaculates. I know the second time around she'd go crazy or at least come before I did. She'd see I really am getting better at it.

If I hadn't read *One Flew over the Cuckoo's Nest* I'd have committed myself years ago.

LOVE LETTER TO MY RAPIST

♥ ♥

Lisa Blaushild

Howdy, stranger!

Remember me? That's okay, it's not as if we were ever formally introduced (ha ha). I'm the girl you beat-up, then poked without permission on my kitchen floor at 164 N. Main Street, apartment 4C. Ring a bell? Sorry the place was such a mess, but I wasn't expecting company. I'm just writing to say "Hi" and hope there are no hard feelings, okay? The bruises and welts have almost completely disappeared, the bloodstains came right out of my favorite sweater with a little club soda, and the couple places on my face where you slashed me easily vanish under concealing cream. No fuss, no muss. After all, it's not as if I'm a fashion model and you've ruined my career! And since statistics prove it was bound to happen to me sooner or later, I'm grateful it happened in the privacy of my own home. That is, at least you didn't force me into sexual submission on a deserted rooftop (fear of heights), in the backseat of a moving vehicle (motion sickness), around children (we'd have had to keep our voices down), near animals (too stinky!), in a cheap motel (creaky bed, no room service), or anywhere in the great outdoors (I don't even like to picnic in the woods, much less do the nasty act there). So mucho gracious for your consideration, kind sir! After you left I wondered, Why *me?* But now I think, Hell, why *not* me? I'm not such a dog! It's flattering to learn even though I'm pushing thirty I'm still considered quite a fetching piece of ass. Besides, you didn't dismember me then store my various parts in your freezer as a souvenir, or keep me chained in a damp cellar somewhere as your love slave. No, you quickly accomplished what you came to do, then you were outta here. A true professional! And I certainly didn't mind that you dropped by unexpectedly without calling first (If I'd known you were coming I'd have shaved my legs, hung out the fancy embroidered towels in the bathroom, and slipped into something more comfortable). A dashing gentleman visitor is always a welcome surprise for a girl living alone (Since I'm unlisted, it was obviously impossible for you to have phoned ahead. But even if you had managed to bribe a telephone company official for my number, still, how could you have honestly introduced yourself without sounding like a fool? "Hi, I'm an escaped sex offender. How about dinner and a movie?" Convinced you were a practical joker, I'd have slammed the receiver down, not even giving you a chance. And you should also know this pathetic fact about me: even if we had made a date, I'd have been a nervous wreck for days in advance, so worried that I'd make a poor first impression, I'd have inevitably developed cold feet and canceled at the last moment, or even worse, cruelly left you waiting for hours on some previously agreed upon street corner, shivering in the cold and wondering what became of me. So you chose wisely to just show up). If you're still having trouble placing my face, perhaps this will stir your memory: they say you used a crowbar to break into my building, then you rode the elevator to the top floor, once outside on the roof you heroically scaled the wall to the rain duct, then lowered yourself with catlike agility until you landed on the fire escape outside my flat with perfect accuracy. Cool! (Do you work out? I wanted to, but realizing with alarm how I look in spandex, immediately abandoned the idea.) I figure you must have really had a hankering for me to go through all that hassle, huh? It was a swell gesture. I mean, let's face it, there aren't many suitors in this day and age who would risk a broken neck to be with the girl they fancy, no matter how much they had the hots for her. Charmed, I'm sure! Not to mention you schlepped all the way out to Queens. That's quite an impressive feat in itself. Did you subway or cab it? My ex-boyfriend (Now don't be jealous. It's over between me and him. I swear.) used to refuse to visit me, complaining that I live way out in the sticks and it's much too inconvenient, and if I wanted to see him he'd insist I prove it by traveling hundreds of miles by bus to another state, climb the six flights to his tiny apartment, usually to have him hurriedly explain that he didn't have time for me that day, then sending me on my way again. Your gallantry sure is a refreshing change! So how's prison life? Have you made any nice new friends? Is Death Row really no picnic or are you able to make the most out of the hopelessness of your situation with, say, some cheery travel posters on the walls and a positive attitude? Try greeting each day with a bright smile and singing an upbeat, life-affirming song. In high school I was voted Miss Optimistic and I've tried my best to live up to that title ever since. As you might imagine, it's a constant challenge to be a universal model of perpetual good cheer, successfully finding silver linings in even the most dire circumstances. For example, I can easily think of more troubling events that can happen to a girl than a mere trespassing on her person. Waiting for the crosstown bus in a heavy rainstorm without an umbrella, for instance, or discovering a snag in one's stocking while on the way to the 7-eleven, now that's what I call a humiliating experience. You were just reaching out. Actually, it's *me* who should apologize to *you*. I wasn't exactly the most gracious hostess. You see, for years I've followed the same predictable nightly routine: after I arrive home from my office job as an assistant to the executive assistant of a large corporation,

I prepare myself a light, yet satisfying supper, browse through the current issue of *Self* magazine, then early to bed. Not exactly the most thrilling schedule, but comforting in its regularity. Naturally, I was startled to say the least at your sudden arrival on the scene! It's not so often a dreamy hunk (Like I described to the boys at the stationhouse, you're an interesting cross between Robert Mitchum and Ted Bundy. Even with that stocking mask on, you still can't hide those beautiful blue bedroom eyes and that fabulous bone structure. Next time, leave it at home!) appears uninvited in my kitchen while I'm sticking my turkey TV dinner-for-one into the microwave, then grabs me from behind threatening to cut my throat if I don't cooperate. (I guess I'm basically an old-fashioned romantic, I still prefer it when guys make the first move. That is, even if it is considered perfectly acceptable these days for the female to be the aggressor and I'd spotted you first, say, at a gallery opening or a cocktail party, I'd never have had the courage to ask *you* out; sadly missing a perfectly fine opportunity to establish contact with another human being, then kicking myself for losing the moment for years to come. Clearly, with me at the helm we'd have gotten nowhere fast!) May I be honest? I'm not about to tell you how to do your job or anything, but flashing that switchblade was definitely an initial turn-off. Now don't get offended, this is just constructive criticism, okay? I thought, Christ, here we go again, another big ape with an ego problem who feels he has to impress a dame with a macho swagger and silly props (Did you have trouble asking girls out in high school? I was bashful with the opposite sex myself. Another trait we share in common). Yet I foolishly overreacted. Rather than rudely slamming my knee into your you-know-what (If you didn't guess, yes, I was suffering from PMS. Unfortunately, you caught me on one of my crankiest days of the month. Now you know, I can be an absolute terror to be around. Watch out!), I should have extended myself and offered you a refreshing glass of lemonade or a square of my delicious homemade Rice Krispies crunch. Gosh, where were my manners? That hospitable gesture on my part would certainly have helped break the ice, eased our awkward initial shyness, and gotten our brief rendezvous off on a much more agreeable start. What good is finally having a man around the house if I'm going to jump out of my skin every time he says "Boo"? In fact, one might assume by my extreme case of the jitters that I'd never been alone in a room with a cute fella before. Well, let me assure you, that is definitely not the case! I have, lots of times and on several occasions even in the dark (You can ask my ex-boyfriend and he'll vouch for me. I'll give you his number). Then you politely asked me not to scream, and like a spoiled child I defied your warning and howled like a siren anyway (Later the neighbors looked away embarrassed and claimed they didn't hear a thing. Little good all that carrying on did me). Ain't that just like a broad? Thank you for perceptively pointing out one of my most glaring flaws: I should learn to keep my fat trap shut! Nobody likes a nagging shrill. I mean, there are ways to beg for one's life without whining and acting real bitchy about it. A humble, soft-spoken plea would have been much more effective. Then I had the nerve to play hard-to-get! A tired old tactic, I'm sure you'd agree. Breaking loose and fleeing from you like a nervous schoolgirl is a shoddy way to treat a guest who'd clearly gone to great lengths to be with me that night (Nothing personal. I was running away from my feelings, still terrified of getting too close and risking true intimacy. It takes me a while to fully trust my paramour. Please be patient with me, my sweet). And talk about tacky! I really spoiled the mood when I grabbed my purse from the counter and desperately hurled it at you, mistaking you for a common thief. How insensitive! Why do I still have trouble believing a guy can be genuinely interested in me without ulterior motives? I totally misread you. Tell the truth, had you ever felt so insulted? In fact, if you'd turned on your heels and climbed right back out on the fire escape, feeling rejected and hurt by my spurning of all your overtures, deciding that you're putting more into the relationship than you're receiving and it's just not worth all the heartbreak, I wouldn't have blamed you one bit. It was early yet, you could still get lucky and break into another, less problematic woman's apartment, or simply lurk in the shadows by the nearest subway exit and stalk an attractive commuter on her lonely walk home. The point is, you could pick any babe out there, why should you take my shit? You wouldn't have been the first man who's demonstrated affection for me that I've subsequently driven away. Give me just a little more time to get used to the idea of "us," okay? Before you came along, I'd given up hope of having a new beau enter my life, doubting that I'd ever meet that special someone who could live up to my unusually high standards. Mother was right. You'll see, she always predicted reassuringly, you'll meet your prince when you *least expect it*. And how's this for a weird coincidence: earlier that same day as I was trying to enjoy my lunch in the crowded company cafeteria, seated alone at my usual table at the rear (You'll be relieved to note that I am counting calories to get rid of that unsightly tummy bulge, so yes, you will be able to walk tall with me wearing a bikini at the beach!), I was suddenly joined by a few of the other girls who work in my office. They sat down with their lunch trays and formed a critical cluster around me, commenting on my pale complexion and dowdy appearance, then proceeded to state what's missing from my life and exactly what I should do about it. "Competition is tough out there," pointed out an anorexic stenographer. "The man shortage has reached a critical low, and the numbers are dwindling at an alarming rate. There's not a moment to lose. You must hurry and get out in the world, then grab the first thing in trousers. Mr. Right isn't going to just show up at your front door one day." No, but how about at the bedroom window? Ha ha! And later after I emerged from the subway and was crossing a busy intersection, an elderly man driving a dark sedan slowed to a crawl, then shouted out his window to me, "Lady, what you need is a good f——!" Well, what a difference a day makes, huh? See, I've never had such casual sex before (If you think I gave you a hard time, just ask my ex-boyfriend how long it took him to get inside my pants. An entire year, to be exact, and only when I was wearing the heaviest flannel nightgown I could find with all the lights turned off). Geez, you'd been in my apartment only a few minutes, and without so much as a howdydo (though I can't hold that against you, I'm lousy at small talk myself), you had me pinned beneath your heaving torso, my panties torn off, thighs pushed apart, you boldly driving in your private part, without the common courtesy of asking first! Or could it be that you did ask and I missed the question, failing to honor you with the decency of a reply? I'm practically deaf in my left ear, so if you posed your inquiry while standing on my left side, you could have shouted your request for a sexual favor through a megaphone and I wouldn't have heard a thing. Or perhaps you asked in a foreign tongue and I mistook it for gibberish. Voulez baiser, no? Monsieur voulez baiser, non? (I did it without permission to a man once. Early one morning as he snored on his back, I climbed aboard, rocking back and forth until the helpless victim woke with a start. Don't tell!) In any case, we couldn't have asked for a more beautiful evening. I used to imagine it'd be wonderful to make love on my terrace overlooking the Long Island Expressway, the lights from gridlock twinkling below like the Milky Way. But you opened up an entire new world to me. It was just about perfect on the cold linoleum, surrounded by my color-coordinated dish towel and oven mitt collection, and the smell of turkey burning in the microwave. You opened up an entire new world to me (Are you married, single, or what? Tell me now before we get further involved. I never go out with married men. A girl's got to draw the line somewhere). And don't worry about neglecting foreplay. I'm not one of those demanding women who hands out a detailed map of her erroneous zones every time she has sex with a man, then shouts instructions like a drill sergeant. You'll have no performance pressure from me. You're a busy man on the go, and I'm grateful whenever you can manage to squeeze me into your whirlwind schedule. Maybe you even had a cab waiting downstairs, ready to whisk you off to an important business meeting (Just my luck, another man who puts his work first! Ha ha. Just a joke), or to a private jet, then some faraway, exotic destination. Besides, who am I to complain about you? I'm sure you have quite a few gripes of your own. I just lay there like a lifeless sack, drifting in and out of consciousness, not exactly the most reciprocative partner. On the other hand, you have to tell me how you like it. I'm not a mind reader, after all. Okay, so it was a quickie. Most couples spend an entire lifetime together and never share what we did in just a few precious moments. They say the first time is never as good. Next time we'll take it nice and slow!

Your pal,
the girl in apartment 4C

PS: Smell the envelope. It's slightly scented with Coco by Chanel.

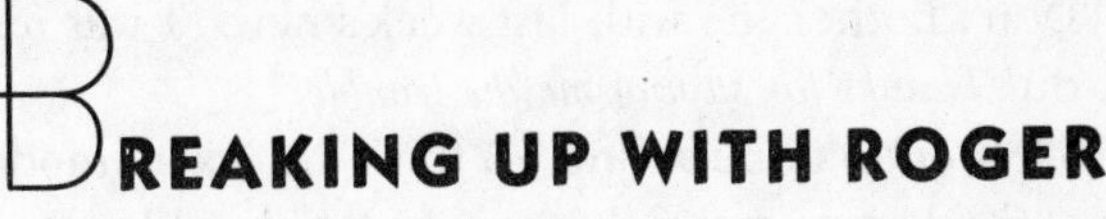

BREAKING UP WITH ROGER

David B. Feinberg

HOW WE BROKE UP I

We broke up over omelets in a rather inexpensive restaurant in the East Village. I was dipping his french fries in ketchup. "Smoking is very glamorous," I said, putting two french fries in my nose à la Brooke Shields, pretending they were cigarettes.

"Maybe you should stop that?" Roger suggested softly. Still, his voice was twelve octaves beneath my own harridan's shriek.

I had ordered an exotic omelet, which arrived with a mound of creamy green pesto that resembled avian feces from a rare and possibly extinct specimen. "Should I be eating garlic? Are we going to be kissing later tonight?" I asked, smearing my Italian bread with gobs of sauce.

"I don't think so," said Roger.

He cleared his throat.

"You'll probably hate me after I tell you what's on my mind."

"Oh, are you going to drop me?" I inquired, disingenuously. "Don't bother me with last week's news. I was *just* about to drop you. *Thanks for saving me the trouble.*"

"Shouldn't *I* be telling *you* this?" he asked, moderately relieved.

"Or do you mean that maybe we should sort of cool down for a while, maybe we shouldn't be talking to one another for a while, you know, try to be apart and think about things and maybe dump one another in a few weeks or so. Is that what you're trying to say?" I questioned.

"Something along those lines," he admitted. "I guess you're not upset as I'd imagined."

"Why should I be upset, you cad, you hypocrite, you imbecile, you hateful scourge of society, you insect, you Precambrian layer of igneous material, you spineless creature, you jerk, you simpleton, you heartbreaker, you infidel, you bore, you know-nothing, you atheist, you Pet Shop Boys fanatic?" I said, as I tossed a glass of Mondavi Cabernet 1987 (a fruity, subtle full-bodied varietal) at Roger Taylor, who was wearing a lesbian-identified lumberjack shirt.

He ducked. The slim and elegant waitperson ("Hi, my name is Gregory, and I'll be your server this evening"), who wore enough Stiff Stuff in his neatly coiffed hair to style seventeen Farrah Fawcetts, managed to catch the entire volume of liquid in a flask which he carried for such occasions.

WHY WE BROKE UP

We broke up for the completely rational reason that we had absolutely nothing in common, aside from HIV antibody status.

We broke up because Roger was deeply committed to a long-term till-death-do-us-part-or-at-least-until-I-run-out-of-conditioner relationship and I, a novice at deep, meaningful, fulfilling relationships, had only read fifty pages of *The Male Couple's Guide to Living Together* in preparation.

We broke up because I was a closet radical who went to demonstrations and shouted in protest and even once got arrested in the hopes of being strip-searched by the policeman of my dreams and Roger was so apolitical he didn't even *vote* in the last election (and if he *had* voted, he would have voted for *Bush*, but only because the name Dukakis didn't sound "presidential").

We broke up because I was a proabortion atheistic kneejerk pinko faggot and Roger was A CATHOLIC who had spent several years unsuccessfully trying to cure himself of homosexuality because of the obvious religious conflict; moreover, Roger was deeply offended by Madonna's video "Like a Prayer" whereas I worshiped her and secretly yearned to lick her stigmata.

We broke up because Roger liked to have fun and I preferred to suffer; because he liked going out to bars and dancing on tabletops and smoking unfiltered cigarettes and eating brunch with other, like homosexuals of his ilk whereas I preferred to stay home in my wreck of an apartment to the point of agoraphobia, reading the works of Schopenhauer, drinking bitters; because he was extremely loyal to a highly selective group of friends numbering three, whereas in all of my relationships I was fundamentally promiscuous and my acquaintances numbered in the hundreds and I'm sure he eventually smelled the rancid stench of my constant infidelity which I was able to conceal so ingeniously that even I wasn't aware of it.

We broke up because he was a virgin and I was a whore; we broke up because I would rush away a moment after ejaculation to wash off the DEADLY SPERMATOZOA and Roger would happily lie in puddles of spunk for days; we broke up because I masturbated constantly—I'm masturbating this very second!—and Roger would rarely, if ever, perform an act of self-pollution, possibly because subconsciously THE VOICE OF GOD was telling him that it was a sin and he would go STRAIGHT TO HELL if he did it, but more likely because it wasn't inherently interesting to Roger.

We broke up because I was a pseudointellectual and poseur and snob and Roger was not particularly interested in printed matter when it didn't concern the internal mechanisms of automobiles: where I read Kafka, Roger read car manuals.

We broke up because I had complained that I didn't have

enough time for a job, gym, reading, movies, plays, therapy, doctor's appointments, the beach, running, AIDS activism, museums, galleries, endless phone calls, visiting friends in the hospital, cleaning the apartment, doing the dishes, the laundry, ironing shirts, making dinner, eight hours of sleep each night, and a relationship; Roger responded sympathetically by casually eliminating the final item of my list.

We broke up because Roger fell instantly, profoundly, completely, and eternally in love with me the moment we met: he told me he was experiencing deeper feelings for me than he had experienced for anyone else in the past eight years since his first cocaine-addicted lover named Larry, the first of three cocaine-addicted lovers named Larry (funny how we all have a "type"); perhaps this may have arisen from the fact that neither is my name Larry nor am I a cocaine addict; and of course, two months later, after I returned from a ten-day separate vacation, he fell instantly, profoundly, completely, and eternally out of love with me; that was, of course, the point where I was gradually realizing that my feelings for him were growing to the point that separation would be unthinkable and I was actually considering releasing the floodgates of my frozen and stultifying emotions for a moment and admitting that maybe, just maybe, I might be in love with Roger; although, as one would expect, I only really fell in love with Roger two weeks after our tragic breakup.

HOW WE BROKE UP II

We broke up over dinner at the Heartbreak Restaurant, down in SoHo.

The walls of the Heartbreak Restaurant were covered with repulsive art that changed every month: last month photorealistic canvases of grossly enlarged contorted faces blanketed the scene; this month, nonrepresentational splotches of violent shades of red. Our table, raised and centrally located, had two spotlights focused on it. The sound system played dramatic music from some unspecified film noir of the forties. On a videoscreen above the bar, I could see Barbara Stanwyck with tears running down her black-and-white profile.

Roger was prompt and sweating slightly. I staggered to our table, having subsisted on vodka and cranberry juice during the past few weeks. The waiter left us separate checks as we ordered, and informed us that tips were requested in advance of service, as very few meals were completed at the Heartbreak Restaurant.

"I have something to tell you," Roger began gently.

"Oh, are you going to drop me?" I inquired, disingenuously. "Don't bother me with last week's news. I was *just* about to drop you. *Thanks for saving me the trouble.*"

"There's no need to be nasty," he chided.

"What can I say? We laughed, we cried, we had good times, we had bad times. If you don't get on that plane, you'll regret it: maybe not today, maybe not tomorrow, but someday. Laszlo needs you more than I do. When you remember me," I said, arm poised with a glass of pink champagne, "and you will, you will, think of me kindly," I continued, tossing the contents at his white alligator shirt and stalking angrily out of the restaurant, to thunderous applause.

HOW WE MET

We met in typical approaching-the-fin-de-siècle manner: at a People with AIDS Coalition Singles Tea. We had both come with friends who didn't want to go alone, hardly expecting to meet anyone ourselves, merely as support. My friend Jim said I would be Rhoda to his Mary. Our friends had both developed full-blown AIDS; at the time, Roger and I were asymptomatic antibody-positive.

The official yenta, a nice Jewish boy with aspirations in the profession of musical theater, asked exceedingly embarrassing questions to the group gathered, to help narrow down our choices. Audience members should raise their hands when appropriate. Who has more than twenty-seven T cells? Who has less than fifteen hundred T cells? Who is currently in a relationship with a member of the clergy and willing to have six to ten additional relationships on the side? Who has never had a relationship that lasted longer than the Broadway run of *Moose Murders*? Who owns an apartment in Zeckendorf Towers? Who lives in a Salvation Army shelter? Who bites their nails? Who has a two-thousand-watt blow dryer? Who has a penis that is ten inches or larger? (Please see me later in the back room for a brief proposition.) Who would have oral sex with a condom? Who would have oral sex with a condom, only if the condom had a penis inside? Who is on aerosol pentamidine? Who owns their own nebulizer? Who rents? Who won more than ten thousand dollars in the New York lottery? Who goes to the gym more than five times a week? Who goes to twelve-step-program meetings more than twice a day? Who uses deodorant on a regular basis? Who shaves more than his facial hair? Who shaves more than his facial hair daily in the Chelsea Gym shower? Who has been in therapy for longer than ten years? Who hasn't been north of Fourteenth Street in ten years? Who has appeared as a model in *Mandate* magazine? Who used to hustle? Who is allergic to pubic hair? Who has slept with more than one thousand men in the past ten years? In the past five years? In the past ten weeks? Who has been disowned by his family? Who has disowned his family? Who likes to wear lace occasionally? Who is currently wearing frilly underwear? Who wouldn't mind displaying it to the group? And so on.

By the time all of the questions were asked, I found that I would have absolutely nothing to say to someone on an initial meeting other than "Your place or mine?"

HOW WE BROKE UP III

One day it just happened. It was over. It ended. After a while I lost interest. We just let it fade away and die. I went home quietly and took an overdose of sleeping pills and turned on Carson. I went home quietly and called up the phone sex line and had a lovely time. I went home quietly and baked a dozen hash brownies and sat there, eating them, watching a rerun of *Sweeney Todd* on Arts and Entertainment. I went home quietly and rented a masseur and had a lovely time. He stole my stereo, my CD player, my VCR, and my personal computer, along with most of my software. I didn't care. Life was meaningless. I made a conscious effort to at least appear upset to the outer world. I failed. It was over. I didn't even notice his absence. I looked in my little black book and easily found a substitute. It ended quietly. There were no harsh words. We both agreed that we had relatively little in common, and although we did have a pleasurable experience it was best to part. It was enough to just go home and cry into my Laura Ashley designer pillows and play Billie Holiday LPs on the stereo and drink absinthe and smoke opium from a hookah and try to forget.

My old flame. I can't even remember his name.

WHAT DID ROGER LOOK LIKE

Roger had deep, bright, sensitive brown eyes; thick, full, sensuous lips; a short, neatly cropped brown beard; and well-groomed brown hair thinning along the temples, indicating a high production of testosterone. He was extremely tall, at least for me: six foot one or two. He looked to be in his mid to late thirties. He was bundled in a plaid overshirt and jacket, possibly concealing several defects, for we met in the dead of winter. His clothing was rather unremarkable, leading me to the mistaken impression that he wasn't overly interested in fashion. His voice was deep and satisfying.

Later I would discover he had a not inconsiderable member, henceforth to be referred to in a voice several octaves lower than my normal range as his "tool."

HOW WE BROKE UP IV

We broke up in a civilized manner. Afterwards, we returned to our respective apartments and shot ourselves with a single silver bullet in the head, between the eyes. Moments before, we had neatly laid newspaper around to catch spills and notified the manservants. We left our wills in plain sight. Unfortunately, we had named one another as executors, and had, in fact, left most of our money to one another. The wills were in probate for years.

WHY DID I APPROACH ROGER

Throughout the proceedings I kept my eye on Roger. He'd occasionally look in my direction. My friend Jim and I came expecting the usual emergency room overflow crowd, the kind of congregation one might find at Lourdes or at one of Louise Hays's evangelical lectures, ready to throw away their crutches and dance onstage with tambourines and ethyl rags. It wasn't quite that bad; still, it was like a bad night at the Barbary Coast: the pickings were pretty slim. Early on during the mass interrogation, Jim and I decided that Roger was the only appealing prospect. Jim threw in the towel early, complaining that Roger hadn't noticed him. I announced my intention to secure him.

So afterward, I walked up, introducing myself. "Even though we're completely incompatible, since you are homeless and I am a complete slob, I would like to give you my phone number."

"I'm not homeless," said Roger, in a deep baritone that reverberated at the base of my spine.

"You didn't raise your hand at any of the questions regarding place of residence," I pointed out.

"I live on Long Island. It wasn't on the list."

In former years, this would have been an automatic cause of disqualification: the red light, the buzzer, the seat-eject, the trapdoor, the shepherd's hook, you name it. However, in the approaching-the-fin-de-siècle manner, one uses a less exacting set of criteria in selecting possible dates. In other words, we've lowered our standards. There was a time when I didn't date men who smoked cigarettes, were in any of the design professions, wore leather pants, had tit rings, appreciated the opera, drank to excess, danced in the gym, or had been in therapy for more than ten years. Now, however, I'm just looking for a warm body to cuddle, hopefully with a life expectancy longer than that of my shampoo. The rest is immaterial.

HOW WE BROKE UP V

Roger and I broke up every week, on Friday. After considerable experimentation, we had decided that Friday would be optimal, giving us the rest of the weekend for what is called by Harlequin Romance a "second chance at romance." We were doomed to repeat our breakup scenes endlessly, with only minor variations in our Twilight Zone of Boyfriend Hell. One week I would break up with Roger; the following week, he would break up with me. One week I would toss a glass of chablis at Roger; the following week, he would retaliate with a glass of Mogen David wine, kosher-for-Passover. Yet, inextricably linked, powerless to resist, we remained faithful to our Friday-night assignations.

HOW OUR FIRST DATE ENDED IN A RATHER TYPICAL MANNER

We promised not to start too fast and ended up having sex on the first date anyway. "You seduced me!" he accused. "It was that look you gave me, with those big brown eyes of yours."

"They're hazel. If only you were paying attention."

"Whatever. It must have been what you whispered in my ear."

At every step Roger hesitated, from the door to the chair to the couch to the bed. Ever the disinterested participant, I was willing to offer no advice, either pro or con. I neither encouraged nor discouraged his advances. On this, I am certain he will dispute me. "I would rather get to know you better," he said, enveloping me in his brawny arms on the couch, kissing me on the cheek, "before we continue."

I offered the suggestion that we contain ourselves to necking and petting above the waist, with at least one foot on the floor at all times. Roger consented. All too soon, we went the way of all flesh. "Would you hate me if I stopped here?" asked Roger.

"Of course not," I murmured, circling his sensitive nipples with my tongue.

Perhaps we were both too passive to stop.

Was it my fault? I mentioned the possibility of a change of venue to the bed, in the interest of basic human comfort. Roger *was* six foot two, and my farcical couch was tiny, a suburban sleeper suitable for Japanese apartments and preadolescents. I had bought this midget divan for the express purpose of avoiding sleeping with a siren from the Midwest who had visited me roughly nine years ago intent on converting me to the wonderful world of bisexuality—she who, like Marilyn Chambers, was "insatiable."

Of necessity, shoes were removed. At that point, it only made sense to continue disrobing. Socks, pants, and expandable watchbands were sporadically tossed in the direction of the couch. I hid under the sheets, burrowing deep down under like a gopher, curling up into fetal position. Roger soon followed.

We were down to our underwear. "Would you feel foolish if we stopped here?" asked Roger.

Answering neither yes nor no, I went to the kitchen for twin glasses of water. When I returned, Roger lay flat on the bed, arms outstretched, legs spread, a pillow replacing his white jocky shorts. His eyes were closed. Following the most primitive of all categorical imperatives, I doffed my shorts and dove in.

Was it a momentary lapse of reason, a convenient case of temporary amnesia, or merely situational ethics of the most abhorrent and venal kind? For some reason, in the heat of passion, I invariably forget the logic behind not sleeping with someone on the first date. Perhaps I should spray-paint it in Day-Glo block letters on the ceiling for such occasions?

We all have our own personal scales of intimacy. Perhaps mine was skewed? It ranged from shaking people's hands, greeting them on the street, having violent and profound sex with them, exchanging first names, sharing recreational drugs with them, pointing out unseemly semen stains in public to avoid undue embarrassment, exchanging last names, adding phone numbers to the quick-dial feature of automemory, naming one another as correspondents in divorce cases, exchanging housekeys, and so on.

Sleeping with someone was rather low on my scale of familiarity. "Don't take it personally," I rushed to reassure Roger, who feared we had gone too far and was consequently banging his head against the plaster. "What happened to you could have happened to anyone."

HOW WE BROKE UP VI

I was coming home from work late one evening. I decided to take the shortcut through Great Jones Alley. I patted my wallet self-consciously. I heard footsteps behind me. I started to pick up my pace. Soon, we were both running. I made a quick left into a blind alley. I was stuck. There was no way out.

He had a flashlight shining on me. I couldn't see his face. And then he spoke, that deep familiar voice of gravel. "This is for the scars you've given me these past six months."

"But Roger," I began. "I didn't mean to hurt you—" That was when I felt something harsh splashing on my eyes. I screamed. Battery acid. I was blinded for life.

WHY DOESN'T ANYONE GO SLOW ANYMORE

Because there just isn't enough time.

HOW WE BROKE UP VII

Once we broke up, we severed all contact. I believe Roger moved to Baltimore the following autumn, with an insurance broker. I remained firmly ensconced in my venomous flat in Hell's Kitchenette. Christmas cards were not exchanged. Birthdays were forgotten. A few years later, it was as if I had never known Roger at all.

HOW LONG WERE OUR FIRST THREE DATES

Roger wanted to stay over. I acceded to his wishes, although my omnipresent infinite list of things to do weighed heavy on my mind.

It was a very long first date.

A few weeks later, I realized that each of our first three dates extended longer than twelve hours. Perhaps we were getting serious? I consulted my horoscope for clues. The enigmatic forecast was immediately covered with the wet quicksand of my memory.

WHEN DID ROGER LEARN MY PHONE NUMBER

Roger learned my phone number by heart after our first date; I always referred to the yellow stickum on the bulletin board, next to the laundry ticket and the film festival schedule; I ultimately didn't memorize his number until about two weeks *after* we broke up.

HOW ROGER KISSED

Every kiss was an event. Roger's kisses were gentle morning dew on my cheeks; teasing passes of a butterfly's wings at my lips; mad B-52 bombing runs on my mouth; kamikaze attacks on my throat; atomic bomb explosions on my nipples; urgent stingray bites on my pelvis; laconic feathers slowly wafting their way earthbound on my stomach.

"Look!" he would say, pointing his left finger toward the ceiling.

"What is it?"

"No, the other way." he'd continue, veiling his approach with subterfuge, throwing me off the track with false promises of Halley's comet. I would turn my head, following the imaginary trajectory of his fingertip to the sky.

He would bring his finger to my lips. "Shhhhhh."

If I turned to look at him, he would warn, "Don't watch."

Shy and secretive, he would make his gentle approach, with all of the stealth of an invisible jet bomber. "Don't move!"

I pretended I was in Bermuda, merely hallucinating Roger. I felt Roger wanted to protect me, rejuvenate me to the point of ebeing too young to realize I was naked. "You don't want to spoil it, do you?" said Roger with his eyes.

Every kiss was magic. I can only fail in my attempts to describe the unbearable lightness of Roger's lips. Thus inclined, he would make his gradual approach. "Excuse me, what's that?" he would say. A piece of lint? A freckle? An imaginary spot? A bull's-eye?

I would feel a gentle, sweet, soft contact on the cheek, as Roger kissed the locus of our deception. "Got it!" he'd announce successfully. "It's gone now."

Who wouldn't swoon?

WHAT WE WERE AFRAID OF

I was afraid of dying.

Roger was afraid of getting sick.

He said he didn't mind dying, it was just the getting sick that he hated.

I said, "Are you crazy? Nobody wants to die."

HOW WE GOT ALONG WITH ONE ANOTHER'S FRIENDS

I hated all of his friends and he couldn't stand any of mine; every chance meeting was fraught with peril. It was safest when we stuck to our apartments and ordered out Chinese, rented old horror flicks, and had copious amounts of sexual intercourse.

The snideness of his friends' responses was unparalleled in the history of queendom. Roger's friends discussed accessories constantly, along with fashion utensils, sexual appliances, household demographics, makeup secrets, interior deconstructionism, and skin care secrets. They all worked in the madcap world of design: remixing music videos, deranging window displays, bending hair, slinging hash, filing teeth, and so on.

My best friend Matthew didn't fare any better with Roger. The three of us met in a Mexican restaurant. Matthew chose that moment to inform Roger that Madonna's latest blasphemous video had changed his life. He then made us move to another table because the lighting was rather unflattering. For some reason which escapes me, Matthew grated on Roger's nerves, although Roger was kind enough not to bring it to my immediate attention.

DID ROGER SLEEP NAKED AT NIGHT?

Of course he did.

WHAT KIND OF UNDERWEAR DID ROGER WEAR?

Roger wore plain full-cut white underwear and I wore gray Calvin Kleins because I took vitamin B and pee stains were rather unattractive. I wondered, "What's the point of having a lover if you can't double your wardrobe?"

HOW ROGER DROPS MEN

"I try to drop men as soon as I know that it won't work out," explained Roger to me on one of our twenty-three-minute post-breakup phone calls. "I don't believe in dragging out an affair. I try to be as gentle as possible in my approach. I usually hint around. I never break up over the telephone. It's always in person; usually over a chef's salad."

"All I wanted was to better my personal record of three months for a relationship," I whined in reply. "I was hoping to break one hundred days. Maybe *Time* magazine would do an article on our relationship, like on a recently inaugurated president. 'Roger and Me: The First Hundred Days.' "

"Everything was wrong from the start with us. The first time I saw you, sort of goofy-looking, slouched down in that chair, an admitted slob, hair all over the place, terrorist pants with fifteen Velcro pockets, not the height of fashion in my book, if you ask me."

"I don't recall posing the question," I replied, stung. "At least I've never been involved with cocaine addicts."

"Maybe it was a blind spot on my part."

"It's not as if I had any fantasies of sex with a grease monkey either."

"You were weird from the start. I should have dropped you immediately. Yet for some reason I was drawn to you. I don't know why."

WHAT I ALWAYS WANTED TO DO WITH ROGER

I always wanted to go for a drive on his motorcycle, with my long blond hair blowing in the wind, hugging him tight around the waist of his leather jacket, holding on for dear life as he sped around a curve. Unfortunately, at the time, I was a brunette with a crew cut. And when I finally found the appropriate wig, Roger had already sold his Harley-Davidson.

Roger had wanted a motorcycle for years, but when he finally got one, he was too scared to drive it with any regularity.

WHO CALLED THE OTHER FIRST AFTER OUR TRAGIC BREAKUP

I suppose it was me.

DOES SIZE MATTER?

"And suppose I had a two-inch penis," asked Roger during one of our twenty-three-minute post-breakup phone calls. "If after you looked into my big brown eyes and boyishly sat next to me on the couch and then seduced me with your lips and took me over to the bed, leading me like the blind leading the blind, and then as we tussled on bed and you caressed my legs, my thighs, my loins, feeling around, very casually, for some hardened *tool*, and then licking my bountiful chest, suppose after you had finally undressed me, taken off my shirt, my pants, then my underwear, you found that I had a two-inch penis, would you have still loved me the same?"

"I probably would have pressed the bed-eject mechanism and sent you out flying through the window onto the hard sidewalks of Chelsea."

"You wouldn't have loved me for my charm, my wit, my sweet loving-kindness?"

"Of course not."

"Well, then, forget it. Forget this relationship. You wouldn't love me for what I am, just for a THING."

"What about me? What about if I had a two-inch penis?"

"That's beside the point," responded Roger, in the sullen voice of a child refused. He paused for dramatic affect, long enough to let the dark and heavy cloud of guilt envelop me. "I was just playing with you," said Roger. "I was just teasing. You can tell, can't you?"

"How long is it, anyway?" I asked, wanting to finally quantify my long-lost lust.

"I actually never measured it. I think maybe eight and a half or nine inches. The last time I measured was when I was twelve. I don't know. It may have grown since then."

HOW I FELL IN LOVE WITH ROGER

I fell in love with Roger over the phone approximately two weeks after our tragic breakup. Let me describe the progress of love: it is a slow and fitful process, fraught with complications; it follows a narrow and tortuous path; it is accomplished through a series of gradual shifts, almost imperceptible; the accretion of idiosyncrasies and minute details of personality; my love, the love of a callous and jaded cynic from the island of Manhattan, was like a snowball in hell surreptitiously gathering frost from the freezer of a poorly maintained Kelvinator in the devil's locker room. And as I gradually fell in love with Roger, he became more and more remote from me: he was firmly resolved to uproot our geminate lust and render asunder the tendrils of our mutual affection. He became impermeable to my entreaties. My methods were inappropriate, my directives invalid, my tactics incoherent, as he remained inaccessible.

Love is Lucy Van Pelt, Charlie Brown, and that goddamned football. Every autumn, Lucy convinces Charlie Brown that she won't pull it away at the last minute. Stupidly, he makes his approach, gathers speed, focuses all of his kinetic energy onto his right foot, lifts, and Lucy removes the ball as he is almost upon it; he kicks the air and falls flat on his back. Charlie Brown is in traction for months; he is psychologically paralyzed for life. Yet he persists in learning nothing from the experience, repeating it the following fall.

WHAT I PLAN ON DOING

I plan on seducing Roger back, so *I* can drop *him* properly.

WHY IT WOULDN'T HAVE LASTED ANYWAY

"Guess what I have?" asked Roger one day, during one of our twenty-three-minute phone calls, about two months after our tragic breakup.

"Thrush."

"How'd you know?"

"I assumed it was something bad," I answered. "I assumed it wasn't something *that* bad, or you would have been more alarmed. Thrush is the least serious thing that you could have. Don't worry; it goes away. It's no big deal."

"I guess I should expect something like thrush with my T cells."

"How low are they?"

"I dunno. They were around one hundred and sixty in January," he replied.

"One hundred and sixty! Why didn't you tell me? If I had known your T-cell count was that low, I wouldn't have even bothered attempting a relationship with you," I lied. "I was looking for a long-term relationship. Two, three, maybe even four weeks! And you obviously couldn't sustain that—it was a physical impossibility."

WHY DIDN'T I JUST LET GO FOR ONCE AND FOR ALL LIKE EVERY OTHER ELIGIBLE HOMOSEXUAL IN MANHATTAN AND QUITE A FEW INELIGIBLE ONES AND GO TO THE SPIKE ON SATURDAY NIGHT AT ONE A.M.

Because I didn't want to meet all of my six thousand ex-boyfriends at once. Every Saturday night there's a meeting of the Benjamin Rosanthal ex-Fan Club. They convene at the Spike at midnight, at the wall by the pool table, to dish me.

HOW LONG ARE OUR PHONE CALLS

When I call Roger, the phone calls are always exactly twenty-three minutes long. Roger picked an odd number, so it wasn't immediately apparent that he was timing me. After twenty-three minutes, Roger will excuse himself: he has to pee, the Lean Cuisine in the oven is done, his mother is at the door, or his other line is ringing, and it is long distance.

WHY DOES EVERY STORY SET IN 1989 HAVE TO HAVE A HOSPITAL SCENE?

Roger, sweet Roger. When I found out about the lymphoma, I wanted it to be anyone but you. Already I was stuck with survivor's guilt, and neither of us was dead. Yet. But what do you expect from someone who wrote the book on the Power of Negative Thinking (How to Lose Friends and Irritate People)? I always wanted to know why tumors are constantly compared to fruits, generally of the citrus variety. Roger had a tumor the size of a navel orange in his liver. As the famous Chinese philosopher Lao-tze once said, "This sucks the big one."

Why did it have to be you, Roger? Why not me? This was the tragic knife in the side, the dagger at one's heart. I'm the personification of EVIL, whereas you were never anything but GOOD, except, of course, when you callously dropped me and three cocaine addicts named Larry and countless others.

So our eventual reconciliation, the first time we actually saw one another since our tragic breakup, which I have magnified into legend, into history, into melodrama, into an archetypal primal scene, took place at a Jewish hospital on the East Side. Were there strains of music in the hallways as I entered, men in somber rented tuxedos playing violins in the airshaft that his room looks out on? No, only silence, soundless television in the background. All three of Roger's hideous friends were there, in solidarity against me. And inevitably, I found myself falling in love with Roger for one last time.

We made out on the hospital bed after his friends left. Roger threatened to hang me from the ceiling, using the curtain tracks, and then grease up his arm. He was just kidding, which was a good sign. In a few days, he'd start chemo. "I guess my hair will fall out," he said, sorrowfully.

"It was bound to happen sooner or later."

"But I'm only twenty-six," he said.

"I know. I know."

I don't know why but I almost cried when he told me over the phone and I stopped myself. Does this make any sense? Does anything make any sense anymore? Seymour, the very last Seymour, died during the weekend when we were waiting for Roger's liver biopsy. Philip and I went out to the hospital on Long Island to say goodbye to him on Saturday. He was breathing roughly, eyes closed. By Sunday he was gone.

WHAT ROGER DREAMS OF

Roger dreams of a lover to take care of him the way he took care of his best friend Bill a few years ago. He still keeps Bill's photo in his wallet. Bill was one of the first to come down with AIDS, back in the early eighties. Bill's mother acted hateful toward him after the death, demanding that he return half of the furniture from their apartment.

Now Bill's mother comes to visit Roger at his home. Although she annoys him, he is too polite to tell her. She thoughtlessly blows smoke into his face. Even when Roger chain-smoked around me, he was always careful to notice in which direction the wind blew. Since Roger got sick, he's lost the taste for cigarettes.

If or when I get sick, I would rather be left alone.

THE FUTURE OF OUR RELATIONSHIP

We will stay friends forever because I'm too lazy to change the preprogrammed phone number on the telephone so I'll keep calling him.

We will never get back together because I have too short an attention span to carry a torch for more than three days and I make it a point never to fall in love with the same person more than twice.

SHIFTER

♥ ♥

Lynne Tillman

BUDAPEST: You exhaust me, Zoran says. I want to say something witty like, You mean, in that Central European way, but instead tell him that I'm hungry. I am ferociously hungry. Hungry in Hungary, especially in those moments when, lightly covered in sweat, Zoran and I lie side by side on the bed in the guest house where we're staying. Not a hotel but a room in a woman's apartment that she rents to visitors like us. I don't mind being a visitor in the abstract but in someone's home it's different, though Zoran scoffs at my compunctions. Mrs. Kovacs is different from a hotel manager as we are her only guests and she watches our comings and goings with something approaching concern. Her business, Zoran says, looking tired. My father once said, You exhaust me. I remember that it was very cold out. We were driving somewhere. He didn't have the defroster on and the windshield was fogged. He said, looking tired, You don't have to entertain me.

There's no physical evidence but it was about thirty years ago that the Soviets entered Budapest, in 1956, something that didn't happen to Yugoslavia under Tito. Zoran says, Tito was a great leader, like Martin Luther King, he adds. We talk about King. Zoran was born just after World War II and remembers hearing about American troops marching into Little Rock, Arkansas, to desegregate the schools. We discuss states' rights and federalism, Alexander Hamilton, the Civil War, Justice Marshall and the Supreme Court, Rosa Parks and *Brown v. Board of Education*. A "landmark decision," I quote, like an anchor on the nightly news. Zoran's convinced that America's racism will mean its demise. We don't have racism in Yugoslavia; we have national, ethnic minorities, and it's very bad, he says. Economically, who knows. But things change. Sometimes he's hopeful. He quotes Gramsci: optimism of the will, pessimism of the intellect. I might easily reverse the two, I say, hoping that he'll enjoy the irony. He lights a cigar and peers at me as if we were sitting at different tables. "A joke?" he asks. "Sure," I say. Not mentioning paralysis of the will, the division of the intellect. "In Haiti," I tell him, "there's a saying: when the anthropologists come, the gods leave." "That is too anti-intellectual for me," Zoran says, "but interesting. Anthropology is anyway a nineteenth-century problem." "I can't think of one problem that isn't technological that doesn't go back at least to the nineteenth century." "Touché," he says.

Sitting in a café, everyone enacting to perfection my expectation of this reality, this place, where newspapers hang from wooden sticks and the aroma of pastry is palpable, I wonder if Zoran feels the hilarious intensity to our political discussions, both of us trying to display understanding like fan dancers. That is, when we're not engaged in that other kind of heated discussion meant to stupefy ideology or, at least, deny it.

I can feel entirely indifferent to the content of what I say. A great postindustrial capitalist ennui engulfs me and sweeps away vestiges of involvement. Leaves me passionless and dissatisfied and incapable of movement. I'm threatened by this constantly. In unfamiliar surroundings the point is to shift voices. I like shifting voices. Love affairs permit those shifts, and when the lover is shifty, as Zoran might be, the ride is bumpy. But if he is a shifter, so am I. Shifting to the right or left, shifty, shiftless. American women wore shifts in the fifties, my mother wore them. I have pictures of her looking shapeless but triumphant. These days her only child is shifting. Or shiftless. Many Hungarians wear jeans and walk tall, their faces sculpted with great high cheekbones which make them appear noble and anguished. I write Ann on the back of a postcard of the Hotel Gellert: I'm in Budapest with Zoran. I met him in Venice. The personal is shiftless and political. Gabors all over the city. I tear up the card.

I wish we were staying in the Hotel Gellert, more of that Old World charm I've been prepared for. Instead Zoran and I have soup in its restaurant. His appreciation of this finer side of life is circumvented by a cynicism that he tells me is common to Eastern Europeans. I sip at statements like these but am unable to swallow them whole. Zoran's cynicism, which he considers a national trait, mixes with a heady idealism and produces a roller-coaster personality that accounts, maybe, for his impassioned speeches and intense lovemaking. I would never go on a roller coaster, that is consciously, I might be forced, maybe drugged and blindfolded and kidnapped, and could be thrown on one and end up screaming, my face a mask of fear as in movies where so many characters seal their fates in love-or-death scenarios on that mechanical ride.

In a bookstore that caters to non-Hungarian-speaking travelers, another identity I can assume, I find an English translation of a story by Mihaly Babits. It's the story of a wealthy boy who every night dreams that he's desperately poor. By day he's served by footmen and butlers, treated like a storied prince. But at night he's the servant, barefoot, hungry, and miserable. His dreams become more real to him than his waking life, a familiar sensation. Zoran has no interest in dreams, insists he doesn't remember them and that if he did they wouldn't mean anything. He thinks I'm superstitious. Babits must have read *The Interpretation of Dreams*, I declare, ready to argue about everyday life and the unconscious, but Zoran merely opens his newspaper.

We walk along the Danube. I glance at Buda from Pest or Pest from Buda. It wouldn't be bad to know I was in a well-plotted movie or novel, where every incident and coincidence has meaning. To be part of a mystery that would be solved. With clues strewn here and there. A mystery that I'd be able to solve. With Zoran I'd like to maneuver cleverly or make an opening that was as subtle as one by a chess master like Boris Spassky. Whatever happened to Bobby Fischer?

They say Budapest is the Paris of the East with its massive nineteenth-century buildings, cafés, and large mirrors. I look furtively at the reflections of Zoran and me. We appear composed and regular. We walk in step. We walk quickly. We seem determined. His chin juts out. Mine does too. He pushes his hair back from his face. Mine falls into my eyes. I take his arm or he takes mine. He opens doors for me, I open doors for him. I wear black, he wears black. We're best when we're in motion.

Which is probably why we fuck most of the time. In this we've both become compulsive. His hand is on my lap or on my thigh no matter where we are. At a movie he throws his coat over me so that he can hold my breast and then slip his finger into my vagina. We rush back to the guest house, and fuck till we fall asleep. In the morning it begins again. Zoran is as good a lover as he was a sightseer in Venice. Here, with me, he doesn't sightsee. He says, with a deep sigh, I am too involved to think. I'm supposed to be flattered.

Our Mrs. Kovacs makes herself scarce. She doesn't go in for jokes, the way Signor Mancini did. That fascist Mancini, I can hear Claudia say, then see Claudia spit into the sink of the coffee shop on the Moscow Road. Mrs. Kovacs didn't introduce herself as "Kovacs, not related to Ernie." She just makes herself invisible or squirrels around the apartment. Maybe she's standing behind a door. Or in the shadow in the hallway, standing in the shadow of love. I hear doors closing and opening, thin squeaky noises. She puts on bedroom slippers when she comes indoors and pads around the living room. She may be listening to our moans and grunts. I clap my hand over Zoran's mouth, he grabs my arm and twists it behind my back. I bite him hard on his shoulder, he pins my other arm down. He won't come unless I come. His insistence, which was at first a sign of sexual compassion and urgency, has become the tactics of a cold war warrior meant to win a wordless battle.

I'm on a roller coaster with Zoran, whose light blue eyes are encircled by coffee-colored rings. "Because of you," he says. "I can't sleep. I can't even smell you anymore," he complains. "We have the same smell. You and I. We are the same." Perhaps that's why we fight so much more these days, gripped by the sense we're falling into a time before words and mirrors surfaced to key us to our separate identities. I can smell myself, I tell him. I can smell my cunt all the time. Even reading or drinking coffee in a café, I can smell it. When Zoran is at the guest house or walking near the Danube, I know he's not with me. Perhaps I have been kidnapped and thrown into a story I'd never read or want to see on the screen. Or maybe I would want to see it. I like romance at a distance.

I know of an Englishman who once attempted invisibility but was not as successful as Mrs. Kovacs. He had a suit made of the same pattern as his wallpaper. He put it on and stood against the wall of his room and called for his landlady. What are you doing up against that wall? she asked. Zoran laughs in a raucous way and I like him again. We get dressed. Mrs. Kovacs hovers near the kitchen as Zoran and I rush to find a cab, to go anywhere. Some kids point at our driver and shout, KGB, KGB. They know you're American, Zoran says perfunctorily. They tease you.

I don't know why we're taking a cab. I suppose we're both exhausted. I tell Zoran a story, the same one I told Charles in Istanbul. I tell it almost the same way, too, as if it's already a myth. I once saw a man coming out of an elevator in downtown Manhattan. I didn't know who he was but his face reminded me of someone, someone I knew. Standing next to me another man said hello to the stranger who just shook his head up and down in return. I asked the man beside me, Who is he? He looks so familiar. That's Ethel Rosenberg's brother, David Greenglass, the man replied. He's worked in this building for years. We didn't speak after that, waiting for the elevator; it was eerie. I look at

Zoran. He seems to appreciate the story and puffs hard on his cigar. The Rosenbergs have never, to my knowledge, been defended, I explain to Zoran, the way Blunt and the Cambridge spies were. That's because, he interrupts, the British are British. I go on, No one, their supporters, I mean, maintains they did it because they were Communists and obeyed their conscience, not country. The taxi driver looks in his back mirror and Zoran shoves my arm and whispers loudly, CIA, CIA. The cabdriver laughs. Zoran sighs, You think too much about betrayal and loyalty. A little later, seated in another café, looking up from his newspaper, he complains, You are like all Americans. There is no way that I can say to him, You are like all Yugoslavians, as I have no idea what all Yugoslavians are like.

To Zoran with his impossibly high standards everything is corrupt but sex. Sex and Renaissance art, the paradisiacal moment he looks back to as if it had escaped the forces of history nothing else does. We mostly agree about America's images of freedom and the rhetoric that makes America America, constructs it, but Zoran sees evil everywhere, in every bit of American life, which he appreciates for its vulgarity. We argue about popular culture and television. He sees mass culture as something that can only bring the masses down. With our differences brandished we challenge and frustrate each other. When things hold together or fall apart, the forms are familiar. The conventions—as well as the anomalies—control our ability to imagine different arrangements. Zoran and I have become mired in arguments and positions neither of us, I bet, truly supports. But daily what we actually support and what we find ourselves defending grow more ridiculous. I defend Hollywood movies as if their contradictions really were heroic, and he defends censorship or government intervention without a trace of irony.

He'd like to undo me. I'd like to undo him. I'd like to build a Berlin Wall that places me in the East and him in the West. As for American vulgarity he makes small exceptions. He says he loves me, even though I drive him crazy. I never tell him I love him, and he says he knows I do, but I'm too young to appreciate it. One of his newer verdicts about me. I tell him he's an elitist. He smiles gravely. Perhaps I've wounded him. I'd like to. Did you sleep with that invisible Englishman? he asks.

If this were a comedy Zoran might be a cranky but charming Eastern bloc intellectual on vacation. I'd be sort of bumptious and well-intentioned, a well-off, but not really rich, white American, condemned to a circle of hell Dante never wrote—reserved parking for the naive whose naiveté is laced with masochistic hope. And privilege, he always says, don't forget that. You Americans are hopeless, he also says. History is full of Watergates. Your people are always so surprised at conspiracy. My people. Our comedy will be short-lived. But the comic will be devastatingly apparent, I think, only later when I examine life without Zoran, even though he and I are still determined to go to his country and this seems less likely every day. But Zoran refers to it, a kind of marker or signifier of progress.

There is no progress, there is repetition. John the New Zealander was very fond of saying that, but I wouldn't tell Zoran because then he'd ask me about John and get possessive and jealous in the most so-called reactionary way.

AGIA GALINI: The sun is strong. So is John. He's the strongest man I've ever known. He also cries easily. He drinks way too much and is, I suppose, already an alcoholic, which may account for the tears. Like when he talks about Arlette, who, from his description, is nothing short of a goddess capable of flight, capable of anything. She wouldn't fly too close to the sun. She knows her limits and because of that is limitless, so he says. He knows Greek mythology, having studied the classics, and quotes Latin or Greek at odd moments, then translates. He's shy about what he knows.

Tina and Graham, the Australians, don't like John the New Zealander but as John and I are together, sort of, they accept him. Graham's acceptance is all of a piece with his winsome ways. Tina, who's of Chinese descent, favors John with a studied kindness that he complains to me is transparent. I like them all. Tina's a designer and hers is a colorful world of fabrics and sketches, and Graham, if he were an absinthe drinker, he'd be closer to Verlaine than Rimbaud. Dog with a paintbrush, he says about himself. I think he's faithful to Tina. His imagination is promiscuous.

In Thailand the ad "Come alive—you're in the Pepsi generation" was translated into their language. It became "Pepsi brings your ancestors back from the dead." The Pepsi generation isn't haunted and hears no echoes from dead relatives. I can make myself live again, be more lively, come alive and that doesn't depend on anyone. But if I need to come alive it means I am dead, not my ancestors. And when you don't know your ancestors, when your family begins at the borders of a new world, there's no fear of being haunted. There's no one to do the haunting. Even if those spirits wanted to, they couldn't find their way. I'm reading Rebecca West's *The New Meaning of Treason*.

The streets are few and narrow, with one broad one that could be Main Street. Shutters are closed because it's so hot. Fans whir and local inhabitants stay inside, waiting for the sun to sink lower in the sky. I'm at the harbor, looking at a ship with a Russian name. I think it's Russian. The ship dominates the small harbor, and I wait for Soviet sailors with white hats on to appear and make my day. If they appear I'll wave to them. I hope they come ashore. An elderly Greek woman in black accompanies a young boy who holds a fishing line but no fish. He looks at me shyly and I smile at the old woman who nods her head and says, *Yá sas*. She exposes a mouth full of gold teeth, like a bracelet. I'd never thought caps could be entirely decorative. I watch them walk away and when I look back the Russian ship is heading out of the harbor.

John is drunk, his long gaunt face white and red simultaneously. He's had a letter from home. From his wife, from whom he's separated. I won't ask him what she's said but he's mumbling about honor and Antigone burying the dead, and I sense he's the unburied dead. We don't, for reasons like these, and others, share a room. Mine is right above his and all night long I hear strange noises. A dog howling, a child whimpering, a man tearing paper or ripping his clothes, a sign of mourning. We haven't slept together since the first time, which was a small and sincere disaster, because he was drunk, he said. We're just companions, romantic companions. Home is far away except when it flies in, airmail, with familiar handwriting on white or tan envelopes. Relics of the near past. There's no place like home. There's no home like the present. I can't give you anything but home, baby.

I'll call myself Rosetta Stone, I tell John, and be read like a book. You wouldn't be easy to carry around, he says. He's going back to Heraklion, where he teaches English to Cretans who want to get better-paying jobs, somewhere off the island. He has a small shack near the water and hardly ever sees anyone. I'm on a vacation from my vacation, he told me when we met. New Zealand is on the map, he also tells me, because we stood up to the Americans. He is, he says, just a visitor, dismissive of other expatriates—he doesn't consider himself one. A Greek boy, a crazy one, he recounts dourly, one that had been passed from foreigner to foreigner, took his revenge on a middle-aged American, a man from New England whose manners were elegant, who was from a good old family that had no money to speak of, who was writing a book that would never be published. John says, One of those Warhol-type hangers-on who just kept hanging on. When the American drank, he turned vicious, as mean as you could get without becoming physically violent. At night he would say the most cruel things to anyone, and the next day he'd be at his regular table for lunch, his shirt impeccably ironed, his face cleanly shaved, a silk scarf around his neck, a soft white hat on his head as if he'd just alighted from his yacht. At that time of day he'd mix his white wine with water and then, and only then, he was extremely witty and even warm. But he had a violent end, worse than words. The Greek boy chopped his head off. Clean off. The Greek—by then seventeen—was sent to jail for eight years and several American and English men left town during the trial. The American had forgotten the custom of the country he was in and stepped over the line with a violent boy. It's not a tragedy, John said, even though it happened where tragedy was born. Then he started talking about Antigone again. It might be a tragedy, I countered, though it didn't take place in one day. Think about having to leave home in order to be able to have sex or to love. Then you think everything's tragic. I suppose I do, when I don't think it's comic.

And though I'm looking at John's face I'm seeing those pins that theater lovers sometimes wear—the pins that were the precursors to smiley faces. A tragic face is in an exaggerated grimace, a happy face in a beaming smile, and one grows out of the other, a horrible birth. Grotesque exaggerations. I can't imagine Greeks walking around wearing them. What are you thinking about? John asks. Home, I say. Yes, home, he repeats. Both the smile and the frown are grotesque, I write on the postcard of a ship in the harbor. I'll send it to someone.

Tina and Graham have found a large pond, surrounded by thick bushes and flowering plants, and if I had a sarong, I'd wear a flower behind my left or right ear. Tina's taken two pieces of Greek cotton she'd bought and fashioned a bathing suit that has a kind of diaper bottom. Graham, who every day seems more glamorous to me, has on a straw hat and loafers. He looks exactly as he should and so does she. He takes off his hat. His peroxided hair soaks up the sun and turns whiter and whiter. His skin gets darker and darker. Tina keeps the sun away, sensibly, carrying a paper parasol from Korea. A magazine photographer would do well to appropriate their images. John wouldn't fit in here. He doesn't blend fashionably into exotic surroundings as they do. But he doesn't have to fit in anymore because he's gone back to work, to his shack and, as he noted, we probably won't ever see each other again. But that, John also noted, is no tragedy, just life. Tina and Graham are frolicking in the pond. Graham's chest is hairless, like my father's.

It would be nice to be able to bury the dead. I don't miss John. People can occupy places in your life but not necessarily fill them. They take up ready-made positions. I sit in my small room and read, content in my fashion, or listen to the sound of the water in the distance, or what I think is the sound of the water.

Tina has made me a bathing suit like hers. We're at the pond again. When you come to London, she says, you'll visit my shop and I'll dress you. I see myself as a garden. Tina is beautiful. Graham gazes at her with such comfort that I feel envy inside me as if I hadn't eaten in a long time. I sometimes can't tell the difference between lust and other kinds of hunger. Oddly enough I'm not obese. I jump into the pond to cool off and feel like a displaced person, one that finds herself in the wrong set, in the wrong movie, and who can't take direction. Tina and Graham float above their worries, I see them doing that. The water is black at the bottom and icy cold at the middle of the small pond which might be in the center of the world. That's an American Indian saying, Anyplace is the center of the world. At the center the water is so cold the blood in my brain moves from right to left, a feeling I often have when subjected to extreme changes in temperature.

BUDAPEST: Hot springs run beneath Budapest. People take healing baths in water heavy with minerals. Zoran goes to the men's side and I go to the women's side. A towel wrapped around me, I approach the pool, which has mist rising from it, the warm water meeting the colder air and making a small fog. The water feels too solid. Faces become visible through the steam. There are seven heads floating on the surface of the water. All of them are wrinkled deeply. I am the only young woman in the pool. I walk out. This experience seems to be a dream, and since Zoran doesn't believe in dreams, I don't tell him. I say it was wonderful, which he loves because the way I say wonderful is very American. He gets excited when I say fantastic.

If I don't remember my dreams and occasionally dredge them up for myself, I might live as if they had happened during the day. Become more ordinarily unhappy than I might have been. Or come to the end that the rich boy in the Babits story did: his waking life continues to be luxurious and ordered but his chaotic, desperate dream life grows, extends itself into, and even takes over, his daily life, his consciousness. He kills himself in his dream, a miserable suicide, and when, in the morning, his servant tries to wake him, he can't. The boy is dead. This makes sense to me.

Some people separate their sexual behavior from their lives, as if one had no relation to the other. It is, I think, a human characteristic to make false categories, or perhaps just to make categories. I knew a woman in New York who had a slave called Michael. She had an all-girl party where he served us drinks and hors d'oeuvres. He held the tray above our heads so that it was difficult to see what he was offering. She yelled at him mercilessly. His daily routine was ordinary enough; he was a computer programmer, and we lived near each other. I was supposed to forget that he chose to be humiliated. As for me I'm finding it hard to separate Zoran's and my sexual dance from our daily life which after two weeks is like a long-playing record, a symphony led by a mad conductor. This conductor—maybe Leonard Bernstein, maybe conducting Mahler—urges us on to greater frenzy and pain, to separate absolutely that embrace from the quotidian. But after a while anything becomes mundane.

I like chicken paprika better than he does. I like oral sex better than he does. I like novels. He doesn't read novels because he wants information. One night or early morning as we argue on the bed in all the ways we do—with our mouths forming words, or with our tongues exploring skin, with our hands clenched as fists, fleshy signs of anger, or with our hands touching private unspoken body parts to make them bring forth noises, to make them speak—on one of these nights I try to prove there might be a relationship between Italian Renaissance art and fiction. There's something about the two of us sitting naked on the bed and arguing and me wondering whether Mrs. Kovacs is crouched near the door listening or pacing back and forth in her bedroom that forces a decision, that asks for a decision. It could be arbitrary, the kind of decision I imagined Charles made when he left Jessica. Not because he didn't love her. Not because he was bored. Just because.

I know I don't love Zoran. Actually Jessica, though a Buddhist, might get on better with Zoran than I do, or because she's a

Buddhist she might. I'd like to send him to her. She might need a birthing partner, or whatever they're called. You're laughing again, he says. I say, This is hopeless. Then he lights a cigar. "You don't know what hopeless is," he says. "My grandfather was killed by the Germans, my parents were starving, and no milk for me to drink. My mother was not able to suckle me from hunger. All of us are waiting to see who will kill us or who will protect us. You know what my first memory is, of my father's funeral. I was three. He survived the war to die of, I don't know, they think cancer. I think despair. Don't tell me about dreams. If I had them what do you think they would be?" Zoran puts out his cigar and turns his back to me. I touch him on his shoulder, a shallow gesture but it's the only thing I know to do other than speak. If I tried to speak it would be even more shallow because I'd try to comfort someone whose pain is shaped by forces I don't know. Selective memory isn't only individual psychology.

I walk to the bathroom which is outside our room and near Mrs. Kovacs's. The light is on in the kitchen and she's standing at the counter where a bottle of Polish vodka, the kind that's available in New York, is open and half empty. I don't think she notices me as I pass her, but maybe she does and simply doesn't care, is oblivious, as Zoran might be now, having fallen into a sleep with dreams as deeply hidden as the past we all try to reconstruct or as hidden as his motives. The next day I awaken to find a note with some money for the room. It's polite, formal. He writes, I've made the decision for us because you are weak. I could visit him in Belgrade, he'd still like that. But, he says, I am married. I am sorry for not telling you before now.

Mrs. Kovacs isn't disturbed by his sudden departure or by my staying an extra day to recover in my way. A documentary filmmaker who wanted to make a movie about the Navajos was asked by the chief, Is it good for the sheep? No, the filmmaker said, it's not good for the sheep. Then, the chief asked through a translator, will it harm the sheep? No, the filmmaker said, it won't harm the sheep. Then the chief asked, If it's neither good for the sheep nor bad for the sheep, why do you do it?

A postcard to Jessica. One to Tina and Graham. One to Sal and Sylvie. Postcards from the imaginary into the impossible real. I don't know why I didn't visit Tina and Graham in London, but I will the next time I'm there. I will not go to Belgrade. At least I don't think so. I remember my father saying, like a film-noir private eye, Don't think you can change a man. Buda it turns out might mean something like a chimney. But Pest means nothing, certainly not stove. Buda was Attila the Hun's brother. I wonder if they got along.

THE KID

♥ ♥

Daytona Beach

I've always been slow. Maybe even retarded. Never had an orgasm until I was twenty-three. And only then because my shrink told me to buy a vibrator. Don't get the phallic kind he said. You won't get off sticking one of those things up inside you. Get the kind that looks like a gun. Bang bang. It worked. And ever since. I've been looking for a man whose dick can move like that.

Needless to say it's been frustrating.

I moaned loudly when I heard they were hiring a single mother. I could hear it already. PTA meetings. Colic. Prodigal babysitters. The gamut. But that was discrimination they said. Citing EOE/M/F/H/V/S and a bunch of other letters. So despite my protest Kim was hired.

She's OK though despite her eternal cheeriness and her kid

is too old for colic. Sharp and witty and a faithful subscriber to the standards of logic. As a similar devotee I often find myself subject to the stresses of contact with unbelievers.

For instance. Men who don't excite me in the slightest try to bed me. Logically I decline. They in turn tell me I'm frigid.

"You have a problem with sex," they say.

"No you have a problem with sex. You're not getting any" is the stock response. Myself I have a problem with boorish oafs. I have nothing in common with the success-driven men who populate the offices, bars, and parties I habituate. Wanting to know not what they do but how they do it. Looking for something perhaps unattainable. To be touched.

Kim entertains me daily; a good contrast to my general aura of gloom and doom. Together we insult the unfortunate pock-faced mail clerk as he continues his pitch to spread my legs.

"Sybil one hour with me and I promise I'll have you singing 'The Hallelujah Chorus,' " says Nolan, who actually has a decent build but is not quite all there intellectually speaking.

"More like *Les Miserables*," Kim says.

"Nolan," I say surveying him, "the irony is I might be able to stand having you in bed if you could shut up and stop being such an asshole for just five minutes."

"Starting now?" Nolan checks his watch.

I am the continual recipient of unsolicited advice especially in the sex department. A walking "Ask Beth." Is my discontent that evident? I haven't come with a man in so long it's pathetic. Are they all incompetent? Am I really frigid? Or just bored with the current state of maleness? At age thirty-five, what's left for me after greedy lawyers, corrupt real estate salesmen, failed artists, unsuccessful musicians, bitter divorcees, absentee fathers, and self-made men who would rather jack off in their checkbooks than let me do it for them? Not a pretty picture. Nolan's looking better all the time.

A man lay on the sidewalk in front of the 222 Club, body twisted, face down. I had to step over him to get through the doorway. Inside I saw in the dim light that Kim had already taken a table.

"Nice place," she greeted me.

"Yeah. How do you like the doorman."

"You seem to enjoy looking for the dark side of things," she said eyeing the clientele.

"That's because the light hurts my eyes."

"Ha ha. I thought you had a date tonight."

"I did. Couldn't face it. Said I was sick. I am." At heart.

Kim rolls her eyes. "What's wrong with this one? I thought you had fun on your last date with him."

"Fun. He's a closet Nazi who thinks Jews control world money markets and are plotting his financial ruin. And a bad kisser. All hard and rough. I want a soft kisser." Swirling my drink. "I want someone to love me soft. Like it was a new experience. And not just an exercise."

"But it doesn't always happen instantly. Sometimes you have to let it grow."

"If I don't feel the chemistry it's not there."

"Then you shouldn't be so obsessed with finding it."

"But what else is there."

"You know what's wrong with you Sybil? You don't believe in anything."

"Well your problem," I return, "is that you believe in everything. Cynicism is ultimately logical."

"But don't you have to base your life on some kind of values? Otherwise how do you decide what's right and what's wrong?"

"You don't. You just do everything and see what works."

"Oh Sybil." Kim sighs, a sigh of the weary.

I hate it when people tell me what's wrong with me.

Thursday instead of a dinner date I went to the mall with Kim and her kid. Scott. He's fourteen, sarcastic like his mother. With whom I am spending an increasing portion of my time. Father black gave the kid dusty skin against wiry blond hair. We had pizza first then they bought shoes I bought CDs. On the way home they let me ride in the front seat with them. As if I were a big sister.

I didn't even offer the poor standee the courtesy of an excuse.

It's getting harder and harder to communicate with people. Forgetting if the aim of conversation is the exchange of ideas or merely mutual masturbation. And if it's the latter. Then one is as well off alone.

People my age bore the hell out of me.

I went to Kim's for dinner one night; she and the kid have been letting me tag along with them like a lost waif. After dinner we watched a movie. I was surprised and pleased when the kid sat next to me and sort of leaned against me as he put his feet up. Kim sat curled on the floor in front of us. Very cozy. What a doll that kid is.

That night I dreamed of lying on a bed with a young boy and as I played with his tiny flaccid penis I had orgasms more intense than ever in my life. I awoke wondering if I had actually come.

I went into the bedroom and scrutinized my reflection in the mirror. Thirty-five is too old to be scrounging the sexual dregs for satisfaction. Surely the dream had been triggered by the kid. Scott. But just as surely it was the innocent expression of the natural affection I feel toward him. Because I've stooped to many things. But that is much too far for even me to go.

It's becoming more frequent, however, and quite distracting as it is now definitely Scott in the dreams from which I wake pussy dripping and racked with guilt. I have difficulty relaxing as we squeeze into the front car seat admonishing myself not to notice how golden brown his cheeks are, or how long his legs are as he sprawls before the television. The kid's as tall as I.

The midnightly trips to the mirror are becoming ritual. Perhaps what I'm telling myself with my searching gaze is that I'm old, I'm old and have no business entertaining a sick attempt at love that can only do harm simply because I've failed so often at the real thing. It's wrong and no rationalization will make it right.

I've taken to inspecting myself minutely for signs of aging as if proof were necessary to bring me to my senses. Discovering on of all places the backs of my knees. Which are not easy to see in the first place. Big blotches of broken veins. When I thought I still possessed a small degree of youth and desirability to save me from a life sentence of loneliness. But there. You see. You are old.

I feel miserable. I can't possibly impose on Kim's friendship and openness when all I can think about is that kid. And I can't be around Scott until I've shaken this insane and perverse compulsion. I have no right to feel this way. But for the first time in my life. I want something so badly that I melt and turn to butter between my legs each time I think of him.

I do nothing but mope and fret. Kim is miffed because each time we talk I feel a stab of guilt and horror in my chest that leaves me breathless and I must turn away. Wondering into what category of deviant I fit. Mentally ill. Or merely suffering from a sexual disorder. Not to mention criminal desires.

I disgust myself. But I can't stop craving him long enough to hate myself sufficiently to stop.

Kim trapped me in the office bathroom having had enough of averted gazes and clipped sentences. "What in the world is wrong with you. Why do you hate me all of a sudden. And you're not getting out until you tell me."

Oh god. I hate it when people are nice to me. Especially when I'm already overwhelmed by unworthiness and self-degradation. How could I think of committing such a devastating crime against such a guileless person?

We talked until a hostile line formed outside. I adroitly avoiding controversy while explaining life poised on the edge of a black pit of anguish and despair. She chiding me lovingly on my lack of goals and clear direction. Perhaps she has something. And the key to happiness is simply mind over matter. Or in my case. Over libido.

I must put this sordid fantasy out of my mind and get on with my life. And remind myself that the crime is not in the thought. But in the action.

Although feeling more control over those rampant emotions I was unprepared for Kim's request to watch Scott while she attended a conference out of town. Surely the kid is old enough to take care of himself for one night. But I found myself saying. How fun it would be. It would be closer to his school. And no inconvenience for me. At all.

This may be just the thing to solidify my self-respect and trust. I feel confident I can pass this test and prove myself once and for all to be honorable, decent, a worthy friend and not a sexual miscreant or child molester at all. I've even managed to stop the dreams. Or at least block them from my memory.

Scott came over I cooked hamburgers he slaughtered me at Risk. Such a sweet and funny kid. Of course I misinterpreted my feelings. The dreams the product of a psyche marred by depression and alienation. Nothing wrong with me that an attitude overhaul won't cure.

After he went to bed I sat mind blank in the darkness. God I need a drink. Anything to keep me from thinking before I fall asleep.

But there he is. "Can I watch TV with you?" And curse him. He slouches beside me and pulls my arm around his shoulders. Wiry gold curls against my cheek. Velvet skin and thin bones under my hand. I can feel the rise and fall of each breath.

I petted his hair absently. Put my lips so softly against his head. Just as his mother might do. He sat up and faced me with a look I couldn't read. Oh my he's beautiful. But not to be touched. What would he do. Don't find out. Something inside me said, "It's not too late." And then it was too late.

Curse me. I kissed him. First steadying myself with a hand on his soft cheek as I leaned toward him. Then the vaguest touch of lips. And I died.

We stared again with no change of expression on his face. I no longer cared about decency or friendship or direction. Only about easing the ache in my heart, the one that throbs between my legs. I pushed him down gently. He went like a lamb.

In a dream I hovered over him propped on elbows nibbling his mouth. Wondering if he's ever kissed anyone. How far will he let me go. And could he have been harboring lewd thoughts of me while I was smiting myself with remorse. My arms grew numb and I didn't know if it had been hours or seconds since we began.

We rocked and rubbed and I marveled at the fragility of his small bones beneath my hands. Oh god I'm coming just squirming against him. Want wells up inside me like despair and like a lab animal that feeds itself drugs until it drops dead I want more.

"Do you trust me." He nodded, eyes wide.

"I trust you." He nodded again. And closed his eyes.

And he let me. He let me stroke suck squeeze fuck and love him like a woman frantic to retrieve just a hint of lost youth, like a sex-starved prisoner of self-imposed celibacy finally liberated. I alarmed him several times with my lack of restraint as I dissolved again and again into pools of orgasm. He weathered it well with a mixed response of awe, fear, and jubilation that shatters my heart to pieces each time I remember.

I loved him until three and he never said a word save the occasional "OK?" or "Here" when a pillow was moved or position changed. His eyes would widen and mouth open as if to speak yet only a small moan would emit. Jesus what a kid. However I will lead a child to profligacy but not truancy and eventually insisted on sleep.

This is the longest night of my life. Too scared and sick to cry. Too ashamed to look at him, to enjoy this splendid sight for perhaps the only time. Finally I laid my face against his stomach hands curved around his delicate ribs and listened to him breathe.

Of course I felt like shit upon sunrise but prepared breakfast anyway. The kid also ate not a bite. Scott. He seemed distracted avoiding my eyes until I sank in front of him taking his hands and burying my face in them. I've thought about this all night. And I still don't know what to say.

"Don't hate me." I intended to sound soothing and levelheaded but come off closer to hysteria.

"No." Eyes down.

"Don't hate yourself either."

A small smile. In spite of himself.

"Oh god. You're such a great kid."

He studies my face. "You too." A corner of his mouth turns up and shreds my heart. I feel dizzy and wonder if it's because all the blood has left my brain and coursed to heat my crotch.

"The most important thing," I continue wobbily, "is that you still be my friend, and that you not feel bad."

This kid has in his face more anguish and wisdom and determinism than any adult I know and he's not letting anything out. "Sybil."

"Oh angel. What." My lips reach for his open palms.

His fingers curl toward my face. "I don't hate you."

I am awash with relief and see him off with a light heart and no melodramatics. He is after all just a kid. And I don't know what I expected or even hoped. But as we said our goodbyes somehow I knew. That he was already gone.

Nerves taut I awaited Kim's homecoming. Somehow I am able to control my delirium in her presence inventing various ailments to explain my foul humor. What I can't deal with now is the problem of approaching the kid—Scott—and risking his wrath scorn or worse yet apathy. Tormented by furtive plans and sick fantasies as well as self-recrimination and abhorrence. And getting horny at the least opportune moments. Whenever my thoughts touch on him which is always. I feel a twinge in my chest and crotch. I can make my chest constrict with anxiety just by repeating his name to myself. "Scott." Ouch. "Scott." Ouch. Pleasure. Pain. Reflexive.

But I needn't have worried about how to act around Scott; no invitations were forthcoming, and Kim's much-too-offhand question informed me precisely where I stood.

"Did you and Scott have a fight?"

I felt as if I had been poisoned. Caustic substances shooting through my veins. "Of course not. Why do you ask."

She assured me he had said nothing but she thought she sensed a coolness in his remarks. Well of course he's playing it cool.

Deception after all is an acquired trait. I must let it lie for now. Let him sort out his feelings. Hoping time will put a damper on mine. But knowing my lust has just been awakened.

My concentration is shot to hell and my attention span shortens by the day. Boarding the subway in a daze I stumble as I fail to mind the gap.

"You all right lady?" A tall boy in a high school letter jacket caught my elbow.

His face was flushed with apple cheeks and I wanted to touch them to feel their heat. "Yes, thanks." But I meant no. I'm not all right. I'm dying. Please help me. I took a seat and watched him lean as the train accelerated. Jacket too thick to distinguish shoulder blades. But short enough to reveal jeans hung loose on tight hips and long thighs and I thought of smooth young skin under my hands. His eyes flicker to mine then away. Please help me. To me you are my life's desire. But to him I was. Just a lady on the subway.

I'm spending more and more time at the 222 Club in lieu of too many unbearable evenings alone at home. Somewhat amused to learn that people actually do pace the floors. But finding no amusement in the process itself. Wanting to be in bed only if unconscious. Because the only one I'd share it with has stricken me from his life.

Not even the offer of dinner at my own sparsely furnished digs could bring the kid out of hiding. Kim explained it as growing up as I tried to mask my hurt. "He is a teenager after all and is probably sick of hanging out with his mom and his mom's friend. He needs to develop more outside relationships. It's normal that he would want to put some distance between us."

I must see him. I can't bear not knowing what or why. If it's guilt or revulsion. Abandoning any hopes of future bliss. Now wanting only peace of mind.

At Scott's school I waited on the lawn near the front gate. In the swarm of kids I feared I wouldn't see him. But there he is emerging from the great white double doors, and oh god a girl is walking with him. I saw them through a fog that must have been tears rooted to the spot and suddenly wishing I were invisible. And when Scott's eyes finally fell on me. My wish was granted.

As if he were ashamed. He acted like he didn't see me. When once his eyes devoured me and his heart cried out. And now he doesn't even see me.

I closed down 222 tonight and was therefore surprised to see anyone out at that late hour, much less kids playing basketball in a schoolyard as I passed. Hoods no doubt. Bad boys. Picking up my thoughts one calls out, "Yo mamacita."

I slowed to cruising speed. Five of them; older than the golden-haired angel and rougher. Probably not a virgin in the bunch. But at this point I'm not too choosy.

"What's up," I say.

"Hey pretty lady." One swaggered to the fence. "Would you like to join us in a quick game?"

"I'm looking to play a game but there won't be anything quick about it."

"Wo! The lady she don't beat around the bush." My friend is coming through the gate around the fence that separates us. "Are you lonely tonight pretty lady?"

"No. I'm hungry." I'm also quite tipsy.

"Wo. What's your name?"

"Sue."

"Very pleased to make your acquaintance Sue. I am Rolando. At your service."

"I'd like to employ your service Rolando."

"Wo. Let me tell my friends I'm leaving."

He joined me on the sidewalk and said, "Where to?"

"We can go to my apartment. Rolando."

"Yes ma'am. Ow," he said staggering from the force of a blow to the upper arm. "Hey. Why did you hit me."

"Please don't call me ma'am, Rolando."

"OK. Geez. You don't have to hit me."

"I don't know. I might."

"Geez. What kind of weird stuff are you into. Maybe I should go back to my buddies."

"Come on. I'll be nice."

"You got any booze here?" Once inside Rolando took a beer from the refrigerator. "Hey where's all your furniture?"

"Drink this," I said pouring two shots and handing one to him.

"No thanks I'll just have a beer."

"Drink it." Putting the glass to his mouth I tipped it in. Spattering vodka on both of us he shoved me away. "Crazy bitch. I said I didn't want any."

"I just want you to have fun." I lurched forward and kissed him clumsily. He didn't seem to mind. His hair was slick and I wondered how I'd keep him from soiling the pillows. Leaving a greasy blot. Maybe I should fuck him here in the kitchen. "Take off your shirt."

Oh no he has hair on his chest and back thick and black. However he is thin nicely shaped bones jutting under smooth brown skin. Standing I pull him to the bathroom. "Let's take a shower."

"No I don't wanna. Where's the bed. If you got one."

"Can I shave your back."

"What. Are you nuts. What am I doing here."

I went into the bathroom and turned on the shower. "Just come here for a second." As he entered, I pounced pulling him me and the shower curtain into the tub. After several false starts he righted himself hurling me across the tiny room and into the door with a loud crash.

"I knew it. I'm getting out of here."

"Oh no." Feeling shaken I began to cry.

"Christ. What's wrong with you now. I didn't mean to hurt you. But you act like a psycho."

"Rolando. Please don't go. I promise I'll be better."

"Christ. You fucking nuts."

"Oh please Rolando."

"OK," he said obligingly once again easily distracted by sloppy but ravenous kisses.

I backed him to the bed and we collapsed wriggling out of our clothes. Oh god I need this to live. Even though it could only be at best a pale imitation. I must have something to fill the yearning vacuum between my legs.

He balked though seeing me reach into a bedside drawer for a rubber. "Aw no. Don't make me put one of those things on."

"You have to. You're a filthy little disease-ridden greaseball."

"What are you talking about. Now you're insulting me. I don't have to take that shit. First you beat up on me. How dare you. You the one who probably got diseases you so crazy. Let me out of here." But I don't think he meant it at all this time. He's ready to slip it in and be done with it.

"I didn't mean it. Please let me."

"I can't do it with one of those things."

"What do you mean. Of course you can." My head was pounding from the collision with the bathroom door. I unwrapped the offending item and tried to roll it on but he squirmed and squirmed until in a few seconds my hands were wet and sticky.

"Oh no."

"Ah. I told you I couldn't."

"Shit," I said totally desolate now. As he got up to dress I sat watching him head in hands. "How old are you Rolando."

"Sixteen."

"Ha. You were too old anyway."

"Lady," he said backing out the door, "you know what you are. You are a real pervert."

A blow from the skies has devastated me. Kim is returning to the East Coast and to her ex-husband. And taking my life's blood with her. In a sense I am relieved at the cessation of falsehood and temptation. But now more than ever I must see him to put right the damage.

"Hello?"

Oh god it's his voice on the other end. "Hello. Scott. It's so good to hear you. This is Sybil. I want to talk to you before you leave."

A second of silence. Then I heard, "Hello. Hello." Pause. Then, "They hung up." And the line was dead.

Having lost not only the sole source of ecstasy in my life but the only person who offered unconditional affection as well I am now thoroughly convinced of the existence of cosmic justice. Kim's absence is no relief. There is no one to convince me of my worth. And I could use some convincing.

However I made an interesting observation during the evening commute as the bus passed a school I must have seen every day for several years but in my warped desperation only just noticed. Several boys indulging in various sport activities or spectating. Possibly a hundred of all ages. And as we crept past in the rush-hour traffic. I thought I saw a head of golden curls.

Perhaps tonight I'll veer by there on the way to 222. I can't fare worse than last time. I may even get lucky and find another dusty angel. Surely there exists another somewhere. After all. This is a big city. I may be lonely. But I never have to be alone.

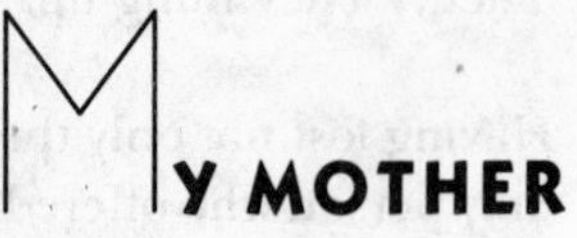

MY MOTHER

Kathy Acker

1. MY MOTHER'S SPEAKING:

I'm in love with red. I dream in red.

My nightmares are based on red. Red's the color of passion, of joy. Red's the color of all the journeys which are interior, the color of the hidden flesh, of the depths and recesses of the unconscious. Above all, red is the color of rage and violence.

I was six years old. Every night immediately after supper, which I usually was allowed to take with my parents, I would say good night. To reach my room, I'd have to walk down a long dark corridor which was lined with doors on either side. I was terrified. Each door half-opened to unexpected violence.

Morality and moral judgments protect us only from fear.

In my dreams, it was I who murdered and simultaneously was murdered.

Moral ambiguity's the color of horror.

I was born on October 6, 1945, in Brooklyn, New York. My parents were rich, but not of the purest upper class. I'm talking about my father. At age six, I suddenly took off for unknown regions, the regions of dreams and secret desires. Most of my life, but not all, I've been dissolute. According to a nineteenth-century cliché, dissoluteness and debauchery are connected to art.

I wrote: "The child's eyes pierce the night. I'm a sleepwalker trying to clear away the shadows, but when sound asleep, kneel in front of their crucifix and Virgin.

"Holy images covered every wall of my parents' house.

"Their house had the immobility of a nightmare.

"The first color I knew is that of horror."

Almost everything that I know and can know about my pre-adult life lies not in memories, but in these writings.

"Religion:

"Days and nights all there was was a sordid and fearful childhood. Morality wore the habit of religion. Mortal sin or the Saint of Sunday and the Ashes of Wednesday kept on judging me. Thus, condemnation and repression crushed me before I was born. Childhood was stolen from children.

"Never enough can be said, muttered and snarled, when one has been born into anger. THEIR criminal hands took hold of my fate. HER umbilical cord strangled me dropping out of her. All I desired was everything.

"Listen to the children. All children come red out of the womb because their mothers know God.

"The night's replete with their cries: unceasing flagellated howls which are broken by the sound of a window slammed shut. Harsh and drooling screams die in lips that are muzzled. We who're about to be suffocated throw our murmurs and screeches, our names, into a hole; that hole is everywhere. They laugh waterfalls of scorn down on us. If any speech comes out of us, it appears as nonsense; when the adults answered me, I puked. My few cries, like dead leaves tumbled by winds, climbed out of my body and vaporized.

"It is a very Parisian garden which I found for hiding myself.

My mother was a great lady. Whenever she walked into the local grocery store which the neighborhood rich used, she'd order whatever young boy she could find to fetch the various items she happened to desire and to bring them to the taxi waiting for her. It didn't occur to Mother that she might have to pay.

If it was my misfortune to accompany her, I'd crawl behind her, trying to be invisible. I didn't know her. Me, an orphan. As soon as she was about to leave the store, as quickly as possible I'd pay the man behind the counter. My face flamed as if struck by sun. I don't know what happened when I wasn't there to pay: at that time events which I didn't perceive didn't take place.

At that time I thought, let them all go to hell.

It's entirely possible that I wasn't the only person who knew that Mother could always do as she wanted. For the Queen of England never carries her own money. Someone's money.

Three or four times, trying to escape her, I ran away. Since my father was so gentle he was subservient to Mother, I also had to run away from him.

I climbed down their back fire escape to the street below. Walked on streets till there was nowhere to go.

"There's a white man behind the spindly trees. He leans into the sky to grasp at the wood and falls down on all fours, a dog. On pebbles. Now he's crawling across the street, stretches out one hand as if it's dead. Trying to become a wall, I hide against one. Sooted ivy and begonias are crushed. Another man rises up; his face burning and lips too red. He walks toward me, hand touching his cock, and another man, aghast, leaps out of a window. His arms beat against the sky as if he's a windmill. Through the froth on his lips, he says, 'They've stolen me.' "

Walked down the streets until there was nowhere.

"A lying hypocritical society turns around the grave of the holes in the garden of childhood."

I had to return to home.

I didn't want to escape my parents because I hated them, but because I was wild. Wild children are honest. My mother wanted to command me to the point that I no longer existed. My father was so gentle, he didn't exist. I remained uneducated or wild because I was imprisoned by my mother and had no father.

My body was all I had.

"a a a a I don't know what language is. I I I I I shall never learn to count."

I remained selfish. There was only my mother and I.

Selfishness and curiosity are conjoint. I'd do anything to find out about my body, investigated the stenches arising out of trenches and armpits, the tastes in every hole. No one taught me regret. I was wild to make my body's imaginings actual.

And I knew I couldn't escape from my parents because I was female, not yet eighteen years old. Even if there was work for a female minor, my parents my educators and my society had taught me I was powerless and needed either parents or a man to survive. I couldn't fight the whole world; I only hated.

So in order to escape my parents, I needed a man. After I had escaped, I could and would hate the man who was imprisoning me. And after that, I would be anxious to annihilate my hatred, my double bind.

This personal and political state was the only one they had taught me. "I'm always in the wrong so I'm a freak. I'm always destroying everything including myself which is what I want to do."

Red was the color of wildness and of what is as yet unknown.

As my body, which my mother refused to recognize and thus didn't control, grew, it grew into sexuality. As if sexuality can occur without touching. Masturbated not only before I knew what the word masturbation meant, but before I could come. Physical time became a movement toward orgasm. I became sexually wilder. I wanted a man to help me escape my parents, but not for sexual reasons, because I didn't need another sexual object. Mine was my own skin.

Longing equaled skin. Skin didn't belong to anyone in my kingdom of untouchability.

I hadn't decided to be a person. I was almost refusing to become a person because the moment I was, I would have to be lonely. Conjunction with the entirety of the universe is one way to avoid suffering.

"Today I don't have any friends. Mother's criticized everyone I've tried to know as being 'nouveau riche' or 'not pious enough.' This idiot finds it normal to run to a priest to ask him whether it's all right for me to play with whatever friend I'm lucky enough to have. No one's ever good enough for her or her priest.

"Mother just hates everyone who isn't of our blood. She uses the word 'blood.' She hates everyone and everything that she can't control: everything gay, lively, everything that's growing, productive. Humaneness throws her into a panic; when she panics, she does her best to hurt me.

"I've taken refuge in the basement. In its stale air. Jesus sits dead in its windows.

"I found safety there, sitting on a horse who was rocking on decaying moleskins or crouching on a red cushion which needed to be repaired. There I told myself story after story. Every story is real. One story always leads to another story. Most of the stories tell how I'm born:

" 'Before I was born, I lived in Heaven. There the inhabitants spend their time imaging a sweet white Jesus who kills President Mitterrand of the United States or a golden Joseph, swaddled in velvet, who plays heavy metal. There're dolls everywhere. But I owned a cap gun which I used to blind pigeons and minutely examined my body. Then I entered a world in which, since God sees everything that happens there, I had to become curious.'

"God followed me into the basement. Though I was curious, He frightened me. I decided that curiosity has to be stronger than fear and that I need curiosity plus fear, for I'm going to journey through unknown, wonderful and ecstatic realms. If there is God, the coupling of curiosity and fear is the door to the unknown.

"For a while there was no one in my life."

I became older.

"Then I adored the maid who was younger than me. One day she told me she was planning to get married and have a child.

" 'I'll dress my baby only in white,' the maid said.

" 'You can't do that,' I replied, 'because you're poverty-stricken.'

"Her face turned the color of my cunt's lips. It was she who was red, not me.

" 'I'm not poor: I work and my boyfriend has a steady job with the subway.'

"The word *work* meant nothing to me; I continued to try to teach her that she was too poor to afford a baby. That she couldn't clothe a baby.

"In desperation Henrietta (the maid) couldn't find any language; finally she located the word *evil*. I was *evil*.

"This word *evil* made me begin to think.

"I remembered how my mother calls her *the girl* and talks about her in the third person even when Henrietta's in the same room. Whereas if I show the slightest disrespect to any of my parents' friends, I'm severely punished. I see that I'm being trained to want only the girls who come from the wealthiest and most socially powerful families as my friends. I see that education is one means by which this class and economic system become incorporated in the body as personal rules. The world outside me that's human seems to be formed by economics, hierarchy, and class.

"I'm anything but free.

"I want Henrietta to explain to me the degree of filth proper to each class.

"After that I fell in love with the gardener. Eight years old, I was no longer human.

"There's the country. I'm learning the names of the flowers of night and those of water, heliotrope and St.-John's-wort, water lilies and all the sorts of roses. I know that there are birds of the evening and those of the night; bats, screech owls, and baby owls fallen out of their nests and drowned in a pail of water haunt my dreams.

"The summer air in the grotto, like a blind cat, walks down my stomach. I had to disappear finally. I pressed myself between a gray-red wall and its ivy growing up from the ground. In there,

I became many-legged, a spider, a hedgehog and raccoon, every animal I'll ever want to be and every animal that is.

"This is what God saw when He followed me into the basement.

"I observed wheat fields, corn fields, clover the colors of flesh, poppy and huge cornflower fields, fields framed by weeping willows and poplars.

"Behind mother's kitchen, a plain which is sparkling in the sun appears. Cricket-rustling and fat bumblebee-buzzing. Filthy flies are fertilizing its pastures. In the full of noon I walk out here. My head bare to the light, the hay scabbed my knees. There was a new taste on my hot lips, lavender and burning skin. I'm journeying in order to know vertigo and enchantment.

"My father showed me all of this and more: dragonflies, the kingfishers, and wrens, the day-flies and all that glistens around them; wild ducks, turkey hens, and all the fish. Daddy taught me the trees and the seasons, tar, the forests and fire.

"Now and forever, I no longer care about religion.

"No religion: this is the one event that'll never change. No religion is my stability and surety.

"Mother's demanding that I see her priest."

I couldn't escape my family because I still didn't know a man who would help me.

For reasons other than escape, I wanted this man to be wilder than me.

When I was twenty-three, it began to be possible for me to escape my parents. I started to remember directly, not just through writing, all that happened to me. A sailor is a man who keeps on approaching the limits of what is describable.

I was wild. My brother was the first man who helped me: I spent an increasing amount of time in his apartment.

It was the days of ghosts. Still is. Not the death, but the actual forgetting even of the death of sexuality and wonderment, of all but those who control and those and that which can be controlled. Since an emotion's an announcement of value, in this society of death (of values), emotions moved like zombies through humans.

At my brother's house I met artists. Romare Bearden. Maya Deren. This hint that it was possible to live in a community other than my parents', a community that wasn't hateful and boring, one of intellectuals, by opening up the world of possibilities, saved me from despair and nihilism.

I still couldn't break with my parents' society on my own.

There Paul Rendier took my virginity. Fucking enabled me to cast off my past; red gave me the authority to be other than red.

Once I had fucked, the only thing I wanted was to give myself entirely and absolutely to another person. I didn't and don't know what this desire means other than itself.

In me dead blood blushed crimson into the insides of roses and became a living color that's unnameable.

When Rendier left me and I didn't know where he was, I had to find him because all that was left of me, all that was me, was to give myself to him.

In order to run after Rendier, I had to break with my family. My father was already dead; he had left me enough money so I no longer economically needed a man. I know that women need men not just due to weakness. I escaped my mother because sexuality was stronger than her.

Then I found Rendier. We lived together one year.

After Rendier, "I threw myself onto every bed as a dead sailor flings himself into the sea. My sexuality at that time was separate from my real being. For my real being's an ocean in which all beings die and grow.

"The acceptance of this separation between sexuality and being was the invention of hell."

Searching, I traveled to Berlin. There I lived with a doctor named Wartburg whose apartment I wouldn't leave. I never saw anyone but him. I had wanted to give myself to another and now I was beginning to. Wartburg put me in dog collars; while I was on all fours, he held me by a leash and beat me with a dog whip. He was elegant and refined and looked like Jean Genet.

At that time, "nobody was able to look for me, find me, join me."

What dominated me totally was my need to give myself entirely and absolutely directly to my lover. I knew that I belonged to the community of artists or freaks, not because the anger in me was unbearable, but because my overpowering wish to give myself away wasn't socially acceptable. As yet I hadn't asked if there was someone named *me*.

At this time I first read de Sade. Perusing *120 Days in Sodom* exulted and horrified me: horror because I recognized my self or desire.

Living with Wartburg ended; I had no money nor friends in Berlin. All I wanted was to be entirely alone. I had strong political convictions so I took off for Russia. There I couldn't speak any language.

Loneliness and my kind of life in Russia physically deteriorated me to such a point that I almost died.

From that time onwards, I have always felt anxiety based on this following situation: I need to give myself away to a lover and simultaneously I need to be always alone. Such loneliness can be a form of death. My brother found me in Russia and brought me back to New York.

I first attempted to dissipate my anxiety by deciding to fuck and be fucked only when there could be no personal involvement. I traveled on trains, like a sailor, and made love with men I encountered on those trains.

My attempt failed. Friends said about me, "She's on her way to dying young." But I wanted more than most people to live because just being alive wasn't enough for me. Wildness or curiosity about my own body was showing itself as beauty. My brother placed as much importance in sexuality as I did. When I met Bourenine at one of the orgies my brother gave, I was ready to try again to give myself to another, to someone who was more intelligent than me and a committed radical.

Anxiety had turned into a physical disease. Bourenine said that he wanted to save me from myself, my wildness, my weakness. He made me feel safe enough to try to give myself to him.

I became so physically weak that I stood near to death. When Bourenine believed that I might die, he began to love me. I began to hate him yet I worshiped him because I thought he protected me. My gratitude has always been as strong as my curiosity, as is mostly true in those who are wild.

Even then I knew that most men saw me as a woman who fucked every man in sight. Since Bourenine wanted to be my father, he didn't want me to make my own decisions. I saw myself as split between two desperations: to be loved by a man and to be alone so I could begin to be. When I met B, he was married. I didn't mind because I didn't really want to deal with an other. Since B immediately saw me as I saw myself, I saw in B a friend and one who wouldn't try, since he was married, to stop me from becoming a person, rather than wild.

From the first moment that B and I spoke together in the Brasserie Lipp, there was a mutual confidence between us.

I had pushed my life to an edge. Having to give myself away absolutely to a lover and simultaneously needing to find "myself." Now I had to push my life more.

Bourenine's inability to deal with what was happening to me turned him violent and aggressive. During this period, B and I met several times and discussed only political issues. As soon as I began speaking personally to him, we commenced spending as much time alone with each other as we could.

Wildness changed into friendship.

I had already written, "No religion: this is the one event that will never change. No religion is my only stability and security.

"Mother insisted that I see her priest to such a degree that I had to.

"Let me describe this Director of Human Morality. (One of the Directors of Human Morality.) While his hands were sneaking everywhere, all he could see in my words was his own fear.

"Right after I saw him, I wrote down in my secret notebook, 'Religion is a screen behind which the religious shields himself from suffering, death, and life. The religious decide everything prior to the fact; religion's a moral system because by means of religion the religious assure themselves that they're right.

" 'From now on I'm going to decide for myself and live according to *my* decisions—decisions out of desire. I'll always look . . . like a sailor who carries his huge cock in his hand. . . . I'll travel and travel by reading. I won't read in order to become more intelligent, but so that I can see as clearly as possible that there's too much lying and hypocrisy in this world. I knew from the first moment what I was, that I hated them, the hypocrites.'

"As soon as I had written this down, I knew that I was dreadfully and magnificently alone.

"I am now seventeen years old.

"All around me are termites, familial households without their imaginations. They would never rise an iota above their daily tasks, daily obligations, daily distractions. Everyone who's around me has lost the sense that life's always pushing itself over an edge while everything is being risked.

"So now there's going to be a war! Hey! Finally something exciting's going to happen! The United States's coming back to life! The government of the United States is realizing that someone's angry about something-or-other and's descending to offer its people a target for their bilious bitterness. O emotionless sentimental and sedentary people, because your government's a democracy and responsible to you, it is giving you a whole race to detest, a nation on which to spit, a religion to damn, everything you've ever wanted. You're incontestably superior to men who wear dresses. Again you will become important in the eyes of the world.

"You Americans need to be right. This war will not only be a pathway to future glory: once war's begun, you'll feel secure because you'll no longer have to understand anything else. You will again know what good and evil are.

"Tomorrow you are going to give your sons joyfully to the desert, maybe daughters if you're feminist enough, because you're emotionless and, in war, you can be so emotionless, you don't have to be. Therefore war allows people to surpass themselves. The English know this full well. As soon as you have tanks and dead people all around you, you'll be able to feel alive, once more powerful, magnanimous and generous to all the world.

"All that your grandparents and parents, educators, and society showed you, the triumphal road, the right way, the path of true virtue—the RIGHT, the GOOD—is only Liberty mutilated and Freedom shredded into scraps of flesh. The raped body. A man's a child who walks down the right road, thoroughly carved out and signposted, because all he can see is the word *danger*."

2. LETTERS FROM MY MOTHER TO MY FATHER:

(The days of begging, the days of theft. No nation who began for the sake of escape and by fire can be all bad. Even if democracy is a myth. Myths make actuality, that's what myths say. Me, I've always been on fire for the sake of fire.

(Listen. They thought they could have their freedom through something called democracy, but they forgot about knowledge and no one's ever had freedom anyways. So now it's all falling apart, this economy, a so-called culture and a society, so-called, and anyway there's never been anything except loneliness, the days of begging, the days of theft.

(This is what the books tell about American history: You can travel and wherever you'll go, there'll be no one but you. Listen, American history says: the sky's blue and every shade of purple and then so bright that your eyes have to be red in order to see it.

(A sun declines in front of you. The sunless air'll make your fingers grow red and there spots will swell. Every possible color in the world'll sit in this sky until evening black spreads over the air or your pupils, and you will never be able to know which.

JOIN THE U.S. ARMY
GET KILLED

(Solitary, mad, deprived of community, depraved and proud of all your depravity, you dream, no longer of a lover, but solely of sex the way a rat desires garbage.

(Stronger than dreams will be your inability to forget what you don't know.

(Specifics: northern California. Myths say, settled by white bums and white prostitutes desperate for gold. Who, as soon as they had found the yellow, tried to decimate all nonwhites. And kept on trying. Born out of attempted murder, loneliness, and wildness. The yellows who survived formed their own gangs. The cities born out of riffraff and, unlike those back East, knew no culture.

(Said that they could never be poor.

(What we're dealing with here is a race of degenerates. A mongrel people who doesn't know how to do anything but hate itself. No wonder they love God so much because God doesn't exist. We're dealing with a people manifestly incapable of manifest Destiny.

(Thieves or imbeciles. Take your choice or chance. Sooner or later some people'll govern these lands, but not until all their inhabitants have died.

(In other words: ungovernable.)

LETTER

Dear B,

Our friendship has no stability. Our meetings are taking place only by chance. Well, maybe that's how things—reality is.

All my emotions, fantasies, imaginings, desires are reality because I must have a life that matters, that is emotional.

I don't want to speak anymore about anything that's serious. I just want to speak.

I'm writing you and I'm going to keep on writing you so that all the fantasies that we have about each other through which we keep perceiving each other will die. After that we'll be so naked with each other that I will be your flesh. You mine.

I don't need to tell you any of this because you already know. But you're still running away from me and I hate it when you do this.

This is what I want to say: When I saw you in the early evening, sometime around 7:30, your friend, whoever was with you, looked right through me. Just as if I was still a child wearing the ring that I had always wanted that renders its bearer invisible. I'm not your child.

If I could be invisible and go everywhere, I would. To outlandish lands and where there are great people.

While your friend was staring through me, you stood up and walked past me without noticing me. I remember the first time we met alone: we talked together for hours, almost until the sun rose, then despite my shyly asking you to stay, you left my brother's apartment.

None of all I've just said matters. That's the point.

All that matters to me now, has mattered to me, to the point that it's painful, is that we tell each other everything. Since I fear rejection more than anything else, I must have trust. Then I won't be able to leave your life and you won't be able to leave mine. Despite the fact that—I'm not going to waste my time trying to explain this to you or convince you that this is true—your world is cozy. Me—I'm nothing. I promise you that I won't blame you for your smugness. You need that kind of crap: images of richness, maybe because you weren't born that way, so you can live confidently in this world. I need to be invisible and without language, animal.

ADDENDUM

If you want to contact me, you'll have to find me.

If you really know me, you can do this.

I started writing you because I believed that if we told each other everything, there could be only trust between us. Then we wouldn't be able to hurt each other so much that we destroyed each other's lives.

I just told you that I despise your bourgeoisie and your wealthy friends.

Maybe it isn't possible for two people to be together without barriers in a state of unredeemable violence.

I think that Mother was still with Bourenine, but I don't know for sure.

LETTER

Dear B,

The more I try to tell you everything, the more I have to find myself. The more I try to describe myself, the more I find a hole. So the more I keep saying, the less I say and the more there is to say. I'm confusing everything between us.

I'm not being clear here.

I don't want to tell you anything.

The only thing that's possible between us is a car accident. A car accident's now the only thing that can deliver me from the anguish that's you.

I'm dumb, wild, and I don't want anyone coming too near me. But the more emotion comes out, the more I want you.

I've been writing down every type of fatal accident I can imagine. Whenever I do this, I feel calm and as if I'm orgasming. I know I have to follow death until its end. That road passes through putrefaction and disintegration.

Whenever I'm traveling that road, I'm calm.

When I'm lying in your arms, I'm calm.

At the same time I have to battle you; there's something in me that has to oppose you in even the most trivial of matters.

I still tell you everything as if I'm more than naked with you. I hate you. My mind's moving round and round, in tighter and tighter spirals. It's going to end up in a prison, a void, destroying itself. I always try to defeat myself.

Until the present I've thrown away my past. As soon as something's been over, I've gotten rid of it; I've acted as if that relationship never happened. I never had memories that I wanted.

Now I believe that, though I'm still doing everything possible to defeat myself, our friendship, to misunderstand you, and to view everything in the worst possible light, you're going to always be with me. I believe you're not going to leave me. I believe without understanding this that you see exactly what I am and that you're guiding me.

At the same time I've been observing that our friendship's

changing me: I no longer know who I am and I'm beginning to see what I am. So when you're observing me and know me and guiding me, you're perceiving I-don't-know-who-anymore. This combination of your eye and I-don't-know-who-anymore is a work of art made by both of us and it's untitled.

Now I'm rational.

I know you hate me when I'm rational because, as you've told me, you don't like it when there are rules. You don't like rules.

Here are my most recent thoughts: When I met you, I was drowning because I wasn't going to let another person be close to me. (This frigidity is named "wildness.") I asked you rather than anyone else for help because I knew that you're an emotional paralytic. Perverse, as usual, I hollered "Help!" so that you'd beat me over the head so I'd finally drown or fall off a crumbling cliff. What I really wanted to do. You're just what I want, B: a better death method.

I decided to tell you everything because, by telling you everything, I'd make you kill me faster. I always want to test everything to the point of death. Beyond.

(Children and dogs squatted in the dirt.

("This looks like the high road to Hell," one kid said.

("From Hell."

(It was a desolate land, a populace who had nothing except government criminals, and now it was going to war. Since no one knew where the country they were fighting was, no one thought anything was real.

(What the weapons might be in this war of the imagination made actual no person knew. Half-buried skeletons of cows, horses with mouths dried open, cats' and goats' legs.

IN THEIR OWN LANDS THE ARABS TEAR OUT EACH OTHER'S EYEBALLS AND RAPE THEIR OWN CHILDREN. IF ONE AMERICAN SOLDIER GOES INTO BATTLE, BECAUSE RIGHT MAKES MIGHT, HE HAS TO WIN.

—SOME AMERICAN GOVERNMENT OFFICIAL

(When a man on his deathbed had told the child that he had killed many men, the child was envious.

(Through the rest of his childhood, the child bore the idol of a perfection to which he could never attain. All he could be was a mercenary.

(Every son is heir to the death of his father: every son needs this death to experience a preliminary death and every son must have his father die so that he can live.

(What about his father's life? When a child inherits the father's life, he inherits his place in the prison of morality and can never break out.

(In other words: we are the children without inheritance.

(He was fucked over as a child. When he grew up, he looked for a trade. Searched. Since he always wore black, people thought him a preacher. But he had never witnessed anything that had to do with God.

(The country went to war, as it always did, in some other country.

(He watched men being killed in many ways and women left for dead and forgotten.

(Then he glimpsed ships. He observed vultures as large as any tree but too high up to be seen in detail. He was too lost to want to do anything but soar.

(One day, he came upon a woman who told fortunes. He thought, as if there's a fortune to be told.

(Asked her about the fortune of the lost. "What's going to happen to me?"

(She gibbered at some night.

(Asked again, "In a society of murderers, how can children be educated to something else?"

(The beautiful woman answered that they should be raised with the wild dogs.

(He replied that life wasn't a laughing matter.

(The woman asked, "How's it possible to be lost? How can anything that exists be lost?

("The cards have been lost in the night. Pull out these cards."

(She turned his cards over: "Your problem is desire. You've

unsuccessfully tried to resolve, dissolve, desire through work. The result of this repression is that either you must go to war or you are at war. The cards are unclear on this temporal point. You're now moving through the negative part of that dialectic; there'll be synthesis when your centralized power has died.")

LETTER

Dear B,

At this moment because I'm perverse I'm telling myself: Without you I'm lost. I'm letting myself realize what I don't usually let myself. And as soon as I see that I need you, I imagine your absence. Again and again I'm picturing you rejecting me. This is the moment I love.

(I never had a father. This isn't correct because, science says, every animal has a father. I never knew my father which fact, for me, is the same as not having a father.

(I'm writing about my father whom I never knew.)

LETTER

Dear B,

I doubt everything.

You're asking me two questions: Do I think that you don't love me because I doubt your love? Do I think you'll never trust me because I doubt?

No.

When I doubt to the point that emptiness sits under my skin and someone or something feels nausea, I begin to be. Everything that used to irritate and still rasps me is now wonderful and desirable.

Of course there are times when I can't bear this relationship to doubt. When I hate that which gives me the most pleasure.

I don't want everything to be complex; I don't want to live in closed rooms like some academic. I want everything between us and everything to be simple. That is, real. Like flesh. Not hypocritical.

But in the past when I tried to kill off hypocrisy, I destroyed possibilities for love.

I will not descend into the night, for that romanticism is a disease.

(My dream: We're kissing, but I feel nothing. He takes my clothes off me, then picks me naked up off the floor. Carries me into somewhere. In there he cradles me as if I'm a child. I grab what I feel to be safety. At that moment he starts systematically hurting me. After hurting me for a long time, he holds me and the world opens up.)

Mother moved into her brother's apartment.

LETTER

I said that I wanted us to be so naked with each other that the violence of my passion was amputating me for you.

Listen. I am not a victim.

I don't know what the end of all this can be.

At the moment neither of us is in danger.

Mother didn't want to live with my father.

CONTINUATION OF LETTER

I want to be clearer about what I just said:

You don't believe that you own me. What you think, precisely, is that you've put me in slavery and I'll always be your slave. You now control, limit, imprison, bar, categorize and define my existence.

I'm hot.

As soon as you saw that I got pleasure from yielding to you, you turned away from me. Then I really lay myself at your feet.

You stated that you were denying me because you needed to be private.

But what's real to you isn't real to me. I'm not you.

Precisely: my truth is that your presence in my life for me is absence.

I'll say this another way: You believe that everything that's outside you ("reality") is a reflection of your perceptions, thoughts, ideas, etc. In other words, that you can see, feel, hear, understand the world. Other people. I don't believe that. I believe that I'm so apart from the world, from other people, that I have to explain everything to every single person to such an extent, in order to communicate at all, that for me communication's almost impossible. Day by day my actuality has become more and more hollow and is now breaking apart like a body decomposing under my own eyes.

You've destroyed every possibility of religion for me and I want you to help me.

(The United States, begun on less than zero, on dislike negation and fire, had inflated itself into an empire. Now, it has returned to less than zero. My mother realized this. The Christ of her mother had taught her that she had no right to exist; love had taught her otherwise. Fuck all of that. My mother thought. She wrote love letters to my father while knowing that they didn't matter.

(Mother said, "Nothing matters when there is nothing.")

LETTER

Dear B,

I've told you that I never want to live with you. (I can't live with you because you're married.) Now something more: I have to be alone.

This isn't rejection.

I'm going to go away from you so that I can find something new, maybe a "me." Then we'll be able to be completely naked with each other and perceive each other as each of us actually is.

Whatever it takes so this can happen.

I know you think that my desire to be alone is just one more instance of how I run away from everything. That I've tried to run away to the extent that I no longer wanted to have a self. (If there is a self.)

This is what I think: In the face of death,

(There's no more education, no more culture [if culture depends on a commonly understood history], and perhaps no more middle class in the United States. There's War.)

when all is real,

(In the face of this very real American death, there is only the will to live.)

I will be able (to have a self) to say something, "I've seen him, I can say his real name. I know that nothing, including this, matters."

In other words: there's nothing.

Because there's nothing, I don't have to be trained, as females are, to want to stop existing.

But: Your desire for me when I see you halts my breath. Want torches my mouth into contortions. No longer a mouth. You're mad.

If only in public I could throw myself on top of your feet and kiss them so everyone would know. But I can't have anything to do with you publicly.

I'm frightened that my ability to go all the way with you, to give myself to you in ownership and at the same time know that everything between us has to be a lie in the face of your marriage will destroy me: my honesty, my integrity. For by railing and revolting against bourgeois hypocrisy, I became me.

It's because of you I now sleep and want to eat. Since I'll not deny my own body, I now know that I can and will lie ignobly, superbly, triumphantly.

(Mother thought that there must be romance other than romance. According to Elisabeth Roudinesco in her study of Lacan, around 1924 a conjuncture of early Feminism, a new wave of Freudianism, and Surrealism gave rise to a new representation of the female: nocturnal, dangerous, fragile, and powerful. The rebellious, criminal, insane, or gay woman is no longer perceived as a slave to her symptoms. Instead, "in the negative idealization of crime [she] discovers the means to struggle against a society [which disgusts].")

LETTER

Dear B,

You want me to live a lie and you admire me for my honesty. Repeatedly you've said that you respect my intelligence more than that of any woman you've ever met and you treat me convulsively and continually like less than a dog. Female variety.

I still believe that you know everything about me and I don't think that you understand anything that has to do with me.

The only conclusion to all this is that reality has reversed itself. The reversement, which is a window, has set me on fire.

My conclusion isn't sweet. You call it "a penchant for the night." But I no longer have a penchant for the night.

At this moment I'm halfway between life and death. And death and life.

I'm now trying to write down something called *truth*. Which isn't *my truth* because I'm not an enclosed or self-sufficient being.

My conclusion: You're no longer behind everything that happens. You, sexual love. Since you're no longer at the bottom of everything, where I know I can always find you, no one can mean anything to me anymore.

I hate our wildness. The only life each of us has is when we're together. Just as I had to escape my family, now I have to get away from you, from the mad rhythm named *us*, from our nights, from *horror*.

FROM THE DIARIES OF A WOLF BOY

♥ ♥

David Wojnarowicz

I'm still a piece of meat like something in the 14th street markets swinging from stinking hooks in the blurry dragqueen dusk. Maybe a hundred dollars to my name, no place to live and I can't hustle anymore. I'm trying to keep my body beyond the deathly fingers of my past but I'm fucked up bad never learned shit of how to create structures other than chaos. I'm attracted to chaos because of all the possibilities and I don't have to choose any of them or die frozen inside any of them but right now all I know is that I am tired, bone and brain tired. I woke up in this guys bed in the middle of the night and realized not a whole lot had changed since I got off the streets. He was an alcoholic doctor I'd known on and off over a handful of years and he let me live with him for the last couple of weeks cooking me upper-class meals in return for me fucking him legs over my shoulders like a video stud. He could have gone on forever like this but the distinct sensation of being made of glass, of being completely invisible to him, was growing and curving like a cartoon wave. So fucking dark I don't even have the energy to throw myself off a building or bridge. Now he's starting to come home slam-down drunk banging into walls moaning and crying falling down in his pristine kitchen and hoisting his pale legs into the air murmuring: Fuck me my lovely. I told him one night he needed some help and he responded by bringing home a hustler from west street and I ended up sleeping on the livingroom floor.

The doctor takes me on a weeks vacation in his station wagon up to the coast of maine. No license but I'm driving the almost deserted interstate north. I haven't slept for about two days and feel sort of drugged, hypnotic lines of the dawns highway wavering like an unraveled hypnotists disk. Kind of beautiful and foliage on the shoulders still illuminated by the tungsten lamps blip blip blip. The doctor vaguely woke up and his hand drifted over the armrest between us and slid over my leg slowly back and forth till I got a hard-on. Then his sleepy fingers unbuttoned my trousers and he leaned over taking my dick in his mouth. There was a car way up ahead of us and another way behind; beacons of headlights circling the hills and the sky still turning; still and black night being pushed up through the sky over the car by quiet surfacing day. My whole body stiffened with my hands on the wheel. I had a hard-on for thirty miles moving my hips up and down finally shooting into his mouth; my eyes closing slightly and dreamily and the sudden surprise as a lone car overtook us and sped past causing me to realize I'd slowed down to fifteen miles per hour.

He rented a motel room somewhere on the breezy ocean. Sort of an oddly beautiful coastline but I knew all this was temporary so I couldn't let myself buy into it. I went for a walk while he slept and climbed through the craggy rock postcard views among postcard families and vacationing heterosexuals. Finally off the sand and up onto this mammoth asphalt parking lot bordering the motel. This guy, young and handsome in an indefinable way; short brown hair, a pair of dark shorts that revealed muscular legs slightly browned from weather and sun, a ruddy color to his forehead and cheeks and nose, he just coasted up on a bicycle and stopped short a distance away checking me out. I was walking under this long canopied bench area so I sat on one of the empty seats, folded my arms over the back of the bench and laid my head on it staring at him sideways. He rolled a little closer and dismounted, standing next to his bike hands thrust deep into pockets for a while. He finally moved towards me one more time then tossed back the hair from over his eyes, a boyish gesture suggestive of a remote past in school days; something that still makes me weak in the knees. He said: Hey, hello. I straightened up and said: How's it going? He gestured: Okay. with his head and then said: Where do ya go around here for fun? I told him I just got into town and didn't know nothing. I felt that blush in my chest as we talked stupid talk never quite revealing our queerness to each other but somehow wordlessly generating volumes of desire. Like some kind of sub-language that makes you just want to splash into it even with all its tensions. He continued loose conversation watching me closely for reactions to his coded words and then finally seemed to abandon it all and said: You want to get together later? We made a date for 11:00 p.m. at the same spot and I walked away wondering how to handle the doctor.

The doctor started drinking after dinner and I encouraged him to go to bed. He finally fell asleep around 10:45 and I slipped from between the sheets, put on my clothes and fished the room key out of his pocket. Every movement noiseless until the barely audible click of the lock of the door. I walked to the bench area overlooking the ocean and stood around. The night was heavy, the water indiscernible in the darkness. The tide was way out so it was just this screen of grainy blackness that contained the rushing hollow sounds of waves crashing way out there. Every so often a lone car would swing to the edge of the lot, its headlights illuminating one patch of ocean in a field of circular light;

and beyond that light one could see the low caps of broken waves spreading in towards shore, illuminated as if by luminous microbes. I walked down onto the sand out into the darkness to see how far I could go before I touched water, leaving behind me the cars turning round and round and the windows of the motel burning along the beach with rectangles of orange light and the flap of banners and flags as the staff hoisted them on poles for the holidays.

I got close to the waters edge when an old ghost of a man materialized and with his open palms stretching out towards me I heard a murmur: Want some action? I turned and walked to the opening of the bay along the coastline, climbing the boulders to the back end of the parking lot. Walking back to the bench area two local toughs: HEY. YO. came up fast behind me, their arms dangling at their sides like whirligigs. Both were kind of sexy but dangerous. One guy with close-cropped hair and a red face said: Any women out here tonight? So they're coming up on me on both sides with that shit about women, spinning their heads from side to side looking for witnesses. I became as charming as possible: Cigarette? As they took them a car spun in the lot illuminating all of us and I took that moment to tip towards the headlights and lose myself among the parked cars. I circled back to the benches and the young guy I'd met earlier was sitting on the hood of his car. He told me to get in and we drove out into the town, parking behind a deserted bank and walking through the streets looking for a bar. He wanted to drink some beers. His name was Joe and he was in town for the naval reserves, a two-week training with a few days off in between. There were no regular bars around just a couple of queer joints with heavy cover charges and pounding disco, so we ended up walking a couple miles down a dark road talking about ourselves and the distances we'd been. We turned back at some point and passed through the town on our way back to his car. The gear-heads were out in their pickup trucks whizzing around the curves of the small streets. One truck sped by a club we were approaching and white ugly distended faces blew out of the side windows screaming: WE HATE QUEERS! I turned to him: Let's go somewhere. Okay? Yeah, he said: We really should. There's got to be a place we can just sit down and have a drink and talk. I was wondering if I had this guy wrong; if that's all he wanted was talking company. I was already drawn in by the movements of his chest and belly beneath his shirt, the movements of his arms and the outline of his thighs in his trousers. I turned to him in the darkness behind the bank and said: Well, what I really meant was that I want to lay down with you at some point. Tonight. In fact the sooner the better; I can't stay out all night. He laughed: For sure. For sure. We got into the car and I was feeling nervous. He startled me by suddenly reaching his arm out, encircling my neck and pulling my face over his. His mouth opening slow and kissing me for a few seconds. He drew away leaving his hand curved around the nape of my neck and smiled, leaned back in for another kiss, and then drew away again. He patted me on the leg and turned the key in the ignition.

He had this shitty piece of plastic that he'd fashioned into a tent strung between two trees in a forest of firs. It was some rarely used campground way up in the hills, no lights just dirt roads among the trees. The car twisted its way along at times illuminating a pitched tent or rusting trailer. He finally swung in between some trees and came to a stop snapping the headlights off. He left his door open a bit softly illuminating the nearby trees. His tent billowed in the slight breeze.

We stood in the dark kissing for a while, then he went to the back of the car and got an old sleeping bag out from the trunk and spread it under the tent. He closed the car door extinguishing the interior light and turned on a tiny flashlight, laying on the ground between us. We struggled to get our clothes off we were so blasted from a bowl of pot he produced as we drove up the hillside. We trying to pull off our pants standing on one leg, tipping over and making crashing noises in the bushes. I was completely disoriented but he grabbed onto my arm pulling me into the opening of the tent his skin so warm. We couldn't stop tasting each others mouths, changing back and forth in different positions; lying on top of each other, moving down and licking at each others arms and bellies and chests. At some point I was hovering over him in a push-up position leaning down drawing my tongue over the wet curves of his armpits when an intense light swept over the tent. I felt like we were in the path of a searchlight. A lot of noise, shouts and the slamming of car doors. I froze with my mouth on his chest and then the light disappeared.

About two in the morning he dropped me off outside the hotel and we exchanged addresses. I entered the room as quietly as I could and saw the doctor still passed out in the bed. I had that rude perfume of sex all over me and needed to take a shower in case he woke. I passed through the darkened room into the bathroom and closed the door, stripping off my clothes and hitting the light switch. I was in front of an enormous mirror that reflected an image of my pale white body covered in dozens of thick red welts. Mosquitoes. Everywhere. I took a hot shower, soaped off and finally crawled into bed without waking the doctor. The next morning the welts were gone. Everything was casual and we left the motel and drove up the coast.

It was falling apart. A hustler moved in and I spent a weeks worth of nights on the livingroom floor. I scavenged for leftovers in the refrigerator rather than sit for sullen meals at the dining table. I'd wake up early and leave for the day coming back only after the doctor and his boy were asleep. He left me a couple of angry letters taped to the refrigerator saying he didn't like the ghost routine and that he thought I should give him his set of keys back. I'd been writing Joe for a while and asked if I could come up for a visit. He wrote back saying he had a four-day break coming up the next week. I called him long distance and he gave me instructions to some small town in massachusetts and said he'd meet me at the bus station. I packed a small shopping bag and left without saying anything to the doctor. I didn't know where I was or where I was going I was just leaning into a drift and sway that I hoped would set me down gentle. I walked around the streets until five in the morning up around the east village and sat on a bench near st. marks church watching dawn coming over the tenements. A pale depressed queen sat down next to me and eventually invited me to his nearby place. It was a filthy room in a tenement with lots of dirty bedsheets and clothes. I stayed there a week till I caught the bus to Ludlow.

He met me at the station and drove to some queer bar on the outskirts of a city. We stood in the shadowy dark near a cigarette machine and hardly spoke; just grinning at each other and sucking on cold bottles. Later he drove us back to his apartment complex where he shared a small place on the second floor with his brother. We went for a walk out in the back fields and woods; down a dirt road where a fat coon kept trying to beat the cars to get across. We followed these rusting steel railroad tracks long ago abandoned in the fall of industry, now lying in the cool evening air reddish brown and swallowed at times by the dense undergrowth. We pushed along through thick nets of trees and bushes catching our feet on vines, past a house down in the distance with a howling yard dog behind a storm fence, down through some forest with a steep incline tumbling down towards a river. Further on we came to where the tracks went over a trestle bridge, over small rapids that merged into a vast smooth curve suddenly broke up on more rocks creating a whooshing spill towards the west. Watching the trees dipping down towards the banks we were forty or fifty feet up in the air tightroping these tracks with nothing but rotting steel stanchions holding us up. There were sounds of leftover fireworks somewhere in the distance, huge bullhead clouds, some rosy from the disappearing sun, others dark and bruise-colored drifting heavily overhead. We sat on a girder, before us the water rushed below giving us the sensation that we were moving at high speeds through the quiet and dying world.

He pulled a little bowl of pot from his pants and lit up. I had a difficult time not staring at his arms and torso, he left his t-shirt back at his place. I was falling, like from the portal of a plane way up in the skies. He had the kind of sexy grace that you want to swim in warm and breathing. In these years I always fell in love so easily; gestures of an arm, the simple line of a vein in the neck, the upturning of a jaw in dim light, the lines of a body beneath clothing, the clear light of the eyes when your faces almost touch. We talked about flying saucers; whether its a physical reality for those who claim abduction or whether its some kind of psychic schism that people have experienced. I was slowly leaning and without any reason suddenly kissed his bare shoulder. He kind of wigged, pulled back in vague shock: Uh uh. Don't ever do that. There's people around here.

Two days later around midnight he stepped out of his bed and squatted next to where I lay on a sleeping bag on the floor of his room. He was wearing shorts and pulled his dick out the leg part and bounced it against my lips. We hadn't mentioned sex since I'd arrived. We got into something quiet and slow, came, and then he slid back into his bed and fell asleep. I was feeling dislocated, my money was going to run out fairly quick what with fast food meals and occasional beers. The feeling of dislocation was really about dreaming too much in this guys movements. There was nothing ahead of me but a return to the streets of new york unless something opened up inside the flow of time and rescued me. I didn't even know what rescue was; a warm belly to lie against, a sudden purpose or meaning to existing, the slap of death, or a drift into something we call loving that probably never existed except in the mythologies of media or the lies of time. It's not just the urge to climb up inside someones skin and fuse in the rivers of blood; it's more wanting to leave the face of the planet, bodies rolling against each other up into the cool spacious sky. But this guy couldn't even verbalize anything that touched his sexuality; he had a look of pain when I strayed near the words so I slid back into my solitary drift, and waited til his hands began to move.

We were going swimming, he lent me a pair of cutoffs which I put on, slightly self-conscious about my hospital-white legs. His legs were darker, sturdier, that's what I recall about first meeting him on the windswept coast, late afternoon beneath the flapping canvas awnings and the lines of his muscular thighs and calfs. Where am I? We're in his two-door car stopping once outside of town to pick up a six-pack and then onto the interstate. It was so many miles further on, finally swinging onto this small asphalt road, then onto an even smaller road that climbed up into the trees and hillsides. He was picking up some kid who wanted to come with us. (telephone call: Is your mother home? Well, then, meet us on the rock near the road.) (hanging up the phone: He's really worried about his mom or sister seeing him going out with other guys.) We pull onto this fucked-up asphalt strip that rolls vertically up another hillside, make a curve and there's this young kid maybe seventeen sitting on a large white boulder lodged in the green lawn. He looked vaguely indian, shorts on and another pair of muscular legs, baby hair mustache almost transparent on his lip. (later that evening: Yeah I met him outside a bar in Springfield. They carded him and he had to stay outside. We camped out in his backyard a couple times . . . yeah, I slept with him once. The first night I met him we talked for a long long time. He didn't have a ride home so we got in my car. Ran out of gas the needle on empty, just outside his home. His mother works in a hospital, father dead. We spent the night in his house no one home.)

Down by the lake right off the road in a dirt patch strip parked with windows open slight breeze easing through. The kid was rolling a meticulous joint on a cardboard cover of a shoebox; gypsy moths, hundreds of them beating soundlessly against the trunks of trees, some flying over into the windshield of the car, climbing inside around the dashboard, on our legs leaving behind a blond powder. Someones ugly poodle dog, hairless almost gray dead skin tied to a tree shivering in the tall grass. Sounds of splashing somewhere else and ripple currents drifting towards us through the windshield. I was smoked up to the point of getting stupid. I got out of the car and drifted to the waters edge, I'm ahead of them and I walk slowly into the lake with my eyes focused on the horizon like a happy zombie; steady, smoothly upright and forward into the dreamy nothingness of future. The waters riding up around my waist, further up around my chest shocking my armpits. I'm so far from shore no glasses on; everything taking on that indistinct look like water cascading over a window, just wobbly form and light and color. Without my glasses color seems to fade because there are no true lines to contain it, it mixes with things and rides outside its surfaces; no density to anything in the world but what I feel beneath my feet.

I dive beneath the water and swim for the longest while beneath its surface slow and quiet down there. I'm aquatic somehow, surrounded by the silences, everything gray beneath the eyelids feeling for the first time so aware of my arms and hands and kicking legs and what they all mean. Surfaced far from shore and lay sideways on the surface seeing the pale bodies of strangers moving waist high in the shadows of a further part of the hidden shorelines.

Later in the shallows of the lake I'm walking on my hands, digging into the sand there. Further out it's silt so soft and deep you know it's black and rich; feet sink up to the ankles. It's a texture thats like the inside of a body when your fingers go wandering. I felt these smooth objects beneath my fingers; I pull them to the surface and it's some kind of freshwater mussels. He's doubtful when I tell him so I toss one to him and he's amazed. Later he holds it against the top of a wooden fencepost and slams it with a rock cracking the shell to bits which he pulls apart revealing tan flesh. I pick up my little camera off the backseat and take his picture. He gets embarrassed: You just take a picture of me? Yeah: I said: Just of you talking. (not of your beautiful chest which I'd love to spit on and rub my dick over.) The car radio is on and the announcer says: The worst riots in England in memory; worst civilian damage since world war two.

Later we drive the kid back home, up the small darkening road of the hillside into the blue shadows of evening. The house is softly illuminated from behind by a back porch light. The kid gets agitated: Uh oh . . . my mother's probably home . . . uh . . . just let me off here and if ya can turn around in someone elses drive . . . I didn't leave that light on . . . she's probably home. We say good night and he whispers: Joe . . . call you later in the week. He turns and runs across the lawn disappearing into the shadows of the porch, screen door squeaking and the bow wow of a dog.

His brother has buddies hanging out in the apartment; they might spend the night since it's heading towards the weekend. He wants sex with me really bad and really sudden. He's trying to get a motel room so we're on the interstate driving miles and miles. Finally he spots a Holiday Inn. I wait in the car as he goes inside to register. I'm sitting there for a long time feeling this melancholy just circle around me. Couldn't tell exactly what it was; part of it I guess is being outside of new york city in a slow place with air and grass and bodies of water to lie down in. Some of it was the slow growing tension of the day arriving soon where I had to leave, almost broke and no place to live. Death was a smudge in the distance; I don't know what exactly I mean by that but lying down inside this cradle of arms in my head was becoming transparent. Sometimes I wonder what planet I got dropped off of; what foreign belly did I get birthed from; this shit is painful; it's like being on a raft way out in the middle of a sea completely alone. I wave my hands in front of me, I know I'm not invisible so why are my thoughts so fucking loud? I'm lost in a world that's left all its mythologies behind in the onward crush of wars and civilization, my body just traveling along independent of brushes with life and death; no longer knowing what either means anymore. I guess I'm just so tired of feeling weary and alien; even my dreams look stupid to me. They belong to another world, another century, maybe another gender that fits the codes of all this shit. I don't know.

He comes back visibly upset, swings into the car through the open drivers window, slumps back: Shit. How could I be so fucking stupid? The clerk asked me if I lived nearby and I told him where and he goes: We have a policy where we don't rent to nobody who lives within a thirty-mile radius of here.

He was upset. I put my hand on his leg and said: Look. Don't let the asshole get you down. So what? Let's look for another place or else just forget it and go for a ride. (I really wanted to try and fuck him.) We drove out onto the highway again and rode for a while in silence. He pulled into a Ramada Inn. He got a room there. Everything calm again. He took a six-pack of beer from the trunk along with a carton of photographs and albums from his days at sea. It was a standard motel room with double beds and cheap thick white curtains, a sink with glasses wrapped in wax paper and a color television with an air conditioner humming behind it.

We're sitting on one of the beds, our shirts off, shoes and socks lying scattered across the floor, our legs resting on each others and stray hands smoothing along each others sides and chests. We're looking at his notebooks filled with kodak pictures of faraway places and naval scenes of boy sailors passing the equator for the first time. Most of the guys are wearing these weird fucking female outfits that only dumb hetero-boys can come up with. Some kind of ritual they do when they cross the equator. Mop wigs and overloaded halter tops and string skirts and underwear of different colors. Some of the photos look like a drunken fashion show with sturdy legged guys with balloons or cloth tits beneath their t-shirts; sort of like a hula nightmare but more sexy. Later in other pictures they're dressed like canines; on all fours with sheets of paper and cardboard curved and strung around their faces with magic marker lines drawn like grinning dogs. One philippine guy has a white t-shirt with a pirates skull drawn on its chest. Another guy is dressed like a hounddog bitch with eight fat papier mâché tits dragging the deck. Other pictures were of all his friends and him bare-chested waist-high in water of a foreign sea with beautiful delicate pink and white flowered leis around their necks. I put my hand casually on his butt and he jerked away. Anyone ever put their hands on your ass? I said. He made a disgusted sound: That's fucking gross; I'd never put my dick in somebodys ass and I'd never let somebody try that with me . . . makes me sick to think about it. Same way I'd never be in a relationship with a guy, maybe a girl but never a guy . . . it just ain't . . . uh . . . normal . . . it just doesn't make any sense. I don't mind playing around here or there but not a relationship . . . I don't know.

Sometimes I wish I could blow myself up. Just wrap a belt of dynamite around my fucking waist and walk into a cathedral, or oval office, or the home of my mother and father. I'm in the last row of the bus, the seven other passengers clustered like flies around the driver in the front. I can see his cute fuckable face in the rear-view mirror. I lean back and tilt my head so all I see are the clouds in the sky. Inside my head I'm looking back with my eyes wide open. I still don't know where I'm going; I decided I'm not crazy or alien. It's just that I'm more like one of them kids they find in remote jungles or forests of India. A wolf-child. And they've dragged me into this fucking schizo-culture, snarling and spitting and walking around on curled knuckles. They're trying to give me a damp mattress to sleep on in a dark corner when all I really want is the rude perfume of some guys furry underarms and crotch to lean into. I'll just make guttural sounds and stop eating and drinking and I'll be dead within the year. My eyes have always been advertisements for an early death.

THE REAL McCOY

♥ ♥

Catherine Texier

He had it all: the narrow hips, tight in worn-out, torn-at-the-knees blue jeans, the tallness, the slenderness, the washed-out blue eyes swimming in tenderness, but just as possibly blurred by myopia, the full lips, the stubborn chin.

She watched him push through the crowd from the vantage point of the low couch on which she had been sprawled for a while, nursing a glass of white wine, tired of standing around exchanging banalities with barely polite strangers.

She tried to guess where he was from: Irish eyes, Jewish mouth, American Indian nose and cheekbones? Or vice versa? She wasn't so good at telling one American from another, although she would never have admitted it. She recognized American men by their gait, the swinging motion of their hips, their slouch. She couldn't tell about the hair either. He had a baseball cap screwed backwards, revealing short brown strands. He didn't take off his leather jacket, just unzipped it and pushed his cap back a notch, kissed a couple of women and slapped a couple of men on their backs and hit the bar. There was no mistake. The way his hips leaned against the buffet table, the way his shoulders hunched, the way he swirled the ice cubes in his glass, she knew she had before her an authentic, pure-breed American, the real McCoy, although she didn't know, not then, not yet, what it meant.

Her miniskirt rode a little further up her thighs as she crossed her legs. Her heart made a little leap when she felt his gaze fall on her fishnet stockings.

She had been living in New York for five years, a French expatriate in the wildest city in the world. Eurotrash, she discovered, was the name New York columnists gave young Europeans like her. She was appalled. She was wide-eyed about New York, the city of hip, of danger, she was smitten by the stench rising from the gutters, fascinated and repelled by the extreme poverty, drunk on the high voltage of the streets. She wrote to her mother it was Calcutta-on-the-Hudson, and although she expressed sorrow and indignation, there was more than an edge of pride and excitement to be living in the middle of such powerful and unrelenting decay.

She had a sense of getting in touch with some primitive urban instincts, abandoning the intellectual Parisian dialogues for a raw, more guttural and gutsy American dialect.

She didn't think she was Eurotrash. The word brought forth an image of young, moneyed English or French debutantes of some gentility or nobility, slumming on the Lower East Side or throwing each other huge birthday bashes in the West Side clubs before crashing in their tiny Upper East Side studio apartments. She had nothing in common with them. She had gone native. She dressed, looked, and ate as if she had sprung in full armor out of a downtown Manhattan sidewalk, without a past or a family. Even her voice didn't betray any sign of the mellow, more fluid French syllables. She passed.

When he saw her from the bar, he thought she exuded a dark, elegant sensuality. There was a grace to the curves of her body curled on the low couch, an artful abandon to her limbs, an attractive fragility to her small-boned frame. She was the type he could go for in a big way, the jet-black hair, the sultry eyes, the pearly-white skin, there was just enough of something offbeat to throw him off and anchor him in the sea of sexually charged faces. He couldn't quite put his finger on it—an innocence, a seriousness under the hip, know-it-all mask, a genuine appetite? For what?

She jerked her head back in what might or might not have been a calculated move and her short, glossy hair swung across her face. He got himself a drink at the bar and leaned back against the table, one foot over the other.

She smiled at him, just short of coyly. He raised his glass, touching it with the tip of his finger, meaning, do you want the same? She shook her head no, pointing to her own glass. It was not a coy smile at all, actually, it was seductive and confident, but in an understated way. He kept his eyes on her while carefully carrying his drink. Someone made room for him on the couch and he slid next to her.

She pursed her lips and slowly sipped at her glass.

He was watching her as if she were a rare bird.

She smiled a wry, lopsided smile.

I've got the same boots as you, she said, pointing to his laced-up British-made model. They're so fucking comfortable.

There was something about her. Did she have an accent? Canadian maybe? She didn't look like a Canuck. He threw both his arms on the back of the couch. She stretched her legs and leaned a little against him.

Where are you from? he asked.

What do you think?

Minnesota? No, I'm kidding.

France.

Oh yeah? You don't sound it.

So they say.

I don't believe you.

Want me to prove it?

He laughed and dropped his arm around her shoulders.

Okay. More hoarsely than he had intended.

She got up and smoothed the tiniest miniskirt over her thin thighs.

Come, she said, pulling him to his feet.

She was a photojournalist free-lancing for the French publications *Liberation* and *Actuel*, sometimes writing her own stories. She'd arrived in New York right after the eighties boom had peaked but there was still enough energy and craziness in the city to keep her running, although the last year or so the emotional EKG of the city, if not of the whole country, had gone flat-line. She felt as if she had been thrown off the merry-go-round into a harsh reality that looked like her worst nightmare. She was getting news from the European front that whatever action there was was happening in Paris and Berlin and it looked like throngs were leaving New York like rats jumping ship, and faster than the East Germans had crashed the Berlin Wall. She had been ready to drop New York like a hot potato but a couple of assignments and a lingering sense of attachment and loss were keeping her in the city longer than she had expected.

On the way to his apartment, he told her he was a photographer and a filmmaker. She laughed, running her hand down his leather jacket, hooking her fingers under the belt of his jeans. She ostentatiously looked at him from head to toe. "Filmmaker" sounded pretentious to her, a bit too Hollywood. Men she met in New York told her they were Artists, Writers, Actors, always with a capital letter heading the word, while it was plain to see they were waiters or salesmen at the Gap. She wondered if they were trying to make themselves sound important in her eyes out of insecurity, but then she noticed women were doing the same thing. It occurred to her these people were inflating their status in a wild leap of optimism and not just out of pure arrogance. Still, "filmmaker" was too much.

And me, I am Sarah Bernhardt, she said.

What?

Oh, never mind. So, what movies have you made? Anything I might have seen?

I work low-budget, he said seriously.

Maybe I'll do a piece about you in a French magazine?

He shared a loft on Church Street with another guy who was always gone, he said. The loft was cluttered with film equipment and wires and strewn with clothes. The overall impression she got was gray and brown, dusty, industrial, like a workplace gone out of control. There was a bed at one end, emerging from under a bunch of clothes and a pile of flat round film cans.

He brushed the clothes aside and carefully stacked the cans on the floor next to the bed to make room for her, then punched some buttons on the stereo.

She loved the way he moved. He had this lanky body that managed not to be angular but sinuous and full of unself-conscious grace. He slouched next to her, leaning against the pillows, but he didn't go after her. She liked that. She felt he gave her room, space. It was something she liked about American men—or was it only some American men?—the way they sent sexual messages but ultimately let you make your move. He had a shadow of a beard and now that the baseball cap was gone she could see his hair, slicked back, with a strand that kept slipping over his forehead and that he pushed back with his hand. She could smell him, no after-shave, no perfume, but a male smell mixed with cigarette smoke and alcohol breath, a mixture she found irresistible late at night.

She picked up his hand and traced a circle in his palm with the tip of her finger. He responded to her. Their hands played together, their fingers ran lines of fire.

He told her stories, holding her hand, he told her about his grandfather coming to America from Poland as a little boy and selling bolts of fabrics on the sidewalks of Orchard Street, he told her about his other grandfather who was a cop and whose mother may or may not have been a Cheyenne Indian. He told her about growing up in Brooklyn and about building an A-frame in the redwood forest in California and living in the backwoods of Appalachia. He told her about moving to a little island off the coast of Venezuela for a year and making his first film there, and soon it became blurry in her mind, at times she didn't even understand his accent and she would just lose herself in his voice, listening to the alternately clipped and drawn syllables, bathing in the same sounds she had listened to watching American movies as a kid, weird, nasal, and jerky, that sounded to her like rock and roll.

So here he was, this beautiful specimen of American male, stretched next to her in this terribly American pose, long legs in denim (do little American boys come out of Mother's womb with their little chubby legs ensconced in tiny blue jeans?), good round shoulders in the oversized shirt, and arms thrown upwards (in surrender?), here he was, offering himself to be picked, sampled, and thoroughly consumed. She put both her hands on his chest and rubbed them up to his armpits, stroking the inward curve of his arms until she felt his open palms and greedily fastened against them.

I want you, he whispered. And he pulled her above him and gently opened her legs and reached up under her miniskirt following the lines of her tights until his fingers found the edge and rolled it down to her hips.

She was kneeling above him, a curtain of black hair hanging in front of her face. Only the tip of the nose and the dark pouty mouth peaked through and she straddled his face, hanging to the headboard of the bed. He felt her small-boned body, lifted the flimsy blouse over her breasts and reached for them, cupping them in his hands.

When she walked back to her small studio on Avenue A the next morning in the raw white light of a bleak December day she felt the mark of his body imprinted on hers like a scarlet letter. She searched for his hands in the inside of her knees and on her neck and on the small of her back and sniffed him under her arms and between her legs.

He seemed mysterious and aimless, although he had a day job selling software in a computer store and kept fairly regular hours and even cooked for himself sometimes in the evenings, which she thought was definitely the mark of a foreign, possibly more advanced culture. Although what he cooked filled her with wonder and very little appetite. Squash and kale sitting atop a stack of millet grains, dark-green seaweed unfurling on a bed of glistening azuki beans that he managed to get off the plate on the razor edge of crossed chopsticks. He was not above washing this down with a double shot of Glenfiddich on the rocks or straight bourbon, and it seemed fitting, somehow, it was a farfetched connection that made the same weird sense as when he drank cold chocolate milk with his eggs Benedict for brunch one Sunday.

But after he had washed and wiped his dinner dishes he roamed the streets of Manhattan late at night armed with a pair of Leica and Nikon cameras strapped across his chest and under his leather jacket and a camcorder at his wrist. He took snapshots and quick takes of urban night scenes, sometimes at his own peril, wandering the arcades of Times Square or tent cities in downtown back streets. He was doing a documentary on street people. He knew them, he said, he knew when things were cool, he knew when things heated up. She feared for him in these strange forays but he was the real thing, he wasn't a phony, she told herself, and that was well worth the fear. It made life worthwhile to have a lover who walked the wild side.

For the French monthly *Actuel* she took photos of him on his night forays, the photographer photographed. They were published as a six-page photo essay, black-and-white grainy shots of his dark gangly frame merging into the night, shards of light bouncing off the leather of his jacket and the metal of his cameras. The subjects of his work appeared in shadows or on the side of the photos or in the background, but probably because of his camera being aimed at them, the eye would focus on the street figures lurking in the night or lying in clusters on the ground. The photos were ambiguous: who were the real protagonists? The voyeur, representing the power class, blazing with sophisticated equipment, or the threatening shadows of the underclass, the dark continent of the street, who could have jumped him anytime and robbed or murdered him?

She was uneasy publishing these photos, although taking them had been a heady trip and a way of sharing his night life and the thrill of danger. For her, he was an integral part of the scene, and she was the real voyeur; she was the stranger observing the natives and reporting about them. She longed to cut all ties to her roots and plunge in.

She moved in with him. His occasional roommate didn't mind her and since the roommate was only paying a third of the rent anyway, his opinion about her move was only asked perfunctorily.

To him she was like quicksilver, impossible to grasp. He would hold her by her small, narrow waist, he would pin her down under him; still she would seem to slide off his grasp. He would tackle her in mock anger and she would let herself go down under him and burst into laughter. She would be standing in front of the dresser pulling on her velour leggings, she would be slipping into her boots, she would stretch her arms up to fluff her hair and he would see the lines of her back and the curve of her delicate neck, and she would turn around and her lips would be bright red, set in that famous pout, and her wrist adorned with a heavy bracelet, she would have donned her street persona, and she would curl backward into his still sleepy arms and taunt him, offering him her shoulders in the opening of her shirt or her sweater, and then she would be out of the door, leaving a trace of subtle perfume behind her. She was a woman that he never could get a full load of. She moved in angular facets like a Picasso painting from the blue period, she was a series of snapshots, she was a fast-paced tape edited to the speed of light. She moved as quickly as her hair would fall across her face or flip back uncovering her neck and her chin. He had no idea what she was about. He supposed she had style. And warmth. If she was happy she'd jump for joy and hug him. She'd hold him tight around the waist and the back—she was too short to comfortably keep her arms around his shoulders—and muss his hair and kiss him firmly on the lips. You're great, she'd say. I adore you. Laughing and inviting. She genuinely seemed to love men. But she was also unbelievably moody, she was either in high gear or in tremulously low spirits. He was crazy about her.

They would meet at the local bar, a dark, damp beer and pool place where she would find him deep into a conversation with the bartender when she swung in. She would climb up the bar stool in her high heels and perch on top of it, crossing her legs high and balanced on one buttock, like a delicate bird resting between two flights. When he wasn't busy shooting his documentary—a long-term project he had started three years earlier and that was dragging on because he had had some of his grants cut—he would cook her dinner or they would go straight to see a weird (she thought) movie at the Film Archives or the Film Forum, or they would watch videotapes at his place and catch a cult movie at midnight at some revival house. Or they would spend half the night at his editing place because you could rent the editing machines cheaper at night, he told her, and he would show her how to cut a videotape. Other nights he joined her late at the studio she rented with another photographer (she was soon to move her photo equipment into his darkroom) and watch and comment as she would bathe the paper in chemicals and see the images emerge out of their fog like ghosts from beyond. With his encouragement she had started a personal portfolio, far from (she said, or, rather, she hoped) the conventions of photojournalism. Like so many photographers before her, she took inspiration from the city, she reveled in its decay, in its tragedy. There's no room for sentimentality in this city, she'd say. (And he would concur. She'd sometimes strike him as being infinitely wise and capable of expressing feelings with a depth and precision he could never hope to approximate.) He liked her "work," as he called it. It had a rawness and an urgency that couldn't be denied, as he put it. She took chances and sometimes had a startingly fresh look which thrilled him. Add to that a certain classical manner which had to be attributed to her European upbringing, and he was predicting her success and recognition.

So now she was a Photographer, she could even entertain thoughts of becoming an Artist. Barely a year with him and she didn't think her confused aspirations were arrogance or egomania. She saw them as legitimate ambition.

They lived a year in next to total bliss. They didn't leave the city other than to cab to the airport (their only extravagance) to fly to Amsterdam, Berlin, or Paris, together or separately. They and their friends called themselves "poor jetsetters." Then, upon their return, they would crawl back into their shabby (but of course they didn't see it that way) downtown loft, which, at that point, had been all but abandoned by the original roommate, who himself had crawled back into another hole in L.A. or in Madrid, expending his creative talents elsewhere.

She was living her American dream. Dipping deep into the squalor and decrepitude of New York, merging with its denizens, belonging to its fabled "mean streets." Belonging to its artists' colony. Being ticket-holder to the coolest Bohemia in the world. Heady stuff.

They were a couple in demand. They looked great together. It was obvious there was a strong sexual chemistry between them. And under the hard black leather and the biker's boots, she kept (in fact honed and polished) the sensuality and finesse of a French woman. And he was a true-blue, dyed-in-the-wool New Yorker who, in spite of his claim to street hipness, liked nothing better than to spend Saturday and Sunday afternoon sunk at the bottom of his couch, two stockinged feet crossed on his coffee table, watching ball games and boxing matches back-to-back with his pals in a rite of male bonding and beer drinking.

For a year they navigated the downtown waters, their sails flapping in the wind, with barely any contact with the outside world (she would say about friends who had to leave Manhattan, even if they only had to go on the other side of the Holland Tunnel, that they were going to "America"), and when he finally got the last leg of his funding allowing him to complete his documentary and when she (almost simultaneously) got a show in an offbeat but on-the-rise art gallery in SoHo, she thought her balloon would burst she was so close to her fantasy.

The day they went to see his family in Rego Park, Queens, she didn't think anything of it. They were going to America and visiting an American family and she was intensely curious: she was going to find out how the natives live. She felt the excitement of an anthropologist departing for the field.

His mother was petite and thin, her hair frosted blue, her eyelids silvery blue, her mouth fuchsia, her fingernails orangey-red, and she was wearing a baby-blue pantsuit matching the color of her eyes. She spoke with the husky voice of a chain-smoker, although there was no trace of cigarettes on the coffee table. His father was tall and quite rotund around the gut, with thinning gray hair, a burgundy-colored polo shirt, green-and-white plaid pants, and white loafers. When he shook her hand she felt his pinkie ring. It had an oval green stone and she noticed he was holding his little finger slightly separated from the rest of his fingers.

Although it was lunchtime, no food was served, and she wondered if there was some misunderstanding. Had they already had lunch? She whispered to his ear that she was starved. He yelled toward the kitchen, Mom! Can we have a sandwich? And the mother came back carrying two plates with a container of a grayish-brown mixture, a jar of pickles, and a stack of bread slices. Chopped liver, the mother pointed to the container with her mandarin-colored nail, eat, eat, I made it myself.

Liver?

Pah-tey, cut in the father. Like French pah-tey.

This?

The mother spread the liver on a piece of bread for her and laid a couple of pickles next to it.

Try it, she said. You'll love it.

It was nothing like pâté, but she ate it, and even the pickles, which were weirdly sweet. She was a good traveler and always ate local food. In Rome, do as the Romans. . . . She would take in the food like the rest.

Without a word, the father flipped the TV remote control from his easy chair and a football game came on the screen simultaneously with the easy chair clicking into dozing position. He and the father fastened their gaze on the screen, while the mother pulled out a needlepoint work from a plastic bag and proceeded to tell her all about their relatives and about her son's success at school, while the father and son alternately yelled at the screen and beat their thighs with their tightened fists, or fell into a deep coma.

There was a collection of knickknacks on the dresser, almost all in animal form: crocheted dogs and bunnies, porcelain cats and owls, sappy maxims brightly embroidered on canvases. She was discovering the meaning of kitsch. Her armchair was getting more and more comfortable and the mother's conversation turned into a monologue peppered with my son this, and my son that, and she turned comatose too until it was time to go home.

In the train back to Penn Station it seemed to her he looked different. His shirt was bulging over the waistband of his jeans. Was it a pouch growing in his midriff? The slouch (the famous American slouch, legs half extended to one side, shoulders leaning the other side) suddenly looked as though it had been carved into an easy chair. So this romantic, passionate man, this filmmaker of the night, of the underground, came out of a brick split-level with wall-to-wall shag carpeting and had been fed chopped liver! She buried her face in a magazine and didn't talk to him until they got back to his loft.

They had their first fight that night. There was a boxing match on TV and he turned on the tube. She was wearing her fishnet stockings and a low-cut loose black dress and no shoes and was lounging on the couch while he was sunk in an armchair, his gaze fastened on the screen, a remote control under his thumb. She struck a few provocative poses, failed to catch his attention, and finally came down hard on him. She said he was boring and turning into a couch potato and she hadn't come to New York to be spending her evenings watching her lover flip the channels on TV. It was so, so . . . middle-class, so, so . . . American.

She tripped on the words she was so furious. What she really thought was that it terrified her, being sucked into an American family, everything that she had heard about, but only seen on TV: the tackiness, the polyester clothes, the vulgarity, the faux antiques, the faux wood, the faux marble, the TV turned on all day long.

He waved vaguely toward the door.

Be my guest, he said. Nobody's asking you to stay.

She stormed out of the loft wrapped in her winter coat but still wearing her thin fishnet stockings and as soon as she walked in the street, her legs felt as though they were being whiplashed by razor blades.

She walked into a little café down the street and huddled in the back far from the front door, cupping a mug of hot chocolate in her hands, pondering how her prince of the night had turned into an ugly suburban toad, a sad twist to the fairy tale.

He, meanwhile, didn't have a clue about what possessed her. Snotty little bitch, he thought, defensively. She had been acting uppity all evening. He felt vaguely guilty but he didn't know of what. He was always tense and depressed after visiting his family, but, all things considered, things had turned out all right. She had been friendly to his folks, and his parents had been on their best behavior, so what was eating her now? Still, he had felt uneasy with her on the way back, as though she had turned alien, moved to a different planet. He blamed her hysterical behavior on her period or a nagging wife syndrome and drowned his wave of guilt feelings in the blue light of the tube and the golden hue of Scotch.

She came back that night and they made love and all was forgiven if not forgotten. But for her—and maybe for him too, although he truly had no idea, most of the time, what his feelings were, particularly regarding women; he'd much prefer to take his cue from his cock, which had a very clear way of expressing itself—the enchantment was broken.

He had just finished his documentary, and he had been invited to be part of a documentary show at the Whitney Museum, but his ambition was to show his work at major film festivals, and he had been turned down. This left him with a sense of futility and failure, although objectively, the documentary was his first real success and an important—if small—step in his career. He was actually more down than he would admit and furious to be dragging his feet. He felt betrayed and unjustly put upon by her nagging about his hairstyle and his clothes, his lack of discipline and direction. He clammed up.

The following night they were invited to a party that promised to be fun, where a lot of their friends were going, and she spent two hours getting ready for it, soaking into a fragrant bath, rubbing her skin with creams and lotions and putting together a killer outfit. The busier she got, the deeper he sank in front of the tube. When it was almost time to go, it became obvious to both of them that he had no intention of moving from the couch.

Aren't you getting ready? she asked, trying to sound relaxed and matter-of-fact. To which he didn't answer.

I am talking to you, she yelled, towering over his slouched body, in a pair of knee-high suede boots and militarily garbed in a brown parka, a thick band of fur framing her pale face.

He didn't bother to lift his gaze, which was fastened on the TV screen; although he tried so hard to blank out her voice he only saw a blur of colors.

I am talking to you. So you're not going to that party? Why are you being so hostile?

She was pacing the floor back and forth, trying to force his attention. And the more she paced, the more incensed she got, the more he withdrew into intense, hostile silence.

You're a louse, you're full of shit. What are you turning into, some kind of lazy bum, always sitting on your ass, getting fat, watching TV, numbing your brain, ignoring me?

Throughout the whole scene, he remained speechless, motionless, a block of stone. Under the verbal assault, he froze all feelings, all nerve endings.

She knew she was hysterical, but his silence infuriated her.

Will you talk to me, for God's sake? Anything, say anything to me. Stop ignoring me!

She came to him, leaned over his shoulder, rubbed her fingers through his hair. She felt him tense up as she did this, which only made her want to push him further. She held him around the chest in furious embrace.

Talk to me, please talk to me.

He braced himself and pulled both arms out, breaking her embrace, and stood up. She tried to make him face her.

Look at me, she yelled, pay attention to me!

He walked away from her. His back was a rigid slab, a wall against which she hurled herself. She pummeled him with her closed fists.

Talk to me, talk to me! I'll make you talk. You're not going to ignore me. I won't let you.

He shoved her against the couch with a sharp cut of his elbow. She collapsed, screaming, Bastard!

Wild, his jaw set, in fury, he grabbed a chair and smashed it —his full weight behind it—against the bedroom partition. The frail Sheetrock gave in with a pitiful crack. Two yawning holes stood gaping while he walked into the bathroom (the only closed room in the loft) and slammed the door behind him.

Asshole!

She stood up, zipped up her parka, and left, as though she had been waiting for him to spend himself, almost satisfied to have pushed him so far that his anger flared up, tangible to both of them.

In retaliation he never made it to the party and remained locked into silence for three days. She waited for him to come around and they made up again, in a flurry of passion. He apologized for his bad temper. She received his apologies graciously.

Every time he talked to his family or even about them they ended up having a fight, but she realized the connection days later and wasn't sure what to make of it. He seemed to lose his shine and his aura and turn into—what? A regular American guy? Isn't that what she wanted? Or did she want the tight blue jeans, but not the chopped liver? Her hero had clay feet. And where did that leave her?

Next time she moved first and after an unproductive exchange of furious platitudes, she grabbed a plate and threw it at him.

He ducked and the plate crashed, not far from the two holes, vaguely star-shaped, that the chair had left in the Sheetrock. He picked up one of the broken pieces and hurled it back at her, but she was already fleeing out of the loft and didn't come back until late at night.

Being a French intellectual (proclaiming oneself an Artist or a Writer can be sneered at in France, but being an Intellectual is alright), she was often given to statements about America's boundless energy and curiosity, and its capacity to renew itself, which of course, she added, led straight to the need to be "born again," over and over. She berated this obsession to rebuild a better, newer, more perfect present, and to erase the past, instead of learning from it and building on it, layers and layers of knowledge amounting to a rich cultural stew. Of course, she would muse, there is something terribly seductive in the eternal vigor of youth. But America is decaying without having even matured.

She had now added a new litany that went something like this: Americans are completely paranoid. New Yorkers won't even drink their own waters. And look at them, as soon as they set foot abroad they get sick! Or: Americans are obsessed with disease and death. They are totally morbid. Having abandoned all sense of spirituality, tradition, and pleasure, they hysterically watch every one of their little booboos (she pronounced the word "bohboh," as in French) blossom into full-blown symptoms and incurable illnesses. Or: Fads are symptoms of America's deep anxiety about itself. Or again: American women hate men and hate being women. They have no sense of style and are deeply afraid of their femininity.

Or this one, that she would victoriously unleash on him at the most vulnerable moment: Americans need to throw themselves into cycles of depression and revival, or binges and purges like bulimic teenagers.

He would listen, bemused, to her rantings, marveling at the energy she could dispel with her mouth and her lungs, while he slouched supine on his bed or puttered around with his equipment or tried to block out the fairly high pitch of her voice in the drowning clamor of a TV sports announcer.

Or he would knock her down and stop the flow of her words with his mouth pressed firmly on hers, and he would unbutton his pants simultaneously, pushing himself into her and whispering: You like American men because their dicks have no memory and no past and they just go for it.

They were really very lucky. They were both healthy, they could support themselves with their work, they were part of the in crowd, in spite of the fights they were still strongly attracted to each other sexually, so why do we find her one early evening sitting on the bathroom floor, her arms tightly embracing her folded legs, sobbing uncontrollably?

Is she expecting her period?

He might have thought that, the sexist fool, hiding his anguish about their relationship behind a reassuring cliché.

But she actually had just had her period. It was over and done with and she was sobbing, for no apparent reason, a sense of dread and doom filling her entire body and surroundings. In the whole loft, the bathroom seemed to be the safest place, and she had locked herself in.

It was the middle of a sultry New York summer and they hadn't been able to go away because, in spite of their doing okay, they couldn't afford to go anywhere else, and relied on the few invitations to the beach or upstate to see some green. The air was so torrid and humid she felt physically trapped. She stretched on the cool ceramic floor, rubbing her sweaty palms on the edges of the tiles. Her heart was pounding and the sweat that ran down from her armpits was not just from the heat but from inside of her.

In the bathroom, on the window ledge, she kept a collection of blue glass bottles and small family photos in baroque silver frames. She had moved in the loft with him, but tacitly they both recognized the place was his. A section of the darkroom was hers, with her filing cabinets and her equipment, and one of the dressers in the bedroom was hers, always overflowing with printed underwear and panty hose in dark colors, and she had a desk in the living room with a mess of papers held down by a huge paperweight, but for some reason it was in the bathroom that she had arranged this modest array of personal objects. In fact, without realizing it, she had made the whole bathroom hers, her expensive Chanel and Christian Dior cosmetics and real boar's hair brushes, gold lamé and black velvet headbands, and silk ribbons, pushing far to the edge his more plebeian shaving foam, jar of Vaseline, Head and Shoulders shampoo, and antifungal athlete's-foot powder.

The portraits in the silver frames were all black-and-white prints of her as a little girl, and of her mother, as a young beauty of twenty-five or thirty and also as a little girl, laughing at the wheel of a 1935 Duesenberg, with a huge silk bow in her bob.

These photos and a few books (among which, Marguerite Duras's *The Lover*, Celine's *Journey to the End of the Night* and *Death on the Installment Plan*, and Baudelaire's *Flowers of Evil*) were all she took with her from France, along with her clothes, in one large suitcase and a nylon backpack.

She picked up the photos and lined them up on the toilet lid, kneeling next to them, staring at them. She hated herself as a child, with rage and contempt, and had enormous admiration for her mother's beauty. But there was one picture of herself that she liked, and it was this little one, a toddler running toward the camera, her arms extended, bursting with life. She stroked the intricate engravings of the frame. It was antique silver, dulled because, of course, she had never thought of polishing it, but when she rubbed her thumb on it, it turned smooth and shiny.

Her heart was pounding so hard she was afraid to stand up. What if it burst? What if her whole body blew apart? She felt tingling in her arms and hands and she was convinced she was going to have a heart attack. She wrapped her arms around the cold porcelain of the toilet and stared at the photos. She wanted to throw herself out of the window or run screaming into the street to escape the explosion in her body, but she was terrified it might make it worse. She knew she couldn't escape herself.

She went to get her camera and snapped the row of silver-framed portraits standing on the toilet lid.

When he came back later that night, the terror had abated. She didn't mention the episode. He hated it when she seemed weak and despondent.

He noticed her drawn face, her pallor. She was tight-lipped and looked jumpy, anxious. But this was not news to him. She seemed to have permanently slipped into a state of morbid anxiety. They both, actually, had slumped into a morose morass. Maybe it's time to break up, he thought, but he quickly hid in his darkroom and forgot about it.

She was engaged in a new project, which had started as a magazine job: a series of portraits of French immigrants, young and old, in the arts and in the food and restaurant business, posing in the context of their work, which was also, in some cases, their family life. They were not photojournalistic, action-packed shots, they were studies in character and background, the facial expressions, the clothes, the family resemblances, and the surroundings revealing more to the viewer than more spontaneous gestures, the way a silence sometimes speaks more than a wordy exchange.

They were a revelation to her, these pastry chefs, these charcuterie entrepreneurs, these older waitresses, even the younger generation of artists, who were her mirror image. With some of them she felt as though she was back in Paris, where she had lived all her life. It was both painful and weirdly familiar. Some insisted on speaking only English to her, which disturbed her. The whole project felt like taking a trip back to the motherland right in the middle of her daily New York life. To bring both of her personalities, the French and the American, together threw her into a panic. Her French self had been a painful exercise in wearing a series of rigid masks behind which she suffocated. Now, with the finger of port or the glass of wine she was being offered while setting up her tripod and lighting, her New York hip veneer started to crack, and in would rush the free language of her childhood. She didn't fight it. The old jokes and forgotten expressions melted from the deep freeze she had kept them locked in and flowed into her mouth. She busied herself with the angles and the light and the lenses, checking the background, the postures, chatting with her subjects, marveling at her own newfound ease.

Coming back from one of her photo sessions, she found him cooking a Japanese dinner, rolling sushi in strips of seaweed with the help of a tiny bamboo mat. His long fingers worked precisely, neatly. It always surprised her that he had that earthiness about him. The kitchen was an oasis of calm in the chaos of the loft. Cooking seemed to relax him. He listened to rock and roll, sipped on a drink. It was usually a sign of good mood.

He offered her a glass of wine and she sat down on a stool, grateful for the gesture of hospitality. This could be home, she thought, leaning against the counter. She had just come from a photo session at one of the city's top French restaurants. After the shoot, the chef and the kitchen staff had invited her to an appetizer of scallops and oysters and a glass of white wine, and that had also felt like home.

This second glass of wine almost did her in. Her eyes were swimming in tears. Why did things feel like home and were never home? It troubled her, this capacity to feel at home for brief moments and then lose it altogether. He seemed at home right now, expertly deep-frying broccoli stalks dipped in batter, more at home, at least more alive, than he had been at his parents' house. Was he homesick too, sometimes, for some imaginary home, or some long-lost haven of warmth?

She didn't know how to talk about these things. Feelings were like air, or like fire. They formed and burst and vanished. You had to ride them, follow the movement. You couldn't really touch them or catch them with words. As a photographer you had a better chance. You could stumble upon that fleeting moment and freeze it, frame it.

What got you into Japanese food? she asked him, while he was laying the sushi in neat little rows on black pottery trays.

I was a Japanese samurai in my past life.

He put the trays down on the kitchen table and pulled on his eyelids with both index fingers. See: there's something, right?

She laughed and sat down across from him at the table. He poured them both more wine.

We should be drinking tea, he said, but I am not a purist.

He stood up and wrapped his arms around her shoulders.

I love you, he said.

She pressed his hands and let go of them.

It occurred to her they were both at a loss for words and maybe that was the reason they had turned to images in their work. Their rage, their tenderness, they had no idea what to make of it. It was overwhelming.

We don't speak the same language, she whispered.

Say what? he asked.

I am a stranger here, she said. I don't belong.

He stiffened.

I thought you loved it here. He meant: I thought you loved me.

She had changed. She was still curvy and graceful and moody. Maybe it was the moods. The moods had become so intense. He looked at her, teasing a piece of ginger with her chopsticks, her curtain of black hair hanging across her cheek.

I got what I wanted, she said.

What's that?

They were both speaking very low, as though by holding their voice back they were not quite saying what they were saying.

I wanted to become American. I wanted to soak it up, feel the fresh blood in my veins.

And?

I did. I felt it. I felt the pulse.

And?

I got it . . . well, some of it: baseball on TV and real American hamburgers and real American hot dogs and dope on the street, guys wearing real Levi's and home-grown sneakers and baseball hats, the low-slung cars hitting the potholes, you know, all that stuff, the Jewish jokes, the black slang, hip hop, freedom, Art . . . I got to step into the movie.

He didn't say anything. He looked vulnerable and hurt, tight.

For a moment she thought he was going to run to the TV and turn it on, drown her voice behind a barrage of sports announcements or gunshots. But he hung in there.

. . . You know. Welcome to America, the most exciting country in the world. I felt really welcome. I was never made to feel like a stranger.

So?

But it's not what I imagined. Or maybe it is. That's the problem. It's just like the movies. But it's for real. People are dying, they are dying of AIDS, they are dying of gunshots, they are dying of hunger, or else they are brain-dead. It's like my face was rubbed into it, day after day. There's no escape.

She poured herself another glass of wine. It was French white wine, a dry Entre-Deux Mers, nice and crisp. The sushi was finished. The black shiny trays were stark and elegant on the natural maple table.

What I am trying to say is that I wanted to be free, I wanted to be rootless, I wanted to be wild.

He looked around. Beyond the tall windows, the city loomed, a huge glittering mass, a tall jungle of buildings.

You got it, he said. This is the wild, lawless city.

She laughed nervously.

You want to go back?

His voice sounded bleached, pale.

I don't know. Maybe . . .

She stopped, watching his face tighten.

No, it's not that. . . .

He stayed frozen.

I fucked it up, she thought.

He was still with her, listening. He couldn't stand being caught vulnerable and showing it. But she looked disarmed, she didn't seem to be out to get him or push him into some admission of wrongdoing.

Not wild enough for you, hey?

His voice had lost its defensive edge. There was the tenderness again, in his eyes.

She couldn't believe they were talking like this. He didn't pull away from her. The only time she saw his face so vulnerable was when they made love, and he promptly closed himself when he went back into his daily life.

The whole city was dropping away from them, the loft, the Brazilian music playing in the background, the food on the table. They were dangerously alone, very close.

When she looked into his eyes, she saw they were still wildly, crazily in love. It frightened her. The desire was overwhelming.

MRS. VAUGHAN

♥ ♥

Patrick McGrath

London 1936, and a young hospital doctor has fallen in love with an older woman, the wife of the senior pathologist. . . .

I, though, had little time for newspapers, or champagne! The weather was damp and chilly, the days were growing shorter, and the frail and the elderly with their rheumatism and influenza and arthritis and bronchial problems were flooding into St. Basil's, seeking care. Then on the evening of December 9, King Edward VIII told Parliament that he was no longer able to discharge his duties as king "without the help and support of the woman I love," and signed the Instrument of Abdication. It was a moving speech, and there was much subsequent discussion of it in the hospital. Some were puzzled, those who didn't understand how a man could give up power for romance. It was the first time a British monarch had voluntarily renounced the throne; feelings ran high.

I was in the flat in Jubilee Road, the night of the king's broadcast. The gas fire was lit but it wasn't enough, for I am a thin man, so I'd put on a jersey, a scarf, and my dressing gown as well. I'd had a perfectly bloody day; Cushing had told me I'd never make a surgeon and again I'd seriously asked myself if he was right. There was a certain untutored deftness with fine instruments that I seemed simply unable to acquire. I was, I suppose, competent enough, but did I, I wondered, have *talent*? The question disturbed me profoundly. I got up and walked about the room to get warm. So the king was abdicating for love of Wallis Simpson. How would it be if I were to do the same—tell Cushing I could no longer assist at surgery "without the help and support of the woman I love"? Ha ha. Someone knocked at the door. "Come in, Mr. Kelly," I shouted. The door opened. "It's not Mr. Kelly"—those familiar tones—and I whirled about: it was your mother! She closed the door behind her, and a moment later we were in each other's arms: her very *being there* shattered whatever thin crusts of reserve and propriety still stood between us. We clung to one another. "Something has happened," she whispered.

"I know."

Something has happened. Dear Dorian, never, I think, can three such simple words have engendered so much happiness in a human heart! We clung to one another in the middle of the room, rocking slightly; eventually we came apart. For a moment or two we hovered there, stranded in some odd void between intimacy and decorum: something had happened, yes, but whatever it was, it was yet to be assimilated. She laid her fingers on my arm for a moment and turned away. She drifted to the window and pulled aside the curtain. I think I must have offered her a drink. "That would be nice," she said.

We sat in the armchairs, pulled up close to the gas fire. She kept her coat on and wrapped her fingers round her glass and stared into the thin hissing flames. Usually so voluble, she was now silent and I, with my initial excitement checked, rather, by her strange, distant mood, watched her, and waited, ready to take my cue from her. "I'm sorry it's so cold in here," I said at last.

She glanced up. "Were you listening to the king?" she said.

"Yes I was, actually."

"I met her once."

"Oh?"

"Small and elegant, with rouged toenails. Neat as a pin, not a button awry, though the funny thing is, she has big strong hands with stubby fingers, isn't that odd in someone so delicate?"

"How do you know her?"

"I went to a cocktail party in Upper George Street. She told me she shops at Harrods and Fortnum's and does her own housekeeping, having been taught the value of a dollar growing up in Baltimore."

"A thrifty woman," I said. Then: "I'm so glad you came. I keep thinking about you."

"Yes, I know." She frowned.

"You know?"

She nodded. "It's happened to me as well."

I wanted to take her in my arms there and then and cover her face and neck and breasts with kisses. She reached for my hand. She stroked it for a moment and gazed at me with great seriousness. "What are we to do?"

I shrugged. I saw no problem. "Celebrate?"

She stared into her glass. Then she shook her head and rose abruptly to her feet. "I must go," she said.

"No, don't."

"I must. This is foolish. What can come of it? I shouldn't have come here, it was a stupid impulse."

"It was a wonderful impulse. Please sit down. Five minutes."

She hesitated. "Five minutes."

Five minutes.

Traces of her perfume clung to my dressing gown. I noticed it as soon as she'd gone, as I wandered about the room, touching things, my thoughts and emotions in turmoil. I clutched the material and brought it to my nose, and smelling her awakened the memory of touching her, and this I concentrated hard upon, animated with as much detail as I could, lingered over as I buried my nose in the fabric of my dressing gown where her face and neck and hair had come into contact with it. Smelling her and remembering the softness of her hands, the warmth of her slim body beneath the thick fur when I first slipped my hands in under it, I became aroused all over again, and felt suddenly cooped and trapped, so I threw on my hat and overcoat and ran downstairs and out into the blustering raw night and began to walk.

I never knew quite where I walked or for how long. All I could recall, later, were dark streets of large houses lost in gusting sheets of rain, water streaming in the gutters, the occasional bowed figure hurrying by in the blur of a streetlight, umbrella slick with rain—striding forward, through the night, my hat pulled low over my forehead and my overcoat flapping about me, I did not feel the cold and damp, for I was wrapped in the heat of erupting emotions that didn't even *begin* to subside until I turned at last into a small pub called the Bell, not far from Jubilee Road, and stood at the counter of the saloon bar, dripping wet and still in high excitement, and bought a large whisky. Only then did I articulate it: I'm in love. I love her. More to the point though, *she loves me*.

This produced dazed bewilderment, the very idea of it, and I found a small table near the fire—the room was deserted—sat down and took off my spectacles to wipe them on my handkerchief, and gazed at the burning coals and told myself again: she loves me. I contemplated the fact that she loved me. How odd it was. Funny really. How had it happened? Small miracle, considering, but there you are, there you have it. She loves me. At last I looked up, looked around, realized how wet I was; then the clock behind the bar caught my eye. I should have been at St. Basil's twenty minutes ago!

The ward was in darkness when I got up there, and silent but for some wheezing and snoring and the odd soft moan. McGuinness was with Staff Nurse Harris (who was on nights) in her office at the end of the ward; he had little to tell me, and after I'd apologized for keeping him waiting he struggled into his overcoat and prepared to leave. "Wet out, then," he said; I must have looked like a drowned rat; fortunately I kept dry shoes on the ward. "Filthy night," I said vaguely.

Filthy night—yes, to McGuinness it would look like a filthy night, to all the world it was a filthy night, but to me, to Neville Ratcliff, no, not a filthy night, a golden night, a blessed night. In the hours that followed I would find moments here and there, little islands of grace amid the darkness of sickness and injury, when this immense miracle of the heart became once more vivid to me. For the first time in my adult life I knew I was loved by a woman.

It began to rain again shortly after midnight, and it kept up almost until dawn. Strong winds blew; there was no moon, only heaped banks of low cloud, and the streets of London flashed and shone in the downpour; every few moments the wind flung volleys of rain at the windows of sleeping houses, and embers hissed in deserted fireplaces, as the rain found its way down chimneys. It tumbled in torrents along gutters and into drainpipes, it went flooding down drains. What few people were about in the city scurried with their heads down from doorways to cabs, their umbrellas ravaged and broken in an instant. It was the same storm system as had been lashing the south coast for days now; in the capital, citizens turned uneasily in their beds, ancient race memories awoken by the violence of the weather battering at their windows and doors. Your mother has described to me her state of mind that wild night. She did not attempt to sleep. She sat for five minutes on the padded stool in front of her dressing table, removing her makeup, then paced the room, smoking. She wore her silver robe over her nightgown; a fire burned in the grate, two table lamps gave off a low, warm glow. The room was deeply carpeted, the curtains were thick. There was warmth, safety, and comfort in this room, but the fingers of danger plucked at her throat—and she *liked* it, she told me, she liked it, it made her feel alive. But it alarmed her too. She had of course never been unfaithful to Frederic before. He would not tolerate it, this she knew; no *mari complaisant*, he. A curious mood she was in, then, with this excitement, this restlessness upon her, and from time to time she pulled aside the curtain and watched the storm sweeping about the houses opposite, and all along the pavement the bare branches of the big old chestnuts flailing in the wind. . . . Then she turned and wrapped her arms about herself, and closed her eyes, arousing in herself the memory of deep and recent sexual pleasure. For I had been a good lover to her. She had risen from the armchair and wordlessly taken my hand and led me into the bedroom, where she allowed me to open her clothing, and without haste, without clumsiness, I had done so, and then my lips and fingers had impressed on her skin a description, or declaration, rather, of feeling that was almost unbearable in its tenderness, in its trembling intensity, for I was inflamed by her; and when I lifted my head from her breasts, she saw (she said), for those few seconds that I gazed at her, before I kissed her throat, and lips, my eyes, and Dorian, *never*, she said, did she imagine she could forget the expression in my eyes at that moment, the utter *glut* of feeling, the love that was in them. . . .

Later she heard Frederic coming up to bed, heard him cross the landing at the top of the stairs, then go straight to his room, and this was unusual, for it was his habit to tap at her door and open it a crack and whisper to her to sleep well, and she liked that he did that, but tonight he did not, and this made her grateful and uneasy at the same time. Suddenly the world seemed fragile. Suddenly it all seemed to shiver, as though great explosions were occurring three streets away. What if this love should destroy us both? She leaned against the wall of her room, pressed her body full against it, to feel how solid it was. Again the fear came. She sat down at the dressing table and stared at her own reflection. Let me understand this, she said to herself. She had deceived Frederic; the terms, therefore, of their life together had changed; therefore her security was in jeopardy. Seen clearly like this it seemed to lose some of its force. This I can control, she told herself. There is danger here, but I can control it. She gazed at herself in the mirror and wondered if she altogether believed it.

By the next morning the storm had blown itself out and she awoke to a world that felt as fixed and stable and permanent as ever. She breakfasted alone; Frederic had left early for the hospital, and you were of course away at school. She ate a finger of buttered toast with just a smear of marmalade and drank a cup of coffee. The fear she had known in the night had largely dissipated; she felt rather gay, rather light-headed. It was a damp, chilly morning but the sky was clear. She knew several women who managed complicated private lives without great distress; all a matter of being clear in one's own mind about what one was doing. She wondered when she would see me again.

And me? What was I thinking, what was I feeling? You can imagine. I was intoxicated with the very idea that I was loved. Your mother had said that "it" had happened to her too, and this was all I needed to know. So exalted did this make me feel, her real presence would almost have been too much; finding her in everything I saw, referring everything that happened to her, I hardly needed her presence, during this brief phase, all I needed was to sustain the feeling. . . .

I see myself in the flat in Jubilee Road; I should be sleeping, but cannot. I pace up and down the faded carpet, I stop at the window and pull back the curtain and peer out—perhaps she will come to me again, perhaps I will glimpse her alighting from a cab below—? At that moment a cab does turn into Jubilee Road, and moves toward the house, and suddenly I'm convinced that *this is her*—this is her, coming to me again!—but the cab passes without stopping and I let the curtain fall back, pace the carpet once more, pause by a rather somber reproduction of a drawing of a seascape at sunset. . . . I would like to go back to that nice little pub and order a large Scotch and so live again the moment when it first had dawned on me that I was loved, but I cannot leave the room, for fear that she will come while I am away.

I fall dispiritedly into an armchair and doze for a while. I am awoken by a knock on the door. I leap to my feet—cross the room—throw wide the door—it is Mr. Kelly, the landlady's husband.

What did that friendly man see? He saw the door wrenched violently open, and looming there before him, one hand on the doorknob and the other clutching the jamb, as though the entire structure would otherwise collapse, this lanky, wild-eyed Englishman in a dressing gown. Mr. Kelly was sympathetic. He understood the essential incoherence of the human condition. "Should I come back later, doctor?" he murmured in that soft lilt of his (he was a Cork man, and a Republican).

"What is it?" I cried.

"The wife says will you be wanting the room done out in the morning?"

"Yes!" I cried. "No letters, Mr. Kelly? No messages for me?"

"Nothing," he said, dramatically. "Not a single one, doctor."

I pushed a hand through my hair and frowned. "Thanks, Mr. Kelly," I said, and turned sadly back into my room, deflated and forsaken.

Time passed. Not a lot of time, by normal standards, but by the clock in my heart—ages, eons, very eternities. I soon became desperate to see her again. I needed to nourish my love upon her being, as though my love were a ravening parasitical creature which if it could not feed upon her would feed instead upon its host, causing agony. I was in agony. Missing her was no state of tranquil melancholy, it was actively, fiercely energetic. There came a moment when it occurred to me that she was dead. This idea rapidly turned to certainty and I began to grieve for her, and now—cruelest of cruel ironies!—I felt I had lost her before I had even known her—grief without even the consolation of memory! The problem was of course that I did not know how to reach her. The idea of writing to her or telephoning her . . . any move on my part, I felt, might embarrass her, or worse. And hadn't she told me not to try and reach her? I was unsure if this had happened or if I was inventing it.

And meanwhile I continued to go to work, functioning as best I could. An elderly woman called Belle Sylvester was found in an alley in a coma one night and brought into St. Basil's. It was our turn receiving from Accident and Casualty, so I had to work her up. A first, cursory examination on the ward gave me no real clue as to what was wrong, though meningitis suggested itself: I was compelled, reluctantly, to perform a spinal tap.

Harris, who was still on nights, wheeled screens round the bed, then turned the unconscious Belle Sylvester on her side and bent her double, knees to head. She was a big woman, fleshy and pink. I settled myself on a chair at the bedside, frowning, uneasy—I hate doing spinal taps, they're so tricky. I scrubbed the skin at the puncture site, painted it with antiseptics, then laid sterile cloths across her broad back, leaving one small patch uncovered. I picked up the big spinal needle and then, with as much delicacy as I could, inserted it. It seemed to be sliding in nicely, until suddenly—and this was what I'd been dreading—there was a horrible scraping sound—I'd hit bone! I lifted my head, looked at Harris, and withdrew the needle. "It's impossible," I muttered, sitting up straight for a moment, unbuttoning my white coat and sweeping the skirts back, then hunching forward on the chair to again slide in the needle, "with her bent double like this . . . to aim the needle . . . accurately—damn!" Again the scraping sound—again I withdrew. I wiped my brow, took a few deep breaths, tried to shake off my fatigue. For just an instant I thought of your mother, and my penis stirred in my trousers. The problem was that if, in my search for the minute box canyon formed by the bony arches of the vertebral column, I plunged the needle in too deeply, I'd pierce a vital organ and kill the woman! I inserted the needle once more, and this time was rewarded by a pulpy feeling. "Yes!" I murmured. I withdrew slowly, allowing a drop of cerebrospinal fluid into the barrel of the syringe, then rose to my feet, feeling rather proud of myself; the image of your mother again sprang into my mind, and for a second or two I was elsewhere.

Your father was talking about dead bodies. "Hypostasis, gentlemen," he said. "Note the discoloration of the skin. It begins to happen about thirty minutes after death, and takes six to eight hours till it's done. Caused by the blood gravitating downward and suffusing the lower capillaries, leaving the upper surfaces of the body pallid. Starts off pink, then rapidly darkens. Ends up purple. Another peculiarity of the body in death, gentlemen, is the appearance of a network of bluish veins, dendritic in structure, just below the surface of the skin. Generally occurs when putrefaction is rapid. Note too the shedding of the skin and the formation of adipocere. This happens when fatty tissue changes to fatty acids. You'll also see bloating as a result of methane generated by decomposition, you'll see liquefied eyeballs, you'll see blistering of the skin, you'll see dazzling changes of color, maggots, you'll even see corpses bursting open. You can never really rely on the dead to do what you expect; it all depends on temperature, moisture, insects, bacteria, oh, a host of factors."

I was down in Pathology to hear what they'd found in Eddie Bell's lungs. Your father was in the postmortem room, standing at a dissecting table in a black rubber apron, talking to half a dozen medical students. On the dissecting table (steel, with a central channel and a hole where body fluids were hosed down) lay the pale, ill-smelling cadaver of Eddie himself, with his thorax split open. Also in the room was a glass-fronted cupboard containing instruments (knives, saws, bone forceps), a table with steel bowls for specimens, and a row of metal hooks with rubber aprons hanging from them, some black, some dark green. It was a small, cramped, low-ceilinged basement room with a narrow barred window at the top of one wall through which a little light was admitted, and a view of feet crossing the courtyard outside. It was very cold, and stank of formalin. "Pathology makes physiology possible," your father was saying, "in the sense, gentlemen, that organic functions are revealed only when they fail." Standing there patiently, waiting till he had a moment for me, I remembered your mother's words. "Don't you wonder," she'd said, "what it is that makes men spend their lives poking through the diseased bits of dead bodies?" I could hear her voice, see her eyes, feel my lips upon her silky skin; and Dorian, at that moment I experienced my first real spurt of antagonism toward your father.

LOVE'S LABORS LOST

♥ ♥

Joel Rose

Love is a pernicious thing. Dolly knew that. She knew that in our society love can be a real danger. For her there were no surprises.

Dolly and Delgato lived in the basement of a tenement where there used to be a shooting gallery. When they moved in there was no longer any shooting gallery, but the idea that the basement apartment once was played at Delgato, until he couldn't resist.

Delgato used to tell how he and Dolly first met when Delgato was nine years old and Dolly twenty-six. She'd found him abandoned, homeless, wandering the streets, and took him in. He loved to tell how Dolly initiated him into the world of woman's pussy. He said she loved him up and took care of him like she was his mother. To this day he calls her "Mommy."

Dolly and Delgato had been living in the same tenement apartment for twenty-seven years. They were not what you would call "spring chickens."

For most of the time they had lived in the building, they had been on the third floor. When they lived on the third floor (the building was a six-story old-law tenement walk-up) Delgato didn't think much about how the basement used to be what it had been, although in his younger days he had been a frequent visitor to the shooting gallery in the basement. He'd been a real dope fiend in his time; and it had cost him two stretches in Sing Sing penitentiary; not to mention a couple of other sentences in lesser institutions.

Dolly was a heavyset woman with gray hair she tied at the nape of her neck with a ponytail holder. In her prime she had been strong and able, a Polish woman with Cree Indian blood, and people on the street and in the neighborhood knew her.

But now that she was past seventy, life and the neighborhood had taken their toll on Dolly. Delgato said she had a "touch of the cancer." Sometimes he would sob and say she needed a heart transplant.

"God help me, Mr. Link," he'd tell me. "I don't know what to do. The doctor says she needs a new heart, but I can't bring myself to sign the papers. She's my baby," he'd weep, "and I'm afraid to lose her." Then he'd ask to borrow a couple of bucks against the impending operation.

Delgato had a real penchant for money. He didn't work, but received social security checks twice a month, on the first and fifteenth. Dolly was on the welfare too. Social services sent her three checks a month, all on the first. One for rent, one for food, and one for disability. When she heard about any money Delgato had borrowed, Dolly was conscientious about repaying it. You had to catch her on the very day the welfare checks came, otherwise you had to wait for the next month, but she always paid, at least when her health was there.

Of late she was always going to the hospital. Usually she returned after a day or two. She'd go by ambulance and come back that way too. The attendants knew her too well and would drop her off in front of the building. Then she'd be screaming on the street, "Delgato! Delgato!" till he came out and helped her inside.

In her old age Dolly had developed trouble walking and had a terrible time getting around. Her legs were swollen twice their normal size, what is commonly called "elephant legs."

She didn't have to be reminded, people who have trouble walking by theirselves in our neighborhood, as a general rule, were not long for the world. Dolly and Delgato's part of the city was like the jungle in that respect. The lions always pick on the wildebeest can't keep up with the rest of the herd. People knew that instinctually.

On her best days, when the sun was shining, Dolly made her way to the corner store or the bodega, shuffling along the sidewalk in her house slippers. She always wore her nightgown outside no matter what the weather. You'd express concern for her health, tell her she was going to her death, but it didn't seem to faze her in the least or even register. She'd go out in a flimsy nightgown that would flap around her like cellophane.

It took her a long time to get anywhere, and usually she didn't go. Mostly she would sit on the stoop and yell for people or passersby (she didn't necessarily have to know them) to go to the store for her or whatever. Sometimes if you was looking for alternate side of the street parking and she spied you she'd ask you to take her to the check cashing around the corner. She'd sit on a newspaper on the stoop, and sometimes pee right there, the pee running into the street. Once when I drove her over in my car she left behind a stained washcloth from under her nightie. When I politely called her attention to it, she said, "Sorry, I got a touch of the diarrhea."

The building where we lived was a city-owned building, which means the city took it over from the landlord, when the landlord failed to pay his taxes. The city is the worst landlord in the city. And the biggest. They own the most buildings, in the poorest state of repairs. But in our building at least it was warm in the winter and there was hot water. Like I said, they'd lived there for more than twenty-seven years. They'd been together, or at least known each other (time out for prison breaks), for forty-six.

Most of that time they'd lived on the third floor. But when Dolly's legs swolled up and she couldn't walk so good, Delgato came down to my apartment in the basement and asked could they switch apartments with me. He told how he had to do something because Dolly couldn't climb the stairs no more. He became emotionally wrought and talked about her cancer and the impending heart transplant.

He said how they were on the list to move to an elevator building, but the city and the welfare couldn't find nothing for them just then, the state of the economy and all, the homeless living on the streets and in the parks and under the bridges, three and four families living in the projects in one apartment already. Delgato said the city and the welfare people was going to move them on the top of the list. But him and me both knew, what did that mean?—nothing. He said maybe they would move back to Puerto Rico.

He didn't have to go through no big song and dance. I was ready, willing, and able to switch with them. I'm the super of the building. My name is Lenkowsky, but everybody calls me Link. Except for Delgato who calls me Mr. Link.

I didn't need convincing because I hated the apartment where I lived. To me it was like a dungeon. The building had been built over a swamp more than a hundred years ago and the basement was so damp in the summer it made my bones ache, and so hot in winter I cooked because the steam pipes and boiler return lines ran through the apartment from one end to the other. No, to me, the basement didn't offer a whole lot of joy.

Right away, soon as they moved down into the basement, things changed. As soon as they settled in Delgato had déjà vu and began to let junkies come by, pay him a few bucks to use the bathroom to get high, or smoke crack in the little backyard.

Sometimes he let people drop off some dope, and then someone would come to get it, and get off in their place for a fee, almost like a house connection. For his trouble Delgato would get himself a little taste off the top, plus a couple of pesos for his own pocket.

On the other hand, the new apartment was better for Dolly. She didn't complain about the dampness coming up from the ground aching her bones, or the heat pouring in from the boiler drying her up. She went through a period of happiness where she stood at the stove all day boiling cabbage, but then her legs were bothering her something awful again from all that standing, and it was evident that her health was failing. She went to the hospital less, but stayed longer than she had before.

Her prolonged stays made Delgato distraught. Dolly was a steadying influence in his life. Although not as worn out as Dolly, he was old and stiff his own self. Some days he stayed in bed all day with the arthritis. He was going to be fifty-five his next birthday, and he had a lot of pent-up bitterness in him and anger.

He didn't get along so well with his neighbors.

In some ways when they was living on the third floor, he'd calmed down pretty much for a number of years, leastwise, troublewise, if not dopewise, compared to what he had been as a young man, or even since he was forty-five. But with Dolly in Beth Israel he run right back out of control, like it was twenty-seven minutes of clean living, not twenty-seven years.

Danger abounded about him. He'd be out stalking the streets with a wild look in his eye, his Mets cap askew, his sneakers unlaced, his plaid coat flapping. When Dolly was infirmed, he wouldn't sleep at night. He'd bring in bad-looking strangers or dopers who would be living in the apartment with him, arguing and putting on the trouble. Three in the morning you could hear them shouting and screaming, and their crack cocaine smoke would waft up the defunct dumbwaiter shaft.

His state of agitation grew. The mestizo woman who fed Dolly's cats while she was in the hospital told me she was afraid he was going to cut off her hands with a machete when she pushed the opened cans of cat food through the window.

One afternoon in a smoky haze he smashed the door intercom because he was convinced a mouse was living in it.

When a tenant from the fifth floor asked him what he thought he was doing he threatened to put an ice pick in his heart.

He told his upstairs neighbor he was going to murder her because she was vacuuming too loud.

When I came down in the morning to straighten the garbage cans or check the boiler, I always had my eye out for Delgato lurking. No one in their right mind would put anything past him. He would appear out of the woodwork and sometimes he was as sweet as could be, asking the time of day, or how was every little thing, or could he get you a cup of coffee, but sometimes he had the glint of insanity in his eye and no one could tell what he might do.

"It's all right," he would say to me when he saw he had startled me.

But it wasn't all right.

I had known him for years, and had been humored by him, and maybe even charmed at times, but now, thanks to the crack, his mind was fucked. One day on the block he went up to a poor woman he didn't even know, pushing a baby carriage, and punched her right in the face for no reason.

He chased a bunch of kids from the projects coming home from St. Brigid's Catholic school with a hammer at three-fifteen in the afternoon.

The only thing capable of keeping him in check and calming him was Dolly's love, and he didn't stand a chance of turning back to his old self till she come back from the hospital.

While she was sick he at first would get all maudlin, tell how she was the one who taught him everything he knew. He repeated the story how she adopted him off the street, how she couldn't get enough of his dick, how even to this day, when she wanted it, he wasn't man enough to deny her.

He told again how he was nine; she was twenty-six. He had been abandoned, left to his own devices, sleeping in the gutter. Delgato was Puerto Rican. His father had brought the family to New York from San Juan when Delgato was five years old. When the father couldn't find work and couldn't feed his family, he beat Delgato as an example and put him out on the street and told him not to come back or he'd kill him.

Dolly espied him on the street three days running, each day getting worser-looking, and hungrier. She said her heart went out to him when she seen him. She asked if he wanted to come live with her. She had been on her own since her own fourteenth birthday. She had run away from her home in North Dakota because her father had been fucking her and it finally dawned on her what he was doing.

He said he took care of her like she was his mother. Like I said, to this day he calls her "Mommy."

She fed him and clothed him. She was forever boiling him up cabbage and cutting in sausage and kielbasa from the Polish meat markets on First Avenue, inviting one or other of her neighbors in to eat and the smell would permeate through the building and inundate every nook and cranny.

The first and only job Delgato had in his whole life, outside the army, was when he worked at the *New York Post* printing plant on South Street. The primary offices was not so far away from the neighborhood where we lived, down by the river, and when Delgato was still a kid he used to hang around down there, sort of like a mascot, and when he come back from Korea they made him a bundler, although he would brag there was some writers he had come to know who said with his stories and gift for gab, he should be a columnist and write a book on everything that happened in his life.

At the *Post* he worked at the foot of an old printing press. His job was to catch the bundles of newspapers as they came off the baling machine and stack them up for a teamster to come and throw them in the big black trucks.

Most everything was automatic. The papers came off automatic, they got stacked automatic, they got tied automatic. All he was supposed to do was watch. It was what they ordinarily called a "plum" job.

If the press shut down, then he was to take the papers off the belt as quickly as he could and stack them off to the side so the machine wouldn't jam.

He worked at the *Post* till he fucked up. He fucked up royally because the guy who was his partner who he worked with on the plum job on the bundler had asked him to get some doogie from East Twelfth Street near his apartment on the way to work where they sold blue and red balloons full of heroin for three bucks. They got high behind the press and the guy nodded out and fell into the bundler and strangled to death, the twine wrapped around his neck about thirty-eight times.

The shop steward told Delgato the union couldn't save him and he lost his job. He also wound up serving a short stretch in the old Men's House of Detention for procurement of a narcotic.

When he come back from that Dolly was living common-law with a black guy, had a little kid with him, another on the way, and Delgato had a nice little heroin habit he had acquired in the Tombs penitentiary.

Dolly's friend beat her without remorse. He wasn't too fond of Delgato either. He didn't relish some squirt white Puerto Rican kid hanging around used to pork his common-law, and put him out under no uncertain terms. So Delgato was back on the street, living by his wits, which weren't too keen then and aren't too keen now.

He served two jolts in Ossining where Sing Sing is. One in '72 for armed robbery and manslaughter. Then another in '76 for murder alone.

When he got out his parole officer got him into an SRO, single-room occupancy, on East Third Street. One day while shoplifting he run into Dolly at the Key Food on the corner. She told him while he was away the black guy had taken a powder and she had had a couple more kids, making four, and the lot of them were all living with her over the same place. She invited him back to her apartment, got him on her welfare as a social disability.

Through her social worker, she got him enrolled into a methadone program on Second Avenue. Once he got used to the regimen, it helped him stay clean for many years. He was very happy then, enjoyed the methadone high, come home, tell her how happy he was.

The four children Dolly had with three different men while Delgato was away was all star-crossed. Three girls and a boy. The boy and two of the girls was dead.

The boy had been killed in a street fight when he was fifteen. He pulled a knife, and the guy he pulled the knife on said, "I don't fight with my hands," pulled a gun, and shot him. He was dead before he hit the sidewalk.

The two deceased girls had o.d.'d. One in a shooting gallery on Avenue C, the other in her boyfriend's mother's apartment in the projects.

The one surviving sibling was a drug user too, but she had a family of her own and wasn't exactly an addict, more like she had a chip. She lived a block away with Dolly's two grandkids, Willoughby and Minerva. Dolly worried because her daughter didn't have the kids in school. The daughter said the city wanted to send them to some special magnet school way the fuck over the west side, but it was too far away in the daughter's estimation, and she didn't want to be bothered, and kept them home instead, while she hung daily by Dolly and Delgato's basement window, calling "Maaaa! Maaaa!" till one of them came out and let her in.

It didn't take a genius to know what she was after.

Sometimes Delgato would take pity on her and wangle a little something for her off one of his house customers. But sometimes Dolly wouldn't let Delgato do that for her, and on those days the daughter would just sit there on the stoop the whole day with the kids, waiting for something to happen, occasionally screaming, "I hate you, Ma! I hate you."

Sometimes, after a while, Delgato would send her to the corner or to the bodega when Dolly's back was turned to get a little bit of coke and dope, c and d, enough for the two of them to inject.

He would rarely go out for himself. He didn't want anybody from the building or his neighbors knowing his personal business.

He thought he was a sly fuck, but he wasn't. People knew, but they was afraid of him. Rightfully so. He might of thought he was getting over, but all he was was a crazy old man getting crazier and more dangerous every day. People didn't need to be told that.

Dolly knew too, although she'd be the last to admit it. She was very loyal, and she loved Delgato, and no matter what he did, she would never, ever betray him. She told him all the time. She'd say, "I love you, Delgato. You're my man." And Delgato would say, "I love you too, Mommy."

Dolly and Delgato.

Delgato and Dolly.

In October, right at the beginning of heating season, the boiler went down. I was in the basement dicking with the burner when I heard a commotion up front at the street end where the electric meters were.

I waited till everything grew silent, then went up there and found all the meters were smashed and busted, the protective glass bubbles lying in shards on the cement floor.

I stared at them for about half a minute, then started upstairs through the airshaft. When I got into the hall I heard pounding and shouting at the front door and saw Delgato standing outside, his face contorted, pressed to the wire-reinforced glass, shouting for me to open up.

It crossed my mind to ignore him, to just let him scream and pound, while I went about my business, but then I went and opened the door.

"What's the matter, Delgato?" I asked him evenly.

"Mr. Link," he said, "if Dolly dies, I'm gonna kill you."

I asked him why she would die just then.

Delgato said because there was no hot water. I told him I was trying to take care of just that. I showed him the dirt and oil on my hands to prove it. By talking quietly I tried to bring Delgato back from the stratosphere to some reality that approximated the building. I said, "It's me, Gato. It's Mr. Link."

"I don't care who the fuck you are," Delgato said. "If Dolly passes, you'll pay."

"I don't want anything to happen to Dolly," I told him. "I'm trying my best. You know me, Gato, I'm your friend."

"No, you're not."

To reassure him I put my hand on Delgato's shoulder and walked him down the stoop stairs. I said, "Gato, I'm going up right now and call the repair man. I live here too, remember? I want hot water just like you do. I'm trying the best I can." I didn't mention anything about Delgato smashing the Con Ed meters. Instead I asked after Dolly, the specifics of her affliction this time.

That softened him, the anger lifting like a veil. "I swear to God, Mr. Link," Delgato said. "I pray to know what to do. The doctor wants to take out her heart. He wants me to sign the papers to give him permission to do it. He says if he don't give her a new heart, that's the end of her. But I don't want nobody cutting out Dolly's heart."

I agreed, said I didn't blame him. "The heart's the most important organ in the body," I said. "An operation like that, that's a risky thing." All the time while I'm commiserating, I'm not believing a word he's saying, thinking to myself, who's going to give poor old Dolly a new heart? People like them, like Dolly and Delgato, people living on society's edge, they don't get new organs.

Before Delgato took off he hit on me for five bucks for a cab to get him over to the hospital. The last words out of his mouth was "I love you, Mr. Link."

Love can be a fickle thing.

Later that afternoon the boiler man arrived. He found the problem right away in the burner ignition. He had the part in his truck and it took him twenty minutes to replace. As him and me were walking back through the basement we could smell the crack, like burning rubber, being smoked in Delgato's apartment. The repairman handed me his bill and as he turned to leave Gato was there staring at us, his eyes glassy. "Did ya see?" he said. "Somebody broke the electric meters. Why do people do something like that?"

Dolly called my apartment late in the day from the hospital. She said she was worried about Delgato. She said she had been expecting him for hours. Had I seen him? I told her, earlier I had given Delgato five bucks to take a cab to the hospital. Hadn't he arrived? She was silent. Then she said, "Do me a favor, honey, don't give him no more money." Then she asked would I do something else for her, go down, see if I seen him, tell him she needed to talk to him.

I asked after her health. She told me she had a touch of the pneumonia and her legs were swollen up worse than usual, but the doctor said she would be able to come home later that day.

I went downstairs to the basement and knocked on the window outside Delgato's apartment. Somebody I couldn't see, but I thought was Dolly's daughter, answered and talked to me from the kitchen, from the shadows.

"Where's Delgato?" I inquired.

"He's here. Wha'd'ya want?"

"Are you Dolly's daughter? She gave me a message for him."

She turned away from the window. "Delgato, man here wants to talk to you."

For a few minutes I heard muffled voices, then Delgato came to the window. He talked from behind the curtain so I couldn't see him.

"What you want, Mr. Link?"

"Dolly called me. She's worried about you. She's said you were supposed to go to the hospital. She wants you to call her right away."

"Okay, Mr. Link."

I told him to send my regards.

"I will. Thank you, Mr. Link. I love you, Mr. Link."

"Yeah, I love you too."

Toward midnight, I was dozing in my chair when I heard a steady pounding downstairs, and then my buzzer sounded, one long incessant note like someone was leaning on it and not letting up. I got up stiff-legged (I'm not getting any younger my ownself), staggered over to the kitchen wall, and pressed on the intercom. "Who is it?"

"It's me—Gato. Come down, man, will ya?"

He was with Dolly's daughter, both of them in an extremely

hyper state. They were standing there, their eyes bloodshot, fidgeting and sweating and looking furtive.

I said, "What's the matter?"

Delgato said he'd gone out and locked himself out of his apartment. Did I have a duplicate key?

He showed me how he had already pounded the shit out of his lock with a brick trying to get back in, but hadn't managed to open it.

"Where's Dolly?" I asked. "Didn't she come home?"

"No," he told me. They were considering replacing her liver and kidneys, so they kept her an extra day.

I slipped my library card between the doorjamb and door and the lock clicked open. Delgato couldn't thank me enough, before him and Dolly's daughter pushed past and hustled inside without a backward glance.

Three hours later I was in a deep sleep under the covers when I was woken up by Delgato screaming, "Mr. Link! Mr. Link!" from the street.

Delgato was marching back and forth on the sidewalk, waving a five-foot-long length of galvanized pipe in his hands.

I watched him from the window for a while, listened to my name being shouted and cursed, then pulled on some clothes and went downstairs and opened the door and stood on the stoop, my arms folded across my chest.

"What's bugging you now, Delgato?" I said slowly.

Delgato turned on me like a beacon. His eyes glowed red like an alien from another planet. He said, "You're to blame for my troubles, Mr. Link. You stay away from my Dolly."

"What? I don't understand."

"You loving up my Mommy," he said. "You loving her up and turning her against me. I know you, Mr. Link. You no good." He swung the pipe, and I jumped back, but not fast enough, and the pipe caught me on the hand, as I threw it up in front of my face, trying to protect myself.

I was stunned by the blow, and retreated into the alcove behind the mailboxes. He cursed me, called me a son of a bitch and worse. "Why'd you do that?" I shouted back at him.

Delgato glared at me, his eyes iridescent, and brandished the pipe as if to hit me again.

I ducked back inside, ran up to my apartment, and came back down with a baseball bat.

"Now hit me!" I said.

Hearing the commotion, a bunch of young guys from the corner rushed over and broke it up. "Don't be hitting that old man," one of them said to me. He grabbed the ball bat out of my hands. "Go back in your apartment. Don't be messing with an old man like that," he said. "He ain't nothing but a crack addict. Ev'ybody know he run the crack house down there."

Soon the cops came. They took one look at my hand and called for an ambulance. They picked up a fourteen-inch butcher knife from the sidewalk between Delgato's feet, and laid it on the roof of the police car, but said they couldn't prove it belonged to him because no one had seen it in his possession.

Delgato was out of jail faster than I was back from the emergency room at Bellevue, where I spent the night, it was so fucking busy. He was there waiting for me when I returned home the next morning.

"I'm so sorry for what I done to you, Mr. Link," he said. "I didn't know it was you I hit until I went in front of the judge and he said your name."

Dolly came home from the hospital that same afternoon. The ambulance workers unloaded her on the sidewalk. She was screaming at them and they pulled her hospital gown over her head to shut her up.

Delgato came out and kissed her all up and helped her inside.

Later her daughter showed up on the stoop. My hand was in a cast and was throbbing me. The bone was split on the middle finger from the knuck to the first joint, but there was no displacement. I was watching the Giants game on TV and heard the daughter screaming outside the apartment, "Maaa! Maaa!"

Hearing her, I looked out the window, saw her leaning over the railing, her hair a frazzle, the two kids sitting on the steps, their bicycles thrown on the sidewalk.

It wasn't a half hour later, halftime, the Giants up thirteen-zip to the Redskins, when a chill run through me, and I wondered why the boiler hadn't kicked in for the afternoon heating cycle.

I picked myself up and went down to the boiler room real careful not to run into Delgato unexpected. When I come through the door I seen Dolly's daughter lying on the cement floor, Delgato standing over her, throwing a bucket of water in her face. I took one look at Delgato, did an about-face, and headed back upstairs, sat down in my chair in front of the TV, and shook.

The girl was dead. I knew that for a fact if I had ever seen a dead person before in my life (and I had seen three in the emergency room the night before). Her shirt was up around her throat and she had looked about four months pregnant. After I pulled myself together I called 911 for an ambulance.

Before they arrived though I began to hear Dolly outside screaming Delgato's name. When I looked out I could see him hurrying away down the street, his back to her. She was shrieking at the top of her lungs, bellowing, "You ain't gonna leave me here with her! Come back here!" The kids were still sitting on the stoop, watching Gato run, too.

Pretty soon an Emergency Service ambulance arrive. They knocked on the basement door, went inside, stayed for a long time. Two more ambulances came, and a detective car. By this time a crowd had gathered. Delgato come back a couple or three times, hanging around on the periphery, trying to suss what was happening.

By this time the Giants had blown their lead and were losing by two touchdowns. Later, a young detective rang my buzzer, asks me to come down. He asks me am I the one who called the ambulance. He shows me three Polaroids of Dolly's daughter floating in the bathtub. He asks if this is who I seen lying on the floor outside the boiler room. I says it is.

"You know her?" the detective asks. He's a young guy with blond hair, a Polish name, and a big pompadour.

I says how it's Dolly's daughter.

"She's some strange bird," the detective says of Dolly. "You know, the whole time I'm in there, all she does is play solitaire at the kitchen table. She don't show no remorse. Anytime I ask her a question, she says, 'Talk to my lawyers.' "

He says, "Her story is the daughter come over to her house, asked to use the bathroom. Unbeknownst to the mother, for the purpose of drug use. Apparently she o.d.'d right there on the toilet. They threw her in the tub to try to revive her."

The detective explained there was no point to press charges because under the law the apartment residents had no criminal culpability, the daughter being a legal adult, responsible for herself, no one can tell their grown child what to do.

He says, "You want some free advice? Why don't you get the tenants together, complain to the housing authority?" He says, "These people are no good. Evict their ass."

It took five court dates. Dolly and Delgato never showed up once. After the daughter's death they holed up in the basement, didn't come out. Court dates passed, one after the other. Dolly or Delgato kept calling up housing court, making excuses, one for the other. "My wife's sick. She got the tubercular." "My husband laid up with the weather, it affects his joints, and he be moaning all night and can't get out of bed. Me neither."

Finally the judge gets sick of it himself, even though he's known for his tenant advocacy. Each and every court date eleven of us building residents traipse down there to show up, plus the mailman who was beaten up by Gato when the welfare checks was late, and the judge finally sees fit to take our depositions.

The judge was not that interested in all the gory details. After the first six or seven witnesses, the bare bones was enough. Despite what the Polish detective said about them having two MFY lawyers, Dolly and Delgato had no legal representation in court. The judge announced he would give them one last chance to offer a defense, and instructed the court clerk to notify them by registered mail to that effect.

In the next few days spring set in on the city and Dolly slowly and carefully made her way to the front stoop, where she took in the sun in her flimsy nightgown, waiting for someone to pass by, run her errands. She must have been having real trouble with her bladder, even more than usual, because she kept wetting right where she sat. At one point I seen Delgato heading off down the block, so I come out, ask her didn't she think it was too cold to sit outside like this, but she wouldn't acknowledge me talking to her. I told her I was sorry about her daughter and the kids. Social Services had took them off and put them in foster care. I said I thought we was friends. I told her that it was Delgato's fault for all this, that he had busted my hand for no reason, that I hadn't done nothing to him. She said that's not what she had heard. I told her, no one who lived in the building had anything against her, if she got rid of him, she could probably stay.

She turn on me then. She say, "Mr. Link, why you tell Delgato that shit, why you tell him you loving me up?"

On the morning of the final court date, Delgato called the judge's chambers, say that Dolly was in the hospital waiting for her heart transplant and that he was laid up in bed with the arthritis and the rheumatism and couldn't move. An hour later the judge announced to all the tenants sitting in the court that Delgato and Dolly had had ample opportunity to respond to the charges brought against them, that he wasn't buying any of it, and signed the eviction order.

Dolly. Delgato. Delgato. Dolly.

Three weeks later the city marshal shows up. A big, muscle-bound guy, his badge dangling from around his neck on a leather thong, his shiny silver gun buckled high on his hip, he stood on the street looking at the building, pursing his lips like he was kissing the air.

He rang my bell and I come down and signed the papers as I had been instructed by the HPD. I warned the marshal to be careful, that Delgato was dangerous. I told him how he broke my hand and when I went down to make a complaint the assistant district attorney had pulled his yellow sheet and saw how he had killed two people. I said how Delgato had punched that woman pushing the baby carriage, chased the school kids, trying to brain them with a wrench or hammer or whatever, threatened to stick an ice pick in the fifth-floor upstairs neighbor's heart, assaulted the mailman.

The marshal's eyes narrowed, he fingered his gun, but knocked on their door and went inside, coming out a few minutes later, shaking his head, saying to me where I was staying out of sight in the hall, "You're right. The guy's a real crackerjack."

Delgato had followed the marshal out onto the street and was standing on the sidewalk muttering to himself, peering into the building, trying to see with who the marshal was conferring.

The marshal warned me to go back inside.

I went upstairs and stood at my familiar place at the window, looking down. Delgato was standing in front of the building, surrounded by their shabby furniture and possessions. The marshal had brought some moving men with him, sent by the city authority, and they were busy emptying the apartment and padlocking it. Social Services had sent a man, but Dolly and Delgato had refused any help, didn't want to hear a word uttered about city shelters.

At the end the movers carried out Dolly's wheelchair and then her, and set her in it on the sidewalk. Delgato stared up the street, then down. He stared at the tenement building, his home for twenty-seven years, at his basement apartment that had once been a shooting gallery.

I watched the marshal come over to talk to him. Delgato took off his blue Mets cap, rubbed his thinning gray hair. He pointed back up the block somewheres, toward the projects. Then he took hold of the back of Dolly's wheelchair by the handles, pushed it forward about a foot and a half, and stopped.

He bent down and hugged her. He embraced her in her wheelchair on the sidewalk, swaying back and forth, then he stood up and began pushing her down the block where he had pointed, out of sight, and away.

CONTRIBUTORS

♥ ♥

KATHY ACKER is the author of a number of novels, including *Blood and Guts in High School*. Her most recent novel, *In Memoriam to Identity*, and the trilogy which makes up her first work, *Portrait of an Eye*, were published by Random House in February 1992. She has worked on several plays with Richard Foreman and a movie, *Variety*, with Bette Gordon. She is currently teaching at the San Francisco Art Institute.

DAYTONA BEACH was conceived the night after her father won the famed race of the same name and has since been around the track a few times herself. Now a myopic recluse in San Francisco, where she writes and rants, she aspires to be Dostoevsky with breasts or to bring about World Peace, whichever comes first.

LISA BLAUSHILD lives and writes in New York. *Asking for It* is an excerpt from a work-in-progress.

TREY ELLIS's first novel was *Platitudes* (Vintage Contemporaries). *Home Repairs* will be published by Simon & Schuster in the spring of 1993. He is in love.

DAVID B. FEINBERG lives in New York. He is the author of *Eighty-sixed* and *Spontaneous Combustion*. He is currently working on a novel and a play.

BARRY GIFFORD was born on October 18, 1946, in Chicago, Illinois, and raised there and in Key West and Tampa, Florida. His writing has appeared in *Punch, Esquire, Cosmopolitan, Rolling Stone, L'Immature*, the *New York Times*, and many other publications. Mr. Gifford's books have been translated into fifteen languages. They include the novels *Port Tropique, Language with Traveler, Sailor's Holiday*, and *Wild at Heart*, which was made into an award-winning film by David Lynch. "Everybody Got Their Own Idea of Home" is an excerpt from Mr. Gifford's most recent novel, *Night People*. He lives in the San Francisco Bay Area.

A. M. HOMES is the author of the novel *Jack* and the collection of stories *The Safety of Objects*.

DOCTOR SNAKESKIN A.K.A. DARIUS JAMES is the author of *Negrophobia* (Citadel Underground). When not devising bigger and better ways to outrage the populus, he watches videos with his lifemate Joy Glidden—who is an outstanding painter—goes to sleep early due to old age, and collects Godzilla toys. He is in the New Orleans O.T.O. Kali Lodge Hall of Fame. Traditional voodooists hold him in disdain even if he is quoted in the instruction manual for the New Orleans voodoo tarot.

LYNNE McFALL teaches philosophy at Syracuse University. She was awarded a Wallace Stegner Fellowship, a James Michener Fellowship, and a National Endowment for the Arts Fellowship in literature. Her first novel, *The One True Story of the World*, was published by Atlantic Monthly Press. An excerpt from it appeared in *The Pushcart Prize XIII*. *Bitter Love* is an excerpt from her second novel, *Dancer with Bruised Knees*.

PATRICK McGRATH lives in New York City. He is the author of three books of fiction, *Blood and Water, The Grotesque*, and *Spider*, and he coedited an anthology, *The New Gothic*, with Bradford Morrow. His work has been translated into more than a dozen languages. He reviews regularly for the *New York Times* and the *Washington Post*. He is married to the actress Maria Aitken.

LYNNE TILLMAN's most recent books are the novels *Cast in Doubt* and *Motion Sickness* (Poseidon Press) and *The Madame Re-*

alism Complex, a collection of short fiction (Semiotexte: Native Agents, April 1992). She writes regularly on art and literature for *Art in America* and the *Village Voice*. She lives in New York City.

WILLIAM T. VOLLMANN is the author of *You Bright and Risen Angels, The Ice-Shirt*, the collection *The Rainbow Stories*, and *Whores for Gloria*.

DAVID FOSTER WALLACE graduated from Amherst College in 1985 and from the graduate writing program at the University of Arizona in 1987. He is the author of a novel, *The Broom of the System*; a collection of stories and novellas, *Girl with Curious Hair*; and a book of nonfiction, *Signifying Rappers*. He lives near Boston and is working on something long.

DAVID WOJNAROWICZ is the author of three books, including *Close to the Knives: A Memoir of Disintegration*. He is also an artist, and has exhibited in galleries and museums worldwide. His work has been included in the Whitney Biennial. He died during the summer of 1992.

EDITORS

♥ ♥

CATHERINE TEXIER was born and raised in France. She moved to New York City in 1981. Her first novel, *Chloe l'Atlantique*, was written in French and published in Paris in 1983. She is the author of two novels in English: *Love Me Tender* (Penguin, 1987) and *Panic Blood* (Viking, 1990). She is the recipient of a New York Foundation for the Arts Fellowship in fiction and a National Endowment for the Arts Award. She is completing a fourth novel.

JOEL ROSE's novel *Kill the Poor* was published by Atlantic Monthly Press in 1988. He is the recipient of a National Endowment for the Arts Fellowship and a New York Foundation for the Arts Fellowship. He is at work on a new novel, *The Sunshine of Paradise Alley*.

Joel Rose and Catherine Texier published and coedited the literary magazine *Between C & D* from 1983 to 1990. In 1988, they edited an anthology of fiction from *Between C & D*, which was published by Penguin as a Contemporary American Fiction paperback original. They live in New York City with their daughters, Celine and Chloe.